"I am bound to you by captivity, nothing more."

Thea stiffened. "I owe you no service whatsoever. My duty is to make certain that I regain my freedom. The sooner the better."

Roderick slipped his forefinger through the iron loop dangling from the collar at her throat. He tugged on it deliberately. "By my law you are bound henceforth. Challenge my authority and you will suffer greatly for it."

His softly spoken warning fell on deaf ears.

What had he expected? She was a black-haired Frank, by nature the most infuriating, stubborn and treacherous race of women on earth.

"Goodbye, Thea. Understand this before my ship docks—no cottage or tenancy or husband do I offer you in Emory. Perhaps in time I will grow weary of you. But until then, you belong solely to me!"

Dear Reader,

When Elizabeth Mayne's first book, *All That Matters,* was released during our annual March Madness promotion, *Romantic Times* called it "...a terrific debut novel." And judging by the success of the book, readers wholeheartedly agreed. *Heart of the Hawk,* the author's second book, is the heart-wrenching medieval story of a woman who refuses to marry without love and a man who has vowed to never love again. We hope you enjoy it.

Honey Logan sets out to prove to her father that she is capable, and winds up handcuffed to a notorious bank robber in *Forever and a Day,* the sequel to Mary McBride's bittersweet Western romance, *The Fourth of Forever.*

Author Miranda Jarrett continues to entertain audiences with her series of stories based on the adventures of the infamous Sparhawks of Rhode Island. Her latest, *The Sparhawk Bride,* is the story of a young woman kidnapped on the eve of her wedding.

Unicorn Vengeance, the third book in Claire Delacroix's trilogy featuring a family whose sons bear the mark—and the curse—of the ancient kings of France, is an intriguing medieval tale of destiny and desire.

Whatever your taste in historical reading, we hope Harlequin Historicals will keep you coming back for more. Please keep a lookout for all four titles, available wherever books are sold.

Sincerely,

Tracy Farrell,
Senior Editor

Please address questions and book requests to:
Harlequin Reader Service
U.S.: 3010 Walden Ave., P.O. Box 1325, Buffalo, NY 14269
Canadian: P.O. Box 609, Fort Erie, Ont. L2A 5X3

ELIZABETH MAYNE

HEART OF THE HAWK

Harlequin Books

TORONTO • NEW YORK • LONDON
AMSTERDAM • PARIS • SYDNEY • HAMBURG
STOCKHOLM • ATHENS • TOKYO • MILAN
MADRID • WARSAW • BUDAPEST • AUCKLAND

ISBN 0-373-28891-3

HEART OF THE HAWK

Copyright © 1995 by M. Kaye Garcia

Books by Elizabeth Mayne

Harlequin Historicals

All That Matters #259
Heart of the Hawk #291

ELIZABETH MAYNE

is a native San Antonian, who knew by age eleven how to spin a good yarn, according to every teacher she ever faced. She's spent the past twenty years making up for all her transgressions on the opposite side of the teacher's desk, and the last five working exclusively with troubled children. She particularly loves an ethnic hero and married one of her own eighteen years ago. But it wasn't until their youngest child, a daughter, was two years old that life calmed down enough for this writer to fulfill the dream she'd always had of becoming a novelist.

To my father—
As my first book celebrated Mother's roots in
Ireland, this one set in German Saxony is for you.
Enjoy!

Chapter One

May 841 A.D.
Fief of Emory, Blackstone Keep

"I say we sail to the land of the Vikings and take back what they pillaged. Death to the barbarians who stole the women of Emory!" Benjamin of Emory, cousin to the lord, punctuated his words by dumping a heavy barrow of wet mortar onto the wooden skid at the duke of Emory's feet.

Lord Roderick straightened. His keen blue eyes swept down the line of men-at-arms who were working in the broiling sun at various levels of the raised scaffolding. Finally his piercing eyes fastened on Benjamin's flushed, unbearded face.

All paused in their labor to hear what answer the duke would give to his last living kin.

"Oh, aye," Roderick said scornfully. Angered because Benjamin listened each time this discussion came up, but did not hear, Roderick spoke loudly enough that his voice reverberated off the stone wall they were building, so that every man among them could hear him. "I tell you the only offense we make is defense. We make Blackstone a fortress! Cease your moaning for what we have not. What we lost, we lost. We build anew. And let God be my witness, no Viking will put ashore in Emory again!"

Roderick spoke with such deadly force that no man dared speak again for a good long while. The scrape of trowels and the grunts of men straining to lift quarter-ton blocks of black granite into place resumed around him. Turning his back on young Benjamin, Roderick tugged on his beard and silently signaled his own crew to begin work again.

Another block of granite waited to be lifted from the trolley and moved to the mortared gap in the curtain wall. Roderick's best friend, Sir Michael of Lozere, bent with him to grasp the stone. The elder Teutonic knight, Sir Deitert, grunted first, then stooped to grasp another side of the quarter-ton stone by its bottom edges. Together, the three men raised it from the crude wooden bed.

Roderick staggered as the brunt of the stone's weight shifted onto him, while the smaller two men levered the corners of the cumbersome rock into the niche. They were adept at their task, a seasoned team, knowing exactly what to do from long practice now. Knowing what to do did not make the work any easier, when it came to laying thousands of quarter-ton stones into the wall Roderick had designed to enclose Blackstone Keep.

Every muscle in Roderick's body knotted and bulged. Sweat-dampened plaits dropped from his temples to his shoulders and twisted into sandy curls that brushed against golden flesh gouged by scars. Half were the pale white of battle wounds long since toughened and weathered into seamless flesh of which he was proud. The most recent welted and thickened from his present efforts. The newly healed scars would sunburn more tenderly than seasoned skin. Of these, he was ashamed. The mark of a whip spoke of weakness.

The duke of Emory did not think of himself as a weak man.

"Move, damn you," he muttered, cursing the stone. Sweat caused his fingers to slip, a thing that never happened in battle, when his hands were sheathed in studded gauntlets. "Lift, with me, men! Push, together! Now!"

His assistants grunted deeply. By virtue of brute strength, the three knights shoved the stone into the gap.

Roderick panted from exertion, drawing his sweat-glistened forearm across his brow. Black-haired Michael of Lozere and bald-pated Sir Deitert each slumped against a shade-bound merlon. Sweat ran as freely down their naked backs as it did the duke's. Michael raised a weary forearm and wordlessly pointed behind Roderick.

Swiveling around, Roderick found Benjamin, his young and thoughtless cousin, shifting from foot to foot. Summoning from his dwindling well of patience, Roderick said, "What is it now, cousin?"

Benjamin flashed him a watery-eyed look of defiance, then broke the silence and fastened another band of iron around Roderick's broken heart.

"In truth, my dread lord cousin, I want you to know it is your lady mother that I miss the most," he said plainly.

Roderick made a strangled noise in the back of his throat. Acceptance of his loss was something Roderick had yet to achieve.

He stood his ground, refusing to weaken, and by the very virtue of his own strength, showing the boy that a man did not break so easily. "Get back to work, Benjamin."

At six-and-ten, Benjamin held all the promise and fair looks to which every Emory male had been born. Ben had the height, but not the breadth of shoulders or abundance of muscle that Roderick had attained in his two score and eight years. Ben's questioning gray eyes steadfastly met Roderick's until the watery excess dried away. Then the boy accepted the order given him, retrieved his barrow and descended the ramp to fetch the next load.

Roderick spent his grief on foul temper, ordering vassals and serfs alike into frenzied activity. Outwardly, his goals were clear—restore the village, plant the fields, build walls of solid black granite, hewn from the cliffs of Blackstone.

The fine wooden manor house that had been his childhood home would never be resurrected. He lived in the scorched and burned keep. It was defensible. If attack should come again...if...if the Norse dared return...he would slay them without mercy.

The squalling for women to relieve the loneliness or the pain of suffering did no Saxon good. No man had ever died from aching loins, and Roderick saw no reason to dwell on what they had not.

The Vikings had been most thorough. All they'd left behind were the dead and dying, the maimed and the injured, and the old crones too ancient to be of any use.

Roderick knew perfectly well what young Benjamin was complaining about. Life in his far-north Saxon fief was grim and heartless without women and young maids to comfort and ease the burdens of such arduous work. They were separated by the wilderness of the great forests from the rest of Saxony, and thus isolated from the wealth and companionship of any neighboring fiefs of the empire.

He flattened his palms on the uppermost stone, scanning the village of charred huts and the gaping stone walls that were all that remained of his abbey. In the village square, his sixty-eight lost and lonely Saxon men toiled together, stacking fresh-cut timber too green to be fashioned into pitchrails and beams to repair their houses.

Roderick lifted his eyes to the clear and cloudless sky and silently asked God what he should do to ease the hungers, aches and pains that grew daily in the restless bellies of ten pages, six priests, twenty squires, thirty men-at-arms and nearly seventy serfs.

From the oldest man to the youngest boy, he'd heard the complaint voiced, more times than he cared to count—*My lord, we are Saxons, not monks. We must have women!* That had been the outstanding refrain since he had returned home to the charred keep on Easter Monday, relieved from four long years of service as champion to Lothair, the Holy Roman Emperor.

Four months later, by the first of August, even Roderick admitted that he felt the same aching need every male in his fiefdom complained about constantly. Meals were bad. The keep was filthy. The only commodity in good supply was ale.

Tempers grew short. Fights erupted frequently. Drunkenness got in the way of work and duty.

My lord, we must have women! became a unified cry from one end of Blackstone to the other.

Even Roderick's men-at-arms had turned feisty and quarrelsome after months and months of doing without. There wasn't a single village whore to service the drunks at Kimball's newly thatched tavern.

The duke of Emory had to do something.

Chapter Two

Feast of Saint Michael
September 28, 841 A.D.
Fief of Longervais, France

As her horse galloped up from the stable, Lady Althea-line Bellamy saw Joclyn drop the hearth rug she was shaking on the white marble steps of Landais Manor. The old nurse ran onto the gravel drive, planted herself in Thea's path and stuck her fists on her hips. Her harridan's cry could be heard from one end of the manse to the other.

"Where do you think you are going, Mademoiselle Thea?"

Thea drew back on the reins. Victory skidded to his haunches and stopped. A clutch of fall leaves and pebbles spewed at the voluminous wools flapping around the old woman's puffy ankles. Thea tipped over her horse's arched neck. Her sister Marie rocked precariously on the stallion's rump, and she threw one arm around Thea's waist, barely managing to retain her seat and her hold of their basket filled with herbs and roots.

Thea caught her breath then scolded. "Joclyn! *Mon Dieu,* you could be killed, running in front of this horse!"

"Kill me! Trample me! Don't let an old woman stand in your way, *ma petite!*"

Joclyn threw her arms wide in a parody of martyrdom, a willing sacrifice. Servants peeked out open doors and wide windows, granting the old woman more of an audience than Thea felt she deserved. Joclyn's act lasted mere seconds before her arms were once again akimbo and a scowl returned to her red face. Thea was not about to question the authority that rang in Joclyn's voice when the nurse repeated, "I asked, where you are going!"

Marie answered, "We are going to Longervais. *Maman* had word Madame Hélène is down with fever. Thea and I would pay her a visit and be back before sunset."

"Going visiting? Dressed like that?"

"What is wrong with the way we are dressed?" Thea held Victory still. They had all worn their oldest gowns for a day's labor in the kitchen. With four sisters to the house, dresses made the rounds as each grew into the other's size.

Thea wore a gown that had originally been Andrea's. Likewise, Marie's workaday frock had once been Thea's. Andrea had their mother's height and bust, Thea her father's thick hair and provocative green eyes. She was slender and willowy, and not a hair taller than Grandmother Lenore. Marie had Lady Lilla's blue eyes and mellow temper and lushly feminine figure. Margareth was still forming, and showed the promise of outdoing all her elder sisters.

"You cannot go a-visiting in servants' garb," Joclyn declared.

"Why not?" Thea tossed her curls. She kept her hair trimmed shorter than all her sisters, hating plaits and bindings. It swung easily round her shoulders, a mass of unruly black curls. "We've been working all day in the kitchen!"

"Need I remind you both you are ladies? What will the duke of Auvergne say about his daughters tramping round the countryside in slovenly attire?"

"Joclyn, we deliver herbs, nothing else," Thea reasoned.

"Papa never notices a thing Thea and I wear," Marie said, joining the argument. "He is much too occupied with the emperor's concerns to attend what we do."

"Humph! You go to swish your skirts around young Cavell and torment the lad. I know it."

"Faith, we do not," Thea told the old woman. "We do a charity to a neighbor, as well we should, not to flirt with squires."

"Father would skin us if we did," Marie emphatically agreed.

"So," Joclyn scolded, "you admit your father would note unseemly behavior. Pray then, what of unseemly dress?" She looked to the wealth of red and autumn-yellow trees marking the river. Long shadows heralded evening at hand. "I don't like it. There has been trouble lately, chickens and geese a-missing, washerwomen gone without a trace."

"What do chickens and geese have to do with Marie and me visiting Lady Hélène?" Thea exhaled in exasperation, then, mimicking her mother's most patient and persuasive voice, said to the old nurse, "Joclyn, we ride to Longervais. Mother would have gone herself were it not for the guests in the hall and the hunt. Besides, the purpose of the day's hunt is to rid Landais of the weasels and foxes raiding the henhouses. No one will notice our aprons. We will be back before sunset."

"Bah! I've too much work to do preparing for Lady Andrea's feast day to stand here arguing with you, minx! Where has Margareth taken herself to? Always you girls disappear when there is work to be done. You are spoiled to ruination, Lady Althealine."

"Faith, Joclyn, your eyes must grow weary keeping track of all four of us. Andrea is in the kitchen tending the bread. Margareth keeps company with *Grand-mère* in her garden. Marie and I have finished our chores. Why so quarrelsome, Joclyn? It doesn't become you."

Joclyn wagged a work-worn finger at Thea. Of the four Bellamy daughters, the second's hoydenish ways distressed her the most. "Dare you to correct me, young lady? Am I the one who rides hither and yon on that vicious beast, sporting a Saracen's dagger at my hip? *Mais non,* I do not. Nor should you. Furthermore, my lady, I can still take a switch to you."

Thea could not resist the urge to tease her old nurse, and she smiled brightly. "*Oui,* you can still take a switch to me, but can you catch me?"

Thea let her stallion dance in the gravel around the old nurse. Sensing what was coming, Marie held on for dear life. Thea's delighted laughter echoed back at Joclyn as the gray stallion thundered out the gate.

Longervais Keep was only a short ride across the well-tended valley floor. Prosperous cottages clustered around every brook. The land was rich and fertile, spawning the abundant grasses and grains so necessary to maintain Picardy's most renowned product—horses. Not just any horses, but Percherons, the stalwart breed newly crossed in Lord Bellamy's lifetime. The Percheron was already recognized as the finest war-horse ever bred.

What fields were not planted in the abundant grains that flourished year after year were fenced into paddocks and grazing meadows for small herds of the massive beasts.

It was upon one such fine stallion that Lady Thea rode with her sister clinging desperately to her. Huge clods of dirt flew from beneath Victory's hooves as Thea gave him his head and recklessly let the wind whip through her hair.

Thea knew the occupants of every cottage. They waved and doffed their caps as Victory thundered past. Behind the mountains, the sun was beginning to disappear. It would be gone from sight before the light faded, prolonging golden twilight in Longervais Valley.

Their visit to their ailing neighbor was short and sweet. With the herbs delivered and some cheer given to the sick woman, both young ladies were eager to be on their way. Thea galloped Victory along the worn path past the river.

From high up in the woodlands came the sounds of galloping horses and the trumpeting of the hunt master's horn. Dogs bayed and barked, chasing quarry.

Marie leaned forward and touched Thea's arm. "Can you hear the horn?"

"*Non,*" Thea answered, barely able to hear Marie's shout above the thud of Victory's iron-shod hooves.

"We could have gone."

"*Maman* said we couldn't," Thea replied. "Not with Joclyn raising such a snort because of Drea's wedding feast."

"That didn't keep *Maman* from going," Marie pointed out.

"I don't expect there is any power on earth to keep Mother home when she wants to go out, least of all Joclyn."

"Maybe Papa," Marie suggested.

"Ha!" Thea knew better. "Just imagine going hunting with all those lords. We could never have kept up with *Maman* and her gyrfalcon."

"That is true." Marie had to agree. "Just think, Thea, by the end of this week, Andrea will be wed. Finally!"

Thea shook her head. "Andrea hesitates over every little thing. I have assured her a hundred and one times, the only man for her is Hugh of Cavell. Tomorrow, our uncle Bishop Henri comes, *et voilà,* the celebration begins! The spits will turn and we will have a week of dancing and feasting." Thea could hardly wait. "I suppose it was necessary that we help Andrea, Marie. You'll want the same for yourself when your time comes."

"And you don't?"

Thea drew Victory to a halt at the river's edge and slid gracefully to her feet. "*Mais oui.* There is no hurry, Marie. There never has been. We have all the time in the world to choose our husbands. Papa says so."

Thea offered a hand to her younger sister, who was not nearly as confident on horseback as she was. Marie dropped beside her and stepped away as Victory dipped his head and took a long, needed drink.

Thea always ran the horse hard, liking his strength and speed. She stroked her hand down his slick, silvery coat. He shivered at her touch, shook his head and whickered, blowing air and droplets of water out his nostrils, then nuzzled his velvety nose against her hand affectionately.

"All I can say is, it's about time Andrea made up her mind." Marie fluttered her collar, cooling her skin.

"You know it is *Maman*'s fondest hope that each of her daughters will marry for love. And that, little sister, takes time."

Marie tossed her braids behind her shoulders. "I know that. Andrea's future is settled. Now it is you everyone is making guesses about. Do you realize Gregory of Merrault has come to Landais looking for a bride?"

"The emperor's champion is looking for a dowry."

"Ah, but that is the same thing!" Marie giggled.

Thea silently asked the Lord for patience in dealing with her younger sister. "No, it isn't, Marie. We certainly didn't need Merrault to visit to have things to celebrate at Landais. Why, for the first time in years there is peace, and our brother Royce has just been knighted. Andrea's feast day is tomorrow, and her wedding follows this Saturday. Not to mention *Grand-mère* and *Grand-père*'s anniversary, too," Thea countered. "It's near dark. Shall we swim?"

"*Maman* says we are too old to swim in the river like children," Marie answered.

"*Oui*, we have grown." Thea glanced at the firm bosom that her apron did not hide. Though younger, Marie was more endowed. A mischievous light twinkled in Thea's eyes. "Are you willing?"

"If you are," Marie said saucily. Anything her bold sister would do, she would do better.

Thea dropped to the bank, releasing Victory's reins. He wouldn't go far, and if he did, it took only Thea's two-fingered whistle to bring the stallion trotting right back to her. An unladylike habit, according to Joclyn, but useful, in Thea's book.

"I guess we had best stick to Mother's advice." Marie sighed, joining Thea at the water's edge to cup a handful of the cold liquid and bring it to her mouth.

"The river is not nearly as private as our glen in the mountains." Thea glanced upstream to a thickly shaded bower. Would her mother object if she and Marie swam behind that thick sheltering of trees? It was as private as the glen. She walked in that direction, sorely tempted by the warm autumn evening. But a girl of ten-and-seven was supposed to be demure and ladylike. Lifting her hems, Thea kicked off her slippers and tested the water.

"Ah, to be twelve again," said Thea wistfully.

Marie laughed. "Well, I, for one, never want to be a child again. Joclyn will be after us both with her stick if we swim here."

"It would be worth it," Thea admitted. "But I suppose we should not test her temper any further today."

She settled for splashing water on her neck and face, then, taking the basket from Marie, plowed barefooted through the salt grass to search out useful roots and herbs.

"Ach! I can hear Joclyn already! *Don't go near the river.*" Thea parted a fall of willow branches and bent low to enter the sheltered cove. "Ah! Where else but at the river would I find willow bark?"

Thea took her knife and slit a branch, peeling away the bark. She sniffed it, then smiled at its tangy aroma. Her eyes sparkled as she regarded Marie. "Perfect."

"You and your medicines." Marie could not be bothered with such activity, not when the collecting of them soiled and roughened her hands. "Tell me, Thea. What think you of him?"

"Think of whom?" Thea wound the flexible bark into a fist-size bundle and tucked it in her basket.

"Gregory of Merrault, the emperor's champion, you goose. Margareth says he is the most handsome knight in the realm."

"What does she know of that? When did she ever go to court to see just how many handsome men there really are?"

"You know perfectly well Margie and I haven't been anywhere. Only you and Drea have gone to court. I tell *Maman* that is not fair. You are only a year older than I."

"A year is a year. Do not worry, *ma petite,* your time will come...sooner than you think."

"Well, the quicker both you and Drea are married, the better for me. I won't settle for a country squire, as Andrea has. I shall have to see all the emperor's knights before I make my choice."

"Court isn't what you think it is, Marie." A small frown compressed Thea's brow. "Mostly it is forever waiting for the emperor."

"You can say that. You even went to tourney last."

"And wished I hadn't," Thea said. Just the mention of a tournament sent chills skittering across Thea's shoulders. She returned her attention to the willow in her hand and slit the thin layer of bark. She did not want to think of such sad things on a happy day like this one. She looked up at Marie and smiled.

"The fairs were most curious. Stalls of merchants spread across every open space of field. Mother did say my head swiveled about like an owl's and my eyes nearly popped from my head. But Papa decided watching such bloody contests was not fit entertainment for his daughters, so now, none of us go. Perhaps you can convince Oncle Henri to remove his threat of excommunication upon all who attend such follies in the future, so you may go. Aha, sweet rush! Come Marie, help me pick the leaves."

"Oh, Thea, must we? That's another thing. No one ever explained to me what *oncle* got in such a snit about at Montigney. And you still haven't said a word about Lord Gregory of Merrault. He looks at you, you know."

"Why should he look at me? Not that, Marie, only the rush. Do be careful. Don't pull up the roots, or there will be none next year."

"Bother." Marie clucked her tongue, then wrinkled her nose at the rank smell of the soggy earth. A small shudder for all things slimy whipped through her. "What about Oncle Henri? What great sin transpired that made him so angry?"

"Marie, use your head. Our bishop uncle has intervened to stop the senseless killing by mortal combat of knights consecrated to God. Death by sport is dishonorable. That's what the king's tournaments have come to. That is why Papa has forbidden us to attend in the future."

"Oh." Marie clicked her tongue. "Is that all? Then why do you ignore Lord Gregory? Are you being coy?"

Thea knelt carefully next to the stand of rushes, her deft hands intent upon filling the basket. "I don't know how to be coy."

"Do you think he has spoken to Papa about you?"

"Pray God, I hope not," Thea said promptly.

"Thea! He is the champion! He lives at court in the best of company, those who serve the emperor. So would you."

Thea's mouth turned slightly downward at the corners. "I have not said I want to live at court. Besides, there is some gossip."

"About Emperor Lothair's niece, Anne of Aachen." Marie giggled salaciously, slanting her eyes sideways to judge Thea's reaction. "I know of it. I heard it all in the kitchen. Do you think it true, that Lord Gregory keeps Lady Anne as his mistress? She was poorly dowered, then abruptly widowed."

An eyebrow peaked above Thea's luminous and wide green eyes. Unlike Marie, she did not participate in kitchen gossip. "Some might think Anne of Aachen holds an enviable position. Mother has explained the advantages of widowhood. However, I doubt that Papa would consider

Merrault suitable for any of us. I would never consider the emperor's current champion husband material.''

"*Current* champion?'' echoed Marie. "Is that why you don't like Gregory, because he killed the duke of Emory at Montigney?

"Lord Roderick did not die because of the wounds inflicted on him by Gregory of Merrault. Though I imagine those were serious enough in and of themselves. The true reason the Saxon was defeated did not become known until after the tournament was over. He suffered a vicious bloodletting before the day's dishonorable contest began.''

"You jest, Thea!'' Marie's eyes rounded in her pert face, shocked. "Who would dare such a thing?''

"No one who knows the truth will say.'' Thea shook her head. "I know it for a fact that the Saxon was set upon at dawn that morning and scourged with a bullwhip until his blood ran to his ankles.''

"Why? Who did it? Gregory?''

"*Non,* I do not think so. If anyone was to blame it was Lady Anne. She wanted the Saxon dead because he had withdrawn his offer to marry her.''

"She did? That's not what I heard. I heard it was a ménage à trois—Anne, Gregory and Lord Roderick. And the Saxon caught her in flagrante delicto.''

"I am not repeating kitchen gossip, Marie. I am telling you what I heard Sir Georges tell *Maman* as he escorted us home. *Maman* was so furious she forgot I was riding close by and, though they spoke in private, I heard their heated words. Sir Georges said Anne of Aachen betrayed Emory deliberately, and Mother agreed. What I couldn't fathom is why the Saxon joined in combat. Men do the most foolish things for their misguided sense of honor.''

"So you would not accept Gregory's *tendre,* even though rumors flood the land that Anne of Aachen is soon to be banished to the convent at Solbert?''

"*Non,* I would not, even were she buried at Solbert today. Suffice it to say the champion doesn't inspire me.''

Marie clucked her tongue. "It's just as well. Margareth absolutely adores him. The silly girl giggles over every word he says to her."

"She's still a child, and will cease that habit when she matures, I hope."

"So, Thea, who will you choose, since you have cause for refusing Merrault?"

Thea shrugged. "No one."

"Oh, Thea, tell me true. Have you some secret admirer that you have not spoken of?"

She cast a quick glance at Marie's expectant face, then shook her head. "I'm afraid not, Marie."

"Surely you have met someone at court. Someone special." Marie's delicate hands formed into fists that she playfully pounded against her knees. "Oh! It isn't fair! It's you who always gets to go, while I am left at home and no one tells me anything. When will *Maman* see I'm not a child?"

"Perhaps on the day you stop throwing silly tantrums," Thea chided softly.

Marie looked at her hands, then laughed out loud at herself. She threw her arms around Thea's shoulders and kissed her cheek. "I do adore you, sister."

"And I you." Thea patted her reassuringly. "You know, most times I doubt I will ever marry."

"Of course you will."

"*Non.*" Thea's head moved in a solemn negation. "I have been to court as many times as Drea. There have been no offers made for me. Papa and I were speaking to that his last visit home. I told Papa that I doubt that any man would ever love me as much as he loves *Maman*. I am not perfect like Drea."

"Thea . . ." Marie rolled her eyes. "You know you are everyone's favorite. You mustn't let such a silly thought take root in your head."

Thea tossed her curls negligently. "I don't know, Marie. I have my flaws, and perhaps others see them more quickly.

I cannot sing, and I play no instruments to bring me the admirers Andrea has. Papa told me that I do not have to marry if I do not want to. It's just as well he feels that way. I am sure Jason will let me remain at Landais as his chatelaine. It is the way of things for unmarried sisters."

"You would let one flaw stop you from experiencing a lifetime of bliss?"

"Bliss? Oh, Marie, you must stop listening to the minstrels. Life is not at all as it is portrayed in their songs. About marriage I am merely being realistic. It would be intolerable to be wed to someone I did not love or who did not love me. If I never find anyone who would have those special feelings for me, then I would prefer to remain unmarried and accepted in the home I have always known."

Thea rose to her feet and brushed clumps of mold from her apron, then wandered farther along the bank. As the light left the valley, she did not see the boat gliding soundlessly across the river.

Chapter Three

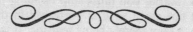

"The Lord has answered my prayers," Benjamin of Emory announced reverently to his companions in the skiff.

This was Ben's first raid. His heart pounded erratically because here, at last, was a greater find than a few measly sacks of grain and seed—women, beautiful and young Frankish women.

From his position at the helm in the back of the skiff, Lord Roderick couldn't help agreeing with his young cousin for once. The gray stallion was definitely the answer to his prayers. His gaze had not left the animal since he'd spied it untended at the river's turning.

"Be quiet, Ben," warned Sir Michael of Lozere, who was more seasoned than the boy was in any type of hunting. "Sound travels over water."

Two chattering maids held Michael and Ben's attention. Their gossipy racket came from a nearby tuck in the riverbank, where willows and shedding cottonwoods formed a cove. Roderick risked rocking the boat to nudge Michael into seeing something other than women. "Look!"

Michael tore his gaze from the lovely maids.

On a greensward below a field of ripe oats grazed a massive gray horse. The beast stared at the three men, twitched its pointed ears and searched the air with flaring nostrils. Apparently unalarmed, it flicked its long, shiny tail and resumed sampling the abundant grass.

"'Tis a fine, worthy gray, eh, Hawk?" Michael murmured.

"Aye, the finest I've seen in a good while." Roderick saw no purpose in remarking on the beribboned saddle gracing the stallion's back.

"I want the one with the braids." Suddenly Ben lurched upright. A sharp punch from Michael silenced him. The duke would not want the stallion spooked.

One maid squealed, drowning out the raucous noise of nesting birds. The other laughed. As distractions, the maids were well placed. The horse ceased grazing, raised his head to look at the girls, then returned his attention to Roderick.

Roderick imagined the stallion found the maids as big a distraction as he did. He glanced into their private, tree-sheltered cove. Even in the half-light of sunset both appeared young and tempting. But their hair was black. For that attribute alone, Roderick dismissed them. He had no use for black-haired women.

Another outburst of laughter made Hawk look at the maids more critically. He focused on the one whose hair flowed freely. She wore a simple gown and apron, though his hawklike vision detected cloth of quality. Her deft hands gathered cuttings from the verdant shore. The curve of her throat and fairness of her skin made him achingly aware of how very, very long it had been since he'd had a woman beneath him.

Whether it was from abstinence or the twilight impression of rare beauty—that one tempted him more than he dared admit.

Tempted he could not be. Not when the real treasure of this sojourn up the river Somme stood before Roderick of Emory, begging to be mastered.

Besides, he had all the women his ship could hold, but a horse, a fine war-horse—for a prize such as that, he would make room! He lifted his Viking helm and settled it on his head. The skiff rocked as Hawk clambered into the shallows. Water lapped against the hull.

Reaching for a coil of braided rawhide, Michael chuckled as Ben began to rise over the waving cattails. The boy's mindless grin proved that he had completely forgotten he was dressed in a barbarian's fur trappings, loincloth and leggings, just like Michael and Lord Roderick. As the boy straightened to his full height, he clutched the wobbling horned helmet to his head.

"By God's ten toes, she is beautiful," he whispered.

"Damn your eyes, Benjamin, you'll scare them to death showing your ugly face in that helmet!" Roderick caught the loincloth at his cousin's hips, yanking the boy down onto his backside. "Get your mind to the work at hand. Forget the women. 'Tis the horse we'll take."

"Horse? What horse?" Ben sprawled over sacks of stolen seed and bolts of contraband cloth. His head swiveled about on his skinny neck like a loose pin on a wooden toy. "Oh."

The boy's surprise brought a flash of white teeth to Michael's lean, black-bearded face.

Ben pointed to the sheltered arbor, croaking in an effort to whisper, "I'll take two of them for a horse any day of the week."

"And you're a damned fool, as well." Roderick's look silenced the youth as he beached the skiff. "Stay with the boat." Equipped with ample rope, Roderick and Michael moved stealthily under the darkening, shadowy trees.

Ben flopped onto his stomach. This time only his hand snaked forward, parting the waving cattails so that he could enjoy an unimpeded view into the private cove. Maybe the girls had come here to bathe, he hoped. He was content with that prospect. They were definitely two uncommonly beautiful maids.

"It is getting dark, Thea. We had better go." Marie sat on a log and hitched her hems to her knees as she tightened the laces on her muddy slippers.

Thea bent over, searching through the grass, "Marie, did you hide my shoes?"

"*Non.* Victory's run off, you know."

"*Non,* he hasn't." Remembering where she'd discarded her shoes, Thea ran barefoot through the salt grass. "They are not here. Marie?"

"I didn't hide them!" Marie protested. "Thea, call Victory. We are late enough without walking home." She picked up the basket and slipped its handle up her arm.

"Oh, bother!" Thea wandered, pressing aside the tall grasses. She looked for her shoes, ignoring how dark it had become. "If I don't find them, I will have to come back tomorrow and look in the daylight." She paused as she straightened and looked up at the darkening sky. "You are right. We had best get home quickly."

Putting two fingers to her mouth, she blasted a shrill whistle that set the nesting birds chattering in the trees.

The unexpected sound startled Ben, nearly causing him to topple backward where he crouched in the grasses, a scant two feet behind the girl tying her shoes. A second shrill signal sounded just as he sprang forward to capture the girl in front of him.

Thea gazed at the shoreline where she had last seen Victory grazing. He was nowhere to be seen at the moment.

"Victory, come, boy!" She parted a fall of willow branches. "That's odd...."

Thea cocked her head to hear Victory's answering call. Returning two fingers to her lips, she gave a third shrill signal that sent the birds scattering from their overhead perches. That noise was followed by the reassuring thunder of Victory's hooves pounding the earth nearby. Behind her, a muffled squeal barely registered.

"I hope Victory isn't in the oats. Mother hates it when he tramples the grain. What are you up to now, Marie? Are you hiding my shoes? We haven't time for games." Turning back to her sister, Thea was startled to see that some sort of horned monster had caught hold of Marie and dragged her into the cattails.

"*Marie!*"

Thea heard Victory's wild, angry snort and the resounding thud of his hooves smashing the earth. Body frozen, Thea's head rotated from side to side, viewing equally horrifying sights.

Two bearded, horn-helmed, half-naked men had control of her horse. A third was vanishing into the cattails with her sister.

"Oh, my God!" Thea gasped. "Vikings!"

Marie cut loose with a bloodcurdling scream. Without a thought to consequences, Thea launched herself onto the Viking that held her sister. Marie fought, as well, kicking and clawing. Both gouged at his eyes with their fingers and pounded their fists into his unarmed body.

The young Viking lost his helmet under Thea's assault. Overbalanced with one girl in front of him, the other pounding on his back, he toppled into the mud. Marie struggled free of his grip. The three of them rolled in the muddy marsh. Marie sat up, wiping mud and muck from her face, screaming hysterically. Astraddle the youth's back, Thea pounded her fists against his unprotected head.

"Run, Marie! Get help!" Thea landed a well-aimed punch as the youthful Viking twisted toward her. The youth howled and grabbed his bloodied nose. "Run! I can handle this runt! He's naught but a skinny boy!"

Taking a page from her bold sister's book, Marie clubbed the downed youth with her only weapon, a crushed basket. Neither she nor Thea were helpless!

Thea almost had the situation under control when the youth flipped her onto her back and pinned her to the ground. He shouted in triumph.

"Run, Marie! Get help!"

"Let my sister go, you brute! Thea! Thea!" Marie bashed the youth with the basket of herbs.

"I've got him! Run, Marie!" Thea ordered frantically.

The youth grinned evilly and grunted unintelligibly.

The earth seemed to tremble under Thea's back. The boy was heavier than she'd first thought. She twisted and got her hand on her knife. Victory burst into the clearing with a rider on his back like the most fearless of war-horses entering into the fray. He emitted a ferocious and terrifying shriek as he reared.

"Thea!" Marie screamed as she turned around and spied the enraged stallion with a huge man mounted on his back. That was ten times more frightening than a boy Viking because Marie knew Victory went berserk when a man tried to ride him. She fell and scrambled backward like a crab, screaming, "Help! Help, somebody help! Thea! Victory will kill us!"

The enraged stallion pawed the air dangerously close to the young Viking's head. The youth was not so stupid as to remain where he was. Scrambling off Thea, he gave her the chance to roll out of danger. She cleared her horse's descending hooves and bounded to her feet. Unsteady and winded, she held firm possession of her deadly Saracen knife.

The second Viking skidded to a halt. He saw the blade in her hands and held back. Wisely, he raised his empty hands, proof that he carried no weapons. Thea tried to catch her breath and think what best to do. With the knife, she held the fragile balance of power. The man backed slightly away from her. The youth nursed his bleeding nose.

That left the most dangerous man of all, the one who had managed to bring Victory's four legs to the earth and held him firmly at bay by sheer force of will. That, Thea knew, was no mean feat. Victory had never tolerated the heavier weight of a man on his back. That was why he'd become her horse.

Thea wiped her sleeve across her mouth as she put her sister safely behind her. Marie shook as badly as the willows, helplessly wringing her hands. Thea fixed her eyes upon the mounted Viking.

The man on her horse broke the tense silence, saying plainly, in more than passable Frankish, "We mean you no harm. Leave. Take your sister and go."

The light was dismal at best, but Thea saw clearly his hardened, uncompromising bearded face and heard every nuance of command inherent in the Viking's deep, resonant voice. He stunned her. She stood where she was, gawking at the golden-skinned barbarian, so magnificent astride her horse. A girding of fur circled his lean hips. A fur cloak swung away from his powerful shoulders. Leather bands crisscrossed his naked chest. Polished armbands encircled the bulging muscles of his upper arms as they flexed and contracted in his effort to keep the horse under control. Awestruck by the terrifying power of the wild barbarian, Thea knew she should take Marie's hand and run.

But she was shaken, not hurt, and something inside her balked at his command.

Victory stamped under the Viking's control. He was a horseman of some expertise to have so easily subdued her mount. Still, she reasoned, she held the knife. It was one bargaining point he could not argue with.

"I said take your sister and go."

"And just let you steal my horse?" Thea felt every bone in her spine straighten. "Nay, I do not give over what is mine."

"Thea! Don't be stupid! Didn't you hear what he said? We can go!" Marie clutched Thea's arm, pulling her back.

"Nay!" Thea shook off Marie's hand. "Obey me, sister. Run. Get Papa. They'll not steal my Victory."

"Jesu, a horse is a horse, Thea. I cannot leave you."

"Go, I said. I can hold them with my knife till you bring Papa and Royce."

"Thea!" Marie's wail was full of anguish. How could she leave, if Thea wouldn't?

"Run, I said!" Thea commanded. Not once did Thea's resolve weaken. "Over my dead body will I let a barbarian steal the finest horse ever bred in Landais."

Marie heard steel scrape against steel. The huge man mounted on Victory was armed. She watched in horror as he drew a sword from a scabbard at his hip. That was the last thing she needed to see to be convinced to run. She turned and fled into the trees.

Thea's heart was pounding too loudly in her ears for her to hear the scrape of steel, but she did see the long, double-edged blade as the magnificent warrior raised it over Victory's beautiful neck. Her weapon was trifling in comparison.

She began to tremble, seeing that she had made a grievous mistake, but she regained her nerve with the thought that she had managed to hold back two of his men with seven inches of razor-sharp steel. They would bleed very deeply if they dared to come near her. She had only to stall for time, delay them from leaving, then perhaps her father and a dozen of the knights visiting Landais would come to her rescue. It was that thought that gave her courage to stand her ground.

"Go." The Viking ordered his men, but his eyes never left Thea's as he resheathed his blade. "We meet at the ship."

The youth leaped into the tall rushes. The other staunchly defended the ground between his lord and Thea. Oblivious of the man on foot, she kept her narrowed, furious eyes fixed on the barbarian atop her horse.

He drew hard on the reins and propelled his heels sharply into Victory's sides, forcing the animal to turn.

"You unspeakable bastard! Get down from my horse before you hurt him!" Thea bolted forward, throwing one hand up to snatch Victory's bridle. "Get off, damn you!"

In concert with her scream, Victory bucked. The Viking held firm as the stallion fought him. Thea drew back from the fight, as horrible as it was to witness. Both man and animal were contorted with purple rage, he to control the beast, Victory to gain release.

The stallion arched and thudded to earth. The Viking's gold helm flew from his head. It landed near Thea's feet, but she hardly noticed. Her jaw sagged in shock, because now that no metal disguised his features, she recognized him.

"*Mon Dieu!*" Thea gasped. "Roderick of Emory!"

Her heart quit beating. It couldn't be! *The Hawk of Emory was dead!* But the Hawk of Emory was unforgettable. Blessed with sun-kissed golden hair, his brow was a strong plane above chiseled cheeks and a proud, Roman nose. But it was his eyes that Thea knew she could never, ever mistake. They had the intensity of a predator's, and now were fixed upon her as if she were the prey he intended to swoop down upon. She wanted to run, but her legs would not move.

Blowing harshly, Victory submitted, dropping his head in defeat. Thea swallowed and found her voice and the wherewithal to approach her winded horse. "Monseigneur Hawk, I beg you, do not take my horse. He is a good horse, and I love him."

At the touch of her fingers on the bridle, Victory quieted. His sides heaved and shivered, and though his legs trembled, he bore the weight of the man on his back perfectly, as if they were made for one another. A tremor swept through Thea's belly that she did not recognize or know the meaning of—but a wild thought raced through her mind, asking if she, too, was made for this man.

"You know of me?" Roderick of Emory rasped. His face twisted, fierce and wild—as magnificent as the animal he had chosen to subdue. His naked chest heaved, glistening with the sweat of his labor. His piercing gaze fixed so resolutely on Thea, made every sinew and bone in her body quiver.

Flesh-and-blood man, no ghost, Thea thought.

"Yea, I know of you. I saw you fall at Montigney, and heard afterward God took you unshriven." Thea crossed herself and added a hasty prayer that her father would come soon.

"Nay, lady, not unshriven, and not taken by God that day, but cast into hell on earth. I take the horse. I have need of it."

Thea's hands tightened on Victory's bridle. She must delay him, stall for more time. "*Pourquoi?* Why do you do this? The duke of Emory has no cause to steal. You have been and always will be Emperor Lothair's favorite."

Her words caused his mouth to harden into a grim and furious line, shrouded by the darkness of his beard. Abruptly he yanked Victory's head free of her containment and shouted. "*Michael, à moi, maintenant.* The maid has recognized me. Bind and truss her and bring her to my ship."

Thea was simply too stunned to move. She should have run with Marie when given the chance.

She turned, her Saracen blade no longer an idle threat. When the vassal tried to grab her, she used it, striking at the hand he sought to put on her, feinting when he lunged to the side. Her long skirts hampered her as she backed away from the advancing, wary man. She tripped and tumbled. He followed, rolling her in the dirt. She felt the blade, gripped so tightly in her fingers, sink deep.

"Augh, damn and perdition!" The dark man clutched his belly.

"*Salaud!*" Thea sucked in air. The jeweled handle of her blade protruded from the man's belly. "*Pour l'amour de Dieu,* you got what you deserved, you animal!"

"Blood of Christ!" Roderick of Emory shouted. "Ben, get you to me!"

Thea scrambled onto her knees, tugging her skirt free from beneath the injured man. "Oh, no! Oh, no!" she whispered, afraid for her own life. Staggering to her feet, she turned to run at last, crying out, "What have I done?"

She had not taken three steps before an iron-hewn arm swept her off her feet and she was pulled across the bow of her own saddle. White teeth flashed wickedly against the golden shadow of the Hawk of Emory's beard.

"You've gotten yourself captured, woman."

It was too late to help Thea. Each knight and squire who tramped over and over the riverbank with torches in hand and lanterns held aloft had come privately to that conclusion.

There was blood on the earth beside the riverbank. Lord Bellamy knelt on one knee, examining the dark stain, his face twisted with rage. His eldest son, Sir Royce, held the sobbing Marie in a protective embrace. Their mother, Lady Lilla, stood to herself, strong and angry, glaring at the water.

"Describe to me again these men who attacked you and Thea," Lord Bellamy demanded.

"'Twas dark, Papa. We had no warning."

"Think, Marie! There is no time for useless tears. What did you see? What did these villains look like? Tell me again."

Rattled, Marie trembled as she answered. "They were huge, hairy creatures. Devils, Papa. All had helms with horns upon them, as big as bulls', and beards, except for the one that attacked me. He was fair-haired, golden, his hair long and curly. He wore a fur pelt on his shoulders and gold bands on his arms. They wore no leggings nor chausses. Instead, they wore...animal skins!" Marie choked on her last words and turned her face into her brother's mail-covered chest, sobbing. "Why did I leave Thea alone?"

Royce Bellamy's arms tightened round his sobbing sister, his own throat too constricted to make a sound.

"Vikings." Lord Merrault stamped forward, leading his war-horse by its reins. His face twisted darkly. He was oblivious of the smashed reeds beneath his sabatons. "We must go after them, my lord Bellamy, before the tide has a chance to turn."

"I've never seen such men!" Marie wailed. "What about Thea, Papa? Where is she? What have they done to her?"

Lady Lilla, whose gaze had been turned to the river for such a long, sad time, finally turned from her watch over the flowing water. "Thea is gone, Marie. I fear you have seen your sister for the last time."

"Non," Lord Roger Bellamy vowed as he rose to his feet. "I will find her. We go after them. Victory has left a clear trail. Lord Merrault, I pray you, go down the river to the abbey. Alert them that Vikings have raided Landais."

"They came by boat, my lord." Lilla pointed to the mashed rushes beneath Merrault's feet.

There were other signs any serious hunter could read. A heavy load had been dragged from the clearing through the short woods, leaving twin ruts in the marshy soil. Elsewhere, Victory's hooves had trampled the impressionable mud to a froth. It was hard for Lilla to read the signs of struggle and injury and not be moved to tears, but for the sake of her three children present she did not give in to them.

Thea's knife lay bloody and forgotten on the ground at the very water's edge.

"You'll not track them, my lord husband." Lady Lilla bent and lifted her daughter's Saracen blade from the damp earth, offering it wordlessly to her husband. Did he wonder, as she did, if it was Thea's blood that marred it? And if so, why had they not found her body nearby?

Their search had been thorough. No other evidence of attack had been found. That provided Lilla no solace.

She put her arm around Marie's waist and drew her daughter tightly to her side, finding some comfort in the safety of one of her darlings. But as she closed her eyes in sorrow, all she could think was *Not Thea. Not Thea. Not the one I love the most.*

"You'll never get away with this," Thea exclaimed.

Roderick drew the horse to a halt on a low bluff over the estuary, scanning the water until he found what he was looking for—the skiff.

Benjamin had good sailing instincts. The skiff cut across the tidewater, tacking into the sea cove under the glimmer of the rising moon. Hawk quieted, each of his senses sharply tuned. The bells at the abbey, several leagues inland, remained silent. No alarm had been sounded, yet.

Thea shifted uneasily, testing the bonds on her wrists. She moistened her lips and repeated her taunt. "Do you hear me, Hawk of Emory? I say you will never get away with abducting me or my horse. You will be hunted to the ends of the earth."

"Be quiet," Roderick admonished her. He was acutely aware of every movement she made. He liked the feel of her bottom cradled between his thighs.

The wind lifted her hair, scattering it against his chest like a soft cloud of silk. Roderick caught the scent of rose water clinging to it. He transferred the reins into his left hand, brought his palm up to cup her chin and draw her body back against his chest.

"Woman," he said as she went still and stiff against him, "I could tarry here, having my way with you, until the sun rises, and none would come to disabuse me of my privilege."

He enjoyed her outraged gasp. She was furious. He tightened his grip upon her stubborn little chin, bringing her full red lips within range of his own.

There was enough moonlight to let him see the luster of her eyes and the paleness of her face against the midnight black of her hair.

As he brought his mouth against the throbbing heat of her lips, her fingernails made contact with his bare belly—sharp talons prepared to rip his flesh.

"Do it," Roderick said against her closed lips. "And I will take you here on this very ground."

Thea's whole body quivered to do something. She opened her mouth to curse him, and his lips swept over hers with the skill of a goshawk diving for a kill. That astounded and shocked her. No man had ever put his mouth to her lips and kissed her. Kisses were to be bestowed upon brows or cheeks or the back of a lady's hand.

Not Roderick of Emory's kiss.

In truth, Thea did not know what to do. The feel of his mouth touching hers was unlike anything she had ever experienced in her life.

Where his mouth was first hard and cold, it softened and grew warm against her own. She tried to break away, but couldn't find escape in any direction. Then she didn't want to escape this bold and shocking touch that was totally unlike any previous touch she'd ever known. She was so distracted by how his mouth felt as it moved on hers that she quite forgot her intention to claw his belly to ribbons.

As abruptly as he'd begun the kiss, he ended it.

Roderick chuckled, put his heels to the stallion's sides, urging him forward, and rode on with his captive, who was unable to do anything to stop him. He had to give her some credit. She had more bravado than any woman he'd encountered thus far in this mad plan to bring wives to Emory.

The horse made short work of the distance to the cove where his ship lay at anchor. Roderick hailed the crew from the rocky shore. The woman relaxed against him for the first time. Roderick realized he would miss her warmth the moment he dismounted.

The beast splashed along the rockbound shallows, tossing its head as if it could take mastery away from Roderick, but he checked the reins immediately. Neither the woman nor the horse would wrest control from his hand.

"You will dismount," Roderick commanded.

Thea jerked around, glaring at him over her left shoulder. "I can't from this height with my hands bound. I will fall and be injured on the rocks."

His fingers tightened on her left arm, shifting her across his right thigh. "You will fall and be hurt only if you attempt something stupid. Now do as you have been told."

Thea wanted him to dismount first. Victory would respond to any signal she gave him while astride his back.

There was one chance they could both be free, because once her horse started running, no one could catch him. All she would have to worry about was keeping her seat.

"I can't. I'm frightened." Thea clenched her knees to Victory's withers, spouting every excuse she could think of. "I can't swim."

"Then you will drown in a foot of water." Roderick immediately changed his grip, encircling her waist, lifting her off the horse's back and dangling her over the side.

Thea reacted immediately, screaming, "Don't you dare drop me in this water!"

He dared. He simply let go.

Thea dropped like a stone into the surf. Nothing but the incoming surf broke her fall. She had no chance to gain a decent footing. One bare foot found a sharp rock. The other slipped on coarse, unstable sand. She tumbled sideways, making a wild, armless struggle to break her fall, and plowed headfirst into the foaming backwash, screaming.

With her mouth full of gritty salt water, she rolled sideways and sat up, sputtering and spitting.

Roderick dismounted, grinning, and handed the horse's reins to the men from his ship who splashed through the shallows to meet him. He cast off his cloak, glad to be rid of the unnecessary warmth. Handing it to the closest man he said, "Use this to blindfold the horse before taking it up the gangplank."

While the four took on that job, he dropped his fists to his scabbard belt and turned to confront the little woman floundering in the shallows.

There wasn't all that much to her, but she was a hellcat. She had managed to right herself to a seated position, and she swung her head violently to rid her face of a clump of wet hair.

Roderick couldn't hold back the laugh that action brought him. A small piece of seaweed draped across her left eye. She blew a furious breath, trying to dislodge it. As he reached down to pick the offending weed from her now thoroughly sodden coiffure, he chuckled again, and marveled at that. It had been a very, very long time since so much as a smile had crossed his lips.

"How dare you laugh at me!" Thea kicked water at the arrogant man, standing with his damned boots planted in the water, towering over her. "You, you... filthy dirty stinking Saxon bastard!"

"Well, well, what a mouth you have, my little naiad." Roderick secured her arm to assist her to her feet, and again she jerked away, trying to evade his touch. That snapped what little patience for her antics he had left. He caught both her arms firmly and hauled her bodily out of the water and shook her. "Next time you are told what to do, wench, obey my command."

Rattled, Thea hissed through her teeth, "I will kill you for this, Emory."

Instead of answering her puny threat, Roderick merely put her on her feet and sent her moving with a firm slap on her soggy backside. Her outraged howl brought back his grin. Taking hold of her arm, Roderick drew her forcibly along with him to the ship.

The craft rocked in the natural harbor, anchored beside a shelf of solid stone that was visible at low tide. Several feet of water overran the rocks at high tide, but either way, the stone provided Roderick a makeshift wharf.

His crew had followed his orders. A plank had been dropped from the side of the ship onto the underwater stones, and the hooded horse was being carefully led up it and onto the deck.

Seeing what was happening to Victory, Thea cast a desperate look back to the shore, praying that someone would come now to rescue her.

The water had deepened well past her knees, tugging on her skirts and legs. Hawk's relentless grip on her arm made certain she kept pace with him. But he had the benefit of having both feet shod. Thea did not. She stepped on another sharp rock and tumbled into the rising tide. Catching her before she went completely under, Hawk lifted her out of the water and tossed her over his shoulder.

"No!" Thea wailed as his hard shoulder dug into her belly. Seawater ran from her clothes into her eyes and blinded her. She twisted, screamed and struggled, bucking more wildly than Victory had on the river.

Roderick clamped his arm over the wildcat's legs and kept a firm hold on her while he waited for his crew to clear the frightened horse safely over the high, moving railing. He anticipated no mishaps where the dumb animal was concerned. The black-haired little witch now trying to sink her damned teeth into his hide was another matter. He was sorely tempted to wade to the edge of the rock shelf and throw her into the deep water. She'd sink like a stone.

He tightened his grip on the back of her thighs and eyed the nicely rounded rump that graced his left shoulder. All that she lacked in size, she certainly made up for in strength. He had to bring his right hand into play to make certain she did not twist off his shoulder. And as he laid that hand on the back of her firm thigh and felt her muscles contract beneath his touch, he began to anticipate the taming of her. He would begin by ordering her to take off her now thoroughly soaked gown.

"My lord Hawk," Benjamin said as he tipped over the side of the ship and waved at Roderick. "Sir Michael's fainted."

"Have you bound his wound?" Roderick shouted, moving to the ramp. The horse balked at the last moment, his iron-shod hooves ringing dully on the unsteady wood.

"Nay!" Ben shouted back. "There wasn't time! What should I do?"

"Wait. I'll be on board directly. Take the horse's reins and pull," Roderick ordered the men crowded around the horse on the deck. The woman kicked at his legs and screamed a curse. He slapped the horse's rump as hard as he could. It bolted over the railing and skidded onto the slippery deck. It was wild and frightened, but boarded nonetheless.

One man had the sense to toss Roderick a rope. He caught it with his free hand, levering himself up the sharply inclined gangplank as the woman straightened. Damned if the fool didn't try to throw herself off his shoulder one last time. He should have seen the move coming.

She literally threw her whole upper body sideways, pulling Roderick dangerously off-balance. The gangplank slipped under his feet and lost its mooring on the rail. She got her wish for release as Roderick went crashing into the water.

He sank to the rocky shelf and stood up. With the tide running high, the water fluctuated to a depth of about five feet, but the current was strong and dangerous, with a vicious backtow. Upright, he immediately looked for the woman.

The gangplank had caught her skirts, and she bobbed helplessly against the hull of the ship and the heavy board.

She was unconscious when Roderick pulled her head out of the water. Bone-limp, she was much heavier than before.

"Toss me the Jacob's ladder," Roderick ordered as he cradled the young woman in his arms, holding her out of the swirling water. The rope ladder scuttled over the sidewall. He scrambled up it and passed his human bundle into the helpful hands of his men, then hauled himself over the rail.

"Is the skiff stowed?" was Roderick's first question.

"Aye, Hawk, and the last cargo lashed."

"Good. Raise the anchor and drop the sail. We're headed for Emory, men."

A cheer greeted that announcement.

Grinning, Roderick took the girl from the sailor that held her. A quick examination proved to him that she was breathing just fine. She had a cut on her scalp, and a small trickle of blood marred her forehead.

"Give me a hand here," he requested as he strode down the deck to the forward hatch. "Raise the grate so I can take this one below. We've a hard night's work ahead of us, men."

Then, with two steps downward into the now opened gangway, Roderick ducked his head and disappeared into the bowels of the ship.

Chapter Four

The hold of the ship stank, of sweat, of fish, of fear. Cool fingers pressed a cup of water to Thea's mouth.

"Please don't scream or shout. My name is Elspeth. I'm from Friesland. I know your name. They called you Thea. Is that right?"

Was it? The best Thea could manage was to nod her head. She pushed the cup away, fighting a terrible wave of nausea.

"Better?"

Whoever the strange woman was, she thought her kind ministering helped. Thea nodded, for her thanks could be no more than a dry croak.

"Your head is injured, and you have slept through night and day. Don't be frightened. I will not hurt you."

"Should I be frightened?" Thea stared blankly at the woman, not recognizing her face at all. A thick blond braid fell across Elspeth's shoulder. "Is this a dream?"

"Yes, well, more like a nightmare, I imagine." Elspeth sighed. "But I don't think so. Three days ago, I was on my way home from market with four sacks of spices Cook sent me to purchase. All I can attest to is that I and my master's spices are here now—captive on this ship."

"Oh." A sudden upward motion jarred Thea against the wall. She raised a hand to steady herself.

" 'Tis Jesse, here beside me."

"How fare you?" asked another voice from the shadows. There was very little light, and Thea could barely make out the pert round face that went with the husky voice.

"Jesse is from Boulogne, and was taken captive first."

"I beg your pardon for tearing the ruffles from your apron. No other cloth was there to use to bind your head. Grant mercy," Jesse whispered hoarsely.

"No pardon needed." Thea found the binding encircling her head. The cloth and her hair felt stiff and rough, as if blood had dried on it. She supposed it had. There was enough pain underneath the bandage to denote a wound of some consequence. She had no memory of how it had occurred.

"Best rest. There's aught else t' do." Elspeth leaned against the bulkhead. Lambs bleated on the other side of it.

"This is a ship." Thea had identified the constant motion at last. She tried to stretch out her legs and couldn't. Another body filled the space before her and groaned at the contact of Thea's bare feet. The woman turned, and a pale head caught what light there was. Realizing that body belonged to another woman lessened some of Thea's rising sense of alarm as she asked, "There . . . there are men here? In the dark?"

"Nay, no men. They are above . . . on the deck. The master does not allow any down here, except one to pass a bucket of water and food after dawn."

"I see." Thea kept her head as still as she could against the constant rocking. "Where does the ship go?"

Elspeth's shoulder brushed Thea's in a helpless gesture. "We don't know."

"It will be a miracle if these Vikings keep this leaky ship afloat," Jesse said as silence settled over the growing darkness.

"Vikings? Are you sure?" Befuddled, Thea wasn't even certain why she asked that question. "How long . . . how long have we been at sea?"

"Five days since I was taken from Boulogne, lady. This coming night makes two for you."

"Two nights..." Thea's voice trailed off into silence. How? Why? She couldn't answer any of those questions. Something made her very angry. Her fingers pressed to her side, feeling for a weapon, certain there should be a knife there. All she found was dampness in the folds of her gown.

She turned her face to the single dim square of light. Unsteadily, using the wall to brace her back, she got to her feet.

"Be careful." Elspeth immediately put out hands to steady Thea. They felt strong and competent. How could the woman be so calm? Then Thea remembered Marie and what had transpired on the Somme.

She sank to her knees, clutching Elspeth's hands in desperation. "Tell me, is there another here like me? A girl with black braids?"

She felt another pair of hands fold warmly over hers and Elspeth's. "Nay, lady, calm yourself. No other such as you with braids is here. I would have seen her."

Thea exhaled deeply, relieved to know Marie was safe. "What of a horse, a silvery stallion with a mane as pale as angel hair?"

Elspeth firmly patted Thea's shoulder. "Fear not about the stallion berthed beyond this wall. There seem to be as many animals packed on this ship as there are women. Best we pray our voyage is a short one."

Thea quieted. Marie was safe. Victory had been taken. That meant she would have the means to escape once land was gained. She dropped her head to her upright knees and prayed a small thanksgiving. That gave her peace. Enough peace that she could doze fitfully for the balance of the night.

Thea started awake, inhaling the pungent animal scents seeping through the cracks in the planks behind her head. It was no more rank than the sour scent of unwashed flesh, sweat and seasickness that clung to the women crowded around her.

A glimmer of daylight shined through the grate on the ceiling. Several women cowered in the deep crevice under the bowsprit, moaning and retching pitifully, begging for someone to bring them water. Thea covered her mouth, lest she also be sick.

Elspeth slept, and the other girl, Jesse, provided her arm as pillow. So it was for all the women. They used each other's body for warmth against the damp, cushion from the hard floor and support for the constant shifting of a boat riding the waves.

Tilting to the stern, rocking aft and up and down, Thea knew she would be sick herself if she could not fetch herself topside into clean air and escape the rank miasma.

Again she levered her body upright, using the rough plank wall at her back. She tested her strength, her balance, and survived without the wall's support. The pain in her head had decreased greatly from the earlier throbbing. She must have clean air.

The square opening onto the deck showed the purple and rose of sunrise. She saw a pathway through the bodies.

The sun had yet to break over the horizon as she clambered up crude planks to the deck, seeing fresh, untainted air.

"Get back below," growled a red-bearded sailor the instant Thea showed her head. He squatted over a cleat, clumsily coiling twisted hemp into a knot, looking no more ferocious than a cooper straining over staves. Thea knew in an instant that she could cow him.

"Some women are sick. They need water and medicine." Thea gulped the clean air. The wind slapped her skirts against her legs as soon as she cleared the last step. The bandage around her head kept her hair from whipping into her eyes.

The man stretched upright, planting his feet apart as if to bar her path, yet he clutched the rigging to keep his balance.

"Get back below." He made a fist with his free hand, as if to strike her.

That he dared even clench his fist in her presence touched a fuse to Thea's temper. She drew to her full height, glaring at him. "Hit me if you dare, cur!"

He didn't. She had no trouble retaining her balance or standing unaided, a feat that enhanced her sense of power over the unsteady man before her. "Who is coxswain of this boat?"

"No coxswain." He waved his sunburned fist at the air behind her. "Lord Hawk holds the helm."

With narrowed eyes, Thea said, "Does he, then? The Hawk of Emory is your liege?"

"Yea, and he will cut you to ribbons for daring to come above decks," the varlet muttered.

Thea cast him a cold glance. She would not go back into that dark pit of misery. Let the other women cower; Thea would feel the wind, taste the salt and see the sun. Not even the uneasy sensation of malevolent eyes boring into her back was enough to force her to return to the hold.

The ship bore no resemblance to the fantastic Viking warships Thea had stared at with morbid curiosity when they were anchored at Le Havre and even as far inland as Île-de-France, above Paris. The hardy crew sprawled wherever they found a stretch of planking, cradle of coiled rope or yielding bundle. To a man, they were blond. None Thea saw were dark-haired. They could very well be Vikings, if one judged solely on the basis of coloring.

The fact that she appeared to be the only dark-haired person in their midst made her feel all the more singular and alone. She moved past the curtaining shadow of the sail and stacks of lashed barrels, seeking the helm, then found it.

There, braced against the rudder, was the rogue. Thea's breath caught in her throat.

The gilding touch of rosy dawn washed him. Thea blinked owlishly, praying the sight before her eyes was a distortion caused by rising sun, moving shadows and light flickering off choppy waves.

In a word, he was magnificent, more the barbarian than any Viking could ever be. What need did he have of a horned helm to make his face more threatening? None. Before her stood a man of war, scarred and hard and beautiful all the same. The harsh line of his beard-shrouded mouth proved there was not a scrap of tenderness in him.

A shiver touched Thea's spine. Her eyes widened. She gaped at him more foolishly now than she remembered doing on the Somme. He had been arresting in the raiment of a Viking, a wild thing, uncontrollable yet controlling all around him. Stripped of all raiment save tanned breeks, he rendered Thea speechless.

Such a man was a dangerous, dangerous *thing* to her. And though her belly knotted and complained of deep hunger, all thought of food fled. It was a different hunger she felt roiling in the pits below her belly.

His eyes focused on the shadow that shielded her. Thea could not decipher their color. Nor did she have to, they would be blue, as blue as rime-laden winter clouds.

Nevertheless, Thea felt the blood within her veins surge to a new beat, and felt the rise of color as it swept upward, staining her throat and cheeks.

"Come out from behind that barrel."

Thea meant to come forward in her own good time. She should have reckoned he was not called *Hawk* for naught.

Locking every bone in her spine, Thea raised her chin and stepped out from behind the stack of barrels. His eyes fairly bored into her.

"You captain this ship, Lord Hawk?" Thea demanded.

He fixed her with a contemptuous gaze, making her conscious of her disordered state and rumpled appearance.

"That is twice you have called me by the name I am called only in battle. How is it that you know of me?"

"I saw you riding bareheaded at the front of your soldiers at the last tourney staged at Montigney. 'Twas forbidden afterward by the bishop of Auvergne for knights consecrated to God to fight unto the death in idle combat."

Lord Hawk considered her words in silence for a long while as doubts about her identity rose unwanted to trouble him—her cherished stallion and dainty ribboned saddle and that gown of hers that was so clearly made of cloth of quality. He hardened his heart. Life was cruel for all men—why should it not be the same for her? He could not go back to yesterday, nor change what was. Nor would he think of this again.

"You know much, little Frank. Who is your liege? Mayhap there is a profit to be made by offering you to ransom."

As a threat, that was devastating. Thea had not given one single thought to such a fate. She could languish forever in some dank prison, awaiting release by negotiation and ransom. Did he dare? Did she dare admit who she was and give him opportunity to hold such an ax over her father's head? Yea, her father was a wealthy man, but she had five siblings yet to be married and established in their own houses. A high ransom could very well turn her whole family into paupers. Wisely, Thea chose to keep her identity to herself until such time as revealing who she was would grant her the best bargain.

"You'd get no profit from ransoming me," Thea told him.

"I knew as much, little Frank. You may as well know I never trouble myself with lesser nobles' petty alliances. I answer only to Emperor Lothair and God himself. Wherein womenfolk of any realm count themselves, I care not. You are my captive, and will remain thus the rest of your days, service charged for the injury you gave my vassal on the river Somme."

Thea's chin thrust upward. He did not dare hold her for revenge. Did he? "Your lackey is dead?"

"Nay, only suffers with a festering wound. Does he die, my retribution will be to see that you follow him to the grave."

"Ha! You can't hold against me the wound he received. 'Twas caused in mine own defense. You ordered the man to attack me."

"You were given leave to depart in safety. You chose to fight for what you could not defend."

"Damn you! Turn this ship and take me back to my home!"

"Rail at me, wench, and I will have you trussed and gagged and thrown back into the bowels of this ship."

"I am not a wench!" Thea yelled, then caught hold of her temper before she lost it completely. "I beg you to return whence you kidnapped me before there are charges brought against you to the emperor."

"The emperor?" he said, without so much as a flicker of emotion passing across the lean shadows of his face.

"Do you have any concept of what crime you commit?" Thea asked him pointedly. He looked at her as if she were the one who'd lost her mind.

"No crime to be counted in emperor's court. Nor witnessed by any strong enough to bring charge against me. Think you that you are able to bring down the duke you see before you? The word of no woman holds sway in any court."

Thea swallowed the hard lump forming in her throat. The law was clear upon the issue of women speaking out against a lord in the emperor's court. They could not, but that did not mean a woman was helpless under the law. She could appeal to her kin to protect her. And they, in turn, could appeal to their liege for redress. Which brought her back to her father and the man he answered to, the same emperor that the Hawk of Emory answered to. What a coil.

"Mayhap no woman can speak against you, but for the theft of a horse, many a man in Longervais can bring charges against you. Don't you fear the day when your entrails are spilled onto the sand and four horses stronger than the one you stole will tear your limbs from your body?''

The Hawk laughed. ''She be a bloodthirsty wench, eh, mates?'' He called to the few of his men that had roused and sat knuckling sleep from their eyes. ''No less than we expect from a black-haired Frank. Do you think your king would trouble himself for a single horse? You are a silly wench if you believe such nonsense.''

Thea's hands fisted inside the folds of her gown. Did he but know the horse was not nearly so important a theft as her kidnap? He thought her no more important than a serving wench! Did she dare give away her true identity?

His upper body rolled with the ship, his shoulders leaning over the rudderstaff toward her. ''Tell me,'' he taunted her with a chilling smile. ''What courtesan of Emperor Lothair's court would kneel in the weeds beside the river, gathering roots and herbs? Eh? Having spent four years at Aachen, I cannot name you one.''

He had a point, and Thea was unwilling to say him nay.

''Ladies order servants to do such tasks,'' he taunted.

''Not every lady behaves as courtesans do,'' she argued.

''Oh, aye, and ladies always wander about the byways unescorted, in tattered hand-me-downs, like you, eh?'' He dismissed her with an autocratic wave of his hand. ''I grow weary of your paltry arguments, wench. Get you below, afore I make move to toss you into the sea.''

Thea defied him at her peril. She could not return to that smelly darkness without succumbing to the same illness that racked the other women. She did not doubt his threat, either. He was cold enough to do just that, toss her bodily into the waves, unless she gave him something else to think upon.

''The women are sick,'' she reasoned.

''They are at sea. It is expected,'' he replied.

''We need water,'' she countered.

''There is no water to spare.''

Loftily Thea argued with a wave of her hand. "There is water everywhere. We need just a little of it. Your ship stinks, Saxon."

Roderick gripped the helm with whitened knuckles. The damned little bitch dared to deliberately provoke his temper. Why he hadn't let her drown when she threw herself into the rockbound tide, he would never know.

"Well? What say you, Saxon?" Thea pleaded.

"One bucket, one woman on deck. You only. You want to serve and comfort, do so."

Roderick cared not one whit for the scornful manner in which she addressed him. It should have meant nothing to him to slit her throat and silence her after she injured Michael. He hadn't been able to do that. Nor could he have left her behind to name him as her attacker. Madness had surely struck him on the Somme.

That she dared defy all reason and present herself topside rekindled his lust. He knew full well why he had not taken the opportunity to silence her. No man in his right mind deliberately did away with a woman he desired.

Thea's pride took a blow at the contemptible choice he offered her. The churl who had threatened her with his fist pointed to an empty bucket on the deck.

"Use that," he snarled.

Holding check on her formidable temper, Thea angrily took the bucket to hand. She called below to the woman named Elspeth and gave terse instructions, ordering scrubbing and washing to begin.

They might be captives, but there was no reason they should remain filthy, or the space they occupied squalid.

Roderick kept his course steady, north by northeast. Good, he said to himself, the black-haired bitch had lost some of her nerve at his cruelty.

It went against his grain to treat any woman so callously. But Roderick refused to allow one ounce of compassion to build for the small woman laboring with the bucket at his rail. He kept watch over her like his namesake—the hawk. The maid worked unstintingly. Roderick saw that as a sign of pride and temper, both flaws in her character.

Once the day became long, her fair skin brightened in the strong sun. For one whose hair was the color of jet, her skin was as white as freshly skimmed cream and burned easily. Still, she preferred to struggle with rope and heavy bucket rather than go below.

His idle crew watched her with uneasy, interested eyes, most with growing admiration. Admiration Roderick could not denigrate in any way. She was the only woman of the sixty he had taken captive in three voyages on this ship that had dared to poke her head out of the hold. The little Frank had caught each man's attention by doing so. Roderick did not care much for that.

It was midafternoon before she drew up one last bucket and took it below herself, and did not come up again.

An audible sigh of relief washed over his deck. Roderick shared that with his men as much as he shared the benefits of the Frank's efforts that day.

The forward hold smelled less vile. The women had obviously done what women did well—cleaned their quarters.

The next morn, she again came up, requesting the same consideration. Her faded gown was clean, the bandage on her head removed. Clean hair whipped about her face and shoulders, unbound and unrestrained. It was the color of pitch, springy with curls.

"She's a beauty." Ben leaned on the railing beside Roderick and grinned. "I wanted the other, but I'll content myself with her."

"No, you won't," Roderick clenched his teeth, cursing inwardly because the damned wench had dared to come topside again. He didn't need this! Did not want the torture of watching her skirts swirl around delicate ankles giving flashes of slender legs to his eyes.

"You said you wouldn't keep any of these women for yourself," Ben said, astonished.

"What I said and what I'll do have now become two different things. That one, I keep. I have a score to settle with her," Roderick decreed.

"But what about your agreement with Friar Laurence?" Ben's brow furrowed. "Aren't all the women we bring to Emory to become wives? Won't the church have something to say if you arrive with women who are not destined to be wives?"

"My agreement with the priest has nothing to do with slaves. That one is a slave," Roderick declared.

Ben couldn't let the argument end at that. "She wears no collar, nor any brand upon her cheek."

"Both can be remedied before we reach home port," Roderick answered.

"You would brand a woman as beautiful as that?" Ben questioned incredulously.

No, Roderick would most certainly not brand any woman, much less one as beautiful as his little Frank. What he wanted of her he would not speak of to his young cousin, either. "Nay, but I am prepared to collar her before taking her ashore so that Friar Laurence's records attest to her status, if my word alone isn't sufficient."

Ben whistled softly. "I do not envy you that task. She does not seem the kind to submit willingly to a yoke."

"Think you I care if she is willing or not?" Roderick coldly brought the discussion to an end. "Get you to Michael. Make yourself useful, and tend to his wound." Benjamin departed. Roderick glared at the sea. He was doing all he could for the knight, yet his fever continued.

"My dread lord Hawk." The black-haired wench brought Roderick from his reverie.

She stood directly below him. He shifted his gaze and found she glared at him with another challenge in her eyes. Both her fists were parked arrogantly on her hips. Her hair spilled about her shoulders, wind-tossed and wild. The laces of her kirtle were partially undone, allowing the wind to play across her smooth, heated flesh, allowing his roving eyes to glimpse the soft, rounded curves beneath.

"What is it you want now, wench?" Roderick felt his body roll forward over the rudderstaff, as if to join with hers. Damn her!

"Have you medicines or herbs on this ship? Fruit of any kind, dried or even withered? Four ladies have skin ulcers. If you won't let them come out to the sun, may I have any kind of ointment you have to treat them?"

"I have none to spare from the man cut by you, wench."

"He is not dead?" She tossed her hair with an arrogance he found irritating. "He should be. Mayhap I was digging mandrake with my knife before you *Vikings* attacked. Did you ever think of that, Saxon?"

As taunts went, this one struck the bull's-eye of the target. Thea noted the whitening of his knuckles. She had his attention with that unforgivable gibe. She had admitted no more than what was true. She had found one rare root of mandrake.

As a charm, mandrake brought a house protection, fertility and prosperity. At the time she could not think of a better gift for her sister Andrea on her marriage than a poppet made of mandrake. It was a pagan thing to do, but Thea had dug up the deadly root with her knife, brushed off the dirt and tucked it inside her basket without telling Marie what she had collected. Of course, she had also followed that by washing her blade very carefully. She was no fool when it came to dangerous roots.

Calmly she stared at the now very, very angry man, and goaded him further. "Do you air the wound daily and keep him from food? Have you drained it, or packed it with healing poultices?"

"What do you know of such things?"

"I know of wounds."

"How to give them," the Saxon growled.

"That, too." Thea withstood his withering glare. Why, exactly, she didn't know. He looked at her with a more covetous gaze than she had noted in Gregory of Merrault's eyes. Only in his case, the Saxon stirred a response inside her. She liked the duel of wills.

"Get below, wench."

"I have a name, *Saxon.*"

Roderick stiffened. He had not forgotten her name, doubted he ever would. Thea, the other girl had screamed. It wasn't likely he would forget it.

Roderick damned the contest with her bold eyes. If he left the helm and stood before her, she would not reach his shoulder. Yet the little vixen stood proud, foolishly courageous. She was not like any of the other women he'd captured. This one contained not a docile bone within her. She made a grave mistake by taunting him. His control was dangerously close to the point of snapping.

She was a Frank. For that alone, he had reason enough to hate her. She had hair the same color as Anne of Aachen, the king's unfaithful, whoring niece. The injury Thea had done Michael would see her death following his. But killing this Frank was not Roderick's fondest desire. Nay, other torments pressed him. A hellcat might be the only salve the demons tormenting him could accept. But not this hellcat.

"I have nursed soldiers of Emperor Lothair a time or two. Take me to your wounded warrior. Mayhap I can help him. I would exchange my skills for medicines for the ladies."

"They are not ladies."

"What makes you so certain none are ladies?"

"For the last time, I tell you it matters not one whit what any of the wenches in my hold *were* or *are*. From the moment my ship puts to shore, all become wives of Saxon serfs. Can you understand that?"

"What's your point? What need have you of so many women?"

"Chattel, parts of breeding pairs, the necessary part to keep my serfs content—wives for the serfs of Emory."

"Is that where you take us—to Emory?"

"Question me more, you will be bound and gagged." The Hawk took one hand from the rudderstaff, raising it palm upward in a gesture commanding silence.

Thea's chin raised at the challenge, and her words, when she spoke, were deliberately hurtful. "Very well. Let your man die, all because you are an unreasonable, clod-pated oaf."

The last word was Thea's. Skirt flapping in the hard wind, she went below without anything to give to the suffering women. She flung herself to a corner, seething over the words the Emory had spoken. A cold chill crept into her spine that had nothing to do with the harsh accommodations, but had everything to do with her private vow that she'd personally kill Roderick of Emory!

Chapter Five

"What has happened?" Elspeth pushed through the crowded hold to sit beside Thea. Only Thea was too angry to discuss with anyone her understanding of their shared fate.

Breeding pairs! Wives for Roderick of Emory's serfs! For the love of God, he saw women as cattle! She had never been so insulted in her life! No wonder Anne of Aachen had ordered the Saxon whipped half to death! He deserved it.

"Did someone hurt you?" Concern was written all over Ellie's face.

"No." Thea stubbornly shook her head. "I hate it here," she complained. "I can't bear staying down here in the damp and the dark."

"Oh, aye, we all do." Elspeth saw something had upset the lady. "We think you very brave for going above and speaking to our comfort. Mayhap you should not endanger yourself for our sake."

"That is kind of you to say," Thea answered. "But don't think I am so selfless as that. I can't bear being confined...nor do I like listening to the others moan and carry on over our fate. It makes me want to slap faces and wring necks. How can any of you accept this fate so meekly? I want to slay every man on the deck."

Elspeth smiled and scooted over so that Jesse could join

them. "Jesse, we have a champion at last. Our Thea would slay our Viking abductors with her bare hands."

"They are not Vikings," Thea declared.

"*Non?*" Jesse's freckles stood out as she paled visibly. "Of course they are Vikings."

"No, they are not!" Thea insisted. "It was a ruse, a trick to lead any that might have seen them off the trail. Every man above is a Saxon, and the helmsman is none other than Roderick of Emory."

Elspeth gasped. "You are certain?"

"I am positive," Thea said through gritted teeth.

"So, what happens to us now?" Jesse asked timidly.

Thea shook her head. She would not compound the Hawk of Emory's insult by repeating it. Jesse and Ellie were incapable of resisting the will of a lord.

Thea would fight! She was not bound by their yoke of serfdom. She was educated, privileged, a lord's daughter. She had traveled all of the empire, been to court and, though she did not aspire to live at court, she had always hoped to marry well and live the lady's life.

The little news she had brought below decks spread like wildfire. The women began to talk freely among themselves, indulging in an endless stream of if-onlys. If only they'd been gently born. If only they'd not been a scullery maid washing clothes at the riverbank. If only they'd not been sent to market. If only...if only, a litany of finding blame for their trouble in something or someone else.

Thea had her if-only, but her regret was tempered by having saved her younger sister. Marie was safe. Whatever else befell her, Thea would not lose her courage to mindless fear, nor blame her misfortune on another. Consequently, she had no if-only that made her chest rise and fall in terrible heartfelt sighs, as did all the rest of the women.

Now that her temper had had a chance to cool, she wanted to know why the Saxon had abducted these women. The Hawk of Emory wasn't a barbarian, not really. She knew some of Lothair's courtiers claimed all Saxons were unfit for the company of better folk, but all the old troubles had ended years ago when Charlemagne made the Saxons Christians.

What prejudices remained were held by ignorant folk, or so Thea had always thought, until the king's tourney at Montigney, which had ended in so much turmoil.

But that did not explain what this particular Saxon was doing raiding Frankish villages, stealing women, chickens, geese and lambs, cows and horses. If the man had truly turned into a brigand, why was he wasting his energy stealing anything less than gold and jewels? It just did not make sense.

Not long after nightfall, the man who handed down the food and water each morning lowered a lantern. The women nearest the hatch cover screamed and clutched each other in terror.

"Where is the black-haired wench called Thea?" the man shouted into the darkness.

"I've gone out for a stroll!" Thea called back to him. She got to her feet and moved into the light.

"My liege bids you come up. Sir Michael lies dying."

Thea hesitated. Did that mean she was to die next? Killing a knight bore a heavy penalty. Each man in a fief bore value to his liege lord, as well as to the king he ultimately served.

Too soon she found herself in a small, stuffy cabin built beneath the helm. It was hung with oil lanterns that swung with the rolling of the boat.

The tiny cabin smelled of putrefying flesh. A single cot held the dying knight, swaddled in soiled linens. His skin was ghostly white against the fulsome black of his beard. Thea got her first look at the injury her blade had caused. A gasp escaped her throat. Her eyes were riveted to the exposed belly wound. Mortified, she thought, *I did that.*

She moved past Roderick and laid her fingers on the injured man's brow. Fever consumed him. Pulling her hand back, she turned to the duke. He glowered at her with a face so hardened her blood ran cold.

"Why have you brought me here? Do you mean for me to watch him die?"

"Yea, wench. So you will know the reason your own life is forfeit."

"All well and good for you, my lord, to threaten my life again, as you did when you took me captive against my will. Beastly oaf, do you plan to let this man die, or will you fight to see him live?"

Thea could see that she tempted the duke of Emory to silence her with his fist. Even she wouldn't blame him if he struck her, but she couldn't bear being forced to stand idly by and watch the poor man die.

Roderick spoke in a strained voice. "Have a care, wench. Yon knight lies dying, and aught can I do to ease his going nor demand his staying."

"Do you have means to boil water?"

"Yea," he snapped in return.

"Then have it boiled a good long time, a quarter of an hour at least. It doesn't have to be fresh, salt will do, so long as it is strained through a cloth and purified by boiling hard. And I must have clean linens, and help to undress him. He is a large man."

"Shrinking in death," Roderick of Emory replied. He sent a man to fetch water, called upon one named Ben to bring linens. That turned out to be the youth who had attacked Marie. As the boy handed over clean cloths into Thea's care, she was struck by how very young he seemed. Hardly older than her baby brother, Jason.

Roderick watched the little witch fly about the bed, stripping soiled linens and now rank clothes from Michael's dwindling body. He did not trust her any farther than he could throw her. He had not forgotten her claim to have used a poison-tainted blade. She showed marvelous strength of purpose by not fainting when she uncovered the wound fully and bent to examine the decaying flesh. Pale of face, she addressed Roderick directly after.

"We must have water and plenty of it. It was not a serious wound at first. No organs were punctured, praise God, but it has been allowed to fester. Had you washed the wound before the fever struck, he would not be dying now."

What his reasons were, Thea couldn't guess, but the Saxon lord refused to help her save his vassal. He stood by, offering no assistance, maligning her with his eyes and probably his thoughts. She could let him rattle her with his hate-filled eyes, or she could ignore him. She chose to do the latter.

She searched through a casket of medicines and herbs the boy, Benjamin, had opened for her, lifting vials, squinting in the poor light to read the markings fixed upon them. She poured brandy on her hands and rubbed them dry. She then took hot clothes from a boiling pot set over a tripod brazier, wrung them out and laid the steaming clothes on Sir Michael's oozing wound.

While the heat worked to draw out the poisons, she bathed the man from head to toe.

An hour of frantic activity had passed before Roderick spoke at all. "Do you think to keep your own neck from stretching at first light?"

"I do not care what you do with me!" Thea snapped. "It has been days since I truly considered myself alive. But no man need die writhing in agony. Be death quick or lingering, his comforts are deserved. Will you lift him so that I may spread the clean linens underneath him?"

Roderick came forward and gently lifted Michael into his arms, cradling his friend's fevered body against his chest. She was quick to strip the linens and replace them. As he returned Michael to the cot, she was ready with sheet and wool to cover him.

Roderick did not want to admit that her efficient manner impressed him. She bathed Michael without any trace of a maiden's blush upon her cheeks. She laid a folded sheet up to Michael's hips, then knelt beside the cot and lifted the soaking cloth away from the wound, immediately bringing another poultice to the gaping hole, packing that with more steaming linen.

These were the actions of a woman familiar with battle wounds. Every few minutes she cradled Michael's head with her slender arm and tipped a cup of cooled boiled water to his mouth. She had a practiced hand for the art of gentle massage, inducing the knight's reluctant throat to swallow.

To Roderick's eye, her claim to know something of treating wounds hadn't been a lie. What kept him silent and removed from offering aid was the agonizing pain his friend suffered.

Were he in Michael's place, with his belly rotting from the inside out, he'd be begging for someone to show mercy and slit his throat, making death quick. Were they on a battlefield, Roderick would have no qualms about doing exactly that to save his friend from the slow and torturous death he was experiencing.

Just as Michael would have done so for him.

Here…on this ship…it felt too much like murder to even contemplate such a deed. There was no honor in death to be had for a man whose last conscious deed was the kidnap of twenty-odd women.

Roderick returned to the helm.

Thea was glad to see him go. She did not need that fierce, uncommunicative man hovering over her shoulder, watching her every move.

Thea's vigil continued long into the night. When she had done all that she possibly could, she knelt beside the bed and prayed that God Almighty and his son, Jesus, would allow this man to live. In the midst of her prayers, his eyes opened. They were as blue as those of her brother Royce.

He smiled weakly, rasping, "Are you an angel, and if you be not an angel, pray tell me your earthly name, fair maid?"

That smile, on his lips of a man who hovered so near to death, amazed Thea. It was the first time any person on that horrid boat had asked who she was. Thea's throat constricted. Her full name and all her titles were too lengthy to waste upon a dying man.

"I am Thea of Auvergne, good knight," she answered simply, giving only her pet name and the place of her birth, which was expected of any soul in this day. "Who are you?"

"Michael of Lozere at your service. Would that I could be." He spoke so softly she had to lean close to his lips to hear him.

"You must sleep, sir knight," Thea said with quiet satisfaction. She had thought the fever turned. Now she was certain.

Reading the stars at midnight, Roderick altered his course, turning south into the prevailing wind, so that he could slip easily and undetected into the estuary of the Weser.

He was wont to avoid being sighted by his most voracious neighbors, the Danes. They preferred raiding Britain and Ireland and recognized the peace accord signed by his father a decade ago. In his weakened state, however, Roderick dared take no chances. Since becoming duke of Emory, he had not been to Flensburg to work out terms for continued peace with Herewald the Walker. Herewald was as avaricious as the Franks. All overlords expected tribute as their price for peace.

To distract his mind, Hawk thought of the work that must be finished before winter arrived. The damned Vikings had left him so little. His efforts seemed so inadequate. He could ill afford the loss of his friend and fellow warrior, Michael. He railed at himself for giving in to his squalling serfs, and damned the day this plan to obtain women for Emory had sprung from his lips.

All the women on earth weren't worth the loss of Michael of Lozere.

In the cabin below the helm, Michael moaned through the night. Roderick relinquished the helm and went to see how Michael fared.

The knight lay naked on the bed, linen covering his loins. His belly was packed with a poultice, and the smell of strong herbs filled the cabin. The maid pressed a cloth gently to his skin, blotting Michael's sweat-soaked brow and face, his beard-shaded throat and dark-tufted chest.

Thea turned when a shadow fell across the bed. She fixed her gaze intently on the Hawk of Emory's mouth, waiting for his words.

"Are you a witch?" Roderick asked.

"If I were, I assure you I'd conjure a means to fly off this boat."

Her sharp retort earned no rebuke as the ship's captain silently considered his friend.

There were signs of change in the raging fever. While Roderick watched, she peeled away the poultice, exposing the wound to Roderick's inspection. He was amazed that the cut no longer oozed. Its whitened edges had neither blood nor yellow matter seeping from them. The flesh still looked raw, grisly.

As he looked to the wound, she spread a salve she had prepared from the medicine supplies onto a freshly boiled square of cloth. This she laid over the steaming pot on the tripod brazier, allowing the steam to soften the thick decoction. While that took place, she stood, folded her hands over her apron and looked straight at Roderick.

"You will not have the satisfaction of hanging me for the murder of your friend. No thanks to you, he is going to live."

Her calmly stated accusation took Roderick aback. He looked at her face, noting that her clear eyes of luminous green stared at him with undisclosed pride in the miracle that she had done.

"Think you to bargain with me, wench?"

"Nay, I'd as soon make a pact with the devil, Saxon. I only tell you that there are spores in the air and things that cause infection that no one can explain. A sick man must have the best of care, clean linens, clean bedding, and all who care for him must themselves wash thoroughly," Thea answered resignedly. She was tired. It took too much effort to keep her temper up.

"A wise suggestion." He nodded toward the man stretched upon the clean bed.

Thea gathered the dirty linens and cloths and asked for soap. Roderick opened a chest and handed her a hard cake of lye. Her gaze fixed on the dirt adhered to his hands, but she took the soap without a word of comment.

It was cooler outside than in the cabin. A shiver caught Thea unawares as she moved to the railing with her bucket in hand. All was quiet as it ever was, on the ship at night, with ropes creaking and water sloshing against the hull. A crescent moon hid behind a bank of clouds. The sea shimmered green and gray, different from any way she had seen it before. No sooner had Thea come to the rail to drop her bucket than her tired eyes caught sight of land.

That so startled her that she dropped the bucket on the deck and spilled out the cloths she needed to wash. The ship moved briskly through a channel of rising mountains on two sides. Directly ahead, there was more land, but also more water, as far as she could see. They traversed an inlet of some sort.

Thea swung about, looking for Roderick. "Where are we?" she demanded once she spied him at his helm.

Even though it was dark and he had only two tin lanterns swinging from the posts that held the canvas awning over his head, she saw him raise a proud, arrogant brow at her question.

"The northernmost reaches of Lothair's empire, little Frank," he said softly, so softly it was almost a warning. "Saxony."

Thea gasped. Had she imagined he would not truly bring his ship to this faraway land? They were nearly to the end of the known world. Swallowing her fear, Thea looked to the land again.

The dark wealth of it surrounded them on all sides. The air held a chill. Farther down the inlet, a blanket of fog covered the shores. She couldn't fathom what place this was they were coming to, but the whole idea of this journey's ending filled her with dread.

She moistened her dry lips, tasting the salt that rimmed them. Thea called to Elspeth to come to the hatch cover. She must warn the women, give them some means to prepare. Her thoughts centered on how to make good her escape when the ship docked. Repeatedly her eye sought landmarks as she tried to remember what she knew of cartography, land and seashores.

There were boats near the land, small fishing boats, three of them. The sight held her enthralled and caused her to hear no commotion behind her.

The captain had turned the helm to someone else and strode down the deck to her.

"Enough water." He grasped her arm. Startled, Thea let go of the bucket. It dropped heavily into the sea, whipping the coarse hemp rope across her palms.

"Why did you startle me?" Thea screamed. Her palms were seared as if hot coals touched them. Yanking free of the man's grip, she glared at him angrily, clenching her injured hands into fists. She swung away to return to the hold.

"I have not given you leave." He caught her arm, spinning her round to face him.

"I need not ask you for it." She had not sought this confrontation with him, but since it had come, she would not be the one to back down.

"You become a nuisance. It is high time you learned your place." Roderick gripped Thea's arm, shoving her ahead of him as he shouted orders to his crew. "Put the grill over the hold to see that none of the other women find their way above decks. She told them we're nearing land."

"I did not," Thea protested. "I said nothing, yet. They have the right to know."

Angrily he lifted her off her feet when she resisted. His arm snapped around her waist like a band of iron.

"Put me down! Unhand me!"

Thea's cry went ignored. She panicked as he neared the cabins beneath the helm, hearing the rude laughs of the crew above her terror.

The duke put his shoulder backward into the door beside Sir Michael's and swung her around inside. Even gripping the frame didn't help her. The door banged against the solid wall. The youth called Ben bolted up from the single cot, his eyes as wide as saucers, his hair sprouting wild all around his head.

"M'lord." He bounded to his feet, leaving behind a rumpled bed.

"Out!" Roderick of Emory said tersely.

"No, do not go!" Thea scratched at the bare arm clenched around her ribs. The boy didn't say a word as he squeezed his lanky body out the door. It slammed rudely behind them. The duke tossed Thea onto the rumpled bed. She landed jarringly on a soft nest of fur. Before she could scramble to her feet, Roderick of Emory loomed over her, both his hands flat against the bedding, his huge body much too close and intimidating for her to dare sitting up.

"I know what you were thinking, wench. You'll remain here the rest of this journey."

"I won't." Thea countered, trying to beat his arms away. She had not been this scared since she was first captured. She wished she had not decided to launder the sick knight's last change of bedding.

"Need you a lesson in the uselessness of defying me?"

"You, sir, are going to hang," Thea hissed. "You press my good nature too far by half."

"Nay, 'tis you who have pressed mine to the breaking point and leave me no choice but to shackle you. You will enter Blackstone a slave, as forfeit for the injury done to my vassal Michael of Lozere."

"I will not!"

"Yea, Thea, here that is all you will ever be. Not a tenancy or a husband will you have, only a master, and I will do with you as I see fit. Now stand up and remove your gown."

"Remove my...what?" Thea shouted. "I will do no such thing! You, sir, tread on very dangerous ground. Do you persist in causing me injury, I will see that you are stripped of all your lands and vassals and serfs and banished from the empire forever. I will even implore the bishop of Auvergne to have you excommunicated."

"Why stop with a bishop, wench? Call down the pope, if you can!" Roderick coldly taunted as he pulled her back onto her feet.

This cabin seemed crushingly small with him raging mockingly in the center of it. She jumped when he dropped his hands to his belt to set his arms akimbo.

"Believe what I say, wench—there is no law you may appeal to higher than myself. I am the duke. Your life is in my hands. Since even gowns for slaves come dear, you will remove yours yourself. Force me to tear it from your body, and I will beat you for causing destruction to my property."

"Why?" Thea implored. "Why are you doing this? I have done you no injury!"

"I cannot have you wandering freely, distracting my crew and getting in my way while we are busy with docking."

"You cannot do this." Thea's face had turned an ashen white. "I won't allow you to bully me."

"I have given you an order to disrobe."

The man advanced another step, closing off escape. Thea stiffened before him, her legs against the unyielding bunk. Her refusal was unconditional. "No."

When the lord of the boat spoke again, his voice was so low and guttural she could barely hear it. Yet the command it contained was more than a warning to her. "I will not be defied by any woman. You have pressed me too far and, hence, will learn the foolishness of disobedience, wench."

"I have a name," Thea declared fiercely, intimidated by his size and ferocity. She could clearly see that goading him only weakened her position.

"I will do as you say." Her fingers fumbled at her laces. She turned her back to the man. What had she done to deserve this?

I am not a coward, she told herself. Defiance straightened her spine and brought her head up straight and proud. She blinked away the tears that had sprung to her eyes, shrugging her gown off her shoulders. It pooled to her narrow waist, the laces caught. She tugged at them more, unfastening the hook, and dropped the garment to her feet. Perverse pride made her swing around in just her kirtle to face the man.

Roderick silently groaned. Even her kirtle was finely made, edged with frothy guipure and more beautiful than any undergarment he had seen in a long, long while. He stared at the swirling lace clinging to her breasts and felt his will soften at the urge to touch her. What more proof did he need that she was a lady? None. Clenching his fists impotently, he renewed his resolve to finish this as he had begun it.

She must enter Blackstone a slave—else she could never belong to him. He wanted her more than he'd ever wanted any woman in his life. They had come this far...past the point of return. He had no choice except to make her his chattel in the only way possible...slavery. He was not free to take a wife into Blackstone, as his serfs and vassals were, not when the needs of his fief required a titled woman whose dowry would be their salvation in the years to come.

Yet, will it nor not, he could not drag his gaze from the heaving motion of her breasts as they swelled and pressed against the kersey and lace clinging to them.

"Hear me well, little Frank." His voice was roughened from unresolved need when he spoke. "I have no wish to beat you into compliance. But I will, should you give me no alternative."

"I have done nothing," Thea whispered, reading the grim set of his mouth. He did not flinch from her gaze. She could not fathom why he stooped to such hateful cruelty.

"Why?" she asked. "What have I done to you to cause me this humiliation? You cannot hold against me the injury I did to your vassal when I was captured. Don't you expect your own women to defend themselves against such an attack?"

"You talk too much." Roderick picked up her discarded dress. She forced him to this end by the very fact that she would not keep herself contained in any quadrant of his ship. But he judged her rightly. With her gown taken away, she would not wander about in her kirtle.

Thea flinched as he unlocked a large trunk and opened it, dropping her dress onto the packed contents.

"What are you doing?" Thea protested, running forward to retrieve her garment. He spun around, confronting her.

The flat of her hand touched a raised scar on his sinewy chest. Thea froze. Her eyes widened, seeing, feeling, the thickened scar that ran beneath her fingers, coiled across his arm to his bare chest, snaking through a matting of golden hair.

She restrained her hands, which had been poised to rip his skin into ribbons, and made no assault against him. Her eyes fastened to his scars in horror. She would have fought him to the death if he had touched her only a moment before. Now she wasn't so certain.

The single lantern hanging from the rafter swayed as the ship rolled, causing the glow of light to shift from shadow to hollow. Her eyes moved relentlessly, from scar to horrible scar, the way her mind ran from rumor to rumor. *He'd been set upon by Anne of Aachen's men and scourged until his blood ran to his feet.* Thea saw and felt the results of that lady's efforts. The Hawk of Emory had healed, but stood marked for life.

Thea gasped as his hand shot out to clasp her neck. Expecting pain, she was startled by the lightness of his touch. His callused thumb stroked across her jaw and up her cheek. Broad fingers tightened in the curls behind her head.

"You are frightened of me?"

Thea denied the obvious. "Nay."

He gripped her neck more firmly, his fingers secure at the back of her head. He brought his other hand to her cheek, stroking it familiarly. There was no pain in his touch upon her skin.

Thea closed her eyes. The tilt of the boat placed her on higher footing than he. She leaned to keep her balance, and he seemed closer. His body heat radiated and enveloped her. His hands against her throat and face caused the oddest sensation within her. His warmth overrode her fear.

Blinking open her eyes, she stared at dark, sapphire blue irises that, for the moment, seemed almost level with her own eyes. Some inner voice whispered that he was not the threat she imagined him to be. The surge of feeling accompanying that irrational thought shocked Thea.

Those hard, callused hands stroking her cheek inflicted no damage. He touched her almost reverently. She saw the strangest look she'd ever seen in a man's eye. Words could not describe what she felt when he put his mouth against her own.

Where moments before she would have fought him to the death if he dared touch her, now she stood transfixed, mesmerized, as his lips glided across her own.

A sign of hysteria burst forth in a giggle from her strangling throat. His beard teased her chin and cheeks. Thea couldn't manage a word of speech. She was being kissed by a man she should despise.

She thought if only she'd been an obedient and biddable daughter, the way Andrea was, this would not be happening to her. She had no one to blame but herself that she had become this powerful man's captive.

Yet, it seemed inevitable that he would kiss her. Fated from the moment she'd first seen him riding so proudly into the lists, bareheaded before his king at the tournament at Montigney. Had she foolishly lost her heart to this man then? And felt that love crushed to bits when he fell under Gregory of Merrault's assault?

"You do not fight me," he said in a voice that seemed more even than it should be, considering the ragged way he breathed.

Thea couldn't muster any answer.

Her hands hung at her sides. She couldn't tell him why her eyes moved from one ragged scar on his chest and shoulders and arms to another. She could not make audible the compassion welling inside her.

She knew intuitively that he was a man who accepted pain without flinching. He would not allow her empathy for all the injustice he had suffered in his life. He was not a man accustomed to kindness, but a man who had been hurt and hurt again. He would scorn her pity.

He lifted her chin and kissed her mouth, then murmured against her lips. "My name is Roderick, Thea."

It was a small tenderness that made her look deeply into the sapphire brilliance of his eyes.

"Open your mouth to me, Thea. I wish to kiss you the way a man and a woman kiss."

"Why?" Thea asked, shaken by the very sensation of his mouth touching her own. Her question was irrelevant. The answer to it, a moan that escaped her captor's throat, conveying uninhibited need.

His answer came as possession. She felt the fire of his tongue separate her lips, and the unspoken demand that she accept his intrusion. He gripped her head fiercely, his dominance forcing her to slacken completely. His hand moved down her back, pressing her against his hard length.

Thea intuited a concept that had always eluded her, the sublime purpose underlying the merging of a woman's body with a man's. It was a union and a reunion. As she had been consumed with compassion for his scarred body, she now felt the depth and intensity of his spirit.

Shivers ran over her skin as his tongue danced against hers, teasing, toying, tormenting, tasting. His lips skittered down her throat, causing her whole body to tremble. His tongue laved her breasts, his teeth nipped upon her too-sensitive skin, making her burn and ache all over. How or when she came to be lying upon the cot, Thea did not know.

All she knew was that her body quickened for him.

His hands continued on a separate journey, finding the soft curves of her bottom, parting her legs to thrust the hard maleness of him into the softness of her.

That pressure that had built within her increased a hundredfold. There was pleasure and pain and need, all mixed into one complete and ruthless assault upon her senses. She acknowledged it by curling into him, accepting full tuition, pleased and warmed, rewarded for the fleeting burst of pain by the comfort of his lips upon hers.

All things outside the sphere of her senses ceased to matter. Then, even Thea's senses ceased to exist, and her entire being focused no farther than the burning furnace consuming them as the ages-old rhythm danced relentlessly toward a crescendo of completion.

She did not hear her gasps of pleasure, or have consciousness of her hands stroking across his bared chest. Everything ceased to be, everything outside of this bonding, this joining of man and woman, had no purpose.

They were bound together by some powerful and moving force, elemental and basic to life itself. A communion of souls that transcended all Thea's experience. He was the man destiny had prepared her for. She gazed deeply into his eyes, locked into the uncontrollable tide that swept over them.

Hardly cognizant of how it had happened, Roderick marveled over how sweetly she had opened to him. No acrimonious tears formed in her luminous green eyes. No recriminations ruined the passionate fullness of her mouth as he fought for his breath, spent but nowhere near sated.

She set her teeth to the corner of her mouth, tugging at it with uncertainty.

He could be lost forever in her innocence and wonder. He could ill afford that. Nor could he risk more ruin brought upon him by another Frankish woman. Never again would any woman rule his life.

Deliberately, he withdrew from her, separating what he felt from what must be. He righted his breeks and got to his feet immediately, pulling her off the cot to stand beside him.

His hand stole upward, dragging the torn edges of her kirtle together between her breasts.

She could not stand unsupported. He kept one hand under her arm, giving her his strength. His heart still beat a war-drum staccato and he feared she could hear it.

More composed than he actually felt, he fingered the torn guipure covering one tumescent breast. The swollen nipple peeked at him, begging to be taken into his mouth. He drew a calming breath inside his straining chest. Seeking the control that had never before deserted him, Roderick felt his blood surge, and he swallowed a shout of primitive triumph over having taken her virginity.

His claim indelibly stamped her as his and his alone. His seed inside her marked her as his possession for all eternity.

She weakened against him, knees buckling, body quivering against the support of his arm.

He bent to the chest at the foot of the cot and flung it open, removed an item, then turned and grasped her arm, drawing her to him. Without explanation, he gripped both sides of the metal collar and expanded it, sliding its rough opening around her slender throat. As his fingers released it, the iron torque snapped into place, tight and cold against Thea's fragile skin.

"What work did you do for your past lord?"

"Work?" Thea gasped. Her fingers clawed at the slave collar. The center of it bore a single loop through which a chain could be threaded. Her puny strength would not remove it. "I am not a slave!"

He took care that she saw no uncertainty in his manner, for there were no slaves in Emory. She would be the first. Given time she would learn he had no desire to continue the role of a slavemaster. She had only to play her part, and he, his, to placate the priests when they went ashore.

Testily, because collaring her shamed him, he said, "You know what I mean. What were your duties?"

"To tend the—" Her voice faltered. *The lessons of my tutors and assist my mother in the running of the household,* she had started to say. She turned her face to the wall and clutched the kirtle across her body. No force on this earth would make her look back at him. *Dear God, what had she done?*

She was the daughter of Roger Bellamy, the duke of Auvergne, a duchess in her own right, second daughter of the renowned and respected Lady Lilla of Landais and Limousin. How shamed her father would be if he could see her now.

Her own wickedness filled her with shame. To have embraced that cold and heartless man and found meaning in his kiss and comfort in his touch was an abomination. Why hadn't she died fighting him? No penance would cleanse her from this sin of lust. Madness had gripped her.

Roderick took hold of her shoulder, turning her around to face him. She tried to hide her trembling, but he felt the quivers shooting through her as his hand tightened on her pale skin.

"Look at me, Thea." He waited for her to raise her eyes, hoping his own bore no hint of his distress. Her beauty stoked the fires of his lust. He was damned twice, for he wanted her again, more than he had before.

But the result was not to his liking now.

A hellcat, he'd expected. A voracious, vicious bitch fighting him, he could have handled. The Fates gave him cruel twists, handing him a virgin who had offered the sweetest surrender he had ever tasted in his life. Why had God given her eyes so guileless, they revealed how deeply he had wounded her? Hardening his heart, Roderick made his voice gruff.

"You did not give me a sufficient answer. What work did you do for your previous lord?"

Utterly shattered, Thea could not find the pride she had learned at her mother's knee to gird her now. "I have been trained to be a chatelaine . . . and a healer."

Roderick's brow arched appreciatively. That explained her boldness. A chatelaine in any Frankish household held much power over the unskilled servants within the manse.

"I have need of a chatelaine at Blackstone."

Thea held herself together by sheer willpower now. She wanted him to go away and leave her to lick her wounds in private. "You have twenty women to pick a chatelaine from on this very ship."

"The other women are for a different use."

"Do not tell me again your use for them. Wives for your serfs. I will have no part of that blasphemy." Tears formed in her eyes, and she shook them away.

"Your consent is unnecessary," Roderick answered coldly. "And you will see to all the duties I assign you once this journey is concluded."

When the last Judgment comes, Thea thought mutinously, but she said nothing out loud.

"Very well." Roderick took his ring of keys to hand and removed one iron key and extended that to Thea. "This will open yon trunk beside the cot. In it you will find needle and thread to mend your kirtle. As you have proven to me that you have need of industry at all times, there are other things needing mending inside the trunk. That should keep you busy until my ship is docked. You will remain here, disrobed to keep you from wandering about, until I come for you."

He paused, expecting some word of parting. He would welcome her spleen; words of hatred would do them both good this moment. Else he would walk out the door and continue to brood, thinking only of the magic that had quickened between them.

She clenched her fingers around the key. When she looked up at him again, the temper Roderick sought to ignite was there, simmering in those beautiful green orbs.

"You did not have to force me to disrobe to keep me contained in here," she said accusingly.

Again Roderick deliberately arched his brow, knowing his arrogance would fan the flames more. "You have not shown a propensity to obey orders, wench."

Thea stiffened. "To this very moment, Saxon, I owe you no service whatsoever. I am not bound to you except by captivity, abduction. Nothing more. My duty is to make certain that I regain my freedom. The sooner the better."

Roderick slipped his forefinger through the iron loop dangling from the collar at her throat. He tugged on it deliberately. "By my law you are bound henceforth. Challenge my authority and you will suffer greatly for it."

His softly spoken warning fell on deaf ears.

What had he expected? She was a black-haired Frank, and they were by nature the most infuriating, stubborn and treacherous race of women on earth.

"Goodbye, Thea. Understand this before my ship docks—no cottage or tenancy or husband do I offer you in Emory. Perhaps in time, when I have grown weary of you, I will trade your bondage to a Danish master for a measure of gold. Until then, you belong solely to me."

Chapter Six

Dragon's breath encircled the ship and blanketed the stone obelisks rising from the murky water. A wide plank stretched from the ship's rail to a rocky shelf, but Thea was afraid to step onto the unsteady board.

The whole eerie sight frightened her, making Thea remember legends of old. She had never believed dragons existed, nor fairies, sprites or trolls, but she saw before her an environment where those fantastical beings could very well exist.

The truth was, though she had been taught their language by her tutors, she knew little about Saxony that wasn't rumor or gossip. Some said Saxons still worshiped their tree gods, naiads in sacred pools, the sun and moon and the elements. This moment, she could well believe a troll lurked under that flimsy wooden bridge, waiting to snatch her bare feet out from under her.

Hawk's firm hand on her upper arm did not allay her fear. Thea shook her head, telling herself not to be silly. It was only fog. The same as she knew it in Picardy. But the wet, soundless element seemed more sinister than any morning fog she'd ever experienced.

"Up you go." Hawk moved without warning, lifting Thea off the deck of the ship and onto the plank. She clutched his forearms, scared, looking down at the water, holding her breath. He stepped up beside her, urging her forward. The plank moved, dipping toward the ship as it rocked. Thea bolted onto the shore, seeking solid earth underfoot again.

She took two steps onto the black rocks and nearly collapsed. Roderick's hands steadied her. "Sea legs," he murmured against her ear. "We'll wait here a moment."

Thea sank gratefully onto a rock, waiting for the hammering pulse in her throat to subside. Hawk nimbly crossed the gangplank and disappeared in a swirl of fog.

Thea strained her eyes to see him. She could hear more, the still and quiet harbor, the ship creaking against its mooring, wood rubbing against stone, the distant chatter of the women as they made their way up the zigzag hill.

On the ship the deck was nearly emptied of its stacks of cargo. All sounds were strangely muffled. She wanted Roderick to return soon because he was the only anchor she was accustomed to, but she also wanted him to fall into the sea and drown.

She could see which way to go up the hill. Tin lanterns marked the meandering path. Thea had no inclination to make that journey alone on her shaky knees. She clutched her arms about her chest, regretting that she had no cloak or shawl to ward off the damp.

Hawk returned to the gangplank at last, bringing Jesse and Elspeth and a girl Thea knew had been seasick the whole journey. They were a sight to behold, woebegone and frightened. Thea's heart turned over, seeing their pale faces mirroring the same distress she felt.

They went strangely silent when confronted by the wobbly board and Roderick's stern order to walk carefully. He waited until they had crossed, then picked up the skinny girl and carried her ashore. There was no time to exchange a greeting. Her two friends might never know how glad Thea was to see their familiar faces, but in that moment when they looked at each other, Thea saw iron collars encircling both Elspeth's and Jesse's necks. That shocked her deeply.

Ashore, Roderick steadied the sick girl on her feet and bade Jesse and Elspeth to help her up to the village. The sick girl had no collar binding her neck.

He turned to help the men bearing Michael of Lozere on a litter. The knight's face was twisted in agony from the jarring movement. Thea held her breath as the precarious transfer from bobbing ship to solid shore was made successfully. She felt a stab of guilt over the knight's suffering, which she had caused.

Lord Roderick drew Thea along at his side, following the litter. The hill climbed steeply, the stonebound path slippery. When she stubbed her toes, she wondered if she would ever have another pair of shoes.

As they reached higher ground, Thea found more important things to think about than her feet. The fog lifted enough to give Thea a view of a seaside market skirting the charred ruins of a village. All the cottages beside the market were scorched ruins. Farther inland, at the village square, the cottages had been repaired, whitewashed and newly thatched, neat as could be.

To one side of the square, a roofless abbey dominated the squat buildings. Beyond the church, if indeed that big building was a church, fields of green crops surrounded the town. The fields should be the brown and tan of ripened grain this late in the fall.

Puzzled, Thea watched the fog recede and the morning sun emerge. Beyond the village stood a fortress high on another steep hill.

The forests that covered the foothills and the higher, faraway mountains sparkled with autumn colors. It hadn't been a forest fire that devastated this town.

To her relief, Lord Roderick paused in the village square. She would never have asked him to stop for her, but her tender feet were glad for the rest. She needed a chance to catch her breath.

While she did that, she watched men come greet Sir Michael and speak with him. But no women of any sort, no mother, sisters, friends or lovers arrived. There were no children, either. None. Thea searched for the babes and toddlers and little ones that were the life and love of a town. There were none.

Her brow furrowed, and she looked at Roderick of Emory. She was more perplexed and confused now than before. What had happened to his village, his people?

The sun cleared the eastern sky and blessed the valley. What was left of the fog clung to the lowlands, but the sun would make quick work of evaporating that. This was a far different valley from Longervais. Where Picardy had rolling hills, Saxony had snow-topped, craggy mountains. Even the trees were different. Here oaks clung to the lowlands, and pines dominated the heights. Thea was more used to leafy elms, willows and hawthorns. Still, it was not an ugly place, though clearly some misfortune had befallen it.

Stacked to one side of the square was the cargo taken off the ship. Men pushed crude, heavy carts forward to be loaded by the sailors from the ship. More brought the many heavy chests transported across the sea. Added to the commotion of work and movement, the noisy and odorous animals milled about, as confused as the women. Thea looked for Victory. She saw no sign of horses of any kind in this village.

Thea's eyes moved southward, judging the lay of the land in that direction. How far north was she? How many, many miles away was Landais? Had Marie made it home safely? Had her parents given her up for dead? Were they hopelessly looking for her in the lands close by? She prayed they would forget her quickly.

Two men came to speak to Roderick. One had a patch over an eye, the other, who was missing a leg, leaned on crude crutches. Across the square, at the abbey, another's sleeve hung empty at his side. The sun glinted warm and full of light. But this village of Roderick of Emory's remained haunting and peculiar. Thea didn't like it, not one single bit.

While the Saxon spoke to his men, his left hand remained firmly attached to Thea's upper arm. No one paid her the slightest attention. In the center of the square, three priests sat before a trestle near the village well.

Thea looked longingly at the well. Her stomach grumbled emptily. She hid a sleepy yawn behind her hand and realized she was so tired she could drop. She watched the captive women move quickly down a line before the priests. They were sent inside the fire-blackened, roofless abbey, which did have new doors and beams set in place to support a new roof. Thea hoped it wasn't going to rain tonight, but if it did, most likely she'd sleep right through it.

Hawk finished his conversation with the two maimed men. Thea had not bothered to listen to anything they had said. Only a few women remained at the trestle in front of the priests. Roderick escorted her to the end of the line, behind Jesse and Elspeth.

"You will wait your turn here," he ordered, then gave her his back and walked away.

Close enough now to hear what the priests were saying, Thea turned her attention to them. One monk questioned a woman from Arles. Another listened to her answers, and the third wrote the woman's answers on a scroll of parchment. Jesse and Elspeth looked at Thea with trepidation.

"How have you fared?" Elspeth whispered.

Thea shrugged. Was there an answer for that question? This was not the place to give it.

"Why are we here?" Jesse was actually shaking. "Do you know?"

"I do not," Thea answered. She saw that the last, a very pretty girl also from Picardy, was sent into the abbey.

"Is that all of them, then?" the priest asked the duke in a resonant voice. Thea listened to the Saxons' exchange. She wanted to make certain she understood every word now.

"All. These last three are slaves," the duke said in Saxon.

Thea stiffened. The malaise numbing her tired and aching soul and body compounded into a volatile mixture of bile, churning in her empty stomach. The monk looked first at Jesse, then at Elspeth and last at Thea. He studied the collar circling Thea's throat, but never once made contact with her eyes. She knew he did not see any of them as anything more than possessions the duke was claiming. That lit the fuse to her temper.

"And you are claiming them, Your Grace?" the monk inquired of his liege.

"Yea, for the purposes of the census, you may question them this once. They will live in my house and be my responsibility all their days," said the duke.

"As you wish, Your Grace." The priest opened his hands and murmured low to his fellows.

"Don't be frightened, girls." The monk spoke passable Frankish and smiled beatifically, motioning them to come forward. Elspeth did as she was bid. Thea refused to move, and Jesse was too frightened. They were sent along by harsh hands against their shoulders. Thea turned about and knocked away the hand of the vassal who'd touched her.

"Lay your hand on me again and I'll rip your heart out with my bare hands," she growled in Frankish.

The monk intervened. "Now, now... It will do you little good to scratch and snarl. They don't understand your words anyway, little one. Come, be calm. This will only take a moment or two. You are weary from the journey. You will find life here no different from the one you left. Be calm, my children."

The priest's words helped Jesse gain her courage. She answered the questions directed at her. Was she baptized? How old was she? Had she ever spoken the vows of matrimony? How many children had she given birth to? What had become of her child? Elspeth was asked the same questions. This was the first that Thea had learned that each of them had small children taken from them, but neither had ever married. Listening to the short interviews, Thea brought her arms up across her chest and folded them purposefully in a stubborn manner.

"And your name, child?" The priest turned to Thea. She said nothing. "I have heard you speak already, so do not pretend you can't. It will do you no good. You must answer the questions. The emperor commands that all who enter our port are counted for taxation purposes."

"Her name is Thea," Roderick said from behind her.

"Year of birth? Do you know what year you were born?" The priest would wait till hell froze before he got an answer from Thea.

"List her age as one score," the duke responded again.

"Sire, she should answer for herself," the priest said.

"She is stubborn and headstrong," Hawk replied.

"Not a good mix, I am afraid. She will sour your temper and cause misery in the fief if you let her get away with behavior a serf may not. Better to apply the lash now, before the assembled people, than to let her ire fester unpunished, m'lord."

"A slave's temper is not your concern, priest."

"Is she virgin?" Friar Laurence asked bluntly.

"She is not. I have used her myself, and can swear that her loins easily accommodate any man's rod."

"Have you no answer of your own, girl?" The priest looked up at her from his prayerfully folded hands.

Thea spoke at last. "I have a question."

"Then speak it," he said.

"Are you truly ordained by vows of holy orders?"

"I am an ordained priest, yes," the priest replied.

"Does your bishop sanction the abduction of women?" Thea's voice cut through the chattering assembly in clear and unmistakable Saxon. Each of the friars gaped at her, as did every vassal and serf lingering in the square.

"I am Friar Laurence, prelate. You speak Saxon?"

"I speak five languages, priest."

"Indeed," he interrupted her. "I am surprised to see one sold so frequently and still be so young. But then at a score, you have been well used for years, have you not?"

Thea gasped at the implication of the priest's words. Worse, her cheeks flamed at the laughter they brought from the Saxon men. She no longer cared to mince words with him, or hold back her temper.

"I wish to know the depth of your involvement in this business of stealing women from foreign lands. I assure you there will be a papal investigation of this, and you will be called upon to answer for your part in this blasphemy."

Thea's audacious statements—all in fluent Saxon—rattled the priest. His florid cheeks grew bright, and his jowls quivered.

"Why, we are just replenishing our s-st-ock." The priest choked on his last words.

"Stock? As in cattle?" Thea charged. "Do you think the three of us are any less human than the other women you have given sanctuary to in yon abbey?"

"The other women are virgins." The priest raised his voice. "These two women have freely admitted they are not. If it is your claim that you are virgin, state it."

"What does that have to do with our being abducted from our rightful homes? Does not each woman you trick with your false words of comfort possess a soul, bound only to God Almighty?"

"All women are the chattel of men, and so it is stated in the Holy Book. His Grace has sworn before us all that he himself had use of you aboard his ship. Are you accusing the duke of Emory of lying, woman? Are you an innocent, a virgin?"

Thea saw the trap in the priest's coldly stated words. She looked at Jesse and Elspeth and saw confusion and fear in their eyes. But then she looked past them and saw all the Saxons gathered in this square, listening now for her answer to the priest. She spun around and found the duke of Emory right behind her.

"Answer the priest," he commanded.

Thea shook her head. Dear God, she shook from head to toe with outrage. "What trick do you play on Emperor Lothair, Saxon? You sailed under the guise of Vikings, yet this is Saxon land." Thea went on recklessly, not caring what the consequences were. She triumphed in the shock her words brought to every Saxon, including the Hawk of Emory. His face had gone as white as chalk, his mouth twisted in a colorless gray line. Her voice bristled with hatred. "Is this not your *benefice commitatus* under Emperor Lothair?"

"And if it is, woman, what is that to you? My word is law in Emory. If I do not champion you, no one will."

And that was the crux of it. Thea cast a look around the assembly and found a full assortment of possible champions near at hand. Serfs, men-at-arms, monks and priests, squires, and even a lone Saxon knight fully robed in the armor of his trade. But not a single man put a foot forward to her defense. Nor would they, for a fallen woman. Thea returned to Roderick.

"I wish to God my blade had been turned on you. I'd have cut your heart out!" Thea slapped the Hawk of Emory with all the outrage she could muster.

Roderick stood the blow, retaliating only by capturing her hand on the downswing. He could have crushed her wristbones, but did not. Injured, she could not work.

"Deitert!" He summoned the old knight to him. "This woman goes to the keep as chatelaine. See that she has irons to hobble her. If she gives you any trouble, flog her."

"I will kill you for this." Thea spoke for Roderick's ears alone.

Roderick's grip on her wrist twisted Thea's proud shoulders into a humbled crouch of pain. "Think to your health, ere I order my whip handed to me and give you the lesson your insolence deserves. Answer the priest. Are you or are you not a virgin?"

"You bastard," Thea whispered, but her head was shaking back and forth, negating everything he'd said.

"There is your answer, priest. She cannot claim what she is not." His seneschal had come forward as ordered. "Take her to the keep!"

Thea was thrown into the grip of an older knight. The bald-headed knight gripped her burning wrist and forcibly drew her away.

Roderick exhaled an audible sigh of relief. He had prepared himself for just such trouble from the little Frank, even to anticipating what he would do if she made a bid for sanctuary to the priests.

The remnants of the timid captives peeked out of the abbey and began to whisper among themselves. They were as Roderick had intended to bring home—serfs, used to the dictates of lords and squires. He paused in righteous fury after this latest upset by the little Frank to question his own sanity. What madness had possessed him on the Somme? What fever had bewitched him into bringing that black-haired vixen home? She had been trouble and nothing but since the moment he laid eyes upon her.

At his side, Benjamin shifted uneasily. "I know you are angry because the woman injured Sir Michael, Roderick. But do you really hate her this much, cousin?"

Roderick turned, confronting kin, priests and vassals all in the same encompassing stare. "Dare you ask me now what I feel regarding these women? Was I the one shouting to the heavens, 'My lord, we must have women, we're not monks'?"

His eyes swept across the crowd, daring any to come forward against him. No one did. "Nay, it was to suit your needs this deed was done. I'll hear no more of it. Father Abbot, see to your pairing with diligence. All the vows will be spoken on the morrow. I'll not tolerate another day wasted over what ills the Vikings did us. Instead of bewailing your losses, your aches and your miseries since the Vikings took all, this land should have been put back to rights. By God, it will be."

"So be it!" Friar Laurence intoned somberly. "To work then, men. Is it not written, ask and you shall receive?"

The anger Roderick held so firmly in check simmered anew. The ragtag remnants of his fiefdom scattered out of his way as he strode through the village, inspecting it from end to end. He cared not that his people saw his fury. None understood the reason for his bitterness.

He was a man of war, trained to fight and give no quarter in battle and siege. Through four long years he'd fought petty wars, winning for Emperor Lothair prizes and bounty, taking keeps and castles from Toulouse to Lombardy. While his arm was raised in service, his homeland had lain undefended, victim to the Vikings' spring attack. They had murdered his parents and stripped his lands bare.

He had come home in April, without the plunder of so many battles lining his coffers. Stripped of his honor by Anne of Aachen, he'd simply come home...empty-handed and broken. Lost, all too much had been lost.

To cast his eye about Emory and see such senseless destruction was bitter gall to swallow. It did not go down Roderick of Emory's throat at all. Now the last of summer had been squandered in the chase after servile women to keep this ragged lot content. That added more bile to his filled-to-overflowing bitter cup.

Not a man sworn to him had the audacity to question if the end justified the means.

Roderick stopped at each cottage in the village to see how this odious plan was working. There would be no more sojourns west or south to bring women to his land. The last boatload ended it. Roderick rued that he had not quit the practice at the last landfall.

Leaving Deitert in charge had assured him that fair treatment of the women of the first two boatloads would stay in effect. He was given no complaints, except those that came from the men who had no women yet. Since he spoke the language of the Celtic women, he was able to question them himself. The shock of capture had worn off most. He found contentment in some; if not that, acceptance of their lot.

The new women would be housed at the abbey overnight while it was decided which of his serfs would be best suited to which woman. That was Friar Laurence's duty. He would make his suggestions on the morrow. The weddings would be done en masse, as had been done after the previous two voyages.

It was midday when Roderick climbed the steep path to his keep, bringing Jesse and Elspeth with him. No one had thought to send them on ahead. Sir Deitert had not come back for them, which told Roderick his seneschal was probably in the battle of his life with Thea.

He expected a bitter homecoming, and with old Armina in charge of the kitchen, he would not find anything palatable to fill his empty belly this day.

October 4, 841 A.D.
Blackstone Keep, Fief of Emory, Saxony

"It matters not to me what use you served my liege upon his boat." The graybeard knight paused inside the keep. He did it apurpose, to give Thea time to look around. "I am seneschal, and I give you now the true reason for your presence here."

His hand swept outward, encompassing a doorless hall of dirt, scum and filth in one motion.

"'Tis to honest woman's work you will apply yourself, cooking, scrubbing, seeing to the needs of this keep. Give me your word you will not step outside the curtain wall."

"Why should I?"

The steep climb had not cooled Thea's temper. She burned to fly back to the village and scratch Hawk's eyes from his head. For the love of God, the man might just as well have branded her a harlot before every soul in his fief. Thea turned sorrowful eyes upon the seneschal, wishing he had not believed every foul lie his liege had uttered.

It was that very look that shattered Sir Deitert's will, for never had a young woman looked at him with such troubled eyes. He cleared his throat and tamped down the empathy that had sprung up so quickly in his heart.

"Mistress, do you not give me your word to stay within these walls, I will do exactly as my liege bade me do. I will get a chain and hobble you, then flog you within an inch of your life for your insolence."

Though it killed her to say it, Thea replied, "You have made your point. I give you my word."

"Good. You do have sense. I thought as much. As you can see, there is much work to do. I will show you where water can be fetched, and the state of our larder. You can make up for your rude display to my liege by scrubbing his chambers and making them fit for him this eve."

Her stare, black with temper, firmly assured Deitert it would be a cold day in hell before she'd lift her finger for Roderick of Emory. "Will you leave me no choice except to lay a strap on your hide?"

Thea's chin rose so high that her throat stood open and vulnerable, despite its iron binding. Could she bait the man to draw his sword and slit her throat? He wouldn't be pressed that far, but she saw she was dangerously close to feeling the back of his hand. That was not at all what Thea wanted. Lowering her hostile eyes, she asked, "What malady befell this place?"

The bald-pated knight shot her a withering look. "No malady chops a man's limbs from his body or burns his cottage to the ground. Vikings came, woman. Ten longships sailed into Blackstone harbor and rendered this land what it is today. Over three hundred men, women and children were slain in one day, the rest were taken into slavery."

"Vikings burned your church, the village and this keep?" Thea asked for clarification.

"That and more," Sir Deitert growled. He had a permanently hoarse voice, and Thea recognized it as one that had been badly damaged by smoke.

"When did this happen?"

"Shrove Tuesday."

Thea hardly dared to think the other questions that came to her mind. It was just as well. She had no need to ask if Roderick of Emory had been present during the attack to defend his home. Of course he hadn't been. He had been at Montigney on Fat Tuesday, laying his life on the line for the king's sport. Small wonder the Hawk of Emory was so embittered. After nearly losing his life to Gregory of Merrault and Anne of Aachen, he'd come home to this. It was enough to sicken anyone.

Thea took a deep breath. She did not want to feel any sympathy for Roderick of Emory. She did not want to see him as a victim of cruelty or injustice. How could she keep her anger burning against him if things kept cropping up to make her feelings twist and turn?

She was the victim here. She must remember that!

She did not ask the seneschal when Lord Roderick had returned and found his fief destroyed. With all the blood she had herself seen him lose, he would not have been fit to travel from Montigney until Lent was nearly over. She asked instead, "How long have you labored at restoring the fief?"

"We began rebuilding in earnest at Easter."

"That wall?" Thea pointed to the dark stone barbican, twelve feet thick and twenty feet high, encompassing the keep.

"Aye, that wall. The keep is the last to be restored."

Thea averted her face. She had seen the village, the abbey and the newly erected fortress wall. What that told her was that the duke of Emory saw to his people's needs and safety before his own comfort. She did not want to see Blackstone in that light. Nor did she want to think of Roderick doing without his comforts because he was more concerned about his people's safety and welfare.

Bringing her focus closer to home, she glared at the soiled floor of the hall. She had to make a decision. Was she going to take this hovel under her wing and make it livable? Or was she going to fight tooth and nail until the moment came when she could make her escape? What, pray God, should she do? She took a deep breath.

"So you are the seneschal to this atrocity. What is your name?"

"Deitert," he supplied. His glare intensified. Thea ignored it.

"Very well, you may call me Thea. I would ask that you assemble whatever servants there are and inform them that I am now chatelaine of this squalid keep. But before we do that, show me where Sir Michael has been taken. I must see to his injury. Then we will begin to see what can be done about this."

For lack of anything better, Thea used the same encompassing gesture for the disorder in the keep that Sir Deitert had used at the beginning of their conversation.

It was then that Sir Deitert delivered the telling blow. "Woman, there are no servants at Blackstone. We have a doddering crone to cook, but your lot is to see to all else." He raised his right hand in a threatening fist. "Do you speak to me again in a tone that implies I should be servant to you, you will do so with as many of your teeth missing as I can knock out in one sweep of my hand. Do you understand that, Frankish bitch?"

By noon Thea had seen it all. She knew the lay of the land inside the barbican, the condition of each and every chamber in the four-story keep, the position and purpose of the outbuildings, and the odds of her making a clean escape.

She was seriously contemplating this last issue. She would not be making any escape this day or night, no matter what the chances were that she could actually obtain freedom.

Victory was as ill as could be. He had not traveled the seas well. The poor beast had blown up bigger than a foaling dame. He would recover eventually, provided the old Saxon named Henry knew as much about horses as Thea thought he did. That was another thing. Old Henry should be promoted out of his immaculately clean stable to majordomo in the keep. He was the only Saxon Thea had met this entire day that knew what cleanliness was about.

Armina, Thea decided, should be taking care of the swine. Except there weren't any swine. Nor were there chickens or geese or eggs, for that matter. They were all going to starve to death long before winter set in with its killing freezes.

So she came at last to the one room in the keep she had vowed never to touch. The lord's bedchamber. Here a little remained of Blackstone's past grandeur. Two walls of beautiful ribbonfold paneling had been saved from the flames that had consumed all the interior wood elsewhere in the keep. No brazier for heat marred the stone floor. Instead, it had its own great hearth and chimney, standing wider across than the span of Thea's two arms.

The only true bed in the keep dominated this chamber. But the Vikings had hacked the canopy to pieces, stolen the drapes, eiderdowns and quilts.

A battered high-backed chair had been repaired and placed before the wide hearth. The chamber had grand windows, but no glass. Unlike Sir Michael's chamber, new shutters hadn't replaced the ones the Vikings had destroyed.

One trunk and a crude washstand furnished the balance of the massive room. This was also the only place in Blackstone that was moderately clean.

Thea could easily envision Hawk in this austere environment. Even with so little furnishing it, it reeked of him. Of the entire keep, his chamber would take the least effort to make clean and truly livable.

Still, Thea vowed this would be the last room she ever cleaned. Roderick of Emory would kiss the pope before she would lift one finger in his benefit. He thought to make her his personal slave, did he? Well, she would just see about that, she thought as she drummed her fingers on the armrest of his chair.

The heavy door had shut of its own accord and weight when Thea entered the room. She hadn't paid it any mind until the moment she decided to leave.

As doors went, it was a good one, newly made of golden oak. She grudgingly marveled over the ornate, scrolled hinges adorning newly carved and burnished oak. It was tricky to open, having hasp, bolt and latch. Someone here knew the ironmonger's skill.

When she pulled on the door, she had heard a loud, audible click. Thereafter, nothing she did would open the blasted thing. Well, she sighed audibly, "Someone will come soon enough and let me out."

Left without a choice, she gingerly sat down on the high-backed chair and waited. She was loath to touch anything, really. She was considered the most fastidious at home, having often scolded her sisters for their disorder. She did not care for dirt at all.

Of course, servants had always seen to the cleaning, and Thea hadn't paid much attention to what exactly it took to remove severe soil. Her mother's instructions had always been toward the management of household staff.

She drummed her fingers, impatient now. The bastard Emory had probably forgotten her. Who knew where his man had gotten off to.

Feeling dirt crusting on her hands, Thea hid them in the folds of her skirt. She smoothed her skirt and leaned her head on her hand.

"Would but this was only a dream," she said with a deep sigh. "And that I could wake up in my own bed and find none of this true."

She yawned and stared at the closed door. "Did I ever dream of a knight sweeping me away on his horse? Well, Thea, this is what your foolish dreams have come to."

Her negative opinion of the huge, square keep couldn't go lower than her estimation of the owner of such disgusting habitation. Roderick of Emory was slime. How could he live like this? Was he blind, unable to see his own filth? Well, why not? He was too blind to recognize a lady when he saw one!

Thea had not slept in nearly two full nights. She was tired. Her explosion of temper upon coming ashore had been draining. Her rage at being publicly declared a slave, and Roderick's implication that she was a woman of easy virtue, returned to haunt her.

Wasn't it enough he'd put her in a slave's collar of the kind found in France? How could he have said the other, too, that he had used her himself?

She knew the position a slave held. The lowest of all, to be used for any sort of work, to have no rights at all. A serf could demand protection by the lord and redress from him. A slave was not worth the raising of the lord's hand, neither for defense nor in protection.

What, dear God, would her mother have done if confronted with such a situation? What was she supposed to do? Would her lady mother help a man who had so badly abused her virtue? Thea didn't think so. But then, her mother was a most unusual woman, and it was not an easy thing to predict how Lilla of Landais would react in any given situation.

Thea slept, but how long, she was uncertain. She was startled awake by something thumping against her foot. Jerking her head up so fast, she banged it on the back of the chair, and found the bastard Roderick squatted before her.

"You were not brought here to lie about useless," he said by way of opening conversation.

Thea just blinked at him.

"I can not tolerate idle hands, or a belly that has to be filled that does not do a full day's work."

Thea moistened her lips. "Then I suggest you purge your practice yard. You've a wealth of fat young squires swinging wooden clubs at one another for lack of anything better to do."

The Hawk's fingers laced together between his spread knees. His head turned to the side, the expression on his face inscrutable.

"What gives you the right to criticize what you see in Emory? Answer me this. What fate would await you, were I to be inclined to send you back where I found you? Hmm?"

Thea's blank stare sharpened severely.

Roderick went on, outlining a scenario for her. "Would not your father beat you for disappearing for so many days? Your master...husband...er, whatever...would be full of rage, and direct his wrath at you."

"I have no master, husband, whatever!" Thea snapped. "I am not, nor ever have been, a servant. I am a lady, you clod-pated jackass."

Roderick bounded to his feet and dragged her out of his chair so quickly her head snapped back. He shook her twice. "Cease with your lies. *Whatever* you had before is gone. You make life anew here. That is the only choice you have."

"A choice I did not want," Thea managed to say between her rattled teeth.

He leaned ominously closer to her face saying, "Few have any choice in what they will or will not do. I am no different. You are coming with me. I will show you and the other women what work needs to be done."

"I won't raise a finger to help you," Thea said bravely.

Roderick's eyes narrowed. "Perhaps you were not completely awake when I told you straight out I will not feed an idle mouth? If you will not work, why then, I shall have to find some other use for you."

He yanked her up against his chest, his fist tightening in the wealth of free-swinging black curls, pulling her head back as his mouth descended over hers.

Thea froze as his mouth covered hers. His lips moved harshly. Hard and demanding, his tongue shot inside her mouth. She drew her hands up, pressing against the hard wall of his chest, unable to break free from this lesson in the

uselessness of defying his will. Her fingers curled into the
fabric of his jerkin. She thought she was fighting him, refusing to be used so basely again. But her body was betray-
ing her again, curling into his in welcome.

Shaken, Thea finally jerked her head free, turning her
face to the side to escape his mouth.

"I will not whore for you!" she said bitterly.

Holding her in the grips of his hands, Roderick inclined
his head above her. "You will do whatever service I demand of you. Do you understand?"

"Perfectly!" Thea bit out that word.

"I thought so," he said triumphantly.

She did not resist when he took her arm securely, leading
her through the gallery and down the stairs to the great hall.
Jesse and Elspeth waited exactly where he had left them and
both were quick to give him the obedience he deserved,
dipping their knees to him. Roderick pushed her to them.

"Hear what I say, wenches. I have heard all the insults
before the village priest that I will tolerate for now. I ask
from you the same as I ask of all others. You will work a full
day, or you will not be fed one single crumb of bread. I want
this keep cleaned. Every cinder will be removed from its
walls, and I will have it restored the way it was! Do you understand me?"

All three of the women nodded, including Thea.

She had no idea what this hovel had been before. He was
mad, insane, if he thought he could just wave his hand and
order it restored. That wouldn't happen in a week of scrubbing. Icily, she inquired, "Where should we begin?"

Roderick looked about like a man possessed. What he
saw, Thea wouldn't bother to guess. He owned nothing in
any direction except filth and scum.

He exploded in a burst of Saxon words Thea had never
heard strung together in such a descriptive manner. She
backed out of range as he raised his right hand and stopped
ranting. The fist she thought was going to strike her pointed
to the corner to the left of the gaping doors.

"Begin there," he said in a soft, menacing voice.

"Very well, there." Thea dropped him a curtsy.

Whirling away from her, he stormed out the huge, gaping hole of the hall's doorless archway. What was left of the twisted iron hinges threatened to decapitate him.

Thea sniffed because the mangled ironwork didn't cut off his head. A malingering dog yapped after him. She drew her fingers through her hair in a frantic motion that gave proof of how rattled she really was. Then she spat on the floor where the Saxon had stood. Jesse burst into tears.

Chapter Seven

Elspeth wrapped a comforting arm about the redhead's shoulders.

"Bite your tongue!" she scolded Thea. "You no longer have the right to say what you will. Go to the whipping post in yon yard if you must, but do not drag us there with you. Fie on your pride, you foolish girl!"

"Foolish?" Thea whirled, astonished by Elspeth's hard words. "You will let that bastard make a slave of you?"

"How can he be stopped? Tell me!" Elspeth's anger rang out. "It matters not what you were before. Today you are the slave of the man who owns this keep. He will do with you what he will. Allow his men to do whatever he will allow. 'Twon't be your wish, one way or the other. Grow up, little girl. I, for one, would live, be that with a collar round my neck or a necklace of finest pearls."

"Oh, Elspeth, do not argue. Please." Jesse dried her face hastily. "Let us see to the chambers, as the lord commands. We mustn't fight amongst ourselves. Come, Thea."

Jesse took firm hold of Thea's hand and pulled her from the hall, yet Thea could not help staring in shock at Elspeth's older and much wiser face. At the scummy well, there were buckets. Jesse drew fresh water. Thea spread the skirt of her dress in the bright sunlight.

Even when she'd put it on fresh to work in the kitchen for her sister's feast, it had been a lovely frock. Its embroidered yellow and pink flowers on white muslin had been beautiful. Though it was old, it was not the gown of a common woman.

She trembled as new rage raised bile to her throat. Was this the lot of a slave of the duke of Emory? That she would be assaulted at his whim? She understood now what he had meant when he said the women had been brought to be wives and breed children to repopulate his decimated fief.

But not her.

Roderick said she would have no husband or cottage, only a master. Was she to be cursed and beaten and ordered about, worked till she dropped in utter exhaustion? She would not be ordered about or stand to have abuse reaped on her head in meek silence.

That Elspeth and Jesse suffered Thea's same fate was another abomination. That they accepted it was worse.

The lord had known exactly what he was doing when he seduced her on board his ship. He'd done it apurpose . . . to strip her of all recourse she might have claimed as a lady of a recognized noble house.

Where in Saxony could she find a knight to defend her virtue, when she had none? How could she prove his words a lie? Oh, but it was a vile and evil thing the Hawk of Emory had done to her.

Without a word, Thea took a bucket and returned to the hall. She knelt on stiff knees and scrubbed the floor. What Jesse or Elspeth did, Thea didn't care.

Let the Saxons try to put her in chains. She would see them all dead before submitting. She'd make a potion of nightshade and henbane or foxglove and calamus and feed it to every man and disgusting youth in the house.

And when they were all writhing in the agony of their death throes, she'd take her horse and be gone from Saxony!

This day had surely been the worst day Roderick had faced yet. He could not imagine things becoming any worse.

One look around this fief had almost convinced him to get back on his ship and sail straight away. To go anywhere the winds would take him.

What Roderick wanted to escape, he wasn't sure. The bewitching green eyes of the Frankish woman, possibly. Damn, but he could kick himself from here to Greece and back. How in the name of all things sacred was he to have known the woman spoke Saxon? He had not considered that she might understand a single word he spoke to Friar Laurence when he brought the three women he had chosen for himself forward.

But Thea had understood every single word.

No sooner had he finished declaring Jesse, Elspeth and Thea slaves to his house than Thea had challenged him. She had called him a liar before every soul present at the abbey.

The little minx had even challenged poor Friar Laurence and demanded a true knight come forward to champion her cause.

To silence her, Roderick had made her tremble in abject fear of his wrath. The right or wrong of his actions no longer mattered. The deed was done. They must all live with the consequences of it. Thank God Deitert had taken Thea away from the village, escorting her to the keep.

Roderick had stayed away from the keep. Why, then, had he gone there hours later, stalking Thea?

Had he found her? No, of course not. That she had turned up missing so quickly ignited his temper. Then it became a quest to find her, a burning quest.

Searching every chamber had been like adding log after log to an already dangerous fire. For the first time since Easter, he'd truly seen the squalor of his house. He'd seen the filth in every room. That shamed him. Yea, he'd been blind to his living conditions. All he'd thought of was making his fortress walls.

What man wouldn't, when he fell into bed exhausted from the harsh labor of heaving one stone on top of the other?

Not a hand had been raised to sweep away a single crumb since his mother's tiring woman, Gerte, died in June. And the truth was, the simpleminded servant had never been skilled at keeping house the way his mother had done.

It was not Thea's fault his keep was a pigsty.

Yea, the condition of his home offended him. Before she had been able to attack him, he had attacked her. In war, a man learned the best defense was a strong offense.

Reason did not assuage his temper. He dismounted and walked Caesar downhill to a running beck. The old horse blew laboriously, exhausted by the gallop into the hills.

Caesar dipped his muzzle in the water. Roderick needed a drink, too. He also needed a bath, a shave, and his hair cut from the barbarian locks that had grown untrimmed since Easter.

He needed a hundred men to harvest outlying fields. He needed every single crop in the ground threshed and stored for winter. He needed time to accomplish it all. Time that wasn't going to be granted. It was nigh onto October. Winter could come howling into Emory any day.

At least he had had the presence of mind to buy salt before returning. They would have meat in the winter, provided traps were set now and hunters went out daily. Game was plentiful in the forest. They would eat, though it would be the same miserable fare that had kept Emory going the past six months.

Roderick's eyes searched a potato field below the brook. The tops were lush and green. Had he not ventured out on this last voyage to acquire women, the digging would have begun weeks ago. He had taken men needed for the fieldwork to crew his ship.

The few people who were left depended on him to see to their welfare, as if he himself could ensure ample food in every larder for winter. They ignored apple trees weighted with fruit that needed picking. Could no eyes but his see the peas and beans withering on their vines?

God knew, he should be breaking heads together right this moment, ordering men into the fields.

He walked alone, Caesar following, and he picked windfall apples for both of them. They both chewed the treat while Roderick examined a field of grain. These oats had been planted late. They were stunted, too green to be harvested. What chance did this field have of maturing? The days were short, the nights definitely cooler.

How could he feel any gladness to be home? Had his father worried about so many little details? Roderick needed someone with whom he could share his burdens. It hurt to feel as vulnerable as he did right now. How easy it would be to sail away from Blackstone. Why did he stay and face the devastation here?

He could return to the service of Emperor Lothair. That would earn him and his vassals the means to survive. He excelled at killing and taking fortresses; he knew no equal in the art of making war.

Here, what did he have? All that was left of his mighty army was three knights, twenty squires, half a dozen pages. He'd given leave to all, save those whose fees were payable directly to him. The others were released from his claim. They had the right to seek out new lords able to keep them in the manner that being to court at Aachen had accustomed them to.

Roderick could not pay the last wage due his men. Those he'd released held his mark. A mark he was not certain he would ever be able to redeem.

No, what he had was a bankrupt fiefdom. And he had added to his burden sixty more mouths to feed through the long winter. Where, Lord, did it end?

Grimly he stared down at his holding from the top of a rise, counting the mushroom tops of every rethatched hut. How were they all to survive?

Abruptly Roderick drew Ceasar's reins to his hand. He mounted the old war-horse and forced his thoughts to other things. He must see to Michael, trapped in his bed. Perhaps tonight his companion could manage a bowl of broth. Michael's wound had healed, but it would be weeks before the knight recovered his strength. Roderick must see to his care. No one else would think to do it.

As the sun fell behind the forest-covered mountains, Roderick rode back to the keep, circling the entire of it, examining the newly finished stone wall that rose twenty feet above the ground. He examined each arrow slit and spear notch, looking for weaknesses.

Last, he came to the portcullis gate, considering it from the point of attack. As the only opening into the bailey, it was the weakest point. All three iron gates were open at this moment. Closed, they were formidable. It would take a massive machine to breach them. An even greater one to assault his new walls. He could be fairly certain no enemy would tunnel underneath the structure. His keep stood on granite bedrock. Inviolate.

The drawbridge across the dry moat rattled under Caesar's iron-shod hooves. Roderick let the horse pick his way back to the stable while he surveyed the inner yard. The groom took the reins from Roderick and bade him welcome.

"Have you oats to feed Caesar, Henry?" Roderick asked as he dismounted.

"Oh, yes, m'lord. Plenty for this horse."

"Do you know if the oats can be cut early?"

"We've done it before, when winter jumped and caught us with our chausses down." The old serf chuckled. "Your father once had the grain roasted to prevent mildewing. Don't worry, Your Lordship. You carry too many troubles on your shoulders."

"There's none else to worry."

"Aye." Henry shuffled into a stall with Caesar. Roderick felt pleased that his stable had been put to rights. It was bare, miserably stocked, but there was order and it was clean. "But you're young to be so solemn and hard, m'lord."

Roderick moved to the next stall, looking at the stalwart gray. The stallion snorted querulously and tossed its head, and would not come forward to accept the stroke of his hand. He had traveled badly. On the morrow, once the gray's legs steadied, Roderick intended to put the Percheron through his paces. He lifted the bar and entered the stall, stroking the beast, intent upon befriending him.

Henry said proudly, "Tha's a fine beast, my lord Hawk. I gave him a physic to move his bowels, and he's right as rain again."

"Yea, I see that he is," Roderick said. He drew his hand back in time not to be bitten by the ornery beast. "He's an untamed one, he is. Rest him well, Henry. Tomorrow will be soon enough to begin training him to my hand."

"Aye, milord, I'll see that he's ready."

Roderick strode to the well in the center of the yard and picked up a bucket, expecting to have to dip past thick layers of scum spoiling the water. There wasn't any scum. That stopped him.

The water sparkled. No slime or mold clung to the inner edges of stone and mortar.

"Damn me!" Roderick dropped the bucket beside the well. His head shot up, and he glared into the growing shadows of the yard. Why did he continue to wash at the well when there was a perfectly good bathhouse?

Blackstone had once been a Roman outpost. Proof of their occupation was the bathhouse fed by thermal springs. But long before the Romans invaded, Saxons had favored the springs and held a liking for being clean.

The bathhouse had suffered more damage than the keep from the Vikings' hands. No roof covered it. A clutch of fall leaves clogged the drain at the far end of the deep pool. Roderick leaped over the side and squatted to clear the clay flue of debris. Then he set to work repairing the sluices.

He could see that they would have to make new copings of fired clay, but the iron gates opened with force, in spite of the rust choking them.

It was full dark when he finally caused hot water to race down the narrow coping and splash over the rim of the pool. Satisfied, Roderick dropped to the floor of the pool. He spread his hands under the stream of heated water and scrubbed his face, and laughed when he bent his head so that the water splashed over his neck and burned across his shoulders.

He sidestepped the puddle forming under his feet, gurgling out the drain. He plugged it with a scrap of tanned deerskin and a heavy rock. As the water backed up, it began to steam around his boots. His makeshift plug held secure.

Pleased, Roderick raised his hands to the chin-high walls and hoisted himself out of the pool. It would take time to fill. But this night, before he allowed one small and fastidious maid to go to sleep, he would introduce her to the one good thing at Blackstone Keep—the Roman bath.

He didn't doubt for a moment that the unlimited supply of steaming water would greatly please Thea. Boiling water looked to be an obsession of hers.

He would begin by asking if she had ever seen a thermal spring. Most likely not. 'Twas a thing that had always made him wonder what force caused such heat inside solid bedrock. To his mind, there was no explaining such a mystery. When he was a boy, his father had told him that the Saxon gods the Christ had surplanted seethed underneath Emory's soil, burning to be free again. What, he wondered, would Thea make of that?

Finished, Roderick put away his tools and went up to his hall. The closer he came to the hall, the harder his jaw set. Having absented himself for hours, he could only speculate on what he would find inside the keep. God help him if the first words out of someone's mouth were that Thea had disappeared.

They had no candles. Torches were used now to light the hall. Since Easter he'd allowed only one torch lit at night, set into the iron holder nearest the stairs. That was so that no one was killed going up or down the stairs at night. He might have come down much in the world, but sleeping in the hall with the dogs was going too far.

He had his pride, though he didn't own a decent ticking worth lying on.

Inside the hall, he found light glowing from eight torches set in each iron sconce behind the dais. A fire burned in the great hearth on the opposite wall. The trestle was wiped clean, and set with pitchers and gleaming pewter tankards.

"Oh, good evening, my lord." A page jumped to his feet, greeting Roderick. "I'll run tell Cook you are come."

Roderick gawked at the clean floor of his hall. The boy ran out before Roderick said a single word. Farther in, he saw Sir Deitert and young Benjamin sitting on the stairs.

"What do you there?"

Ben grinned. "We didn't want to dirty the floor until you'd seen it."

Roderick stared at the spotless floor. How long had it been since he'd seen it so? It was a miracle. "Is that food I smell?"

"A knight's life is not an easy one, my lord," Deitert answered. "It seems your return has set a few fires to burning more hotly than I could stir in your absence."

Roderick's attention was drawn to a commotion at the rear door. His cook, old Armina, tottered in from the kitchen with a tray balanced in her hands. Steam rose up into her face. Stepping inside, she bobbed a curtsy. Behind her came Elspeth, the quiet blonde who seemed so resourceful. She curtsied with tray in hand, more skilled and gracefully than old Armina.

"Will you sit, m'lord, so we may serve you?" Armina asked as she grudgingly waited with the heavy tray. Roderick had long since excused her rudeness. The old woman had wet-nursed his father, and was now plagued by arthritic joints. She wouldn't move farther into the hall until he sat. That was the custom. If he did not sit, the food would be taken back and kept hot, awaiting the lord's pleasure.

Roderick hardly knew what to say.

"I say we eat," Ben said with anticipation.

"Good idea." Roderick led the way.

The three went to the table and sat on the long bench beside each other. Only then did the two women come forward with their steaming trays. One contained a roasted redfish, stuffed with grain dressing and spiced appealingly. The aroma from it was very tempting. The other tray held an assortment of beans and lentils, swimming in peppery sauce, seasoned with shallots.

"A feast," Ben declared, and reached for the pitcher of ale that the redheaded Jesse brought to the table.

"Who made this meal?" Roderick asked, for it was not the kind of fare that had come from his kitchen recently.

"We all did." Jesse beamed. She saw him smile, and thought right then and there that she was in love with him, or at least that she could love him, if that were ever her lot in life. "But it was Thea who remembered how to season and cook the fish."

"Is there more?"

"We will make you more, if that is your wish, my lord," Elspeth answered cautiously. In her experience, it was better the lord thought there was more fish than for him to know his cupboards were as bare as his hall. It had taken much effort to bring this much to the table.

"No. I wasn't asking for myself. You must also eat. Where is Thea? Has she run for the woods already?"

"Thea is in the kitchen, m'lord," Elspeth quietly answered.

"Go and get her."

"Yea, m'lord." Jesse ran from the hall. Elspeth went more slowly. Old Armina shuffled out, muttering.

Chapter Eight

Thea stoked the kitchen fires beneath the ovens where her twelve loaves of rye bread were to bake. She wiped her hands on a cloth and surveyed the cleaned kitchen.

Now she might eat something that came from it, provided the filthy old woman did not touch any of the food. She poured herself a tankard of Saxon ale and quenched her thirst. That was the only thing in abundance, and the heady brew did much to kill her hunger and soothe her tired limbs.

She had another batch of dough, this of coarse wheat flour, started from the leavening left over from the rye. Rolling out four wedges of dough, she sprinkled each with stolen spices— cinnamon, honey and nuts—and rolled the dough into logs. When they had risen again, they would be baked for sweetmeats for the morning.

"Thea, the lord says you are to come to the hall," Jesse told her as she ran into the hot kitchen.

Thea blew a strand of hair off her cheek, turning the last dough ball onto the flowered board. "Tell him you cannot find me."

"Thea!" Jesse said, alarmed.

"Tell him you can not find me."

"You will provoke him. He was glad for the meal, and would give you his thanks."

"Tell him you can not find me." Thea slammed her fist

into the risen dough. Frightened, Jesse turned around and ran back from whence she came.

Satisfied, Thea hastily shaped the loaf, then wiped her hands before hoisting a heavy kettle of soaked lentils onto an iron hook and swinging it over the fire. They would simmer all night. She put a lid on the kettle and hurried out of the kitchen.

Thea needed no lecture from the Hawk of Emory, telling her how much else there needed to be done.

But it was dark now. She must find a place of her own to sleep...where she could spend the night undisturbed by any of these Saxon bastards...especially their lord.

Her earlier inspection had already convinced her the stable offered the most places to hide. The man in charge of the stable was the only competent worker she had met this whole long day.

Inside old Henry's orderly domain, Thea found him still at work, making pens for the stock brought up from the ship. He doffed his cap to her, smiling a toothless welcome. "Good e'en, mistress."

"Have you eaten?" Thea asked. "We sent supper to the hall."

"Aye, I do not eat to the hall. I have this." He showed her a piece of dried meat, broke it in two and offered her half. Thea took it, thanked him, then asked if he would show her the horses now.

Henry proudly showed her each of his lord's horses. Emory's collection was pitiful, only seven battle horses and six mares, one of which was in foal. The last Thea looked at were a chestnut gelding prancing in a well-cleaned stall and a war-horse aptly named Caesar.

The war-horse was as fine an animal as any she'd ever seen, though as old as Methuselah. He was powerful, huge, and not very friendly, especially as far as Victory was concerned. All the horses were well looked after, the stables clean and fresh. "You have plenty of hay?"

"A good crop, mistress, drying in the loft, and yon stacks you see about."

"Do you have a boy who can chop hay tomorrow? They need fresh pallets in the keep."

"I will see it done for you."

"*Merci beaucoup.*" Thea looked over the cows. There were more of them than there were horses. Henry assured her there would soon be a dropped calf or two and cream would be available for cheese and butter. She thanked Henry for his time. He went back to work on his pens.

Left alone, Thea slipped inside Victory's stall. The stallion immediately recognized her, whickering a greeting.

"Oh, Victory!" Thea threw her arms around the great horse's thick neck. "We are so far from home!" She burst into tears, unable to hold them back any longer.

He snorted, tossing his head angrily, as if he were answering her. Thea's fingers tightened on his mane. She hiccuped once, then shook the useless tears from her eyes. Crying would not get her home again. She dashed the wetness from her cheeks and patted his firm withers, then scratched his throat where he liked to be scratched.

The horse stamped loudly against the hay-strewn floor. Thea thought it his way of telling the other horses he was the best loved of them all. As far as she was concerned, he was. He called again, then reared on his hind legs, pawing the air.

"Come away from that horse," a cold voice commanded, "before he kills you!"

Thea spun around to find Roderick of Emory raising the bar of the gate. Victory crashed to his forefeet and charged him.

"No!" Thea commanded, then put two fingers to her mouth and whistled. The stallion stopped just shy of mowing Roderick down, snorted and swung his head to Thea. He ambled back to her grudgingly and stood waiting for his reward. "Good boy." Thea had nothing to offer him except her praise. He wanted more, and nibbled at her skirt.

Roderick held back, shaken. When the huge beast reared, he'd feared for Thea's life. He forced himself to stay calm and in command, and strode to her side. She smothered the horse with cooing affection, affection that should be put to better use soothing Roderick's temper. Such a display ruined a war-horse. He said nothing until he had secured a firm hold on the horse's bridle. Once he had that powerful, undisciplined beast well in hand, he could deal with the woman.

"Get out of this stall." Roderick ordered. "Now!"

Thea's hands stilled on Victory's head. He continued to nibble at her skirt, looking for a pocket with an apple or a carrot. She glared at Hawk's barbarian face. Giving Victory one last affectionate pat, she dropped her hands and left the stall.

"Do not come near this horse again. Do you hear me?" His eyes never left Thea's. She tipped her nose up in the air and haughtily barred the gate.

Roderick remained holding the horse's head firmly down, talking softly in the beast's ear, getting it used to the new sound of commands spoken in Saxon. He checked the animal's forelegs, making certain it had not injured itself. Then, satisfied with its response, he provided a ripe apple for a reward.

He left the stall, secured the gate and turned to confront Thea. She hadn't moved a foot away from the animal's stall. Her arms were crossed over her chest. Her chin was set rigidly. He wouldn't be surprised if she splintered a tooth, she ground her teeth so hard. He quirked his brow. "You have something you want to say, wench?"

"For the last time, you misbegotten son of a Saxon troll, I am not a wench!"

Then she flew at him with her hands in fists and struck him in the face, screaming Frankish curses at the top of her voice. Roderick laughed, never having heard so many generations of folk vilified, past, present and future. Roaring with laughter over her puny attack, he ducked under her

arms and caught his arm around her hips and hoisted her
over his shoulder.

"Mayhap you're right," he told her. "You'd never hold
your own in a catfight with other tavern wenches."

"Put me down!" Thea pounded her fists on the top of his
hard-as-a-rock head. That only hurt her hands. She caught
hold of both his ears.

"Tempt me not, Thea. Pull my ears and I'll retaliate by
biting the breast before me."

"Oh! You are the crudest man I have ever known!"

"Eh, but I am the only man you've ever known!" Since
she'd thought better of pulling his ears, Roderick hiked her
higher. She folded in half, assaulting his broad back with
those delicate hands. He laughed again as he strode resolutely out of the stable, because she'd given him the perfect
reason to take her to the bath. They both smelled like horse.

Small pools of light streamed into the yard through the
windows in the keep. Thea pounded on Roderick's back. He
marched resolutely past the portcullis of that high, dark wall
of granite surrounding his keep.

Thea's heart sank a little when she saw that the iron gates
were shut tight. The night's watch hailed him as he ambled
past. She'd not escape with Victory this night.

More important, where was Hawk taking her now, and
for what purpose?

Roderick had sent two pages out during supper to check
the depth of the water, put torches in the Roman bath and
lay out linens, ale, soap and his robe. Tonight, he intended
to relax in the company of a certain maid.

All through his meal he'd brooded, especially after Jesse
returned and stuttered a confession that she could not find
Thea. He'd called Jesse over her lie, correctly deducing that
Thea evaded him deliberately. He could admire her crafti-

ness, but thought it time she learned he was known to have crafty instincts, too.

Thea's heart stopped when she realized he was taking her inside the old, abandoned Roman bath. What was he going to do? She pressed her hands against his shoulders, straightening her body, and looked fearfully around the ruin. She saw the torches reflected in the surface of steamy water in the deep pool.

A small gasp of surprise escaped her lips as Hawk slowly lowered her from his shoulder. He might have thought her surprise was for the way he deliberately let her body slide against his. It wasn't. It was the steaming water that beckoned to her weary and sore body. Her feet touched the tiled floor. Thea dragged her gaze from the water and squinted her eyes fiercely at Roderick of Emory.

"I will *not* scrub your back," she declared imperiously.

Roderick straightened, feeling like a giant, the way he towered over her. Her chin was up in that haughty way that so reminded him of the disdainful mannerisms of the ladies of Lothair's court. He did not like it when Thea made him think of court, or the ladies there. She wavered under his glare, losing some of her nerve for a fraction of a second.

"Pray tell me, when did I ask you to scrub my back?" Everything about her touched his pride, but he remembered that he did not want to fight with her this night. He wanted her...compliance. Yes, that was what he wanted. Confounded, he said, "Mayhap there is something I would to speak with you about that can only be done here in the bath...without interruption."

Amazed at his own glibness, Roderick was gratified by her reaction to his tightly spoken words.

"You do?" A small frown knitted adorably between her brows. She pursed her full lips in uncertainty.

"Yea." Roderick nodded gravely. "You accomplished much, little Frank. It has not gone unnoticed how you marshaled this household and made use of what resources we have. It is my understanding that this bath could also be used as a washhouse. But it would be arduous work for you women to fill this great pool to do laundry. Mayhap you would discuss with me a few renovations I have in mind."

"Discuss with you?" Thea eyed him warily.

"Yea." Roderick again took her arm and turned her toward a tumbledown wall, deep in the shadows. "Mind where you step. The stones are sharp."

She glared at the rocks and debris, regretting that her bare feet were more tender tonight than they had been when she climbed off the boat. But her pride would not let her show any sign of weakness in front of Roderick of Emory.

"I have been thinking that this room could be cleared and the wall repaired. Tubs could be made to fit on the benches." Roderick improvised on the spot.

"What kind of a room was it?" Thea asked. It was really too dark to tell. Only a little light fell beyond the wall from the torches in the bath.

"A steam room, originally. Romans favored steam rooms, cold baths and hot baths, as well. The cold bath can't be rebuilt. My new wall covered most of it. But this could be made into a washroom fairly easily. What do you think?"

"Oh." Thea moved to the low benches made of smooth, undamaged stone. "I think that is a wonderful idea. It would work if the tubs could be made just so high. Why, it would save time, and be ready for use any day."

"Except the Lord's day," Roderick countered soberly. "We attend mass on the Lord's day, and the kitchen is closed."

"Oh?" Thea studied him, uncertain what he meant by that. "Is it your habit to fast all day?"

"Nay, we but eat cold foods, prepared the day before. We come together at the abbey. Sometimes there are games or contests to spend the time pleasurably in the forenoon afterward. There are many new . . . *folk* to get to know."

"I see." Thea mentally counted the days and concluded that the Lord's day was three days away. She planned to be gone before then, but it was good to know in advance what she needed to be prepared for.

"So you think it will do?" Roderick offered her his arm to escort her from the unused chamber. "It would take much longer to rebuild the old washhouse, which was more conveniently placed behind the kitchen storehouse. I won't build any structure of wood again."

"I take it the old washhouse was of wood, and it burned to the ground when the Vikings fired the keep?" Thea asked. It was the first time she had made any mention of Vikings to Roderick. He cast her a sideways look that bordered on the menacing, which unnerved her enough that she forgot to mind her step and stubbed her toes on a sharp rock. "Ow!"

The complaint escaped before she had time to control it. Roderick immediately snatched her off her feet, lifting her over the crumbled masonry.

"You don't have to carry me," Thea insisted, struggling as his arms tightened underneath her knees and across her back. "'Twas only that I stumbled."

"Yea," Roderick said tersely. "I could see that, little Frank. You are the most stubborn and arrogant little baggage I have ever had the misfortune to meet. You could have at least come to me with a pair of stout shoes."

"Merde!" Thea swore under her breath and counted him very lucky that she didn't take advantage of his proximity to smash his arrogant nose. He bent, setting her on the rim of the tub, very near the wide steps that led down into the steamy water. She immediately scooted away from him, but not quickly enough to escape his determined hands. He took hold of her right foot, pulling it to his lap as he sat down beside her.

Examining her dirty and bruised toes only made the dark scowl on his brow deepen. That the dainty foot he held was scraped, bruised and filthy reminded Roderick of his poverty. What kind of a man was he that he couldn't provide a

pair of shoes for a woman he bedded? Wanted to bed...
wanted very badly to bed this moment.

"Do you mind?" Thea declared icily, tugging on her foot,
which he held so lightly. His touch bothered her; she
couldn't take tenderness from him. Jesu, but the horrible
man had plagued her thoughts the entire day. Why hadn't
she stolen a knife from the kitchen to kill him?

"Yea, I do mind, wench." He tugged back and raised his
eyes to look straight into those sea green orbs of hers. Now
her expression was all tight and fierce, as if she wanted to
strike out at him. He chuckled inwardly at that amusing
picture in his mind. That reminded him that she'd made fists
of those small hands and tried to pulverize him. He took
hold of her hands and examined them, as well, fearing she
might have broken every bone. She had done a good job of
bruising and scraping them.

"You are going to soak these tiny feet of yours."

He moved her foot away from his lap, mentally thanking
the gods that she sported no deep cuts.

"Oh, I am, am I?" Thea's eyes flashed dangerously as he
pushed her foot toward the steaming water.

"I said it, so you will."

"Humph!" Thea snatched her foot out of his loose grip,
while he made the mistake of trying to catch hold of it again.
His movement gave her one advantage, and since he was
seated with his back to the water while he'd placed her on
the rim facing it, she put her foot in his chest and shoved for
all she was worth.

The expression of rank surprise on his face was a priceless sight. Roderick of Emory...the great Lord Hawk...
champion of the holy Roman emperor...tumbled backward into his own pit of steaming water...his huge, wind-
milling arms of no use whatsoever to prevent his fall.

"Ha!" Thea laughed, scooting sideways, clear of the
great splash of water he caused with his floundering. She

evaded getting completely drenched, though her skirt took a bath.

He got his feet beneath him too quickly, while she couldn't straighten her face or stop the laughter that spilled out of her mouth. What had there been to laugh over for the past week? Nothing, nothing at all.

He shook water from his head like a mangy dog, flipping sopping hair out of his eyes, but didn't pause for a single second before taking firm hold of her ankle again.

"Don't you dare laugh, you little witch."

"Laugh? I wouldn't dream of it." Thea clamped her hands over her mouth. Clumps of his beard stuck together. His tanned tunic creaked. He was a sight for sore eyes, drenched like a drowned rat. "I won't say it serves you right and you look in need of a bath."

"I can well hear that you won't say that." Roderick's fingers pressed into the flesh above her ankle. "So you won't hear me say you are more in need of a good soaking than I." He reaching forward, caught hold of the laces of her gown, his wet fingers tugging on the knot.

"Alas, wench, since I am naught but the poorest man on earth, we cannot wrestle over your lone gown. If you care to have something to clothe yourself with on the morrow, you will sit very still while I undo your laces."

Thea froze. "You said you brought me here to discuss the repairs," she accused.

"So I did," Roderick answered. "But as you have insisted upon seeing that I bathe, I shall have company. Yours."

He had deft fingers, Thea realized foolishly. Her gown came loose in what seemed only the blink of an eye. "No." She shook her head. "I won't bathe with you."

"Thea." Roderick clucked his tongue. " 'Tis foolish you are. I have already touched and seen your body. Have you forgotten so quickly?"

His eyes bored into hers, holding her gaze as though she were under some kind of magical spell. She moistened her lips and shivered as he gathered her skirt and pulled the loosened garment over her head. Too late, she broke the spell and thought of modesty, hugging her arms to her chest to prevent his removal of her kirtle.

"Here, now…" Roderick's fingers tightened at her waist, lifting her off the rim, drawing her into his watery embrace.

"Oh, 'tis hot!" Thea threw her hands around his wet shoulders as the water encircled her legs and hips, causing the skirt of her kirtle to billow and swirl.

"Yea." Roderick could not draw his gaze from her eyes. He was acutely aware of each movement she made, the way her legs floated and grazed against his, the pressure of her hands against the hard planes of his shoulders. Her fingers stole upward, pressing against his neck. "Will you kiss me, Thea?"

Chapter Nine

"Nay, I will not." Thea lowered her gaze from the intense heat of his eyes. They burned much hotter than the water. "'Tis unseemly."

"Nay, 'tis the most natural thing in the world."

"But..." She turned her face away, only to be caught by his hand upon her cheek. What was happening to her? Did the man only have to touch her to melt her will?

"Ach, Thea." Roderick propelled himself backward, sinking into the water to his chin, drawing her body closer to his, aroused by the feel of her legs parting in the deepening water to take support against his. He bent his head, kissing the corner of her mouth she worried with her teeth.

Again he was struck by how little there was to her. He allowed one hand to slide down her back as his mouth opened over hers. He found two deep dimples above the firm, round globes of her buttocks.

"My lord," she protested against his mouth.

"Yea, dear Lord above," Roderick intoned reverently, "but you're as sweet to taste as honey."

He caught her cheek and chin between his thumb and fingers. Thea resisted the coaxing pressure of his lips with all the will she had. "Nay, you mustn't."

"Yea, I must," Roderick said. "This is the reason I brought you here."

He parted her soft lips in a demanding, stirring kiss.

Thea gasped at the electrifying shock of his lips stroking her own. That wondrous magic could not be happening again! Her mouth found no objection to the tuition of his lips. She yielded to the probe of his tongue, mesmerized by the gentle way in which he held her and kissed her.

Roderick quelled the shout of triumph in his throat. She was warming to him, yea, though slowly. He allowed his lips to glide over hers and his tongue to explore the depths of her.

Her hands snuck upward across his shoulders and onto his neck, her fingers winding into the wet hair that clung to his head. A little moan sounded in her throat, a moan of pleasure that assured him she liked being kissed as well as he liked to kiss her.

Her mouth was deep and hot, deserving exploration. He tasted her. She was sweetly warm, flavored of ale and the herbs she had used liberally to season his food.

Quietly, he taught her his way of kissing. She had had no idea what a sensitive orifice his mouth was. Roderick drew out the lesson as long as he could bear it. But before madness overtook him completely, he pushed her away, sitting her on the steps that dropped into the deepest end of the pool.

He gathered her sore feet against his chest. She said not one word while he took a hard bar of soap in hand and slowly washed each delicate foot.

Thea was too stunned to ask him what he was doing, or to make a protest that he should stop. His strong hands worked the soap higher on each of her tired limbs, massaging the taut muscles in her calves, soothing and deeply stroking the tiredness out of her thighs.

"Does that feel better?" he asked.

"Oh, yea." Thea nodded as he put the hard cake into her hands.

"I vow you will not object to finishing the bath with your own two hands. Allowing to your tender sensibilities, I will grant you privacy to bathe, while I stand guard for you at the door.''

Her eyes were so wide with surprise that Roderick almost chuckled out loud. He wanted her eating out of his hand, and soon she would be. But he kept his face quite solemn as he walked up the steps and stepped out of the pool. He caught up a linen to dry with, shedding only his wet jerkin. "I will grant you ten minutes to complete your ablutions, then return for you, Thea. Do not dawdle overlong in the pool. There is much to be done on the morrow, and we must sleep, too, sometime this eve.''

Roderick strode out of the torchlight and disappeared from Thea's line of sight. He rubbed his head, draped the toweling around his neck and sat on a conveniently placed bench outside the bath entrance. While the water in the pool had been hot enough to subdue his ardor for her greatly, the night air stirred his blood.

He had the perfect view of the pool and the young maid bathing. She had accepted his assurance of privacy without question, and stood on the steps to remove her kirtle. His heart accelerated when she looked to the dark doorway, making certain she was alone. Roderick knew the torch-light did not extend far enough to illuminate him, and there was no moon yet.

Her kirtle was no impediment to his view of her. The fine kersey clung lovingly to all of her curves. Water had made it nearly transparent. He smiled as she shivered and pulled the garment over her head. She was ever careful with what she possessed, folding it and laying it to the tub's tiled edge. Then she stood poised for a moment on the topmost step, reminding Roderick of the statue of Diana that had graced this bath years ago. The damned Vikings had even stolen that.

He did not want to think about the Vikings. He wanted only to watch Thea as she bathed. She surprised him by diving gracefully into the deep pool. He marveled at how well she took to the water, swimming the length of the pool several times before settling to the steps to soap her head, arms and legs and wash her body. She had lied to him about being unable to swim when he'd abducted her. He wondered how many other things about her would prove false. Time would tell.

Charmed by her spriteliness, Roderick vowed to take her up to Kirrel's Mountain in the afternoon on the Lord's day. He wondered what she would think of the waterfall and the natural pool. It, too, was fed by hot spring currents, though the waterfall was cold as the melting snow cap that caused it.

After she had rinsed her hair, she washed both gown and kirtle, twisting the cloths together to remove the water from them. Roderick took that as his cue to reenter the bath. She looked up at him and dropped into the water to hide her nakedness from his view. He retrieved his robe from the marble bench and held it open wordlessly, waiting by the steps for her to emerge from the water.

Thea wished she had heard him return. She'd have put on her kirtle to have some sort of covering over her body, but she understood well enough that he was making a silent, courteous gesture by offering her his robe. The bath was very dark, the torches guttering now. So she made the decision to emerge from the water. She could not hold his gaze—that would be too bold by far—but he paid her nakedness no more attention than any trained lady's maid, enfolding her in the soft, absorbent cloth immediately.

She stuck her arms inside the voluminous sleeves, and was swallowed by heavy cloth with the nap of Venetian velvet. It dragged on the tile floor, and the sleeves hung well past her hands. Roderick's hands tightened on her shoulders, drawing her against his chest as he fastened the belt around her waist.

"I must hang my gown and kirtle to dry," Thea said with almost painful shyness.

"Of course." Roderick secured the knot at her waist and released her. She hurried to the task she'd set herself, draping both from the nearest length of line in the adjacent yard with sturdy wooden pegs to hold them secure against the breeze.

Roderick doused the torches and brought the mugs of ale his page had provided him to the nearby bench at the well.

"Come here, Thea. Sit with me awhile. 'Tis a fair night. The stars are full, and the moon is on the rise."

Done with the only task Thea could think of using to evade him, she stared at the quiet corner of the yard where he sat. "I shouldn't... I mean, I must find a pallet and a place to sleep."

Roderick stared at her levelly. "You will sleep where I tell you to sleep, Thea. Come here."

That was said as an order, and Thea knew she would have to obey him. Obedience was much too ingrained in her. She joined him on the cold stone bench, wary. She cast nervous glances at the hall and the portcullis opposite it, finding the watch on guard and movement inside the hall.

Roderick handed her one tankard, brimming with ale.

"I think I've had enough of your wicked brew. It went straight to my head earlier in the heat of the kitchen."

Roderick smiled wryly and inclined his head toward the well-lit hall. "You are not the only one whose head is affected by Kimball's brew. I don't know how long it has been since I heard that song sung. Deitert has a pleasant voice for church songs, but he's no minstrel with a love ballad."

Thea's fingers tightened on the cup in her hand, and she took a sip, frowning and concentrating. She swallowed the mouthful of ale and shook her head, then fingered the wet curls clinging to her neck. She felt tangles in her hair and knew it needed brushing badly, then feared she must look a fright to anyone's eyes.

Roderick took a longer drink than she did, then set his emptied cup at his feet. "Ah, there is the moon." He raised his arm and pointed to the high wall.

"Oh, I see it, *maintenant.*" Thea said, slipping naturally into French. *"C'est très belle."*

"Yea," Roderick agreed. The orange globe was very beautiful. "Harvest moon. Is it not always that color this time of year?"

"I think so." Thea nodded agreement. "But it will be more beautiful in two more nights. Then it will be full." Saying that reminded Thea that she would need the full moon to guide her on her journey home. Determined to keep her thoughts to herself, she brought the tankard to her mouth and gulped its contents. She couldn't allow herself to soften. Roderick of Emory was her enemy. He had to be. She couldn't allow his few moments of kindness to weaken her.

"Yea, you are right about that, too." He took the empty cup from her hand, placing it beside the other.

His breeks creaked as he stood up, and Thea looked down at his feet, remembering that he had tumbled into the water fully clothed. His leggings and boots must be full of water still.

"'Tis time for bed." He scooped her off the bench without further ado, cradling her in his brawny arms exactly as he had done earlier.

"I can walk," Thea insisted.

"Of course you can. But I can also carry you. Now, be quiet, Thea. I'll hear no more arguments this night."

She was tempted to tell him that she never argued. It wasn't well done to argue and cause discord unnecessarily. As she could see no purpose to be gained by stating such, she kept her silence, even when he entered the crowded hall with her in his arms.

At the steps to the gallery, Roderick paused to tell his men to hie to bed. On the morrow he would need every available pair of hands to mount the new doors for the hall. The squires groaned, but Sir Deitert squelched their complaints with orders to clear the hall.

Thea tucked her flaming cheeks under Roderick's chin, glad no one had made any mention or notice of her.

Roderick resolutely mounted the stairs and deposited her in his chamber without any more words. All evening he'd been thinking of how to soften and woo the little termagant. Thea yawned deeply from the center of the bed.

She looked to him like a drowsy cat, sated by a full belly. More fool he, for thinking he could entice her into a more giving disposition by plying her with Kimball's ale and the soothing comfort of his Roman bath. He had not stirred her senses for pleasure as he had his own. He'd lulled her to sleep.

After closing and locking his chamber door, he had to tend the fire in the hearth. The scent of pine resin lingered above the odor of smoke as he stirred the embers and laid more wood on the grate.

Though this evening was still warm from the day's goodly heat, by morning the chamber would be as cold as ice. He turned from that task to find the woman he wanted most desperately to bed sprawled facedown across his bed. She had not removed his robe or gotten under the thin covers. Moreover, she snored.

Roderick sighed. At least he could content himself with her acceptance of his touch and kiss earlier. Not that that satisfied him. He sat on his high seat beside the fire, unlacing his leggings and boots, laying the leather garments by the hearth, where they would dry by morning. He stood to unfasten the laces on his wet breeks, shivering as he pulled the leather off his shanks. There was water in his basin, and soap beside his ewer. He washed and toweled briskly, glaring at the beard he had yet to trim.

All the while he readied himself for bed, he listened for some indication that Thea's sleep was lighter than it appeared. She was small of stature, and yea, Kimball made a potent brew, much stronger than Roderick had ever tasted in Franconia. But he'd tasted Frankish wines that could humble many a man his size.

Damn me, Roderick groaned. Perhaps he was not a virtuous man, but lust laid a heavy burden on him. He could not continue to suffer endlessly the pains and agony of enforced celibacy. He was no more monk than his Saxon serfs.

Thea's soft snores continued once Roderick moved into bed. He turned her onto her side, though she did not wake. Her eyes remained closed and her mouth slack. The fire in the hearth was bright enough to allow his inspection of her features. No scowl marred her brow, nor did any sullen grimace spoil the generous curves of her mouth. She was lovely, he realized. Pretty and, yea, very, very young.

Tendrils of her drying hair clung to her throat and cheeks. He moved them away with his forefinger. Her skin was finely created, moist and translucent. Faint freckles dotted her pert little nose. For one whose hair was so dark, she had wondrously fair skin, like milk, fresh-drawn. He let the pad of his finger trace the fine arch of her brow, then smoothed back the wild curls that feathered around her face. She could not sleep in his robe.

It wasn't her comfort he thought of as he unfastened the cloth belt, sat her up against his chest and stripped the robe from her inert body. It was his coffers. There wasn't another like it to be had, and he did not wish to turn his great, clumsy body over in sleep and tear the flimsy thing.

Roderick leaned her against his chest as he drew the covers back, laid her down and tucked the rough wool and cotton sheeting loosely around her shoulders. He wasn't anywhere near ready to sleep.

He tied his robe around his own body and went down to the hall, returning with a pitcher of ale to numb his own rampant needs. He sat beside his fire using his knife on a stout piece of rawhide that Aldus, his tanner, had given him that morning.

Roderick held the leather against the soles of Thea's feet, traced their outline with a piece of charcoal and cut simple sandals. With an awl and a few strips of doeskin, he fashioned a rude-looking sandal.

He drank a second glass of ale as he strung the laces. Opening his trunk, he searched for a matched set of stockings that had been given him a long time ago but were too small for his feet. They were too large for Thea's. Even so, he folded them onto the crude shoes and placed both on his trunk at the foot of the bed. The ale did what the day had not done—fogged his mind enough that he could no longer think or plan or reason sensibly.

Lying in bed, he could not sleep. The bed was cold without his fur rug. He was damned to be cold this night, because someone had forgotten to bring his fur up from the ship. He would send for the bear rug first thing on the morrow.

The little woman curled against his side offered so little body heat as to almost be of no value sharing the bed. She felt bony, all elbows and sharp little knees. Even though she had enough of his ale in her to make her snore and sleep like a dead woman, she also sought warmth and dug her toes into his knee, wiggling them, seeking to burrow underneath his weight, where the warmth was greater.

Roderick turned onto his side, settled her against his belly and closed his eyes.

In sleep, she nuzzled down against him, tucking a cold nose into his arm. He let his fingers travel over the contours of her face, learning it thoroughly by touch alone. Her cheeks, her chin, her long, slender curved throat that seemed so frail and vulnerable. That same neck that refused to let her noble head bow before him, that he had so cruelly put an iron collar around.

Gently, without waking her, he spread open the ends of the slave collar and removed it from her throat.

Her skin was rubbed red and raw from its weight. He kissed the most vulnerable wound. She slept on, oblivious of him.

"Life was once good here, Thea," he said. Memories came to mind, too painful to dwell upon. He shook his head. Bothered by the direction of his thoughts, Roderick cleared his mind and tried again to will sleep to come. He couldn't sleep. One thing that did not keep him awake was regrets. He didn't regret stealing her, not one bit.

Chapter Ten

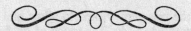

Hours seemed to have passed, but it might not have been that very long. Hawk could not tell by the night, knowing only that the fire in the hearth burned lower and the chamber had turned cooler.

Thea stirred, rousing partly, and, feeling the chill outside the blankets, burrowed face forward into Roderick's throat, seeking his warmth, aware of him for the first time in hours. Her eyes fluttered and she realized she was sleeping in his bed, naked.

His hands made the most comforting and restoring exploration of her body, massaging aches and bone-weariness of the hardest day she'd ever known. His fingers sent comfort surging through her leaden limbs. Comfort and frissons of heat.

Roderick's fingers splayed across the deep hollow at the back of her spine and kneaded the tight musculature until she arched against his hand like a cat. Her belly made complete contact against his. She could feel the press of his rod against her flesh. A shiver swept through her as she raised her arms and encircled his shoulders, drawing her own body closer to his.

That was the one signal Roderick needed to know that she accepted his suit. Thea sighed as Roderick's touches became bolder, unaware that the building aches he stirred inside her could not be satisfied by touch alone. She needed something more. Now fully awake, she harbored no resistance to him within her.

He kissed her deeply, his tongue plunging inside her mouth. His hands were wild where they touched her as he had on his ship, fingers plucking upon her breasts, stroking firmly across her belly and pressing deep into the warm, moist heat that kept building and building between her thighs.

She knew she was very wicked to allow him such complete liberty with her body. The touch of his fingers upon that secret, private place caused waves of tremors through her body. She dared not ask him to stop, in case he would.

His assault upon her senses was so powerful, she couldn't have borne it if it had ended abruptly. Her nose was full of the strong, washed scent of him. Her mouth still throbbed with the taste of his tongue. Every inch of her skin was alive with anticipation, hungering for his next stroke or caress.

He pressed one hairy, grizzled knee between her thighs, opening them, and his hand cupped what seemed like the only part of her that mattered anymore. But she was wrong about that, because he raised his head from hers and lowered his mouth to her breast, touching the tip of his tongue to her nipple. His lips followed, opening over the throbbing orb and closed firmly upon her. She felt his teeth and tongue as each abraded her so-sensitive nipple. He drew it taut within his mouth, and at the same time his thickened shaft entered her body. All of it was her undoing. She had never felt such wondrous pleasures and pains—which were not pains at all.

Roderick moaned at the tightness of her sheath, resisting yet yielding to his invasion. He could hardly concentrate on anything except his sensitive, lengthening rod as it began to penetrate her body. He hardened, even, shuddering as her slick, wet heat tightened fiercely, proof of how completely aroused she was.

He could not continue this agonizing torture. He released her breast to kiss her mouth softly, adoring her, soothing and satisfying her. It was completely foreign to him to behave so, to caress a woman until she quivered with desire. Furious and mad lovemaking, quick assault and conquest, he was skilled at, but to wait and woo a woman slowly, gently... no, in all his days he'd never done such a thing.

He must take his release. But even now, when he could have ended this self-torture, he held back, taking pleasure from the slow dance that built with the heat of a kiln-dried fire, stoking flagrant embers between them.

He was acutely aware the moment her floodgates opened, a silent signal that she was ready to be ridden as hard as he dared.

Never had he known such a woman as she.

Robbed of his sanity, he had the presence of mind to give her space to breathe as he drove home between her thighs, caught up in the eternal rhythm of man and woman. His whole body strained to reach the pinnacle, which came with shuddering exhaustion. He collapsed upon her, unable to move, or breathe, or think.

Her fingers stirred in his hair, and she turned her sea green eyes up to his. They seemed to reflect all the satisfaction he was feeling.

"The priests must be wrong, m'lord," she whispered, and raised her head to bestow on him a kiss of peace.

"How so?" he managed to say, struggling with the effort to regain his breath.

"Love so perfect as this could never be a sin."

Her statement made Roderick drop his head to her shoulder as he stifled a groan. Why had she said that?

"Love?" Roderick gasped, raising his head to nip the tip of her shell-like ear. "Love does not exist, Thea. Mistake this not for anything more than what it is—lust."

Thea swallowed back the feeling of being cheated. *Lust,* he had called it. Lust was one of the seven deadly sins.

"Is there not something more?" she asked.

Roderick managed to make the dryness in his mouth abate enough to give himself the power of speech again.

"More? Woman, if you realized how long it has been since I have satisfied my lust, you would not ask for more now." Roderick raised his head from her throat and kissed the softness below her ear.

Thea swallowed harshly. She wanted to ask if that was all she was to him—a wench he'd bedded. But she knew the answer would hurt her more than anything she had thus far suffered at Roderick of Emory's hands. Abruptly she pushed his greedy mouth away from her throat and swung her legs out of the bed.

Roderick caught her arm, "Where do you go?"

Thea cut him a hateful look. "To find some godforsaken corner of this keep where I may sleep unmolested."

Roderick's hand tightened above her elbow. "I have already told you where you will sleep, Thea."

"So that I may continue to whore for you? Nay, Saxon, I think not!" Thea jerked her arm, but did not break his clasp.

"Damn you!" Roderick yanked her back to him. "I have not offered to pay you, wench."

"The devil you haven't, Saxon. You have sworn to me not to give me a morsel of bread, do I not labor a full day for you! Well, I will not spend my nights laboring beneath you to earn my rest. Do you have any idea of the insult you do me?"

Roderick caught hold of her struggling arms and pressed her back onto the bed. "Insult?" he shouted. "Why, you self-important little bitch, I do you no insult taking you to my bed. I have given you an honor no other woman in this fief can claim."

"Nay, Saxon, you use me. I come from better stock than one who equates it an honor to whore for the man of the keep."

"Be silent!" Roderick roared. Thea closed her mouth with a snap, inwardly fuming, insulted to the core of her being. She was a Bellamy, by God, his equal—and better in rank and position, but for this shame he'd heaped upon her.

Even were she to gain her freedom this very moment and somehow find her way home, she was ruined, soiled goods no decent man would have. Thea's temper smoldered as she thought of telling him once and for all who she really was. But she would not say the words. She, a Bellamy, had been made a slave. A Saxon's whore.

Roderick slowly loosened his grip upon her upper arms, leaving her lying on the mattress. The imprints of his fingers stood out against her flesh. Damn, but she was a haughty creature, full of her own misguided pride. Did she think he would surrender his heart to be trampled under her feet?

Roderick held his temper in careful check.

Little did she know that there was no heart inside the Hawk of Emory. His heart had turned to stone long, long ago.

Love! He snorted, hating the very word.

Abruptly Roderick heaved his body out of bed. He tossed the covers over her.

He strode to his trunk at the foot of the bed and, before his hand could open it, spied the shoes he'd made. He took them and the stockings in hand, needing the tactile feel of something other than warm, giving flesh to quell his raging temper.

"I have made you shoes, Thea." She sat up, holding the sheet before her breasts, staring at him with those intense, penetrating eyes that made him think she knew each of his most mortal sins. Roderick tossed the shoes and stockings onto her lap.

"They are not much more than rude sandals, but you will wear them anyway." His voice was gruff. He saw a flash of hurt in her eyes.

He opened his trunk and pulled out a fresh pair of breeks and sat in his distant chair to lace up leggings and boots. She looked out the window and saw that morning was still hours away.

"Why did you?" she asked.

Roderick made his voice hard and gruff. "Did I what?"

"Make me shoes?"

"In this rockbound land, bare feet invite injury. Those who sicken cannot work. Go to sleep."

Was that all she meant to him? Was she just a body brought here to labor for him? In his keep, in his kitchen, and here in his cursed bed? Thea wanted to ask him those questions. Pin him down specifically on what his use for her really was. But instead, she asked foolishly, as if she cared, "Where are you going?"

"Out. To check the watch."

Thea was still awake when Roderick returned to bed. He laid her damp dress and kirtle on the trunk but said not one word as he cast off boots, leggings and breeks.

It was too early to rise. But as far as returning to sleep, that was impossible. Thea was much too upset by all that had passed between them to sleep.

This time, as he got into bed, he took care that he did not roll to the center. She had missed his warmth. He made no offer of that comfort to her now. In truth, the more she pondered over that sense of communion, of souls touching between them, the more she thought it only a figment of her imagination. She did not feel it now. And it was obvious he did not feel it, either—if he ever had.

She doubted that he had ever felt anything for anyone.

Troubled, Thea watched the sun break upon another foggy dawn. He confused her deeply. Why had he brought up her clothes? Why would he make her sandals? Why was there such powerful magic between them when their bodies touched? Did that magic happen to every person when touching another in such a sexual manner?

Roderick turned over in his sleep. Thea lay on her side, staring out the window. She decided she served no purpose lying abed.

Rising, she discovered she had not a stitch of dry clothing. She could hardly go start things in the kitchen naked. It was much too cool to put on wet clothes to do the same. The only option she had was to get her gown and kirtle dry as soon as possible.

Roderick awoke cold, fumbling for his bearskin. He found only thin sheeting. Foggily he searched for Thea. She wasn't the same as his bearskin or his wool blanket, for that matter, but she was some warmth. Warmth that had rudely been taken from him.

He opened his eyes on the new day and stared dumbly at the scene before him.

She knelt before the hearth, wound in a cloak made of their only blanket, breaking gray embers into red coals to shove under another split of hardwood.

With each thrust of the poker, she muttered under her breath about the crying shame of waking to a stone-cold chamber without a single servant who cared for the lord's comfort in the whole of godforsaken Saxony.

Roderick winced. The heat she created by stirring the coals did not satisfy her pique at doing for herself what she thought others ought by duty to tend to. She knelt before the growing fire, spreading her gown's skirt before her, examining the fabric for stains, bunching the cloth between her palms and rubbing it to remove any soil. She fussed over the task, because she had naught else to wear.

Roderick laced his fingers behind his neck and glared at the undraped canopy, listening to her plaints and miseries. His poverty stung him bitterly. There was naught he could do except feel the bite of her unguarded tongue.

More painful was the bare-bones truth of his body. He had awoken in greater need this morning than he had felt the night before—wanting her.

It was a matter of will to him about whether or not he would assuage the turgid ache stiffening his shaft rigidly outward from his body. No woman was going to lead him around by his rod again. No Frankish woman, and especially not one whose hair was the color of midnight.

Anne of Aachen might have made a fool of him, but he would not allow another to play havoc with his heart again.

He rose from bed without a word. Dragging his robe over his tumescent body, he stalked to his chest and searched for his cleanest tunic. Aggravated, Roderick strode up behind Thea and dropped the garment into her lap.

"There," he said gruffly. Let her taste his morning temper, as he had just tasted hers.

Startled, because she had not heard him rise, or even realized Hawk had wakened, Thea caught hold of the fabric as she turned and looked up at him. Her fingers touched the finest of court samite.

"What do I with this?" She looked at his face, particularly his mouth, which was compressed in a flat line inside his beard. Had he told her to mend it?

"Wear it," the lord said through his teeth.

"Wear it?" Thea repeated just to be certain. She dropped her gaze, ashamed that he might have heard her complaints. She must remember that her habit of talking to herself left her open to censure.

"Are you certain? It's much too fine for the use I would put it to." She spread the cloth over her lap, smoothing the golden threads woven into it with her fingertips.

"For the love of Saint Peter, wear it, and don't argue with me. It's a gift. On you it will fall past your knees. Even without your kirtle underneath, it will be suitable."

Wryly Thea had to admit he was right. She could save her kirtle for her long trip home. With a girdle, the tunic would do, since he had given her fine stockings to cover her legs. But she was not used to exposing any part of her legs, even in stockings.

She wondered if there might be a skirt somewhere, or fabric to make one from. Not wanting to ask for more than he had already given her, Thea hastily pulled the tunic over her head and stood up, discarding the wool blanket she had taken from the bed.

"'Tis indecent for a woman to go about unskirted," she said timorously, unwilling to look directly at the man she had been so intimate with the night before. Were that sense of communion there to shield her, it would have been easy. Without it, she could not bridge the gap between them. He did not seem to care much for looking at her, either.

And why shouldn't the man reject her this morning? Thea wondered silently. What was she to him but a servant? She touched her throat, aware for the first time since rising that he had removed the collar from her neck. It lay on the floor at his side of the bed.

She did not think she could bear it if he made her stand still before him while he put the cursed collar around her throat again.

She made busy with folding the wool blanket.

"Grete's clothes are somewhere. Armina must know where they are. Ask her where she put them."

Roderick hoped his words affected disinterest as he poured water from the ewer into his basin. Draped in his tunic, Thea looked more like a page than a woman. At least her dress enhanced her figure. That lone gown was becoming worn and sadly tattered.

The state of her wardrobe brought all Roderick's failings to mind. It rankled, because a man of his position should at least be able to clothe any woman he bedded.

Stiffly Roderick glared into the small square of mirror, intending to hack at his face with the blade of his knife.

Thea finally hearkened to the mood of the Hawk of Emory. She remained unable to read the nature of his scowl. What was he so irritated about? And who was Grete? It was on the tip of her tongue to ask both questions. She held back instead and marched militantly to the bed to strip it, thinking it was industry he wanted most of her.

"You will have clean sheets and a new mattress this night, I promise you, m'lord."

Roderick made the mistake of turning to see what she was doing. She chose that moment to bend over the bed and reach for the far corner of the soiled sheet.

The samite rode up her hips, exposing the soft white underflesh of her thighs above the knots she had made in the top of her stocking. The sight arrested him, hardening an already swollen and aching need. It was too much to bear that his body so ruthlessly betrayed him.

Roderick's knife clattered in the ewer, and he gripped the washstand with both hands, bending over it, groaning. "Get out of here, now!" he ordered, then ground his teeth, closed his eyes and dunked his head in the basin of cold water.

"What?" Thea turned, gripping the sheets that were rolled into an easy-to-carry bundle, staring round-eyed at him as he raised his dripping face and head. "Have you cut yourself?"

"No. I have not cut myself. Go!" Roderick jabbed his fist at the door. "Leave this chamber, *now!* See you that my bed is restored by eventide, and that you are naked in it. You'll not blame me for your sore backside if I must go looking for you another night."

She gawked at him like a witless idiot, while he stood there, nearly spilling his seed onto the rush-covered floor.

Thea swallowed. Her lips parted so that the pink tip of her tongue could moisten her mouth. Was he angry because she had not said thank-you for the tunic? Gratitude was more than she could give.

"Mayhap... you would like for me to shave you." Thea offered.

Roderick groaned. "Just go."

Thea hesitated a moment longer, then, confused, fled out the door.

Angered and unsatisfied, Roderick turned his face to the mirror and glared at the ugly visage it presented him. He was damned if he'd shave this day. His hands were too unsteady to hold the blade without slitting his throat.

Chapter Eleven

Immediately after he went downstairs, Roderick sent for Ellie and Jesse and removed their slave collars. He handed all three collars over to his seneschal, saying, "Sir Deitert, make it known that I have freed each of my slaves, and see it recorded in the abbey records. Elspeth, Jesse and Thea are no longer beholden to anyone in this household.

"Do they wish to acquire husbands from the remaining unmarried men, they may act in their own interest, petitioning me for approval of their choice.

"Henceforth, they will be paid from my coffers a fair wage for the service they do my house so long as they remain here."

That said, the duke decreed he was traveling north to hunt and check his traps. Elspeth packed his provisions. Thea watched him leave on Victory. He did not pause to tell her goodbye, nor did he even acknowledge that she was present.

He did not say when he would return.

Each night of his absence, Thea retired to the duke's chambers, as he had ordered before he left his house.

Formally there were certain things lacking about the manner in which he had freed them. It came as such a shock that Thea, Ellie and Jesse could talk of nothing else after he left. Thea came to some conclusions of her own.

Lord Roderick had not assembled his household and elevated her to the role of chatelaine by his command. That was a glaring omission on his part. In essence, he had left her in only one position in the house, that of his leman.

By abruptly departing so soon after granting their freedom, he had forced her to wage her own battle, claiming what authority she could by default, temper and sheer dominance over the other occupants of his keep.

Together, the three women concluded that nothing had changed except that they were now freed of the discomfort of the collar they had worn.

Thea decided that so long as she was stuck in this miserable land, she was not going to starve. So she ordered the butchers to slaughter the three wildest sows, demanded that the smokehouse be fired, and stayed exceedingly busy sorting the carts of produce and grains that were being brought to the keep for storage.

She had the keep fumigated with camphor and sulfur, the pallets burned and new ones made from fresh straw and pine needles.

When one of the squires presented her with Lord Hawk's mangy bearskin, she had it removed from the keep and dunked in the Roman bath. It had to be rinsed four times before the long black fur regained its sleek, luxuriant luster. Then, of course, it had to dry. With the days growing shorter and cooler, that would take awhile.

The Lord's day passed very quietly. There was a mass celebrated, and a lengthy sermon in the roofless abbey. A cold meal followed in the village square, with the majority of the food supplied by the absent Hawk of Emory. Which meant that Thea, Jesse and Elspeth were too worn-out to mingle much with the villagers.

Naturally, the Saxons who had lived through the Viking attack were strongly bonded by their common past, and Armina fit right in with them. Armina also carried tales. She took great joy in gossip, spreading whatever news she had.

She had lots to say over the doings at the keep this past week.

Sunday seemed the longest Thea had ever had to live through. She felt very deeply the censure of the community's goodwives. It wasn't in the nature of married women to suffer a leman in their company. Thea did not ask Jesse or Elspeth if they had felt the same censure she had on Sunday. They were not forced to sleep in the Hawk of Emory's bed. Thea couldn't speak of it.

Monday morning, work began in earnest once again. All day the green depths of Thea's eyes had flashed moody, murky color. Elspeth finally asked what was troubling her as they stirred the bubbling caldron of pig fat.

"If you must know my thoughts—" Thea blew a wisp of hair that had come free from her kerchief off her damp brow "—I am thinking of home, and trying for the life of me to remember the ingredients necessary for making soaps and shampoos. Those were tasks done by... others."

Thea stopped herself from saying her mother's servants.

"Soaps?" Elspeth drew the wide paddle across the bottom of the iron tub.

"Yea, soaps," Thea snapped. "Without a goodly supply of that commodity, this keep will shortly return to last week's squalor."

"Mayhap there are others about who know the secrets of making lye from ashes. I'm sure the abbot has recipes," Elspeth suggested.

"There are many recipes for soap. I don't wish to wash my skin with the same harsh lye used for bedding."

"Why don't you go down to the abbey and talk to Friar Laurence?"

Thea stared at Elspeth as if she had lost her mind. It did not bear mentioning that she could not just walk out the portcullis. Sir Deitert would have to be summoned, and Thea was in no mood to put up with him.

She would rather think about soap.

There were all kinds of soaps, hundreds of them, Thea recalled. There were the rich cakes she and her sisters used to make generous lather to shampoo their hair. And those of oatmeal to soften their complexions. Oh, she thought, there were creams and lanolins and ointments. All could be refined and made, if she knew how or had paid attention to such doings at home. Making soaps had never been important. The lowest of her father's serfs tended to such things, for it was hot work, miserable work, hard work.

Everything made Thea think continually of home. The ache grew inside her heart and, try as she might, she could not imagine it being assuaged by a kiss from the duke of Emory when evening came.

If he deigned to kiss her again.

If he ever chose to return home. And when, she wondered, did I come to think of this disastrous place as home!

What am I going to do? Her fingers traveled to her throat, lingering where his collar had injured her. He had taken it off. The damage done by it could not be mended.

All the people of Roderick's fief had seen it. She would forever be the lord's slave, *with or without* the iron round her neck.

Sometimes she hated Roderick of Emory. Then she would remember how she felt when he wrapped his arms around her. His lips soothed and consoled her so completely, she seemed to have given up nothing. She had gained more than she'd ever dreamed possible for herself. She had touched love, felt it, and returned it to him as gift.

But the sad truth was, what he felt was not love.

It was only lust.

Roderick of Emory did not want any part of the love a foolish Frankish slave had offered to him. In her heart, Thea believed that even if she told him exactly who she was, how he felt about her would not make one whit of difference. He called her "little Frank" in the same scornful, insulting way she called him "Saxon." He wouldn't care how many titles she had following her name. To him, she was just Thea, his slave.

Every waking hour she swore she would not make the same mistake twice. She would not fall in love with him. She would not debase herself again.

What had happened between them that night was a once-in-a-lifetime thing. It could not repeat itself. Lust, after all, was not love.

It took three days to complete the soap-making. Bright and early Thursday morning, they turned to making candles.

In the forenoon, Victory's iron-shod hooves rang on the drawbridge, announcing Hawk's return. Thea bent over the simmering kettle of tallow, testing the strength of the scents she was adding to the mix. Elspeth nudged her arm.

"He's come." Ellie pointed to the gate.

Thea straightened and reflexively smoothed her hand over her skirt. She'd forgotten she was wearing his tunic. There was nothing to smooth.

She watched Victory canter toward the stable. Her horse showed a new air about him. His neck arched deeply, and his noble head was high. He looked magnificent. Old Henry hurried to take the reins and hold the horse while Roderick dismounted. The packhorse Roderick had taken with him was heavily loaded with bundled furs. Before he dismounted, his sharp gaze swept the busy compound, seeing all and sundry diligently at work, noting what tasks they were doing.

His eyes passed over Thea as if she were no more important than his cooper straining over banding a barrel, or the blacksmith at his hot and noisy forge.

Swallowing a bolt of disappointment, Thea returned her attention to the wax. The shoe felt awful on the other foot. Roderick of Emory refused to acknowledge her. Well, she could do that, too.

Hoping to hide the tears that suddenly blurred her eyes, she looked up at the overcast, blustery sky. Storms were in the air. She managed to control her voice, asking Elspeth to make the test dips. They had all their racks prepared with lengths of cut cotton cord. They both gave a small shout of triumph when the tallow adhered to the strings, stiffening and fattening with each successive dip.

"It would appear we have a successful batch." Elspeth paused to retie her hair away from her face. More of the fat renderings were being taken care of by a village woman called Griselda and her daughter, Trude.

The peasant mother and daughter badgered each other as they worked in an easy, teasing manner. They had hips as wide as the caldron, and lusty voices that gathered Saxon boys around them, just to hear what outlandish thing Griselda might say next. Both welcomed Roderick warmly, and he responded with a cheerful greeting of his own. He laughed easily, joining in the banter and high spirits.

Thea picked up another improvised rack the smith had fashioned for her. There were twelve wicks dangling from each rod. A temporary cooling rack had been fashioned of planks of wood. Still, the work was backbreakingly tedious.

Her eyes strayed again to Roderick. Hawk moved with eloquent grace from one work station to another, inspecting a whole row of barrels. He paused to speak to his ironmonger, whose forge glowed with heat. For the duration that those two remained in conference, the ring of the hammer against the anvil did not thud dully in Thea's ears.

She tried to keep her eyes and thoughts on what she and Elspeth were doing, but her gaze kept going back to him.

Hawk towered over the blacksmith. He wore breeks and a sleeveless jerkin, and Thea could see the glint of fair hair glistening on his forearms from the ample glow of the forge. Her eyes widened as she realized his arms were as brawny as the smith's.

The warmth of a blush stole up her cheeks. She remembered exactly how those strong arms felt when he held her naked against him.

Thea scowled at the vat of tallow.

"At home we only used beeswax," Elspeth said. "It can be softened and cut, rolled around the wicks. The light is more pure and brilliant."

"And the smell next to heavenly." Thea stopped to flex her shoulders. "I'm tired, and we've only started."

"You don't get much rest at night, do you?" Elspeth said without looking up from the wicks.

"Do you?" Thea asked blandly.

Elspeth shrugged. "Aye, well, I do well enough once Sir Deitert turns over and begins to snore."

A stain of color spread into Thea's cheeks that had nothing to do with the heated tallow in the caldron. Thea took another frame, and they dipped it five times, then set it aside to cool and went on to the next.

Elspeth gave the crowded yard another nervous glance. She really only felt safe when Sir Deitert was about. He had ridden off some time ago on the chestnut charger.

Jesse came from the bathhouse, having hung the day's laundered linens. She stopped at the kettle where Thea and Elspeth worked. "Mmm . . . smells nice," Jesse said.

" 'Tis bayberry," Elspeth said. "Thea crushed the leaves for oil and added it to the boil."

"Where do you get your ideas?" Jesse wondered aloud.

"We did it to home," Thea answered simply.

"Oh, home." Jesse's chest rose and fell. She looked sorrowfully at the wide-hipped Griselda. "My mother is like that, all red-faced and rosy and as gruff as a hedgehog, but lovable, too."

"Don't start," Elspeth warned her.

"You can say that," Jesse replied. "I miss my son."

"You can have another here," Elspeth said practically.

"How can you tell her that, Ellie?"

Elspeth looked to the clouds forming in the north. "My son was taken from me a year ago by his father, to be raised in the manor instead of the quarters. The same thing was to happen to Jesse's boy, and she knows that. Don't you?"

"I don't think my lord would have made me part with Jacob until he was old enough to be pledged."

Thea had never thought of that before. But it was true. Even in her own home, when a servant birthed a child born of the household, the babe wasn't the woman's to keep. She gazed at the two women, now of exactly the same class as she, and they all looked enviously to the woman serf and her daughter.

Marriage was the only protection a woman could ever hope to have. For the first time, Thea regretted how fickle she had been. Love was the province of the minstrels. Mayhap her sister Andrea had it, but she would never know of it herself.

"How far north do you think we are?" Thea asked offhandedly.

"We came on a boat. How should I be able to guess the distance?" Elspeth watched Thea scowl. Lines appeared on her brow. Lines that shouldn't be on a face as young as hers.

"Saxony is not that far. I saw maps in my father's house." Elspeth said sharply. "What if you did? Forget it, Thea."

"What if we stole a fishing boat?" Jesse suggested.

"The three of us?" Elspeth laughed aloud.

"We could stay to the coast, follow it," Thea said. It was an outlandish idea, as silly as could be. Elspeth's solemn eyes twinkled for once.

"Aye, we be candlemakers today, sailors on the morrow!" Elspeth said. "Imagine, we could just skim right along, hoisting the sail and shouldering a long oar, following the coastline, dying of thirst and puking our toenails. We should plan this well, my ladies. Go a month from now, when the first wave of morning sickness hits us."

"What is that?" Thea said.

"What happens to every woman's stomach when she discovers she's with child." Ellie did not mince her words.

"You mean a babe?" Thea said in shock.

"Yea, little one, a babe."

"But we do not have husbands," Thea argued simply.

Elspeth was too intent on the work at hand to look to Thea's face. Has she seen her innocent expression crumble, she might have softened her next words. "A husband? Ha! You have a man, do you not? He boasted before the priests how deeply he'd planted his seed within you. He'll plow you again and again until a child is formed."

"But I thought..." Thea's voice trailed off. "It is done that way?"

"Babies are a consequence of a man's pleasure."

Thea dropped her end of the wick holder. Dear Lord, how blind had she been? Even her own mother had armed her with all the information she needed to know. Did she make use of it? No! More fool she. "We must not delay our departure," Thea said meekly.

Elspeth caught the holder and put it back in Thea's hands, looked to her face, and saw the shattering knowledge awakening in her. Ellie shook her head.

"The damage is done. Running away will change naught."

"It would stop the planting."

"Oh?" Elspeth's brow quirked. The girl knew nothing. Ellie took a deep breath, sighing. "Look to the garden, Thea. Seeds are planted long before the shoots appear. Some seeds take root. Some wither. Has your flow begun?"

"Nay, but it is not time, not till the quarter-moon."

"Well, there you have it. You wait and see if it comes again. If it has stopped, the seed is well seated, and a babe will grow."

Thea reached for another rack of wicks, turning furiously to work. "How many times does it take? How much seed? It takes a lot of seed to plant a garden."

"I do not know."

"Nor do I," Jesse added. Her face reddened darkly as she admitted, "My liege took me many times before my son was conceived. The other maids thought I was lucky because my menses came regularly. Then, when he had lost interest in bedding me, they stopped, and the babe still grew."

"He lost interest in you?" This was another concept Thea could never have fathomed before now. But it was clear Roderick had lost interest in her.

"Aye. He did. I loved him true, and he no longer wanted me. He'd fancied another prettier than I. Still, he claimed my son. Did me right by that, and did not cast me from his house."

Thea frowned again, thinking to her own home. There had been no servants bearing children that her father had claimed. But her brother Royce showed great interest in women, switching affection from one to another as if he were determined to kiss every maid of a certain age in the Empire. He was never true of heart, casting off one to seek another.

Thea looked at Elspeth's pale beauty and Jesse's sweet vivacity and saw them as rivals for the first time. "We are all three taken for slaves of Roderick of Emory."

"Yea. 'Tis time you realized that." Ellie nodded.

"And he may have us, any and all? You would submit to him if he wanted you?"

"Thea, he is lord. Of course we would." Jesse blinked at her, as much to say it was a foolish question.

Thea swallowed. She had refused Merrault because he was inconstant. He had come to Landais seeking a bride, when it was known that he kept Anne of Aachen as his mistress. Was there any man faithful and true outside of legend or song? Thea wondered if her father was as faithful as she had always believed he was.

"And will if it suits him, or any other woman that crosses his path in this fair land. He is no different from any lord," Elspeth informed her.

"Then my course is set. I will leave here." Thea closed her mouth to say no more. Elspeth raised her head and stared at Thea with pity in her eyes.

"Ninny! You cannot leave. I can't. Jesse cannot. This is where we will live until the end of our time. No champion will come forward to rescue you. No Franks come to this

land. They and we are not welcome. Better that you turn
your thoughts to God and pray that the good man who has
claimed us remains strong and resolute. Else the Vikings will
come again, and we will have a cruel master who will not
care if we are beaten or abused sorely by his men."

"Sailing a boat cannot be all that difficult. It looked easy
enough to me," Jesse said cautiously, not liking to see her
two friends disagree.

"As easy as making candles?" Elspeth's eyes flashed at
Jesse in a silent admonition to stop encouraging Thea.

"I won't stay here another night." Thea thrust out her
chin and did not look up at Elspeth's scolding face.

"What do you know of anything?" Elspeth argued.
"What have you learned? Nothing save the sweetness of the
master's bed. You've plied well enough to get him to take
the collar from your neck. He teaches you, but you are too
dense to see what is right before your face. He is the duke of
Emory. Look around you! They burned his keep to the
ground, but still he holds what is his. The man will not let
you go. Do you run away, he will loose his hounds and hunt
you to the ends of the earth."

Elspeth wiped the ends of the rack and handed it back to
Thea. "Today, we are candlemakers. What are we tomorrow?"

Thea glared at the pot of tallow in simmering silence,
while all of Ellie's words sank in like a stone.

"Tomorrow we are scullery maids, culling potatoes and
layering them in straw in the cold cellars."

"Grand." Elspeth smiled.

Thea said nothing more.

"Here, let me take over," Jesse told her. "Go inside for
a bit, Thea. Get a drink of water and a bite of bread. The
fires are too hot on you."

"I'll go wash walls." Thea relinquished the chore gratefully. After she had gone, Elspeth looked harshly at Jesse
and said, "Do not encourage her with her wild ideas of escape."

"She is most unhappy here. She's not like us, Ellie. She was raised to a manor. I don't think she's ever worked so hard in her life."

"She works no harder than you or I."

"But what if we could escape?"

"You could not, and you know it. You may as well spit into the wind."

"If I went with her, I am certain she would see that I was rewarded handsomely by her family. She is a lady. You know that as well as I, Elspeth."

"Then let her kind defend her. It is not our concern."

The hall was empty. Thea looked about for what to do, and settled on the stairs, scrubbing the risers one at a time. Her thoughts were dark. She could hardly process all this information she had gained. Frequently she sat back on her heels, counting on her fingers, trying to apply the logic she had learned from her tutors to her situation.

Surely it took many, many beddings to make a child. She thought of the horses her mother bred, and the times a stallion would be put to a single mare. It was so simple and obvious. How had she missed the connection?

As she sat on the clean stairs, her hands became idle and still in her lap. She thought of the last night she had spent with Lord Roderick in bed. Heat seeped into her cheeks as she remembered just how free she had allowed him to be with her body. Had she no pride left? Where had that goodly trait gone? She was a Bellamy. Every time she gave him such freedom with her person, she allowed him to plant his seed deep within her.

She had thought no further than the sweet moment between them, needing his succor. Again her hand rose to her throat, to skin that was relieved of the weighty collar.

Even without the collar, she recognized that she belonged to the Hawk of Emory. Did he but stride into his hall this moment and snap his fingers, she must obey him.

She brought her focus to the hall that surrounded her. Day by day, more of it regained its luster. The inlaid floor was now a thing of beauty in itself, for the contrasting squares of black and white marble shone with the polish that she had concocted and helped to buff.

Her efforts had accomplished that. There was so much more waiting to be done. She saw the hall not as it was now, or as it had been when she first looked upon the squalor. She saw it restored to glory.

A great house rising from the ashes. And she saw herself as the center of this house, yea, as queenly as her mother ruling Landais.

But she was not the lady of the keep.

That honor would go only to Roderick of Emory's wife.

She made the sign of the cross and folded her hands. Bending her head in prayer, she recited a mea culpa and an act of contrition for her sins of lust and pride. Her soul was in mortal danger.

The duke of Emory would never marry a slave. Nor would he elevate such a lowly soul to a position of honor at his side. Mayhap on the day they met she had been his equal, but no more.

She opened her hands and stared at her reddened, callused palms. They were no longer the hands of a noble lady. They looked as rough and red as Jesse's when she finished each day's wash.

Thea laid her hands against her belly. She could never bear the shame of birthing a Saxon bastard. She was a Bellamy. A Bellamy, by the grace of God. Yet Roderick of Emory's flock of stolen women shunned her at church because she was his leman.

For the love of God, how could she have made so dreadful a mistake? Why hadn't she given him her name outright? Because she'd feared he would hold her for ransom? At least ransom would have been an honorable fate. Again, when he brought her ashore at Blackstone wearing a damned slave's collar, her pride had blinded her.

She could have demanded sanctuary from the priest, had she only given the man her true name. She had been so furious, so insulted, she'd flatly refused to give any Saxon her father's name to revile.

What a fool she was!

She vowed to herself, the name Bellamy would never be soiled by being spoken on Saxon lips.

Yea, anger and pride had propelled her.

What good would come of telling the truth? None. The damage done her was irreparable.

Worse, the more time she spent in Emory, the more she felt sorry for these people. She could not hate Roderick's vassals or his people. It was not their fault the Vikings had attacked and destroyed, killed and taken what wealth they had.

She had tried to hold anger and outrage close to her heart, like armor against the Hawk.

But she had failed even at that.

She had spent each of the past five nights shivering in the Hawk's empty bed, longing for him. Wishing he would return. Aching for him to come back and take her in his arms and fan the embers of desire inside her to a consuming heat.

Now that he was back, she knew without a doubt that she would debase herself completely.

Did he walk inside the doorless hall this very moment, she would be at his feet if he so much as crooked his brow at her.

And what did he give of himself? He did not have a single smile to give her.

Oh, she must leave Emory.

Leave now, before winter set in.

Thea vowed to keep her own counsel from here on out. She would not look to Elspeth or Jesse for any aid. She would go...this very night...at a time when no one went looking for her or thought of her at all. During the evening meal, when every man and boy sat to the table and ate to his heart's content.

Chapter Twelve

The storm broke when Thea reached the quarry at the edge of the harbor. The wind howled and screamed around the cliffs of black stone. Victory's hooves rang against the granite with every step. The lightning and thunder frightened Thea the most. She could withstand the rain, even a pouring deluge, but Thea had one great fear that had remained with her since childhood—lightning.

It was raining badly when she dropped from her saddle and took Victory's reins in hand, leading him down the rocky path into the heart of the quarry. In the flashes of light, she spied a shack near the pier.

On the one hand, she feared going down to the level of the sea, but on the other, she feared being struck by lightning while riding across the cliff.

She also feared stopping this early in her journey. She was not out of sight of Blackstone village yet, or the watch tower on March Island, though at night and with a storm sweeping inland, she doubted anyone spied her or her remarkable horse.

Victory was glad enough to reach the shelter of the rude lean-to. He shook like a dog, releasing water from his coat, and nudged Thea's belly, asking for affection. She rubbed his forelock and scratched his nose.

"We'll be all right, Victory. We've a long journey, but we're strong and young."

Thea tied his reins securely to a sturdy post supporting the roof and searched about in the dark for useful things. There were rags, and several rough crates that contained quarry tools.

She found flint and dry kindling. Nothing to eat, but she consoled herself with what she had brought with her. The flint and striking iron would be helpful on her journey. The rags she used to rub Victory down.

He had been well fed when stabled that afternoon, and she had likewise eaten a good supper before striking out on this journey.

Thea had decided to wend her way homeward by staying to the coastline. When she took Sir Michael his supper tray, he had confirmed what Thea had heard about the land south of Emory. He had said his home was seventy leagues south, through the wilderness.

On her one Sunday spent at the village, Thea had deliberately eavesdropped on several Saxon hunters talking about getting lost in the great forest. Men had died when they were caught trying to cross the mountains, if sudden winter storms swept in from the north. Her own studies with her tutors had taught Thea that many rivers made passage southward between Saxony and Lorraine very difficult unless one went as far as the abbey at Ulm and crossed the bridge there. The Weser, the Ulm and the Moselle rivers were much deeper and more difficult to cross than the pleasant Somme that she was accustomed to at home.

She shrugged aside any concern for the natural barriers she might face later in the journey. She had problems to concentrate upon right now. She removed her saddle and set it on a crate, drying the leather thoroughly. Henry had kept it in good repair.

The silver bells adorning her saddle tinkled merrily. They were as good as coin. She could use the bells to barter for food and shelter if she came to towns and settlements. She might even be able to barter the saddle for passage on a ship.

That was her hope for getting home the quickest, before winter truly set in.

Rain pounded on the roof of the lean-to. Thea curled up in the driest spot, wrapping her arms around her knees, and watched the waves crash over the short pier. Each bolt of lightning made her jump, but she was not a child. She wouldn't let the storm unnerve her.

She had vague memories of the most terrifying night of her young life. She thought now that she must have been little more than a baby. She did not remember exactly being struck by lightning, though the story had been retold to her many times. What she remembered was the lights shooting across the sky, and running to her mama, crying and clawing at Lady Lilla's skirt until she reached the safety of her mother's arms, burying her face in her mother's neck.

They had both been struck. Thea remembered the light, white and blinding, and the overwhelming sound that seemed to come from inside her head. Then, afterward, there had seemed to be constant ringing inside her head, like distant church bells. It had taken weeks to finally abate.

Just thinking about that episode from her childhood made her hear that ringing now. She shook her head, but the sound inside it continued dully. She shook her head again and pressed her hands against her ears.

It was only the storm.

Victory stamped restively and flicked his tail. Thea slid off her dry perch. Better that she think about keeping him calm through the storm.

She ran her hand down his flank, and he turned his head, whickering deeply. She heard that clearly. Heard him snort and blow and stamp his forefeet. She heard the *clang, clang, clang,* of a bell.

"What?" Thea cocked her head. She heard the steady clatter of the rain on the ramshackle roof, the splash of it striking the ground. *Clang, clang, clang.* "What is that?" she said aloud.

It wasn't the undertone ringing inside her head that came and went at random. She cupped a hand to her ear and listened to the baffling sound on the wind, the *clang, clang, clang.*

A church bell? Puzzled and intrigued, Thea moved to the edge of the shed and peered into the darkness.

The storm was not so bad now. Rain came steady, in wind-driven sheets, slanting across rocks and cut stone. She heard the wood around her creak.

A sheet of lightning rolled across the heavy sky, brightening the sea from one side of the harbor to the other. The island watchtower stood out for just a second in the wash of light. But there was something else out there. Thea felt her heart lurch. A boat. No, a ship.

She became very still, forcing all her attention on the island where Roderick had built a narrow tower twice the height of his keep, waiting for the next ephemeral rush of light. Her heart beat more rapidly. A bolt of lightning ran out of the sky and struck land clear across the mouth of the harbor. A jagged, blinding arch of light, and in it, for less than a heartbeat, a huge ship was outlined against the black night.

It was a ship!

The image seemed to fix permanently in Thea's eyes. She had seen ships like that before…in Le Havre…with dragon prows both fore and aft. A Viking ship!

"Dear God, no! It cannot be a Viking ship!" Shielding her eyes, Thea ran through the heavy rain to the end of the rough pier. She could see the tower clearly, for the island was not very far across the water. The ship was there, on the opposite side of the island.

Another flash of lightning gave her a glimpse of the sail. It was shortened. It was stripped. A whole row of oars cut downward into the water, moving in precision.

Another clip of lightning revealed it again. The oars were up, stroking in unison at the water.

Thea nearly swallowed her tongue. She looked to the village, where warm lights glowed in the small windows of each rebuilt house. Beyond stood the stark outline of Blackstone Keep. Wide open and vulnerable. She had snuck out the portcullis, stealing her own horse. The gates were wide open!

"Oh, my God. What have I done?"

She had drugged every soul in Blackstone Keep.

Panicking, Thea ran back to the shed and snatched up her saddle, heaving it onto Victory's back. Her hands shook so badly she could hardly thread the cinch, much less tighten it secure.

Vikings! Roderick would be killed. Dear God! She closed her eyes and pressed her forehead against Victory's side. What should she do? She must warn them. Wake them.

Untying the reins, Thea clambered onto Victory's back. She turned him immediately to the steep path she'd carefully led him down on foot. Digging her heels into his sides, Thea urged him up the face of the cliff.

Roderick of Emory's keep was silent as a catacomb. Only two dogs ran out to bark at Victory's hooves as Thea pulled the horse to a skidding stop outside the gaping doors of the great hall.

"Oh, God!" she exclaimed as she dropped from Victory's back. She tied him to a hitching post in the pouring rain. For a moment she stood on the bottom step, staring at those huge, massive doors that had just been moved into place late that afternoon.

They could not be shut and barred. The carpenters had to make more adjustments and trim them.

Thea struck her wet hair out of her eyes and ran up the steps. The sight that greeted her inside the hall was worse than she had imagined.

Men and boys sprawled wherever they had sat when enforced sleep came upon them. A few had made an effort to go up to their beds. They hadn't made it past the first few steps toward the gallery.

Another loud clap of thunder made Thea turn back to the great doors. There was nothing Thea could pull shut against the rain. The storm slanted indoors, driving her backward, making puddles under her feet, soaking and staining the newly washed and polished paneling affixed to the walls.

Drenched to her skin, Thea shivered from more than just the wet and cold. What if she could not wake them? How could she possibly lower the portcullis all by herself? She didn't know how to work the mechanisms. She didn't have the strength. She clutched her hands to her arms, shivering, admitting she did not like storms. Lightning and thunder frightened her. She must find Roderick. He would know what to do.

A cold claw sunk into the flesh of her arm. "Where did you go?"

Thea startled, screaming. She whirled about to find only Armina, bent as if an ague touched her old bones. Her hand clamped on to Thea's bare arm. Thea consciously swallowed down the lurch of her heart to her throat.

"Where did you go?" Armina's lip curled like that of a snarling dog. She pointed to the trestles. "Look you yon. See, my lord's men snore in their cups whilst you tippy-toe about in and out the door. Ha! So say I."

"Where is Lord Roderick?" Thea countered. "Wake them. Get a bucket of water, if necessary, and throw it in Sir Deitert's face. Rouse him now, Armina. I must find Roderick. There are Vikings at the gate!"

"Vikings!" Armina screeched. "Liar! 'Tis enow to roach me hair. 'Tis poison, witch. You poisoned every man within the hall."

"Nay, they are drunk, Armina. Have you lost your wits?"

"Ha!" She shuffled to the nearest trestle, where Sir Deitert sprawled across the board. A tankard tipped in his hand. Ale spilled onto the floor. At his feet, three pages slept on the rushes, oblivious of the liquid trickling slowly onto them. "Nay, 'tis poison. Mayhaps you can explain this bit of fruit."

She withdrew a severed root of henbane from the pocket of her wrinkled apron. Panic overwhelmed Thea. Vikings approached their shores, and the only other person awake at Blackstone wanted to argue.

"I tell you, there are Vikings in the harbor. I saw two ships near the island. The warning bell was ringing. I heard it clear at the quarry."

Armina's eyes narrowed to slits in her wrinkled face. Thea gulped as the crone held up the root.

"Oh, you damned fool. Throw that rutabaga away. There is no time to argue."

"*Rutabaga!* Ha!" Armina dropped her hand to Deitert's shoulder, shaking him rudely. "Poison it be. Wake, old man. Wake before the reaper robs ye of yer life."

Armina quickly realized no power on earth was going to wake Sir Deitert this night. Armina pocketed the root and cast Thea a telling look. "Think you can escape the Hawk's vengeance? 'Twill be a joy watching you wither on yon whipping post. Yea, and a long-overdue beating it is, ye witch. We'll see then, yea, we'll see."

"Fine. Don't help." Thea turned to the steps, running.

"I keep the root, witch. Proof for the priest. Proof for the Hawk. 'Twill break your fast on the morrow." Armina shouted as Thea ran from her. "Verily, ye be witch! Past time the lord knew it!"

A fist of cold dread tightened around Thea's heart. She reached the gallery.

"You'll eat poison on the morrow, witch!" Armina's scream echoed in the silent hall.

"Hag," Thea whispered under her breath. At Roderick's open door, she stopped, shaking from head to toe. She pressed her forehead to the stone wall. She could almost feel the Hawk of Emory wielding a strap against her. Her hand came to her face to wipe away a sheen of sweat.

Squaring her shoulders, she entered the darkened room. He sprawled across his black bearskin, one arm thrown across his eyes.

Panic tightened Thea's chest. Her knees buckled out from underneath her. She sank to the floor beside the cold hearth, her eyes fastened to his long form. "What do I do? How do I wake him?" She whispered in despair.

Thea chewed upon her lower lip, worrying her fingers together. "Damn that old woman!"

Thwarted, she saw her only hope of ever returning home turn to ashes. Outside, a bolt of lightning rent the sky. A hard, screaming wind tore at the new shutters, slamming them inward against the wall. Thunder exploded, so loud it could have awoken the dead.

Thea jumped up and ran to the window, taking hold of the heavy shutter and pushing it against the driving wind that blew it inward. Elsewhere in the keep, a heavy door banged. Roderick sat up abruptly, scraping his sword out of its sheath in a reflex action.

"Who is there?"

He was awake!

"It's I, Thea!" She managed to hold one shutter in place against the wind, but could not reach far enough across the window to catch the other. She wasn't tall enough.

Roderick stumbled toward her, his sword point scraping on the floor. His long arm shot past hers and brought the opposite shutter secure.

The cold rain soaked his face in that moment he leaned across the sash.

"Milord—" Thea swallowed. Her nerves were frazzled to the nub. "Milord, there are Vikings in the harbor."

"What?" Roderick's blue eyes blinked twice. He stared at her blankly, as though incapable of holding a single coherent thought.

"Vikings." Thea gulped. "Two ships. I saw them. In the harbor. They've come as far as the island. The bell. The warning bell. It rings. We can't hear it here because of the storm.''

Roderick hands came to her shoulders. He shook her. "What did you say?"

"Vikings. Two ships. In the harbor. Dragon prows. I saw them. They have come back, milord."

"Sweet Jesu!"

His fingers bit into Thea's flesh. "You're wet to the bone. How? Why? What were you doing out in the rain?"

"Milord." Thea clutched at his forearms, holding him for all she was worth. "Milord, you are going to kill me for this, but I must tell you the truth. Your men are all asleep. I made a sleeping potion and fed it to one and all in the pasty pies— so that I could run away. I saw the ships when I got to the quarry. Vikings come, milord. Vikings. We must bring the villagers to the keep and shut the gates."

"Roderick, is there trouble?" Sir Michael staggered through the darkened doorway. "Do you need me?"

"Yea, Michael, you're damned right I do." Thea winced as Roderick's fingers dug harshly into her flesh, setting her aside. "You will remain here."

Roderick released her and turned to his war chest, yanking the top open. "Get sword and armor, Michael, if you are able. It may be only you and I to defend all that is left of Blackstone. God help us all."

"Milord!" Thea ran to him as he struggled to fasten his hauberk alone. She quickly did up the buckles down his back and caught the back of his aventail, pulling it smoothly down the back of his head, onto his shoulders. "Let me help. Mayhap I can wake the others. Armina is awake, too."

As he buckled his leather baldric at his hips, Roderick faced her. His eyes cut Thea to the quick with the coldest stare she'd ever felt.

"You have caused all the damage Emory can bear. Remain here. Do not cross my path again this night. Heaven help you if Vikings breach this door. You may have found your match in treachery at last."

He took sword and shield in hand and strode from the chamber, slamming the heavy door shut, shouting for Michael. Both sounds reverberated in the silent room, but Thea still heard an ominous click as the Saxon's lock fell into place.

Thea could hardly draw a breath into her tightly constricted chest. She paced the cold room, rubbing her hands into the sore flesh of her upper arms. A shiver crossed her back. Another crack of thunder shattered the peace.

She was doomed.

Thea went to the door and laid her ear upon it, listening for sounds that would assure her someone else had been roused. Thank God, Sir Michael had not come down to sup in the hall. Though what good the weak knight would be against a horde of Vikings, Thea couldn't imagine.

She stayed listening at the door until she heard footfalls in the gallery. And voices, the excited chatter of boys, and the deeper tones of squires roused from her deadly slumber. Enough went up and down, bringing clanging arms, shouting from floor to floor. Thea managed to pull in a shaky draft of air. At least they all would not die by having their throats slit while they slept.

She knelt to the hearth then, taking the iron poker in her hand, and stirred the cold embers. The chamber was as cold as ice. Her teeth chattered. She uncovered a clutch of red embers and laid scraps of sawdust and minute kindling on them. A small, bright flame burst forth. To that single flame, Thea carefully fed more fuel until it was a strong enough fire to add splits of slow-burning hardwood.

It would be a while before the fire warmed the chamber. Thea sat back on the rushes and unlaced her sandals, then removed her stockings. They were filthy and clumped with mud. She removed her tunic and spread it across Roderick's high-backed chair, near the fire. The samite would dry. It seemed on fire as the gold threads caught the light in the hearth.

Naked and shivering, Thea went to the washstand and filled the ewer. She washed carefully, from head to toe, then took the wool blanket from the trunk at the foot of the bed and sat before the fire to warm her feet and hands.

It was going to be a long time till dawn . . . if she lived to see it.

Herewald the Walker wasn't delighted to be first to test Roderick of Emory's defenses. It was bad enough that the storm had driven him to seek shelter in Blackstone harbor, but to be run aground by the wind on the Hawk of Emory's pileworks, well, that stung Herewald's vanity as a Viking Dane.

"Damn me, Hawk, you could have sent word to me what you were about," the huge Dane said, then added a few fresh curses to warm the chilled morning air. "How do you expect me to get my ship off those rocks?"

"In truth?" Roderick grinned. "I don't. It's my plan to plunder any ship that tries the circuit around the island. You saw the buoy markers, didn't you?"

"By Odin's thumb, yes, I saw them. But we were too busy reefing the sail. How was I to know I'd find so foul a welcome in Blackstone Bay?"

"My lord—" Roderick clapped the Dane on his back and gave him a helping hand onto shore from the rescue boat, "—considering what the *Nordmanni* did to Blackstone this spring, Odin must have been with you all through the night. Just beyond the rocks that your ship is grounded on are rows of pikes that would have ripped your hull to shreds. You had a narrow escape. Welcome to Blackstone."

"Humph!" Herewald grunted. Now that his feet were planted on firm ground again, he put his huge fists to the belt circling his waist and stood straight and tall, surveying Blackstone.

"My compliments, Hawk. You've done a fine job rebuilding the village. I see every hut is rethatched. And what is that circling your keep?"

"A barbican, my friend. Built on the order of the Roman garrison, but bigger," Roderick declared proudly.

"You do say. Impressive, Emory. Very impressive. It looks to me as if you've closed up tight as clam." Herewald rubbed his ruddy hands together. "You'll have to give me a tour of all your defenses. I might borrow some of your ideas. I like it. I like the looks of that wall very much."

"Thought you would." Roderick turned to Sir Deitert and Sir Michael. "Sir Michael, would you escort Herewald's men to the hall? See they are made welcome and fed. Deitert, I'll leave you to organize bringing our good friend's trunks."

"You'll like what I've got in those trunks, Roderick. Least your womenfolk will. Bring them along quickly, Deitert. I've brought you a thing or two special, as well."

"I'll see to it immediately," Deitert promised gravely.

"Well, now, Roderick, I want a closer look at that gray horse." Herewald turned back to Roderick and swung a favorable arm across the young lord's back. "What a splendid beast. It looked big enough to support a man my size."

Roderick ruefully studied Herewald the Walker, who had earned that title when he was twelve years old and so big no horse could support him. "Victory's all of twenty hands high, my lord. But I won't part with him."

"Eh? We'll see about that. Have I told you how we thought it was a spirit, flying up the cliff face? My men called it a Valkyrie's mount. Someone guessed it was a woman riding him. I'll have to meet that sprite, too. Come on then, give me a tour, and start with that abbey of yours. They make the finest wine I've ever tasted."

As the two men started up the path from the harbor, the Saxon men who remained in the village let out a collective sigh of relief. Herewald was a good neighbor, for a warlord Dane. Sir Deitert sent a man up to the keep to have the gates opened and advise the women that they could return to their houses safely now. Otto should escort them down and pass on word to Lord Emory's kitchen that a decent meal needed to be laid to the table forthwith. There were hungry men coming.

Friar Laurence was overjoyed to see his uncle Herewald again, and gladly showed the Dane chieftain through his abbey. Herewald was appreciative of the renovations completed during the summer. He stood admiring the new trusses and beams on the peaked roof of the abbey.

"Well, boy, it looks like you have some industry to you after all. Never were good for nothing except falling to yer knees in ecstasy, whatever that is. What say you, Roderick, shall we have some of my nephew's wine?" The huge Dane clapped Friar Laurence on his back so resoundingly he almost knocked the monk to his knees.

The priest, the duke of Emory and the Dane sat to the abbey's refectory table, visiting for most of the morning. It was such an agreeable morning that Roderick managed to forget the terror of the night before.

At least it remained in the back of his mind for the majority of Herewald's visit. He gave the Dane a tour of the village, walked him up to the keep and showed off the workings of his drawbridge and portcullis gate. They spent the afternoon on Roderick's ship, towing Herewald's undamaged but grounded longship clear of the rocks and harboring it in Blackstone cove, next to the village, for the night.

Herewald's crew planned to make themselves free at Kimball's tavern for the evening and spend the night on board their ship. Herewald and his best man, Osgood, were invited to sup at the keep.

It was late evening when they arrived at the keep. Roderick ushered the two Danes to his stable first and showed off the Percheron stallion.

Old Henry had seen to the stallion's few injuries from the reckless and dangerous ride attempted during the night. *Up and down the damn cliff, for God's sake,* Roderick thought to himself. It remained unsettled, the score between him and one stubborn, willful Frankish maid.

Over supper, Herewald praised how well Blackstone had recovered from near annihilation. Herewald was renowned for having a sharp eye for beautiful women. As the evening dwindled to a close, the Dane drove a hard bargain, demanding the first colt sired by Roderick's new stallion as repayment for his years of aid and protection and continued goodwill.

Roderick could hardly deny the Dane that. With luck, Victory would sire as many colts and fillies as they had mares to put him to.

Having expected some sort of payment demand when he realized who had come visiting, Roderick wasn't overly surprised by the agreement they came to. What knocked the pins right out from under him was Herewald's on-the-spot offer of two hundred gold marks for Roderick's beautiful black-haired Frankish slave.

Chapter Thirteen

Thea had no idea what time of day it actually was when she hearkened to someone keying the lock to Roderick's chamber door. She was so hungry she felt faint. What little water had remained in the pitcher, she'd consumed hours and hours ago.

The door opened as she stood up, smoothing the green samite down her sides. She wanted to look as presentable as possible for Roderick, praying that for once her looks would stave off the beating she knew was coming.

Sir Deitert swung open the door and stood aside for Jesse to carry in a tray. He nodded wordlessly to the younger girl and shut the door, keying the lock from without.

"Oh, Thea . . ." Jesse blinked her wide astonishing eyes. Each freckle on her face stood out against the paleness of her skin. She set the tray on Roderick's trunk and hurriedly embraced Thea as if she were her dearest long-lost friend. "'Tis such news I have. Such a night we've had. We were terrified to wake up and find barbarians in the harbor. Lord Roderick hid every one of us in the cellars. We've only just come out, and to such a commotion. We need you quick, in the kitchens. You must hurry. I've brought bread and cheese, for that was all I could make up quick. Come, I'll help you change."

"Change? Change to what?" Thea asked dumbly. Half

of Jesse's words had gotten lost in the crushing bear hug she'd bestowed on Thea.

"To these clothes," Jesse said, as if that explained everything. "Hurry."

Thea reached for the bread, wolfing it down to quiet her roiling stomach. Jesse shook out some sort of sleeved undertunic. Chewing on the morsel of rye bread in her mouth, Thea popped a cube of cheese between her lips and licked her fingers before reaching out to touch the fine cloth Jesse displayed.

"Where did you get that?"

"I don't know." Jesse motioned to her own new clothes with a nod of her head. "Sir Deitert brought them up from the abbey and bade us all make repairs to our appearance. There's a guest of importance whose ship ran aground last eve. It wasn't Vikings."

"It wasn't Vikings?" Thea choked on the words.

"Nay, 'tis friends. A neighboring lord. A Dane, they say. You know I cannot follow all the Saxons say. Come, quickly."

The cheese lodged in Thea's throat. She could not swallow it up or down. She reached for the dry cup on Roderick's dresser. *It wasn't Vikings!* She had aborted her one chance at escape, and the intruder wasn't a Viking!

The lump of cheese slithered painfully down her throat and lodged like a stone in her empty stomach. Numbly Thea stared at the closed shutters, wishing she'd risked just one look outside during the long day. She should have followed that one look by jumping. Jesse tugged on Thea's tunic, pulling it off over her head. Then the new, rich silk undergown slithered down over Thea's body.

"Oh, it's perfect for you." Jesse's capable hands tightened the laces at the small of Thea's back. She lifted an overgown that was two pieces of the finest green wool Thea had ever touched. It had same-cloth love knots sewn at intervals across the shoulders and down the joined sleeves, which allowed glimpses of the long-sleeved undergown to show. Jesse quickly did up the laces on each side, as she had with the undergown.

"The color matches your eyes. Come, Thea, put on the slippers. See if they fit. I'll let Sir Deitert know you're ready."

"Ready to be beheaded?" Thea asked, taking soft kidskin slippers from the tray and trying them on her feet. She sat on the edge of the bed to tie those laces and marveled at the smoothness of fine leather against her feet again.

Sir Deitert swung open the door and bowed gravely to Thea. "Come, I will escort you to the hall." He offered his arm.

This is very strange, Thea thought. Jesse snatched up the tray and followed them out and down the steps.

A horde of strange, barbaric-looking men filled the great hall. Men whose blond hair was as long as Lord Roderick's and whose beards put his to shame. They were all giants and looked fierce and hungry and very dangerous. To Thea's wary eye, they looked just like Vikings. If they were Danes, then wasn't this keep in a state of siege?

Or had Roderick surrendered?

Thea's grip tightened on Sir Deitert's arm as he walked her slowly across the hall to the side door that opened onto the kitchen yard. Outdoors, Thea took a relieved breath and turned her head to Sir Deitert.

"My lord, are we under attack? Who are those men?"

Deitert's strong jaw tightened visibly. "Woman, I pray you, hold your tongue with me. Were it my decision as to what to do with you this day, you'd be feeling the miseries of the damned. You are to see that the evening meal is the best repast ever placed before Lord Roderick and his guests. That is the only reason I have taken you from your chamber. The other women say they are not up to the task of serving a king."

"A king?" Thea followed each and every word Sir Deitert said, because she dared not take her eyes off his mouth.

"Yea, the king of the Danes, Herewald the Walker, is come to Blackstone, madame." Sir Deitert stopped at the kitchen door. "Hear me well, Thea of Blackstone. A man of mine is set to follow you every step you take this day. Do you put one foot in the direction of the stable or the portcullis gate, I will flay you with a strap, whether there be guests in this hall or no. Do you understand?"

Thea stared into his cold, wintry eyes. "Yes, my lord, I understand." She caught her skirts and gave him the obeisance he deserved on the spot.

"When the meal is ready, you, yourself will come to the hall and serve it," Sir Deitert curtly ordered, and swiveled on his heel, stalking back to the hall.

Elspeth exhaled a sigh of relief as soon as she saw Thea enter. "What have you started?" Thea asked.

"A venison haunch, and potatoes are baking in the lower ovens. We've bread rising." Ellie raised her fingers to her moist brow, looking flushed and rattled. "What else, Jesse?"

"Armina's snapping beans, and I've culled the fresh apples. There's cheese from the smoker."

"Excellent." Thea pushed up her sleeves. "Tommy, send to Otto for six of his best redfish. Are we to feed all the men I saw in the hall?"

"More, I think." Elspeth didn't have a number. "There were more that came from the harbor to break their fast. They've gone out to bring the king's ship from the rocks."

"Well, what we're going to need are some sauces to make what we have seem fit for a king, then. Armina, what is your favorite cheese?"

"One that ain't been poisoned by you, witch."

"That means we'll use the pot cheese. Arnulf, run to the larder and bring two of the bigger crocks. You know which ones."

"Yea, lady." The second boy took off running.

Elspeth took over turning the spit. She looked at Thea, asking in French, "How far did you get?"

"Not very," Thea answered, setting her mouth firmly. She was not going to fall apart. Not now. No matter what. "The stone quarry. I saw the ship and came back to warn Roderick."

"Fool," Elspeth said condemningly.

It rained again that night. A cold, chilling rain that began steadily at sundown and promised to continue through the night. The king looked like no king Thea had ever seen or imagined. He was dressed in leathers and wools, worn and serviceable. He was as big as Roderick in height, paler in coloring, and his eyes were so dark a blue they looked violet. A fan of pale lashes surrounded them. Thea judged him to be more Sir Deitert's age as she came to the table with a loaded tray and bent in a curtsy, then stood silently, offering him the first choice, as protocol demanded that she do.

Herewald of the Danes stared at her and turned to Roderick, leaving Thea holding the tray in suspense. They spoke in a language she could not follow at all. Finally he returned his attention to the tray of braised redfish Thea offered and took for himself the most succulent slice. Thea curtsied and moved on to Roderick. His eyes looked black as apple seeds as he wordlessly waved her offering away. It galled Thea to drop him a curtsy as deep as the king's, but she had to give him that respect before moving on to serve the others.

The meal was agony for her. Once she came into the hall, Sir Deitert's watchdog did not allow her to leave again. Instead, the other servants ran back and forth in the pouring rain, bringing the covered trays, which Thea got to serve around the boards. It was not a pleasant experience.

The Saxons who had been tricked by her potion the night before had as sullen glares for her as she had gotten from Sir Deitert that afternoon. The Danes had grins and quips that she couldn't understand. Finally the last course was served and the ale pitchers refilled and set on the tables where the pages could easily serve for the balance of the banquet. Sir Deitert rose from the table, bowed to both king and lord and came across the hall to escort Thea back upstairs.

Holding her long skirt with one hand, Thea looked straight ahead as she mounted the steps. "I trust you found the meal satisfactory, Sir Deitert?"

This time she did not look at him to gauge his answer. One did not need to lip-read a grunt.

The seneschal brought a key from the ring on his belt and unlocked the lord's door, opened it and held it for Thea to enter. Thea swept past him with her chin up, silently willing him the blackest void in creation.

He did not shut the door immediately, forcing Thea to turn round and look at him.

"You asked about the meal, Slave of Emory. I feel compelled to tell you that it was more than satisfactory to Herewald the Walker. He has offered Lord Roderick a considerable purse of gold coin for your collar. My understanding of Danish is that the offer was accepted. Sleep well, woman."

The door closed on those harsh words and locked irrevocably. Stunned, Thea couldn't move.

"Sold!" Thea turned on the fireplace, glaring at the miserable bed of coals that no one in this stupid keep ever thought of replenishing but her.

"Sold! Why, that cad! That heartless bounder! That son of a Saxon whore! How dare he! He cannot sell me! Damn him, he gave me my freedom! And you, you bastard—" She raised her fist at the place where Sir Deitert had stood and delivered such cutting, cruel words. "You know he did!"

There was no one to reply to her words, to refute or challenge them. The door was shut, the shutters were closed, and the cheery fire she'd tended to ward off the day's chill and damp had died to the point that the chamber was cast in Stygian darkness.

Feeling more alone and miserable than she'd ever felt in her life, Thea saw another of her proud resolutions fall by the wayside. She sat in Roderick of Emory's high-backed chair, covered her face with her hands and cried. The tears were accompanied by floods of remorse and recriminations.

She had come back because she couldn't bear the thought of something happening to Roderick. She loved him. She hadn't wanted him harmed in any way. She'd come back to save him.

So, too, she realized she had left because she couldn't bear to remain here, loving him without feeling any sense of her deep feelings being returned by him.

He'd sold her. Thea raised her head and wiped her face with the backs of her hands. She searched inside her for her pride, needing the thin armor it provided to continue living. She must survive. She must never let him know how deeply he had hurt her.

Finally, she stood up, her chin as firm as her lips, all the tears shed that could be allowed to fall.

She knelt on the cold marble stones lining the hearth and built another fire, feeding it with care, watching the sparks crackle and sputter, the flames dance on the new logs. The heat reached out to warm her cheeks. The glow of firelight stretched to the dark corners of the room.

"I'm tired," she said, admitting that much. Dusting off her hands, she stood and carefully removed the new gown, folding it so that few creases would mar it the next time she had opportunity to wear it. She loved the feel of the undergown, its softness and the way it hugged her body like a silken caress. Her mother had gowns like this, but she had said her daughters were too innocent for such revealing clothes.

That Thea also removed and carefully put away, laying it inside the trunk, next to Roderick's tunics. She took out his robe, brushed it and laid it over the arm of his chair, where he liked to sit and remove his boots and leggings. Then she completed her nightly ablutions, said her prayers and went to bed, going back on another vow and covering her body with his warm, heavy fur.

She closed her eyes and told herself very firmly that she had spent the whole night before worrying herself sick. She would not waste another night with such frantic behavior.

Sleep was hard to come by, but she disciplined her mind by reciting the same prayer over and over again. She was sound asleep when Roderick came to bed.

The chamber was warm as toast. Roderick folded himself into his chair, dropping both arms on the armrests. He felt the velvet of his robe under his left hand. Glancing at it made him aware that Thea had laid it out specifically for him, had placed it here where he could see it and clothe himself after he'd undressed and sat awhile before the fire, as he liked to do each night.

He did not allow himself to look where she slept. He refused to let her beauty soften his resolve. Until Herewald departed on the morrow, Roderick must keep his wits about him. Maintaining the balance of power between himself and the powerful Dane was a tenuous thing. This night, Thea had put a serious dent in Roderick's armor.

Herewald was serious. He wanted Thea. His first offer had been doubled, then later tripled. Herewald didn't just want an unusual, pretty woman to add to his collection of wives and slaves; he craved the exotic, in the manner that older men often craved young and beautiful maidens.

As powerful as Herewald was, Roderick knew the man's prowess had dwindled down the years. He frequently exercised his right as lord and master to take any virgin bride before the groom.

Herewald would not have Thea.

But as Roderick stared into the flames, he could not convince himself that he would ever have Thea, either. Because what he truly wanted from her was not just her body. He wanted her love. All of it, without reservation. Complete and total. Loyalty, honor, all the things that he could not give her in return.

The state of his coffers were such that he could only keep her as his leman. That was the position she held. Thea could never be anything more.

This cold, wintry storm that had arrived so fiercely marked the change of the season. He had this winter to get his house and fief in order. He had until the first of spring to see next year's crops well planted. Then he must hie himself back to Aachen. This time seeking a well-dowered lady wife.

Yea, he could keep Thea, would keep Thea. Her skills were already too valuable to him. Even with her tempers and moods and wildness, she provided him an asset his keep could not survive without. Within Blackstone's high walls, she worked like the bravest field marshal, managing, subduing, ordering, accomplishing that which had been impossible to do without her.

Grimly, Roderick hoped the wife he selected came to him with half the skills Thea wielded.

That thought brought him back to the present. What was he to do about her latest treachery? And how was he to see that she never betrayed him again? The fire did not provide him any answer.

Roderick rose and took another log from the woodbox and laid it to the fire, nudging it by hand over the hottest coals. He sat back on his heel, brushing off his hands, watching the sparks fly as the bark on the splits ignited.

"Did you sell me?" Thea asked the back of Roderick's head. He pivoted, looking to where she sat in the middle of his massive bed. She gripped the fur to her chest, waiting for his answer with bated breath.

"Sell you? Who spoke of that to you?" The shadows hid his face, the fire backlighting his hair to a golden halo.

"Sir Deitert let me know in so many words that he is very angry with me for my deceit last eve. You have not answered my question. Have you sold me to the Dane?"

Roderick rested his forearm on his bent knee, his right hand hung relaxed and loose to the inside of that joint.

"No."

"Oh." The sound escaped very softly from Thea's mouth. With it went all the wind of the towering arguments she had instantly prepared when she realized Roderick had come.

" 'Tis not over, the haggling."

Did he actually shrug one shoulder, as if those words had no consequence? The calm that had come with his first answer faded. Thea leaned more forward, staring very hard at his mouth, needing to see the Saxon word he gave her.

"Haggling? You dicker over the price?"

Roderick studied her stricken face. The light was too poor for him to be certain of whether or not she paled or blushed, but he could see how large and fearful her eyes were. He saw the quiver in her chin.

"Not I. But Herewald is a determined man." Roderick cast up his relaxed palm in a gesture that implied he was open. "He will make another offer in the morning, which I will also refuse, hence he will seek you directly. Seduce you with promises of jewels, more gowns and soft furs. He knows all the soft ways and words that I do not, and will offer you things I cannot begin to give you. What have I but this barren land, this keep of stone and these two hands? Herewald shows me for the pauper that I am."

Abruptly Roderick stood. Thea's eyes followed his rise, remaining fixed with the intense stare he held upon her. Now she didn't know what to ask.

His hands moved to unstrap his sword belt. Thea tucked in her chin, looking at the shiny black pelt that covered the whole bed. The fur was long and supple; she had combed and brushed it intensely during his absence. She could not look up at Roderick as she asked her last question.

"My lord, will you make me go with him?"

His scabbard clanked on the hard floor. Thea heard the whip of his jerkin laces as he yanked them free.

"Nay, Thea." Roderick threw the garment clear across the room. His hands dropped to the bed, fists now, large and powerful, pressing into the mattress. Thea raised her eyes fearfully and saw the anger in his face. "Do not go near the man... or I will kill him."

She swallowed, held by the emotion raging in his eyes. "But, what if... it is as you say... and he comes to me?"

"He is liege lord, and I owe him allegiance. I cannot stop him taking his pleasure. Walk carefully on the morrow. Encourage him, Thea, and you mark his hours upon this earth and bring Blackstone into war."

"I am innocent in this," Thea protested. "I did but serve a meal, as I was commanded by your seneschal. I have spoken not one word to this man to encourage or discourage him. I do not even know the language that you spoke with him, and was not privy to any of your council, even though I might have been in the same hall for an hour or more."

Roderick caught her chin and held it.

"Do you think it was the sight of you gowned this eve that stirred Herewald's lust? Nay, lady. He saw you last night and thought you a Valkyrie leading the way to Valhalla on your silver charger. He is a man besotted by a dream. For that I cannot forgive you."

"How could he have seen me? The storm was raging. The ship was far away."

Abruptly Roderick let go of her chin, straightening, towering over her. His hands moved to the belt that secured his breeks and unfastened it with jerking motions. He sought control over his voice. He did not want his words or hers heard outside his chamber.

"How many ships did you see?"

"I saw... two. Two ships."

"There was only one on the rocks, Herewald's longship. My man at the quarry went out with his fishing boat. So did my guard in the tower. I met Herewald within an hour after leaving you locked in this room last night. He saw you from less than two leagues away from the harbor and watched you ride like the wind.''

Lamely, Thea could only say, ''I didn't see the fishing boats.''

''No. No, but you brought panic back with you to the fief. You disrupted the village. You poisoned my men, my boys, myself.''

They had come to the crux of the problem. Again Thea averted her face, to ask, ''What will you do?''

Roderick returned to his chair to bend his knee and unlace his boot. ''I wait.''

''Wait?'' Thea brought a finger to her mouth to worry a nail. Then she jerked it away, seeing it as a certain sign of her weakness.

Roderick dropped the shoe before the fire. ''I wait. Herewald sails at high tide. Then, you and I will have a reckoning.''

He meant to keep her on pins and needles, fearing his punishment, dreading it. Thea moved off the center of the bed and lay down again, pulling the covers over her breasts. She would rather have it over with now. Let him expend his temper, whatever that was going to be.

He came to bed, and the ropes creaked beneath his weight. Thea's whole body stayed rigid for some time, but then she summoned the nerve to turn and look at him. His hands pillowed his neck, and his eyes were wide open, staring at the ceiling.

''Why do you think of yourself as a poor man, my lord? You have wealth beyond what most men can dream of. Your land, your people. This strong, impregnable keep. Resources that you can call upon, forests and plentiful game, stone and the skill to use it, loyal men and your own strength. Is the only judge of man's value that of the coins that line his coffers?''

''Thea, be quiet now. I wish to sleep.'' He scowled so fiercely at the ceiling that Thea retreated closer to the edge of the bed. Abruptly he turned his head, directing that scowl at her. "No. Sleep is impossible for either of us. Is that not right?"

"I believe that is so."

"We must talk."

"Of what, my lord?" Thea asked timorously.

"Why did you do it?"

Chapter Fourteen

"Do what, my lord?"

"Poison my entire household."

Thea's eyes went round as saucers at that accusation. "I never poisoned you. 'Twas only a sleeping potion I prepared to give me time enough to escape the house."

"Go on. I will hear it all, if you please." Roderick exhaled deeply, his patience tried but not exhausted. "Do not provoke me. I, for once, would have only the truth between you and me. Armina condemns you as a witch."

Thea's shoulders rose with the depth of her long breath. She was not completely reassured. He had not raised his hand to her, but he was close to doing so, she knew.

Roderick took Thea's chin firmly between his thumb and forefinger. "Are you a witch? How is it that you know of healing herbs and potions?"

He had asked for honesty between them. The truth was the one thing Thea could never surrender to him.

"'Tis required . . . where I come from." She could have said, *required in my lady mother's home.* Seeing to the health of all the serfs meant the lady of the manor must know healing arts. "I proved my knowledge of the healing arts upon your ship. That does not make me a witch."

Roderick harrumphed at that declaration. "'Tis good that I took you from France. They have no tolerance for the like in that land. Here in Saxony, we respect those more tuned to yon spirit world.''

''I am not a witch. I do not invoke spirits, and only say my prayers to the Christ, as taught by Mother Church.'' Thea shifted uneasily. She started suddenly and raised a finger to her nose as a sneeze assaulted her. Roderick caught the edges of the blanket and tucked it round her more firmly.

''Wonderful. Now you become ill. What next?''

''What do you care? Only because I wouldn't be able to work?''

''No. For other reasons. I want no harm to come to you, Thea.''

His words made her sigh again, for the greater harm was done her. How could she deny that there was something here between this man and herself? A bonding that defied explanation. She was vulnerable to his every whim. ''How will you punish me, my lord Roderick?''

His broad-boned hand came to her head, and strong fingers spread into her hair. ''The punishment will suit the crime.''

Instead of drawing away from him, she burrowed into his chest, seeking his warmth. Roderick gazed over the top of her head. ''Do you hate me so much?''

Thea wondered how he could ask her that and expect a truthful answer. Did she hate him? At the moment, his strong arms made her safe and secure. His occasional kiss was as sweet as red wine. His ways were rough, yet inside she couldn't believe he truly meant her harm.

''Nay, my lord, there is something about you that keeps my hate from turning bitter. Though it pricks me often.''

''Aye, it goads me as well, little Frank.''

Thea turned her cheek against his shoulder, hearing in his voice the same malice that she gave vent to when she said the word *Saxon*. That they came with bitter prejudices about one another's peoples had never been more apparent.

"It would seem to me you should have many reasons to be thankful to we Franks," Thea said stiffly. "You rule this province by the grace of a Frankish emperor."

"Nay, Thea, 'tis mine by right of birth, and will be my son's after me. No Frank or Roman or Viking will take it from me."

"What did it look like before the Vikings came?"

"I do not dwell on the past. All that was, is gone. I build now to suit myself. A fortress with four keeps this size at every corner of it, all hewn from the black stone that comes out of my mountains. I will build a castle like none ever seen, and fill it with my sons and daughters, and their sons and daughters."

Thea studied his face. She sensed his distancing, his delving into a vision that only he could see.

"I swore when I came home to the destruction that if I must, I would cut each stone with my bare hands and lay them one onto the other, until the village, the abbey—even my harbor—is so well fortified that no enemy will dare to assault its walls. And so I have done, as Herewald learned last night. I am not finished. There is much more that must be done."

"How did you learn such things?" Thea asked. "Not even Emperor Lothair has a palace so well protected as Blackstone."

"There are ways, forgotten by many, now. The Romans knew many secrets. I spent my youth here, where their skills are most wonderfully displayed. The cobblestone brick that leads to the harbor was Roman-laid, upon firm foundation. They paved and graded roadways, smoothed sands and mortars upon it and set into place each brick.

"I know their secret for mixing sand with limes and plasters that harden into stone. My cottages are not made of mud and straw, but of brickstone, and spread with hardened plaster both inside and out. They can lose a thatch roof, but the walls remain, solid, strong. I use the skills I know to rebuild."

"But you haven't the men to build a true castle."

"I have a hundred backs, all that bend and lift and stoop in one form or another. That is one reason we had to have women, to relieve the men of the necessity of toiling all day just so we might eat. Now that every cottage has a woman looking after it, when the harvesting is done, I can begin to build again. Walls of the like you cannot dream, with pinnacles and arches, notches for archers, bowmen. I will design a battlement on the roof that will keep the walls secure. And, if that is not enough, I have one thing more that will make my fortress impregnable—Greek fire."

Thea knew what he was talking about, for she had listened to her father describing the terrifying light and fire that turned the night sky into day. No one knew the secret of making it, or so her father said. The keep under siege where it had been used for defense had gone under in a consuming fire, and no one had survived the burning inferno. Hackles rose on the back of her neck, a premonition.

"I do not think I want to know what that is." He thought her nothing more than a serving wench, stolen from France. It was best she stayed exactly that.

"No, you do not, truly," Roderick agreed, saying no more about it.

"How long will it take?" Thea changed the subject.

"I have less than three years. It will be done by then." Roderick spoke with finality.

"Three years?" Thea did not understand the time limit. She thought of that amount of time, considered it and where she might be in three years' time, then felt compelled to ask, "Roderick, how long will you keep me here?"

"Till morning, of course."

"No, here in Blackstone. How long?"

"What are you asking me?"

"How long the terms of my bondage to you are. I know you are thinking of how to punish me for the crime I did against you last night. Will you set a limit to it?"

"A limit?" Roderick said wearily. He felt cheated by her lack of true contrition. She sought to manipulate him even now. She deserved a beating the moment Herewald cleared the harbor. His men, whom she had tricked, would lose respect for him if he did not deliver speedy justice for the wrong she'd committed.

"Yea, can you not bargain with me? Give me some means to hope to truly gain my freedom?"

"Who has freedom? Name me one man or woman who knows what that truly is?"

"You split a fine hair. Do you claim you don't release people from your service? Give leave to depart Blackstone?"

"Yea, I have granted many such, for trusted service, loyalty. Rewarded valor in battle, and other reasons. I would not do so for you. Your fate was sealed with me when I saw you on a riverbank. 'Tis my desire for you that made you my slave. And my desire for you that made me remove my collar and take back the words that made you slave to Emory. But so long as I live, you will remain thus, bound to me and Blackstone."

Undaunted by his words, Thea leaned heavily against him, her breast crushing against his chest, her fingers straying along the long column of his neck.

"My lord, you are the duke of Emory. You must take a wife and sire heirs for your province, a full line of sons and beautiful daughters. What will become of me when that happens? Do you think to take a lady to wife and have her tolerate me, perched upon your knee as I am this moment?"

Roderick took Thea's hand and held it from him. He saw her ploy. How she turned the tables on him! The picture she presented was incongruous. A moneyed wife of noble blood, to sire sons and daughters upon. A slave to his heart, curled upon his knee to stroke and pet and listen to her purr contentedly or scratch and howl in temper. The two did not mix, fine lady and treasured slave. He thought to squelch

Thea's impudence with a blunt answer. "I will still keep you."

"And a wife?"

"Wives can be managed, just as poorly tempered lemans can."

"Then you would set two against you."

"Do not worry about such things, Thea. It's beyond your ken, and a year before I make such a move. The future is my concern and not yours."

Thea bowed her head, and her mouth set into a deep pout. When she raised her chin, Roderick was shocked by the rude defiance that blazed anew in her eyes. "Will you hear me tell the reason I ran away from you?"

Roderick's jaw went up, his head inclined in a study of her. "Say it." It was a challenge.

"'Tis three women slaves you took to castle keep. A blonde whose wiseness shatters me. A redheaded girl of comely figure and sweeter temper than my own. They tempt the eyes of all your vassals. 'Twas pointed out to me that you may bed any of us three and do with us as you wish. Those women think you a handsome rogue within your rights, and accept their lot. But I do not."

"What do you mean?"

"That I cannot share you with any woman."

"You think to bind me?"

"Nay, my lord. I only warn you. I am of a jealous bent. Do you take Jesse or Elspeth or any other woman to your bed, I would bide my time until the seasons were with me, and then I would go home. Nothing you could do would stop me."

"So! You are telling me it is the threat of winter that stopped you on your reckless journey."

"You know that I came back to warn of danger." Thea felt no fear any longer. She would tell it all, if need be. "Know you this—I do not fear the distance of the journey nor do I fear the hazards, only the season. Had it been spring or midsummer, I would not be here, awaiting any sentence from the duke of Emory. I am strong enough inside my spirit to withstand your wrath. You have declared me publicly your sole possession and forbidden me to enjoy the company of other men."

" 'Tis by my rights I do so. You were taken in capture by my hand. 'Twill be as I will it, and no other will touch you in any form."

"So you say. You have taken sovereign rights and stripped me of my own. I have yielded. 'Tis not to that I argue. Hear my words, Roderick of Emory. I will not share you with another woman."

"Oho!" Roderick laughed bluntly and brought his hand up solid on Thea's backside with a pop. "It would take a lusty wench to keep me from straying. It has never been done before."

"Do not challenge me to such a task." Thea put her hand behind her back to remove his palm. "I would well meet the duty, were I of a mind to do so. But I will not if you play me unfair."

"You are a bold wench." Roderick sternly admonished her. "Too bold, I think. For I might agree to such frugality, were the rewards to my person suitable. But for a stingy brat who hies herself well away from me, there is no consolation. Ere the night is long, I will pry your thighs apart and lay them open to me and give you penance for your crime. You will squirm in high discomfort all throughout the morrow. Not for the imprint of my open hand or any strap laid upon your back, but for the well-seated plying of my shaft between your thighs. Mark my words, little Frank."

Thea gasped. "You treat me like a strumpet!"

"Did you not just make the challenge to satisfy my lust to prevent all others from making claim?"

"I meant to—" Thea snapped her jaw shut. "Promise me to limit your lust and take no other to your bed, and I will do anything you ask of me."

Roderick raised his finger to her so-defiant chin and stroked it down her throat, to the crevice between her breasts. "Have you learned that a man whose pleasures are serviced with sweet charity and fulsome willingness rarely looks to another?"

"My knowledge of this is limited to what you have schooled me. I have my demands. You have yours. Promise me to be truehearted, and I will surrender to you every time you beckon to me. Be it in your chamber, your kitchen, yea, in any portion of this land you own, I will not refuse you ever."

"Without spite? Withholding rancor? Setting aside forever the bitterness of captivity?"

"Aye," Thea solemnly promised. "I will submit to you upon those terms, if you agree to two conditions of mine. That you take no other woman to your bed while I occupy it. Second, when the time comes that a lady wife must come to manor, you release all claim upon me and set me free where you found me."

"No. You ask too much."

"I cannot ask for less, my lord. You not only hold the balance of my life and soul within your power, you cut an insidious road into the heart I vowed to seal against you. 'Tis not only my body you threaten against my will, but my love you are ferreting from me. I can give you all I have only once. 'Tis the way I am. When you are done with me and must take another for the needs of your fief, you must release me from your bondage."

"You ask too much!" Roderick pulled the blanket downward, exposing her body to his gaze. "You are regarded by all in Blackstone as my slave. No demands may you make upon your lord and master."

Thea's eyes lit again with defiance. "I offer you peace between us. My compliance with your every wish. Instead of taking me as an enemy, let us be as allies. I will put your house into order. Blackstone will become the finest manor in the north. I will not cheat you or withhold a single talent of mine from your benefit. All I ask of you is that you release me when your use of me is ended."

"You offer? You demand! Nay, you command! With arrogance befitting a queen. Nay, Thea. 'Tis not your will empowered here. 'Tis mine. What counsel is this, that I should take your words in earnest? Who rules here? You or I?"

"Your law is absolute. You may do whatever suits you. Even if it suited you to pardon a woman who has committed no crime against you."

"I cannot do that."

"Why?"

"For the simple reason that you cannot be trusted. Do I turn you loose in France to sew seeds of discontent against me? I do not know to what lengths you would go to see me scorned, and will not take the risk."

"I would give you my word, here and now, to never harm you in any form. Not by design, or thought, or word or deed. None, no harm. Do you release me to my people, I would never repeat your name. I would swear absolute fealty to you, upon the souls of my entire family. I would not betray you, Roderick of Emory. I give you my most honored vow of that right here, as God is my witness."

Thea reached for his sword beside the bed and drew it to her, kissing the relic of Saint Peter embedded in the handle to seal her vow.

"I swear upon my very soul. I shall never reveal your identity, nor shall I cause you harm, as God is my witness."

As moving and earnest as her pledge was, Roderick held himself aloof from it. He took the sword from her hand, his face coldly serious. "You have given me no measure to judge your word or your most solemn vow."

"How can you say that? Have I not seen to every order you have given me? Was your keep not cleaned and the larder fattened? You did not make me swear not to run away. Nor did you extract a promise from my lips when you removed your collar from my neck. You did so as a convenience to yourself, so your lips were not roughened by the metal I was forced to wear. One more thing—had I wanted

sanctuary at the abbey, I could have had it. It is in my power
to ask the abbot for it anytime I so choose to ask. But I have
not, because something ties me to you. I can be trusted.''

"Your fine protests and arguments do not sway me in the
face of your proven malice. My most worthy knight nearly
died from a wound you dealt him. This very day, all that live
within this keep are victim to your dabbling in the blackest
arts, mixing potions and concoctions that put the mind and
body to sleep. Now it suits you to strike a bargain, pledging
your soul, aye, even those souls you do not own, your family's.

"Lady, I am bewitched by your very words. Where is the
truth in your sea of glib madness?''

"Oh.'' Thea groaned, and held back from pounding her
fists against his bare chest in outright frustration. "Fine
counsel you would make for the condemned man, my lord.
You twist each fact and turn each truth to suit your own
selfish purpose. I ask for a boon, and you give me forfeit?''

"You do not deserve a boon.''

"I did not deserve to be taken captive from my homeland only because I recognized your face. That is the true
issue between us. I beg you, give me the means to prove I
can be trusted. Or set a length of time upon which my integrity can be tested. If I play you false, deny me. But if I be
true, then swear with me.''

"I am amazed you admit your integrity is in question.
You would try to strike a bargain with the devil. I cannot put
aside your poisoning of my house. Yet you plead for a test.
I will give you one.''

"Name your price.''

"All that you promise me must be given from this moment hence. The liberty and the pleasure I would have of
your body, your full cooperation in every bedding. The
submitting to my hand, my whim, yea, even my mood. Up
unto anticipating my next turn. Within my house, you will
comport yourself with modesty before my men, you will see

to all the work that must needs be done. You will do it without rancor, without scowls or petulance or temper. You will do all I ask of you and more, and come to me with the same loyalty as my faithful hounds show. Even to the kissing of my hand after a well-earned beating. Do you set any discord within my house or between us, there will be no agreement to be sworn."

"And the length of this test?"

"Until Epiphany."

"So be it," Thea agreed. "My word is given, sworn and pledged already. I yield every talent I possess to you from this day forth."

"Aye, so be it," Roderick declared solemnly. "Do you play me false, there is no further agreement between us. You will be collared once again, the iron welded fast, and you will remain my slave until the day you die."

"But do I pass your test, you will give me your solemn word that when you go to Aachen seeking a wife, you will return me to that place where you abducted me?"

"I give my word only when the test is done. I mouth no promises until then. Nor will I swear to provide what is beyond my power. Before I would swear any vow, I would have my own conditions met."

Roderick lifted her from his lap and set her aside. He strode from the bed to his chair, donned his robe and sat once more before his fire.

Ruefully he wished he could freely make a promise of the kind she wanted. Her eloquent arguments this night proved once again that she came from an unusual background. Did she know what all she gave away?

He did not press for her identity. In truth, he did not want to know it. To what house she was attached, her liege, her parents, or any particulars of her past, he could not afford to know. It was unlikely her family had influence at court, but there was always an outside chance that they did. She had been a barefoot serving girl clothed in faded dress and

apron, come to bathe in an open river. Only by believing
that could he continue to hold her to him.

It soothed his conscience to think she had had a generous
lady pass down a kirtle of fine worth. How else could he
love her freely? He had wrestled with the same problem each
day that he'd been out hunting and checking his traps. He
had returned to his keep to possess her, to take that which
his conscience had kept him from taking from her thus far.
She dreamed of love and wanted it from him. He had no
love to give her.

Thea was his woman now, and that was as far as he would
allow his thoughts for her to be concerned.

Thea did not say anything as he banked the fire for the
night. When he put his knee into the bed, she relinquished
the lion's share of the mattress. As he stretched out facing
her, his hand came to the bearskin and tossed it aside. The
fire in the hearth matched the heat in his eyes as he gazed at
her breasts and white belly.

Roderick remembered his earlier promise. That the only
forfeit she would pay for her trickery would be to revel all
the morrow from the tender abuse of being well used, sore
and aching from lovemaking.

He was not of a mood to deny himself any longer. He
caught her roughly and pulled her beneath him. His mouth
descended upon hers, taking ruthlessly what it was she owed
him.

Where before he might have had to coax apart her lips and
spread her thighs, now she yielded willingly. He was not easy
on her. He didn't want to be easy. He needed hard passion
to slake his need, and he took it, taking care only that she
was aroused deeply, softened and stretched by his fingers as
well as any woman could be, before beginning the final assault inside her fortress.

She demanded as much and more by touch and direction.

There was no quarter to be given, for the war between
them continued, and the weapons they chose to use were

their bodies. Entwined, twisted, heated and frantic. He plunged into her, seated himself to the hilt, and caught her cry in his mouth. He cupped her shoulders within his arms, holding her to him, feeling the ache and tremors that ran through her body so acutely he almost disgraced himself with lack of control.

Kissing her, tasting and loving her, he waited, bound and hurt himself by the tightness of her sheath fitted round him. Then, slowly, he began to withdraw, until he was nearly free of her wet heat. Her eyes opened wide and her fingers clutched his hair.

"Don't leave me," she begged.

"Leave you? My lady, our joust has just begun."

Thea closed her eyes, marveling at the intrusion that came again, and again, and again. She wound her arms around his broad back and held on to him for dear life, going with him on the wild spiral upward to oblivion. His sweat pooled and slickened on her belly, adhering their flesh together. She didn't know what the building, agonizing pressure was inside her own body, but when he pushed his hand between their bellies and put his fingers to the burning nubbin centering all her pleasure, she exploded.

Roderick caught her cry of pleasure in his mouth and drove deeper inside her, plucking the tiny orb between his fingers, hearing her pleasure, feeling it. Then he could hold back no more, and his control snapped. He rode her hard, harder, straining, every muscle in his body contracting all at once. Shouting in triumph, he released himself at last and collapsed upon her.

Thea said not a word as his full weight dropped on top of her. It wasn't a crushing weight. It felt right, perfect. Her only fear, from the ragged, jagged tone of his breathing, was that he had expended himself too much and might die in her arms. Her fingers tightened against the hard muscles of his neck, bulging against her fingertips. "My lord, are you well?" she asked fearfully.

It was too soon to be able to speak, but Roderick nodded his head against hers, sought her mouth and kissed her in gratitude. Then, conscious that he was crushing her, he rolled onto his back, bringing her with him. She laid her ear against his heart, threaded her fingers in the bristly hair coating his chest, and sighed contentedly.

His rod was still achingly rigid. He knew the cause was the enforced celibacy that had tormented this past year. He gave in to it. This night he would satisfy his raging lusts once and for all. He stroked her head, smoothing and tangling his fingers in her curls.

His fingers tightened on her head, his arm encompassing her shoulders. She felt so perfect, so right for him, and he marveled over that, because she had grown not an inch, nor had she gained a stone.

Then he began the duel again, for he had a rod so stiff it felt as if it would never soften. It was hours later that exhaustion caught him and he fell asleep with Thea wrapped tightly in his arms.

When he woke, Roderick found the fire had been stoked and Thea wore a blanket wrapped like a toga arourd her. She stood at the opened windows, looking out upon fields that were battered down by two nights of hard rain.

The rose of dawn made her cheeks simmer with fair, healthy color. Hearing him stir upon the bed, she turned and approached him, the blanket parting slightly to give him a long view of her shapely white legs with each step she took.

He propped his head upon an elbow, watching her with interest. She stepped gracefully onto the dais and dropped into a deep and formal curtsy, bowed her head, then looked up to him with a morning-fresh face that would have suited a king.

"My lord," she intoned, a hesitant smile edging the wide corners of her mouth.

Amused, Roderick swung his legs out of bed. "Well, what further justice do you seek this morn, wench?"

"I make no demands upon you, Roderick of Emory. In truth, my lord, I was standing at the window pondering my fate. Armina has busied herself with taking my wash lines down from your whipping post."

Roderick took her word as fact and brought himself erect, towering above her. "No demands? No bargains? No commandments on what you will have? What you won't have?"

"Nay, my lord. I yield."

Her answer suited Roderick. He put his hand out and assisted her to her feet. "See to my water, then. I would have it heated well, if I am to carve this blasted beard from my face."

Chapter Fifteen

The balance of the early morning Roderick spent watching her move and stoop and bend. She was a pleasure to watch, a feast for his eyes. He was a little wary of this woman he treasured so greatly. She had so many skills and talents he had never thought to find in an ordinary woman. Bewitchment, he solemnly advised himself, was a luxury he could not afford. Her true reward to him was yet to be uncovered.

Yet he wanted her greatly as she bustled about, heating water over the fire, bringing soap and toweling to the rude table he set beside his chair. She held his knife with an experienced hand and bent close to ply the blade against his skin, filling his nose with her scent. Her touch was light, but sure, as she mangled the corner of her delicious mouth, concentrating upon her task.

Each time she turned to clean the blade in the basin of water, her toga slipped a little farther down her torso. Roderick eyed her smooth arms, her slender throat and the white mounds of her breasts. As she neared the end of her task, scraping smooth the last stubble left beneath his neck and softly tracing her fingers across his now revealed chin, he snuck his fingers into the woolen folds. She twisted to rinse the blade while Roderick held the wool tight. The knot broke free, and the whole blanket dropping to the floor at her feet.

"My lord!" she exclaimed, dropping the knife. The metal rang on the marble hearth. Roderick didn't give a second thought to the blade he would have to sharpen. He cared only that he did not step on it as he rose, her hips clenched in his arms, the taunting crest of her breast captured by his mouth.

Thea gasped with surprise and pleasure as he strode toward their rumpled bed. She stroked his smooth cheeks with both her palms, admiring his handsome face as he laid her on her back. He retained possession of her nipple, drawing the areola deep inside his mouth.

She was achingly aroused, had been from the moment he rose so magnificently from bed and stood towering over her, his rod fully erect and frightening to behold.

His control was admirable, even now, as she parted her thighs to accept him inside the tender portal within her body. He drew his head back, tugging upon her sensitized breast, sending tremors shooting into her belly.

"My lord, do not tease me." Thea raised her knees upward, clenching his ribs, trying in vain to draw him to her when she could not. His chin raked across the wet, hard and throbbing bud, tracing a pathway between her breasts, only to torment and encircle the other before taking that inside his mouth, as well. Thea's fingers tightened upon his jaw, tugging in a wasted effort to move him.

Roderick caught her wrists and pulled her hands from his face, spreading her arms away from her body, holding them pinned to his bearskin cover. He was not of a mind to be ruled by her passion for quickest release.

As she plied her blade across his face, he'd realized that winter was upon Emory. He would have all the long, dark and cold nights ahead to teach her each pleasure their bodies could share. This morning he concentrated upon worshiping her breasts, suckling to draw them hard and full, imagining that they would run with milk into his mouth.

Perhaps, such arduous attention might even stimulate them to grow, so that they filled his hands when he touched her.

It was a thought that intrigued him. An experiment he would enjoy exploring morning, noon and night.

She arched against him. Small, she was so achingly small, compact and perfect, yet strong beyond belief where her thighs fastened to him, narrowing his waist. Her head twisted from side to side, and she cried out, "No more, no more, I beg you."

Roderick released the throbbing, pulsing nipple he held in his mouth and raised his head to look at the flush covering her throat, spreading to her cheeks and forehead. Sweat-damp hair clung to her face. She looked wild, driven, frantic.

"You cry for peace, Thea?"

He watched her struggle as she sought for composure, her reddened lips trembling and moist, inviting him to taste other pleasures.

Thea looked at him through slitted eyes, wary of the power he held over her body. She could hardly bear to look at his beautiful, too-handsome face. She wet her lips, swallowed and tried to speak, but the words came out deep and husky, from a voice she scarcely recognized as her own.

"I do not know what I cry."

Not releasing his firm hold upon her wrists, Roderick moved up her body, centering himself, poising his shaft at her hot, wet entrance. "You will tell me if I am hurting you?"

"You could not." Thea clamped her teeth onto her lower lip. His shaft parted her chasm, only the head entering. She felt herself stretch, and it wasn't enough. "Give me more, please."

"Bring up your knees, Thea. Lock your ankles behind my back, as high as you can." She obeyed him immediately, making Roderick feel the opening and deepening of her chasm. "More," he coaxed, sinking no more than an inch into her. It was the sweetest inch he'd ever been given. She arched and pulled against him. It came as natural to her as breathing.

Roderick released her hands, stroking her limbs inward, until his hands covered her breasts. He put his elbows to the bed, keeping his chest levered hers, and began his slow descent into her, stroking and rubbing her breasts. Her nipples were hard and hot as her nubbin. He took both between his fingers and thumbs and massaged and pulled them to the same rhythm that his shaft rode in and out of her.

And all the while he could, he watched her accept his pleasure. She screamed and cried out, twisted and buckled beneath him, her whole body becoming so slippery he could hardly contain her. But by then, he could not contain himself, either. The game drove them both to completion. His seed shot forth with burning heat, drenching her womb, rocking him with the force of his release.

Spent, he could barely breathe.

When she could, Thea scooted to the edge of the bed, thrusting out her foot to snare her blanket with her toes. On his back, with one hand pressed against the receding hammering in his chest, Roderick watched her agile toes grasp the corner of the blanket and draw it to her with monkeyish skill.

"We need a bath, milord," she announced with a delicate flare of her nostrils.

"Aye, but not together, wench," Roderick said. "We would smell the same emerging from the Roman bath as we would entering."

She gave him a round-eyed look that encompassed his turgid member, which responded immediately to her gaze. "Surely not, milord. Oh." She hopped off the bed and hurried to the basin, wrapping herself modestly in the wool. "There still remain guests to your house whose fast must be broken. Forgive me if I must see to other duties, as well."

Roderick laughed deeply, stretching and arching his back. "See to it, little Frank," he said affectionately. She cast him a glance across her shoulder.

"You do not object?"

"Nay." He rolled onto his side, propping his head on his hand to watch her ablutions. "I will have you to myself again, once the tide has run."

Thea grinned with spontaneous delight. "So you shall." She washed, dressed and was gone much too quickly, leaving Roderick to rise at his leisure and brood.

He had lots to brood about, knowing that he was being lead on a merry chase after a swinging skirt. Given the seriousness of their discussion last night, Roderick prayed whatever charm it was this small Frankish woman possessed would fade. It would be no problem for him to take her back to the Somme and let her fly to her father's wrath.

It was to the possibility of a father's wrath that he had given some thought in the night. Did he give his word to release her, he must be certain of her lifelong pledge to never do him harm. In the time that remained before he was forced to take a wife, Roderick judged, the little Frank could produce a child. Were she to breed, he would not release her before the child was weaned. The child he would keep. It would be insurance against her having a well-seated liege lord who could cause him harm at court. If she proved barren, and his feelings for her did not change, he would have to rethink granting her the release she wanted. He could ill afford a mischief-making woman at his back.

To his mind, her longings to return home proved she had little foresight. Her immaturity seemed boundless. The family she was stolen from most likely would not accept her back into their fold. Her long absence could be a source of high disgrace. If they had little means, it would be impossible to dower and arrange any kind of marriage for her. Nor could she be consigned to a convent without a dowry.

If she would give better thought to her plight, she would see that leaving Blackstone might be the worst thing she could ever do.

On the other hand, Roderick held no illusions that she would hold to her sworn vow. Her stubborn pride allowed for nothing less. Provided she adhered to his conditions, he would give her the pledge at Epiphany, knowing it would bind him, as well.

The time was a long way off, in any event, consequently not meriting more thought. Other than devising a satisfactory forfeit that would absolve the anger his vassals and servants harbored for her and yet not compromise his own tenderness, he gave her no further thought as he washed and dressed for the day.

Thea saw Roderick of Emory next when she laid the trestle for the morning's repast. He was standing next to the Danish king; their heads were bent in earnest discussion. The Hawk of Emory wore his finest tunic, a rich blue samite the same color as his eyes. It was fur-trimmed, as royal as any garment she'd ever seen worn at court. He was so stunningly handsome, she could but stand holding her laden tray, gaping at him.

She gazed lovingly at his mouth, remembering the taste and feel of it, thrilled inside because he had allowed her to remove his thick, obscuring beard. Firm and wide, his upper lip curved and dipped into turned-up corners. It was a mouth that could smile well if he wanted to. As he listened to Herewald speak, she saw deep lines appear in his cheeks that might once have been devilishly handsome dimples. Now, they seemed to be deeply etched crevices, weighted down by his many burdens.

Something about that touched Thea, and set her thinking. *If I could make this man smile occasionally, or lighten his burdens in any form, God would forgive my sin of loving him without sacraments.*

It was his jaw and chin that most intrigued her. As large a man as he was, he had no spare flesh anywhere about him.

His jaw revealed the truth of that, for there was no round-ness to it. It was all angles, sharp and strong below his ears, lean and spare until it came to his squared-off chin. He was mightily handsome with those sapphire eyes like beacons that could penetrate any of her armored defenses. He turned them on her, motioning that she was to come to him.

"Oh, no," she murmured under her smile. She set the heavy tray on the trestle, wiped her palms on her apron and hurried to him with grave questions in her eyes.

Dropping both lords a curtsy, Thea looked up to Roder-ick's solemn face. "You have need of me, my lord?"

"Yea, Thea." Roderick spoke in modulated French. "King Herewald wishes to speak with you. You will give him your attention, and forgive his poor accounting in French."

"*Oui, Monseigneur Hawk.*" Thea dropped him another curtsy and brilliant smile, then turned her attention to Herewald the Walker. His face was as red as beet juice, giv-ing her the impression he had been holding his breath for minutes. "How may I help you, sire?"

The king cleared his throat, then spoke halting French with a rough, gravelly tongue. "Mademoiselle Thea, my good friend Hawk does not care . . . much for my attentions to you. I made him a most generous offer to purchase your indemnity. Alas, he says you are a free woman, able to choose which of us you would prefer. I am a wealthy man, and could provide you with all the earthly treasures women delight in. Would you consider my suit?"

Thea looked to Roderick, but his face was schooled to show her nothing. She lowered her eyes, giving the king a small curtsy. "My lord, forgive me. Monseigneur Hawk does not speak the truth. I am deeply indebted to him, and am not free to seek another protector, no matter the riches you would honor me with."

"You refuse?" Herewald barked, stunned.

"*Mais non, monsieur le roi,* not refuse. Only bound by ties that are not tangible."

"How can this be?" Herewald looked at Roderick, puzzled. "You prefer this duke to a king? Ha! Roderick, you are a dog…a very lucky dog. Mayhap the woman loves you and will not speak of it to me. Mademoiselle Thea, I beg you accept the gift I have presented your lord. I will not take it back. It would insult me to do so."

Confused, Thea looked from one man to the other. King Herewald pointed to a large trunk placed beside the gallery steps. "Look. See if it suits you."

Roderick stiffly nodded that she should do as the king bade. Thea knelt to the trunk and lifted its ornately carved lid. The smell of roses wafted up to her nose. Inside were bolts of the finest cloths, richly embossed Venetian silks, fustians, lace, linens and wools in every color of the rainbow. Thea let her fingers stray across the fine nap of the dark blue fustian, seeing a new tunic for Roderick.

"Oh, my lord Herewald, you are too kind by far. Of course I will accept it. *Merci.*"

Herewald jabbed Roderick in the shoulder. "There, did I not tell you so? What woman does not want cloth? Good. I am satisfied. You may keep her for now, Hawk. Mayhap when next I visit, the bloom will have worn off the rose and she will think I am not so old or uncomely."

"That will be all, Thea. I will have your gift carried upstairs. Now, Herewald, no more talk. Let us eat."

"Ah." The Dane grinned cagily, reverting to his own language. "I had you worried, did I not, Hawk?"

"Not for a moment," Roderick smoothly replied. By the time he and Herewald were seated to the table, Thea was gone from the hall. Roderick confidently thought she would make herself very scarce for the rest of the morning. He wasn't incorrect.

More rain came after Herewald sailed out of Blackstone harbor. The fields were so wet and soggy, the men could not go outdoors. They idled away two days at the trestle table. Benjamin adeptly sketched his idea of a comfortable chair and bed for his room. One thing led unto another and, before the weather cleared, there were sketches for all kinds of new things.

Sunday was so bright and clear that Roderick ordered everyone to mass after holding an impromptu court that morning. He lifted Thea onto Victory and rode to the abbey, bringing all the parchment drawings in a leather packet. After service, he and Friar Laurence discussed the making of such things, while his household joined the celebration in the village, all except for Thea.

She waited for Roderick. Armina cast her a triumphant look at the abbey gate, grunted, then shambled into the village square to enjoy her earned day of leisure. Thea was not allowed outside the curtain walls unless accompanied by Lord Roderick. That was the forfeit he had been forced to levy upon her for her attempt at running away.

It was too soft a levy for Sir Deitert, who knew the depth of her crime, and Armina, who had presented testimony and the root. Armina wanted blood drawn, and she drooled to see Thea's back shredded. Sir Deitert simply did not want to bother with keeping track of where Thea might be. Roderick's edict satisfied him, in that he knew if the maid broke his restriction, he would deal severely with her.

Presented with the root and a no-longer-appetizing pie, Roderick had thanked Armina, then invited her to look around and see all the hale and hearty fellows. The worst that anyone had suffered was a good night's sleep, with no ill effects. He had declined further punishment.

"The old lord would have whipped her."

"My father never had to count the serving women to this house on one hand, as I do. Let it go, Armina. I suffered more ill at your hand in the kitchen than I have at the Frank's."

"She's a witch, I tell you. Bewitched you, cast you under her black-haired spell. The devil works through her."

"Then we'd best go to church and see to our souls.' Roderick had ended with that. Armina had shuffled to church, displeased and grumbling, but now that she thought Thea an outcast in the village, she was happy.

Roderick finished his discussion with Friar Laurence, and the woodwork was ordered, for the monks had tools and two skilled carpenters. He lifted Thea onto Victory's back, mounted behind her and rode away from the village, ostensibly to inspect the fields.

Hail had damaged some of the grains. The cool nights had caused the stalks to dry, and it finally looked to Thea as if the last harvest were ready to begin. It looked that way to Roderick, too.

Roderick informed her that threshing the grain was the hardest work, in his estimation. But for that afternoon, it being fair and mild, he turned Victory toward the mountains to show Thea the valley from above. He came eventually to the pool and waterfall high up the mountainside on an overlook of black marble.

Roderick had packed lunch, a skin of wine, cheese and bread. They swam together and made love on the pine-covered ground, then ate and looked at the peaceful valley below.

"This is a perfect place," Thea said at last, when she was sated on every level. "I can see why you love your land. Your people are good people, too, Roderick. It is a shame what the Vikings did."

"It's the price of living here." He gazed into the distance and twirled a straw between his fingers. "It has happened time and again. Attila the Hun ransacked us, and burned half the forest in his wake. Charlemagne did the same a hundred years ago. I have seen my share of such plundering in the name of Lothair. When it happens, we start anew. I am not the first Emory to face making a new beginning. Life goes on."

"So it does." Thea thought his mood very serious. There was only one thing missing from such a perfect day, spent with a man on such intimate terms that he shared his thoughts and she her own. Neither of them spoke of love.

* * *

The hard work of the harvest was shared by all. The grain was winnowed and threshed and stored. Four cows gave birth, and the supply of milk at the keep was abundant. The women made cream, butter and cheeses of every sort they could remember. The abbot made copies of all his recipes and sent them to Thea, who could read, and thus, many forgotten skills were renewed.

During this busy time, a genuine fondness evolved from their mutual agreement. True to her word, Thea held nothing back, and when they made love it was perfect coupling. At night they slept close to one another, arms and legs entwined. She saw to Roderick's every need, even to the point of being able to anticipate his next word, his arrival home, and to read the signs in his eyes of desire, day or night.

In the days that followed the harvest, a different pace came to the work at hand. As it became colder, the women of the keep rarely strayed outside the hall. The men left every day. True to Roderick's word, every man and boy labored at building and enlarging Blackstone's defenses.

The ironmonger never seemed to cease his labors. The ring of his hammer against heated steel went on all hours of the day. He forged new weapons, armored chestplates Roderick designed. He made gates and iron chains, locks and pots and pans, linkage for hauberks, sabatons and greaves, grates for the fires, and a new chandelier for the hall, which Roderick designed to go up and down on a pulley. That way, anyone could set candles into place and light them.

Roderick ordered thin iron strapping and brought that upstairs to his chamber. Thea sat sewing while he worked with a mallet, pegs and adze, making a webbing beneath the straw mattress. It was firmer than the rope lattice, and Thea slept without rolling into Roderick's side at night. She gathered goosedown and made a ticking, and the bed was infinitely comfortable, a fine place to while away a long winter night.

They were all so busy, no one noticed how the season had changed. The last of autumn was truly gone, and winter's fury came in cold snows that made everything white with wonder.

They had shoes. Boots and slippers, warm fur-lined leggings and soft soles that kept feet and legs warm and dry.

The furniture came up from the abbey's workroom shortly after its new roof was finished. It came a piece at a time, and Friar Laurence always accompanied the cart. Thea thought it was so that he could be invited to sup, which he always was.

By the time the first hard freeze iced the harbor, there was plenty of wood laid in. The boats were dry-docked. The supply of ale was monstrous, for Kimbell's hop and barley crops had been exceptionally good.

The squires and pages returned to the training at arms for a portion of every day. Sir Michael was in charge of that, seeing that the boys trained and exercised daily.

Every woman in the village was given a task to fulfill within her home as winter progressed. Those who knew how to spin, did so. The threads were passed to the three weavers, and to others who could knit or crochet. A quota was demanded from each. Their finished products were brought once a sennight to the keep and counted and stored.

Cloth was cut as it was needed and made into garments. Though colors were limited to dark earth tones, no one lacked suitable outerwear. Thea kept records of all supplies coming in and going out. She accounted for each pair of woolen stockings, every fur, every barrel of ale and wine. Not a single thing escaped her careful accounting.

Roderick often sat down to look over her simple handmade ledger. Until Thea started keeping track of everything, he had had no idea of what it took to daily see to the well-being of his people. Even a skin from a squirrel brought in from the traps in the woods was tallied before it went to Aldus to be tanned. The date that same skin returned to the storehouse, Thea entered it again.

He surprised her when checking her ledgers by correcting numbers or finding an error she had overlooked. Nothing escaped Roderick. She was amazed to find him literate. She had thought Saxons ignorant. He spent much time working over his own parchments. Though he did not show Thea the drawings and plans he labored over, he often spent hours talking with Benjamin, Michael and Deitert, discussing what it would take to build the things he drew.

Beyond the curtain wall, a stack of felled hardwoods kept growing. Sometimes Thea felt imprisoned. Were it not for the ritual of Sunday mass, she might have lost all hope.

The day before the Epiphany, a heavy snowstorm kept everyone indoors. Roderick sat down with Thea's ledger, then took it upstairs to the storeroom. He returned to the hall, amazed by the wealth of furs his hunters had collected, and the variety of them. "I could turn into a merchant this spring instead of a pirate."

"Best see to your defenses," Deitert advised. "The Vikings may return, expecting just such industry to have been made."

That statement made Thea very uneasy.

"Do not worry, Thea." Roderick patted her hand. "They'll not make shore if they do come."

She wondered if his quiet boast would prove true. Herewald had grounded on one side of the island. What if the *Nordmanni* were smarter?

She waited, not saying anything about their bargain or the test she had been put through, although it was all she could think about. She didn't sleep a wink that night, so many, many questions plagued her mind. Would Roderick remember? What if he was displeased? What if he knew instances where she had failed to live up to her vow?

The morning of Christ's birthday dawned clear and cold, and because it was a holy day no meal would be served before they went to church. Roderick arose first, lit a candle in their still dark room, and built the fire. He turned from that task with a smile motioning to Thea to come and sit with him in his chair. She brought his bearskin from the bed to cover them.

With the bearskin loosely draped around them, Roderick took her hands in his, and for a long, silent moment, contemplated her work-roughened palms. His expression was solemn when he raised his chin and looked deeply into her eyes.

"It is Epiphany," he said. "This is the day we are to have a reckoning." Thea nodded, unable to speak for the dryness in her throat. Roderick lifted her hands to his mouth and kissed her fingertips. "Are you going to ask me if I am satisfied with your pledge?"

Thea shook her head, no. She was too afraid he would answer he had found her lacking. Roderick sighed. He bent his shoulders, stretching to pick his sword up from the floor where it lay every night, within the reach of his hand as they slept.

He unsheathed the heavy sword, bringing its gilt and jeweled shaft between them. Thea shifted into the crook of his left arm. He gripped the handle, exposing the full length of the polished blade.

"You have kept your pledge, Thea, and proven to me that your word is as good as your bond. You have yielded all that I would have of you, even unto the pleasure of your body in each joining of it with me. I promise you, that on the day I leave Blackstone and return to court to seek a lady wife for this land of Emory, I will return you to the riverbank wherein I took you, my slave and captive. As God is my witness, I do so swear to you that I will do this."

He brought the hilt to his face and kissed the relic, just as she had done. Then he put the sword away and gathered her again close to him inside the fur rug.

"You have my pledge, Thea, my oath upon our agreement." That was all he said. Nothing more. He leaned close and placed a soft kiss upon her temple.

Thea kissed his mouth in deepest gratitude.

"Know you this," Roderick told her, when their lips parted from the lingering, sweet and moving kiss of peace. "I would that the way of this between us, would never change. And if I were not so constrained by the needs of the people of Blackstone, I would live in this same, rich poverty with you, all the days of my life."

Thea silently nodded acceptance, then, without further ado, smiled and went happily about the work of seeing to needs of another day at Roderick's keep.

The winter lengthened and, as it did, Thea became aware of subtle changes at the keep and in the village. By the end of February, it was obvious every woman in Emory appeared to be breeding—save old Armina and Thea.

One snowy morning, Sir Deitert and Roderick went out together, and Elspeth spent the whole time they were gone fraught with nerves. Thea asked her what was wrong. Elspeth confided with a stricken face, "Sir Deitert has chosen to ask Lord Roderick for permission to marry me. I have begged him not to bother with such a request, but he insists. He does not want our child to be born a bastard."

"Oh." Thea wondered how she hadn't noticed Ellie's thickened waist before. She didn't know what else to say.

Always one to comfort, Jesse gave Elspeth a warm hug, telling her not to worry.

The men didn't return until late in the afternoon, bringing a snowy flurry inside the hall with them as they stamped their boots and shed their heavy cloaks. Sir Deitert looked across the hall at Elspeth and winked. Between him and Lord Roderick, Friar Laurence looked like a small brown hedgehog as he shook out his wools and dusted snow from the top of his tonsured head.

Roderick called everyone in the hall to attention by announcing, "Gather round, my friends. There is to be a wedding celebrated this very moment." Then he cleared his throat and beckoned Elspeth to him, saying, "Provided the bride is willing. Tell me, wench, will you have this old graybeard? I gave you leave to choose any Saxon who remained unmarried. Is this the man you will have?"

Elspeth threw her arms around the older knight's erect shoulders and kissed his grizzled face before one and all.

Friar Laurence spoke the vows and gave the blessing. And the winter afternoon withered into a snowy evening spent celebrating in good company.

Thea moved as though by rote, completing the tasks she knew so well by this time, but the wedding had disturbed her. Not that she had anything but the very best wishes for Elspeth. It was Roderick's reaction to the wedding that she could not ascertain a clue to until after they had retired that night.

They had a roaring fire in the hearth. It made the chamber too warm for a change. He stood at the open windows, looking out. Thea drew a shawl about her shoulders and joined him, wondering if he would say what troubled him.

She looked at the same sky he studied and saw cold clouds and swirling snow fluttering down into the bailey yard. The night was quiet and calm, peaceful. Down in the village, trails of smoke steamed into the sky from the fires burning in each little house.

"Is something wrong, my lord?" Thea drew her shawl closer about her shoulders.

Roderick pivoted on his heels and stared down at her, his face a mummer's mask, giving no sign of his thoughts or his feelings.

"Are you breeding, Thea?" he asked bluntly.

"No, my lord." Thea shook her head, watching very carefully for any trace of emotion her words might elicit from him. His expression remained aloof.

Abruptly he turned and closed the shutters securely, blocking out the seeping cold from his bedchamber. He took the long shawl from her and grasped her shoulders, holding her naked body at arm's length for an intense study.

"When was your last flow?" he asked, as if they discussed the depth of the snow on the window ledge.

Thea couldn't find words to answer him right away and turned her face away, shaking her head. "It . . . I am never regular. It can come anytime, when I least expect it, or not at all for many months."

Her answer deeply disappointed him. Roderick drew her against him. He should have noticed, he supposed. He seemed to spend an inordinate amount of time looking at her face or considering the waspish tightness of her waist.

"That is too bad." He dismissed her modesty as he swung her into his arms and carried her to the bed. "All the women are breeding. I suppose I tire of being asked if I do not do my duty."

"Do they dare to ask you such a thing?" Thea questioned as he tucked her beneath the warm coverlet, undressed and joined her. He folded his hands behind his head and lay staring up at the ceiling. He considered what kind of babe she might produce.

For all her lack of size, Thea was of robust health. She never complained of sickness. He counted the time they had left. March, and, if spring came late, April, before the harbor was free of ice. Had he enough time to impregnate her, thereby entrapping here at Blackstone for another year and another year after that before the child was weaned?

Lying beside him, she didn't say anything. When he turned and placed his hand upon the soft curve of her belly, she neither drew away nor cuddled closer to him.

"I want a son from you," Roderick said with flat conviction. He let his gaze remain on his hand, spread across her belly. "Yet you are too small. I can span your hipbones with my hand."

Thea chewed upon her lower lip, thinking. She wasn't really afraid, but she was apprehensive. He was in a strange mood, one she had not seen before.

Before she could puzzle him out, he shuttered his face as he so effectively did and returned to the contemplation of the ceiling, his hands behind his head.

"You are displeased with me?" Thea asked.

"Nay, you please me, Thea. I admit only that I have begun to wonder if you might not be barren."

Thea bit her tongue before any sharp retort might launch from her mouth that would ruin all her hard work. He could not possibly know how difficult it was sometimes, not to give vent to her temper, not to cross him and to put up with his often inconsiderate squires. But her vow to him was to cause no discord in his house.

Roderick continued. "Emory needs children in every house. Why should this one be any different? Were Armina capable, I would expect her to produce more sons, as well. As it is, the old crone can see to diapering and rocking cradles."

"She'd not see to mine," Thea said without warning.

"Oh?" Roderick cocked a brow upward. "Suppose we wait until there is a babe to fight over, little Frank. Then you can bring out your claws in your cub's defense. Armina raised seven strong sons and four daughters. Mayhap she's not as skilled as you, but she was a good breeder, and her sons were hard workers every one. Did you ever think to what she has lost?"

Thea could not say she had. She thought to what Roderick had said for a while, wondering if he was chiding her for lack of charity. It was certainly true the old Saxon woman and she were never on very good terms. Thea did her best to stay away from the woman. That kept her end of the bargain secure. *It was a mighty order to cause no discord within a house.*

"What was it she and her family did for you?"

"Raised the woolliest sheep you ever saw."

"Don't you think she is too old to be put to that work again?"

"Aye, she is." Roderick left it at that.

In the morning, Thea went out to the kitchen and put her own hands to work scrubbing the pans and pots that Ellie dirtied. Armina shuffled to take her place, her arthritic joints complaining at her movements. "You should see to the spinning today, Armina," Thea told her. "There's wool that must be threaded in the hall."

"And who'll wash the pots?" the old woman asked, as cranky as ever.

"Tommy will help, Arnold, too. It is time those two put in a full measure of work here in the kitchen. Go, get a stool and sit before the fire in the hall. Roderick said you know how to make a spindle sing."

The old woman cackled. "That I do, witch. I still can, too. I'll show you."

When she had thrown a shawl over her shoulders and gone out, Elspeth stopped her stirring and questioned Thea. "What are you up to now?"

Thea relinquished the washing of pots and pans to the two boys. "'Tis not me, 'tis Roderick's order. You boys see that Ellie and Jesse want for nothing here, understand?"

"Yea, mistress," they both answered. Satisfied, Thea helped put the finishing touches on the morning meal and saw to its serving within the keep.

To her surprise, Armina did know how to spin the complicated spindle that Saxon women held under their arm and worked with both hands free to twist and pull the wool into thread. She spun an even thread, far better at it than anyone else in the house.

Able to sit within the reach of the hearth's warmth, the old woman delighted in the busy comings and goings of the occupants of the house. Her gossipy old heart was right where it wanted to be, in the middle of things. As the days passed, she grew less quarrelsome.

Roderick followed his own agenda, insisting his men do the same. They trained in arms early in the day, then took advantage of whatever natural heat the day might bring by working upon the battlements afterward. Often they went trekking out on the thick ice in the harbor.

Every Sunday at church, the women gathered, talking of their coming babies. Elspeth joined right in with the chatter, and gossip, happy to be bearing Sir Deitert's child. Jesse wasn't sure who the father of her baby was, claiming that the joy of mothering a new child was satisfaction enough for her.

By the ides of March, the midwife was up to her neck in women lying in or about to deliver. The last of the cold was over, and the scent of spring flowers filled the air. The best time had come to gather herbs and replenish the keep's depleted medicinal stocks. Thea prowled restlessly inside the high walls of Blackstone, aching to explore the becks and the woodlands in search of herbs and roots. Though she spent her energy on the kitchen garden, that did not satisfy her need to hunt out cinquefoil, *aunée officinale*, or fennel.

Roderick was much too busy supervising construction to take Thea outside his keep to gather roots. Each time she planted a subtle hint about how low the stocks were in the medicine chest, he replied that maybe tomorrow he could find some time to take her up the mountain.

Tomorrow, Thea feared, would be too late.

Chapter Sixteen

June 842 A.D.
Emperor Lothair's Palace
Aachen

The chancellor's chamber was filled with brilliant morning light. On his desk, stacks of sealed letters had collected for over a month. Lord Roger of Bellamy had taken leave of his liege, Emperor Lothair, for personal reasons.

He strode into his chamber now. His servants bowed, greeted him deferentially, rushed to divest him of the elegant cape around his shoulders, to bring his chair forward and to see to his every comfort.

Word had preceded the chancellor's arrival that his latest voyage had ended in failure. No one dared be first to broach the subject with him. All faded into the background as quietly as possible, leaving only the chancellor's secretary to take the brunt of his terrible anger.

Lord Bellamy folded his hands behind his back and stood at the wide-open windows. The slant of the sun should have warmed him, but he radiated a coldness that kept Griswold from making small talk or conciliatory words.

Gazing at the park ablaze with roses and rioting flowers did nothing to alleviate the winter binding Lord Bellamy's heart.

How long he stood there, watching dew melt and birds dance airily over the emperor's garden, Roger did not know. He shook his head, clearing it, trying to come to grips with duties he'd left untended. First the letters, then.

He was too restless to sit in the high-backed chair. Opening the topmost scroll, he cast a glance at his secretary, who had not made a sound since he came into the chamber. He cleared his throat as he broke the seal.

"Well, are you going to speak, Griswold? Or are you just going to sit there quivering, dripping ink all down your blotter?"

"I did not wish to intrude on your reverie, my lord chancellor."

"Humph." Roger scanned the document as he unrolled it, saying dryly, "I can hear by the sounds outside this room, the emperor thinks nothing of intruding."

The document was a tax roll. Roger cast it to Griswold. "Have you opened none of these in my absence, man?"

"My lord, I would not break a seal on a document meant for your eyes only."

"Well, break all of these, *maintenant*." Lord Bellamy lifted the entire lot and put them in Griswold's arms. Several spilled onto the floor, for it was a goodly stack of papers needing attention. "Read them, record the taxes in the king's ledger, then bring back only those needing my attention directly. Now, go. The emperor comes."

Griswold scraped and bowed his way to the antechamber. Alone, Bellamy collected his thoughts, rubbed his broad fingers against his brow and listened to the commotion beyond his office door. He was not surprised that only the emperor felt free enough to intrude on a grieving minister.

When the emperor intruded, it was with the greatest show. Bellamy could hear it coming.

Servants ran ahead of Lothair, throwing open doors and heralding his passage. Since one room in the palace opened into the next, it was like a great wave sweeping the second floor. Bellamy could see it in his mind's eye, for he'd been privy to the circus for so many years it had lost its effect on him. Ah, but old Lothair loved it.

Within every chamber through which Emperor Lothair passed, courtiers and servants rose, dropping whatever they were doing to bob like fishing corks, abasing themselves as His Majesty marched resolutely toward his destination.

As the outer door of his suite was breached, Bellamy straightened. The emperor would find no chinks in his armor. That was a truth every Bellamy lived by. At last, his private doors burst open.

"His Majesty, Emperor Lothair," the herald cried.

"Roger! I came at once." Lothair strode inside.

"My liege." Lord Bellamy dropped to his knee, his fist pressed to his heart in an age-old salute. Lothair's hands immediately clasped his shoulders, urging Bellamy back to his feet. Lothair embraced him and kissed him on both cheeks.

Roger Bellamy was taller, more erect and more kingly-looking than the wildly dressed, extravagant older man.

"By my bones, you were gone a long time."

"Yes, my liege. I was."

"And you found Althealine?"

"No, sire."

"No?" Lothair already knew the truth from the runners who had preceded Lord Bellamy to the castle. "But we were so certain the leads were fresh and you would find her this time."

"So I was." In his heart, Lord Bellamy was a realist. The time had come that he must make his family come to grips with their loss. Thea was gone to them forever.

"Then you found nothing in Friesland? The Viking shipwrecks rendered you no better hope?"

"My king, since September last, I have personally investigated every rumored sighting, every shipwreck, and questioned every harbormaster in the empire, from your northernmost boundaries to the southwestern tip of the continent. Sir Royce and my youngest brother, Lord Augustine, have covered every port from Barcelona to Constantinople. If Thea had been sold or traded, I would know it."

"Then you conclude the Viking kept her."

"Nay, sire. I must conclude my daughter is dead. I have just come from Landais, where I ordered memorial masses to be said daily for her soul and advised my brother, the bishop of Auvergne, to request papal masses spoken in her memory."

Lothair's pale eyes filled with compassion. He had had no prior warning of this. He reached out again to his lifelong friend and embraced him. "Accept my condolences, Roger. They come tardy and unwillingly given, for I would not have such sorrow afflict you. I know how deeply you treasured your daughter. Few men love their children as you do. I hope someday your grief will lessen."

Lord Bellamy rubbed a mist from his green eyes and straightened with purpose. "Well, we have had a troubling year. I have informed Lilla that the grieving cannot continue. Life must go on. I have two other daughters to see established in houses of their own. And my youngest son, Jason, has just been accepted as a squire by Lord Merrault. Spring has nearly passed, and it is a time of renewal. I must count myself a lucky man to have lived two score and ten years and never had to face such personal tragedy before. It hasn't been easy, but I am not so foolish that I cannot number my blessings, as well."

"You speak as if your life has been a bed of roses, my man. I know better." Lothair pressed Roger's shoulder, then released it and waved to the sunny window box. "Forgive me, I'm going to sit down. We have much to discuss, and I fear this will be a lengthy visit. Are you up to it?"

"By all means, my liege. Forgive my rudeness. Sit, please." Roger moved aside his traveling valise so that the emperor could make himself comfortable. "How may I serve you?"

"Well, I have several problems you can help me with, Bellamy."

Lothair dropped onto the cleared settee, and the warm morning breeze immediately began to play havoc with his shoulder-length curls. They were well streaked with gray, just like his curly beard. Daily he lost more of his once leonine fullness. In contrast, Roger Bellamy's closely cropped hair was black as pitch. The emperor envied his chancellor's wreath of tight curls, which, despite its inherent darkness, had yet to show a trace of gray.

Bellamy waited while Lothair took time to phrase his words. "You remember that blasted tournament we staged at Montigney on Maundy Thursday?"

At ease with Lothair in a way that few men were ever allowed to be, Roger rocked back on his heels and barked, "You mean that monstrosity that nearly got us all excommunicated? How could I forget it?"

"Humph, yes, well, if you could control that sanctimonious brother of yours, who thinks his calling to God grants him license to be pope of Aachen, we'd all be in a lot better graces. That's beside the point. I had an emissary from my brother, Louis the German, visit while you were gone."

"What's our pretender up to now?"

"No more and no less than he always is. He's ordered his dukes to secure Frankish brides. Ulm is married to Madeline of Normandy and the heir to Weser is to take Clare of Boulougne, Alfred's youngest daughter. That leaves only the duke of Emory unattached."

"I was afraid you'd say that." Roger thrust out his jaw and stroked it with his fingers. "What of Anne?"

"She remains at the convent at Solbert."

"I take it, then, she delivered her bastard."

"Yes." Lothair glared glumly out the window. He had been, himself, a virile, healthy man, having sired three healthy sons to inherit his empire from him, but more and more his thoughts turned to a different vein. Having been a king since he'd come of age, and now standing on the threshold of being crowned emperor of the Holy Roman Empire by the treaty Bellamy negotiated at Verdun, he could not help but ask himself, *Is that all there is?*

Lothair pulled himself out of his reverie and studied his chancellor gravely. "'Twas a son...a fine healthy son. Did I tell you Hawk returns shortly to select a bride?"

"I gathered that much, since you mentioned your brother Louis's order that his vassals take Frankish wives."

"Ah, well, Hawk returns under duress, with a heavy burden of taxation levied by Louis to induce him to choose quickly. And when all of this is done and the next generation takes our places, I want the Hawk of Emory married well, to the best blood we have to offer. You spoke of your younger daughters. I want them both brought to court, presented to Roderick."

If Lothair had been anything less than a monarch, Bellamy would have drawn his sword right then and run him through. "Sire," he began, "the daughters I retain will be married inside my realm." Bellamy bit off each word he spoke. "My wife could not bear it if they were hundreds of leagues away, never to be seen again. Neither, sire, could I."

Wearily Lothair raised his hand. "I know, Roger. I know that. And you must understand the position I am in. I cannot have the strongest young dukes in the empire beyond my control. You know what Hawk is capable of. Not one castle he laid siege to failed to surrender. The man is the most brilliant warlord since my grandfather, Charlemagne. Louis's emissary informed me, Hawk has completely restored and rebuilt Blackstone in *less than a year*. It is the strongest fortress in the north.

"King Herewald of the Danes grounded in his outer harbor, and we have just had word arrive that six *Nordmanni* Viking longships never made it to his coast the week following Easter. He ransomed the survivors of the Viking longships to Herewald and kept their cargo and their ships.

"I and my sons need Roderick bound securely to us. That is why I've chosen your house to sponsor his bride."

"You expect me to use my daughters as bait to trap the man? Do you know what you are asking, sire?"

"Can you give me another solution? You know Louis. Word comes he builds his army bigger every day. Do you think a treaty scratched upon any paper will keep my crown secure upon my head? Louis and Charles grow bold over their paltry win at Fontenoy. Damn my eyes, but if I'd had the Hawk of Emory fighting at my side, we'd have not lost that battle, Bellamy."

"My king." Bellamy took a deep breath. "The treaty I am negotiating secures your crown as Holy Roman Emperor."

"Aye, I know, I know." Again Lothair's eyes fixed upon some sight in the distance beyond Bellamy's ken. When the king resumed speaking, his voice was thick with emotion. "Think of the consequence of war, Bellamy. With men such as Ulm, Emory and Weser fighting against us, we'd lose much more than Merrault lost for me at Fontenoy. Then where would your family be? What would happen to your sons, your precious daughters? Your lady wife? Have you another solution, give it to me. I would accept it."

Bellamy paced the chamber, saying nothing. The king waited and watched.

"I will endow the daughter that marries Emory the duchy of Lorraine as a wedding gift. I believe Hawk would accept that. Only Lozere lies between Lorraine and Emory. Louis will be mad for the match. He will see it as the greatest concession."

"The duchy of Lorraine belongs to Anne of Aachen."

"Nay, the kingdom of Lorraine belongs to my son, Lothair. I promise only the duchy to Anne's bastard son, who is the blood issue of Roderick of Emory."

That privy information rocked Bellamy. "Not Merrault?"

"Nay, not Merrault. You have only to look at the boy to know he's Hawk's blood. Do you want to see him?"

"Nay, Lothair. You're a wily fox, but I know when you are speaking the truth. What of Anne?"

"Anne," said the king with finality, "is dying. She could be dead even as we speak."

"How so?"

"The pox. A visitor to Solbert took sick of it. I have all this on the best authority, your brother bishop. Henri writes it is God's almighty justice on the wicked."

"What of the boy? Is he free of disease?"

"Of course. I never sent him to Solbert. Anne didn't want him. She'd have drowned him if she had the chance. As it was, I had to keep her under guard, else she'd have gone to every witch in the land until she managed to rid herself of the babe."

"My liege, this is a fine kettle you toss me into. Do you tell Hawk of the child?"

Lothair shrugged. "Perhaps. Eric is a charming imp. Louisa and I grow quite fond of him. What else was I to do with him? He is my blood kin, a prince even if he is a bastard."

"And you would give his birthright to my house?"

"Well, as loyal as you Bellamys are, I don't see it that way. This will all work out, in time. I see a hand greater than mine moving events forward."

"God save us," Bellamy murmured. Then, louder, to the king: "Know you this, Lothair. I wed my daughters close to home. Neither Lilla or I could stand losing another. My house has not been the same since Thea disappeared. I agree to this proposal of yours because you are my liege, but no daughter of mine will be forced to wed. Not by you, nor by me."

"And again I tell you, dear friend, I wish to God you had found your Althealine. But as you said when we first began to speak, life must go on. Neither you nor I can stop that. Your other daughters must marry someone. Roderick of Emory will make a fine husband and give you grandsons aplenty. You won't regret the alliance."

"Surely you cannot think I hold any objections to such an alliance. I could list for you a hundred benefits it would bring to my house off the top of my head. The thing that concerns me and makes me hold reservations is the happiness of my daughters, which comes first. If my youngest were to announce to me she wanted marry Lilla's Moorish hawk master because she is in love with him, I'd approve the match.''

"You jest?''

Bellamy wanted to prove a point. He hoped he had, but inwardly he smiled because Margareth's hawking instructor was over sixty years old, and a more monkish man could not be found. "Nay, sire. You don't know my Margareth.''

She had never once said that she loved him.

There were moments when it seemed to Roderick the declaration was on the tip of Thea's tongue, almost ready to spring forth from her.

Yet, as carefully as Thea managed everything, she managed never to let slip, even in the greatest throes of passion, those three little words, *I love you.*

Roderick dallied all through the spring. Daily he threw himself into tasks that could not be completed for years, delaying the inevitable. Then his hawklike watch upon the harbor was rewarded with a test. Six Viking longships grounded, and the war party that had come to plunder were taken captive. Sir Deitert had predicted the marauders would come again.

For two days they had war in Blackstone harbor, but the outcome was as predictable as could be, with Roderick's fine attention to defense. Seven Vikings were taken alive and held prisoner until Herewald came and bartered for their lives. Roderick was glad to be rid of them. And more glad for the excuse they had given him not to sail this spring.

So intent was he upon keeping watch on his harbor that the party of riders coming from the south almost slipped in unnoticed. His liege lord, Louis of Germany, came on his progress, inspecting Roderick's repairs and seeing to the state of northern Saxony's defenses.

Louis stayed a week and levied grief upon his leave-taking. Impatient for the crown he felt owed him before he tottered into middle age, he spoke eagerly of going to war in the near future. He gave Roderick until the first of June to sail to France.

There were only two conditions to the heir to the throne of France's benefice. Roderick was bid to evaluate Lothair's strengths and fortresses on his northern frontier. The second was that Roderick would make an alliance inside a powerful Frankish house. Louis craved alliances that would pave his way when the day came he took Lothair's crown.

Like the single grains of sands in an hourglass, Roderick's time with Thea was running out. Each night when he held her in his arms, he loved her as well as he could, for she had given him everything in her pledge. Not once had she turned to him in spite, berating him for anything.

Elspeth delivered a fine, healthy baby girl the last week of May. Deitert was so besotted with the babe and his wife, Roderick couldn't help but envy him.

Thea had been with him nine months the day they sailed. It wasn't anywhere near long enough. He did not want to let her go.

It was so odd, their leaving. Thea had come down to the wharf with everyone from the keep. Goodbyes were lengthy, well-wishes long. As Roderick's boat prepared to leave the dock, Thea turned to Elspeth and Jesse and thanked them for all their help, then very calmly went up the gangplank.

Roderick had prayed she wouldn't. How he'd prayed that. Let her kiss him goodbye one more time, cling to him desperately, as she did each night, but let her turn and run back to stay on the shore. He'd have given anything to see her do that. He'd have had something to return to then. For the amount of respect and companionship she did give him was great.

She came on board and looked at him, and he nodded his head, and she went to the cabin without ever looking back to the stunned faces on the shore.

* * *

So much had changed. So much remained the same. The scent of columbine hung in the damp evening air. Lilies and fiddlehead ferns crowded the riverbank under the abundant overhang of leafy elms, poplars and willows. Full summer had come to Longervais Valley, ever the same to Thea's well-acquainted eyes, yet unique and new.

The skiff rocked as Roderick bent forward, pressing the tiller, avoiding the swift-running current that ran in the center of the wide stream.

Thea's heart hammered in her chest. It was nearly dark, yet there was so much golden light remaining. It gilded the green grass, the leaves of the trees, the verdant hills. She could see it all, yet she saw so little, because it hurt to take her eyes away from the man she loved with all her heart.

The small boat glided past the shadow cast by Longervais Keep. It looked different to Thea's casually inspecting eyes. Were the walls higher? She could not remember.

Roderick studied it as they passed, then said they had added a rampart and drawbridge. Thea wondered what changes had been made at Landais. What if her family was not there? Her heart skipped a beat. The painful knot in her belly tightened.

It has been so long. Maybe, I won't recognize Landais. Turning to Roderick, she saw his jaw was locked, his mouth rigid. *If only he loved me.*

I will not cry when we part. How many times this day had she sworn that vow?

Now the skiff edged closer to the shore...to a thick stand of trees with one huge cypress leaning over the water. Her throat closed tight.

The entire journey south, she had consoled herself with one thought: *I will be home, a free woman, no slave nor leman any longer.* The soft rocking stopped as the bow of the boat nudged into the black dirt on the shore. Thea said a silent prayer at the ending of motion. Her stomach was ever uneasy late in the day.

Her nausea had begun during the last week of Lent. Roderick's Saxons took the fasting before Easter most seriously. She had felt it each evening since and misjudged its cause, because it was not the morning sickness Elspeth had warned her about. Fearing Roderick would divine what was wrong with her, she hid the increasingly evident signs of pregnancy. She knew she took something away from Roderick that he would never part with if he knew the truth.

How good she had become at keeping secrets. Thea thought back at the time when she used to say anything that popped into her head.

"This looks like the place to me, Thea," Roderick said. He threw a line up on the shore, dropped the sail and caused the small boat to rock as he tied it up to an elm.

"It is the place." Thea managed to speak. A wonder that was. He stepped out, extended his hand, then placed her feet solidly on Frankish soil.

"I shall walk you safely home."

Thea shook her head no. Tears flashed out of her eyes, and she threw her arms around Roderick, hiding her face against his chest.

"No, my lord, you must not. I have made you a vow to keep secret your identity. Do you accompany me, you might be recognized. I'll be fine. Everyone knows me. They will think I am a ghost. Take care, my lord."

"Thea, you don't have to do this." Roderick clung to false hope to the very end. "You know I would always care for you." He could think of nothing else to say. Rigidly he held back the words *Do not leave me, I love you.*

How or when this woman had caused such feeling to germinate in his fallow heart, Roderick did not know. But she had. She had nurtured the seeds of love from her first kiss until this last. He felt winter coming in the ice encasing his heart.

Thea clung to him, kissing him more fervently than she ever had, seeking his taste to take with her. Then, with a strength of will she'd thought she no longer had, she removed his hands and smiled up into his granite-hard face.

"You are a man of your word, Roderick of Emory. Go now. Your friend Michael waits your return at the mouth of the Somme. I pray you have good luck at the king's court. I will remain your loyal servant always. Godspeed, m'lord."

Another kiss would have broken her will, Thea turned from him, breaking through the bower of trees. The ache in her heart weighed so heavily it nearly crushed her. Pride held her shoulders up as she strode through the trees. She forced her spine to straighten and raised her head, making her chin firm and her steps unfaltering.

With each step she took away from him, Roderick longed to reach out and grab her. His knuckles turned an ashen white against the dark bark of the elm as he held himself checked to the ground where he stood.

His sworn pledge made him let her go.

She went deeper and deeper into the woods, farther from him.

His throat was strangled, locked by the pain reeling out of his heart. He was hurting, and no sound came from from his lips until Thea passed out of his sight, hidden by the trees flanking the river's shore.

"Thea," Roderick's voice barely echoed a bullfrog's croak. "Look back at me."

But she did not. The land he'd stolen her from had swallowed her up.

How familiar it all was. Blackberry bushes thickened along the well-worn paths, heavy with unripened fruit, yet abuzz with bees and stinging wasps. Farther down, the path widened over a noisy, babbling brook, full from a recent rain.

The trees were denser, Thea thought. With each step through the woods, she could hardly stand the wait before she reached the broad, centuries-old Roman road she knew so well.

She began to run at the gristmill, idle this time of year. Not a soul lingered about when there was no grain to be milled. Beyond the mill, the woods loomed thick with new saplings, seeming to fill all the spaces where she and Victory had carved their own pathways.

Then, all at once, the white walls of Landais loomed ahead of her. Thea screamed before she was even within the gate. "*Maman! Maman,* I am home! *Maman,* Papa, Joclyn, Andrea! *Maman!*"

Geese and servants squawked in the yard as Thea ran across it, scattering pea gravel under her feet. The doors to the hall stood wide open. Thea thought her hammering heart would explode as she stumbled up the steps.

"*Maman!*" She stopped in the doorway. Her eyes swept the gallery, with its arches and golden light spilling into the hall. On the stairs, running as if her skirts were on fire, was Lady Lilla.

"*Maman,* I am home." Thea cried.

"Thea!" Lilla screamed.

Shouts came from everywhere at once. Screams, shrill voices, booming voices, cries and tears. Her mother's arms wrapped so tightly around her, Thea could not breathe.

Lilla could not believe her eyes. She clutched Thea to her bosom, kissing her dear face, then held her back and examined every inch of her. Then she burst into tears, rejoicing. Cry... why, they cried until they laughed.

Old Joclyn took Thea's return the worst. The old nurse collapsed in a heap on the floor, blowing into her apron, weeping uncontrollably.

Marie, who had once been as bold and daring as her sister Thea, could not let go of her.

The air filled with so many questions asked at once; not a one could not be answered. The expense of emotion overwhelmed them all, especially Thea. With a mother's wiseness, Lilla ordered a strong tea brewed and put her daughter to bed.

"You are as thin as straw, and so...so..." Words failed Lilla of Landais again. "Rest, my darling. Oh, you look as if you need it. We will talk another time."

Even though Lilla knew her home was the safest place on earth, she sent for Bellamy's seneschal and ordered guards placed at Thea's doorway and below the windows of her room. For the first time in nearly a year, Lilla ordered the gates of Landais closed. She had never given up hope that her daughter would return.

Conferring with Sir Georges, she bade him ride to Aachen with all good speed and deliver Lilla's message personally to Roger of Bellamy.

Another vassal she sent to Concordia to inform Sir Royce and Lady Andrea their sister had returned home safe and well. The last she dispatched to Auvergne to let Bishop Henri and Lord Augustine know their prayers, masses and pilgrimage had not been in vain.

Then she squared her shoulders and went into the west wing, where her elderly parents lived in relative peace and comfort in Lilla's crowded household.

She bade her mother sit down, and gently woke her elderly father, giving them the news in the kindest way she could. Their hearts were not as strong as they used to be. Both had declined in the year since the tragedy had struck.

Chapter Seventeen

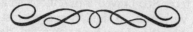

Marie sat on a rush-back chair, waiting the eternity it took for Thea to awaken. Even when she pinched herself, Marie couldn't believe what her eyes told her was true.

Thea lay in her bed, sleeping through the rising dawn. She turned often, restless and troubled, crying out in another language. Marie thought she recognized some of Thea's words... from lessons they'd shared with the same tutors. To her chagrin, Thea had more skill with tongues than she did.

Marie recognized endearments, *my sweet, my darling one.* Stilling the rocking chair so that she could listen better, Marie swore she heard her sister mumble the name Derrick. Or was it Eric?

Troubled, Marie paced the room. Had she not promised her mother to be with Thea when she woke up, Marie would have fled Thea's bedroom. The guilt of deserting this sister the whole family loved so dearly weighed heavily on Marie's narrow shoulders.

She could not think of what she and Thea would have to talk about when her sister finally woke. Nor could she bear to face the hatred Thea must surely bear her.

But Lady Lilla insisted Thea must not waken and find herself alone without a family member there to greet her. If nothing else, Marie always did as her mother bid.

Thea awoke. When she sat up, Marie understood the reason for the vigil. Total panic flooded her sister's face. "Where am I? Sweet Jesu, am I really home?"

"*Oui!*" Marie joined Thea on the bed, hugging her with gentle, reassuring arms. Thea's arms tightened so fiercely in return, Marie could not breathe.

Thea relaxed her grip and held Marie at arm's length, examining her face. She braved a tremulous smile and said, "Ah, Marie, we are so, so similar, and yet just a little different from each other. How have you fared, dear sister?"

Marie could not say anything as new tears dashed from her face.

"*Non, non, ma petite...*" Thea drew her close and kissed her brow. "I beg you, do not waste tears on this happy day. I worried so for you. How I feared you had come to greater harm than I. I'd have lost my mind with grief, if not for my faith in God that told me you were safe."

"Oh, Thea, I blame myself for everything. If I had not hidden your shoes, nothing would have happened to you. Not a day has passed that I haven't shed tears for you and prayed for your safe return. I'm so sorry. I should never have left you alone. It was unforgivable. Do you know that Papa wouldn't even beat me to make my guilt any less burdensome? Oh, Thea, thank God you've come home!"

Marie burst into tears, and it was some minutes before either sister could manage to speak again. As in old times, Thea pulled herself together first, comforting her younger sibling, absolving her of any unnecessary guilt.

"We are both of us safe and together again." Thea hugged Marie again and kissed her cheek most tenderly. "Now, no more tears. None. Here, let's dry our eyes and swear not to cry anymore."

"It's not tears of sorrow that I shed, but tears of joy. How fared you, sister? How did you come to be returned to us?" Marie asked the questions everyone wanted answered. "You must tell me everything that happened to you."

Thea sighed, moving her hands through her hair to smooth and untangle it. She shied away from looking directly at Marie's inquisitive blue eyes. As many confidences as they had shared growing up, she could not burden Marie with the truth. The corners of her mouth twitched, and she said, "So, you did hide my shoes, you little devil."

"Oui," Marie answered. "I'm sorry. I won't ever do something so foolish again."

"Ah, well." Thea smiled, harboring no ill feelings for something so trivial. "I am much more to blame than you are, Marie. I can't answer your questions. Maybe I will never be able to talk freely of what happened to me in the past year. I was very, very frightened at first. But the man who took me was not completely unkind. We came to respect each other in many ways. He gave me his word that when he took a wife, he would return me to where he'd found me."

"Oh, Thea." Marie's eyes watered again, and would not stop. "You look so hurt."

"Aye, I am, sweet sister. This homecoming has been all I desired. I have learned one thing from my experience—we must treasure each day that we have together."

"Why?" Marie looked confused. "This man will not come back for you . . . will he?"

"Non, non. He will not. As you and I have always shared our most secret thoughts, I will tell you, I expect my homecoming to be of short duration."

"Why?"

"I fear Papa will banish me to a convent when he knows that I am bearing a child."

Marie's eyes widened, and she looked down, searching Thea's night rail for some outward sign confirming her sister's words. "Papa will not punish you for that!"

"Shh, Marie," Thea said, laying her fingers to her sister's lips. "I have told you, now you must keep my secret until I have gathered the strength to tell *Maman* the truth."

Marie stiffened righteously. "*Maman* will not let Papa banish you for any reason. Nor will I. And you are foolish to even think that he would."

"Now, Marie," Thea said admonishingly.

"No, Thea, you listen to me. You do not know how Papa has searched for you. Time and again he went away. The entire kingdom has been scoured high and low. No cottage door was not thrown open by his vassals. He went to sea, three times, searching the coasts, everywhere. Royce and Oncle Augustine did, too. They went south, to Genoa, and as far east as Constantinople, seeking every port where the Vikings might have traded or sold you. Papa will not send you away, even if you had come home with ten bastards in your arms."

Thea shook her head, remembering her pledge when first captured. She would never harangue herself with if-onlys.

"You know, Marie, I never told my captor who I was. I was so angry in the beginning, and proud. I was afraid that if I told him who my father was he would hold me for a ransom so dear that it would have endangered the whole family. Then, as time passed, I vowed to keep the Bellamy name from being sullied in any way. Now I have come home bearing a child. Soon even the sight of me will be a cause of shame to all of you. I wanted so badly to come home that I did not think past my own selfish wishes. I think I have made a grave mistake by coming home."

"No, Thea, no, don't you ever think that. Don't say it. We love you. Landais will always be your home. This is where you belong. You couldn't have wanted to stay with that awful man."

"In that, Marie, you are very wrong. Leaving him was the hardest thing I have ever done."

"You came to love a barbarian?"

"A barbarian?" Thea paused to consider, taking time to consider what had happened on the river through Marie's eyes. Thea could not twist the truth to this, her dearest sister. "In all honesty, Marie, the moment I first saw him, I think I loved him."

And that was going far back to the tournament at Montigney, when Thea had first laid eyes upon Roderick of Emory. "But leaving him tore my heart from my breast. If he had loved me even the smallest bit, I'd have not come home at all, Marie. I will never forget him, nor ever love another."

"You came to love a Viking this much?"

"Oui."

Thea gazed off into space. The simplest answer was always the truth. Her words guarded, her thoughts her own, there really was nothing more to say. She was home.

Roderick must have realized the impossibility of another woman coming to Blackstone. A lady who would deserve her rightful place at Roderick's side by marriage and vows between them. Thea had no place in Blackstone Keep now. It was better this way.

Thea looked toward the day that she would not feel the pain she felt right this moment. She had given her word and lived up to it, had withheld nothing from Roderick of Emory.

As she had feared that night so long ago, when they had made pledges to one another, he had stolen her heart completely—and crushed it just as thoroughly.

Were it possible to recover, Thea would turn her efforts to that end.

Oddly, she did not fear her father's wrath any more than she doubted her mother's love. When Lord Bellamy came a week later, Thea met his rage with a surfeit of calm.

"Where were you taken? What was his name? What did he do to you? I will annihilate the man, crush him, ruin him! Tell me!"

It was easy to look into her father's eyes and say nothing. It was not defiance. To nearly every question, Thea did have an answer. "I don't know."

She could not say truly how long the journey was, for several of the first days she had no conscious memory of. "Vikings" sufficed. A cold green land of mountains and water and snow and ice. It was all true.

In the end, she explained, "Papa, he was an honorable man. His reasons in the end more than justified his crime against me. Because he came to care for me in some small way, he released me. More than that, I cannot tell you. Is it not enough for you that I am home?"

Lord Bellamy prowled the solar. His heels would have made an endless racket if the slate floor were not spread with Turkish carpets. He clasped his hands behind his back, deep in thought.

Lilla did not want to intrude on him. No, really, she did not want his intrusion on her. Experience told Lilla that Roger would stop pacing soon. Just as she knew that when he did, she would not like a single word he said.

At the archway at the end of the room, where the shutters stood wide open, granting access to the warm sun and summer breeze, her husband ceased his pacing. He turned abruptly into the alcove where Lilla was steadfastly cataloging another potion. She felt his raging temper penetrate her island of calm. Yea, their whole bedchamber reeked of the approaching storm.

Then he spoke.

"Lilla, Thea protects her abductor."

Lilla lifted her head, deliberately putting her quill aside, taking time while she stoppered her ink to gather her thoughts. "*Oui*, my lord husband, I know that."

"And you accept it?" The mounting thunder in Roger of Bellamy's voice edged toward violence.

"Roger, for *me* it is enough that Thea is home. Why must you have more?"

He exploded. "Woman, how dare you ask me that?" Lilla winced. His shout surely could be heard all the way to Longervais. "I want answers to my questions. I cannot let such a crime as this go unpunished. At a moment's notice I can move an army against whatever Danish or Norse kingdom harbors the abductor of my daughter. I would crush them, once and for all. End this attacking of innocent peoples...this bastardly raiding! If Charles the Bald hadn't gone groveling before the curs and paid tribute to keep the Norse out of France, do you think they would have dared sail down the Somme and kidnap my daughter? I want Viking blood flowing under my feet!''

"Husband, it was within your capabilities to have done that last year. You could have struck when the rage was hottest in your blood. Now, why would you want to go and get yourself killed, drag your sons along, your son-in-law, your nephews and brothers and the sons of hundreds of our friends? Your missing daughter is safe. She is home. All you lost was one horse that no man could ride. That should be enough for you."

"Damn it, it would be, if Thea were the same. But she is not.''

His fist slammed into the stone wall with such force Lilla feared he surely had broken his hand. But if he had, he was so blinded by rage that he could not feel anything else.

He moved away from the illuminated window and came to sit on the damask-covered settee beside her. He took her hand and gripped it within his own callused hands.

"I have never felt so powerless, so useless and so vulnerable in my entire life as I have since that day Thea disappeared.''

What that admission cost her powerful husband, Lilla tried not to judge. It gave her a foundation to build upon, and she took the small advantage.

"I, too, have felt powerless, my lord. It is a miracle that Thea has returned. Perhaps what you see as change in her would have happened anyway. For she was young and so impetuous, so strong-minded. She's now a woman grown."

"But she has been hurt. I cannot abide the terrible sorrow I see in her eyes. It breaks my heart.''

"I know. I see that, too. We must give her time...time to recover. We all need some time to come to grips with this."

Time, Lord Roger thought, wincing, was a luxury the king would not allow him. Not when he was pressing a union between Bellamy's house and the Hawk of Emory. Seeing his strong-willed wife's frame of mind, Roger kept his own counsel. With Lilla, it was better he do that.

Bellamy took only Marie when he returned to court. Lord Bellamy found he could not bring up the topic of marriage and husbands with Thea, and Lilla still insisted Margareth was too young. So he settled for Marie, bringing Joclyn along to serve her. They arrived in time for the weeklong celebration of the emperor's feast day.

The court pageants lived up to everything Marie had imagined them to be, full of pomp and circumstance. The emperor was as sly of an old fox, as she had been told.

So many handsome lords and knights hunted wives of wealth and beauty at Lothair's court, they scared Marie to death. Being painfully insecure, Marie wished Thea had come along to lend her some courage.

At least her father kept residence outside of the palace. There, a normal life could be had in the house Roger Bellamy owned. Not as normal as at home in Landais, but then, this was the capital.

After meeting His Majesty, Marie thought the emperor was disappointed in her. He had addressed her as Althealine. Her father had informed him that she was Marie, and that Thea had declined the emperor's invitation. For a fleeting moment, Lothair had seemed quite displeased.

Marie had lived in Andrea's and Thea's shadows for so long that in the blink of an eyelash the feeling of not measuring up to their beauty came and went. And when the long-awaited time at court had arrived, and she was the sole Bellamy presented, Marie had been much disappointed.

In fact, after three visits to court, she elected to stay home when her father went back for the evening revelries, which upset Lord Bellamy more and more each passing day.

Marie could not figure what troubled her father and began to ask when she could go home.

What Marie did like about the city was shopping. The merchants, the markets! In that she found her element. Each morning, as soon as she could prod Joclyn out the door, Marie went with a large basket in hand to stop at the vegetable mongers, to look in at the lacemakers, to see the cobblers and importers. Lord, to see everything all over again!

Her father disapproved of haggling. Joclyn thought it common. But Marie loved bargaining over even the most minor purchase.

Joclyn accompanied Marie to the market, for a lady did not go anywhere without her chaperone. Nervous, Marie carried her personal safety one step further, insisting on being accompanied by one of her father's strongest vassals. Louis of Longervais had been Marie's personal guard for nearly a full year now. Marie's boldness had never been more than an imitation of Thea's courage. She'd lost what nerve she had, the day of the Viking attack.

Thus escorted, Marie plundered her way through the marketplace, spending her father's money.

"Oh, Joclyn, look at this cloth! Have you ever seen such a beautiful shade of green? Feel its texture!"

"That is as rare a velvet as I've ever seen." Joclyn stroked the nap. "Why, it would be the perfect color for Thea, too. You could each have a dress made, for there is ample on the bolt."

"Forest green. I must have it," Marie said, and waved to the merchant to catch his attention.

As the thrill of negotiations began, Marie became engrossed with the quest to get the very bottom price. She noticed little else.

Sir Louis's attention had been drawn to a hostler's stall, and Joclyn fingered another length of imported fabric, then spied another at the next stall.

The merchant remained quite firm over his price. He would not discount the cloth, even for the entire bolt.

"Very well," Marie said huffily. "Keep your fabric. I will look to another's stall and find just as good or better."

"This cloth is worthy of the court!" The merchant wailed, realizing he was about to lose a sale.

"And hence your price of three times its value," Marie declared. "No, I have made my final offer."

"My children should starve. I should be out of business if I took offers like that." The man beat his breast as if in pain.

Under the market archway, Michael of Lozere watched in great amusement as a black-haired miss made the cloth merchant miserable. At first, Michael thought the girl was Thea, but then the girl turned and Michael saw the braids that coiled and coiled and coiled about her head.

Fascinated, he drew closer, close enough to hear the young girl's words. Her voice sounded so familiar, and her profile mirrored Thea's. Michael recalled that long-ago evening when a girl so similar to Thea had been with her at the river Somme.

How enchanting they both had been in the last golden light of day. The other had worn lampblack braids that tickled her bottom. Could she be the sister Thea called Marie?

Michael's fanciful idea lingered in his head. Logic told him such coincidence was impossible. Yet the maid had caught his eye, and he wanted to know who she was.

The pretty maid picked up her basket, her chin raised in a haughty denial of defeat. Ah, but to have such a willful miss of his own...to tame and tease. Sir Michael approached her from behind. Just as she left the cloth merchant's stall, he reached out a gloved hand to prevent her flight.

The minute he touched the girl, she screamed. It was not the startled cry of one surprised. The girl screamed in abject terror. Out of the stalls, leaped a woman of many years, shrieking like a banshee. In the blink of an eye, a tall knight drew his sword, jabbing its point in Michael's chest.

"Oh, my baby!" Old Joclyn drew the girl into large protective arms as Michael rapidly retreated.

"Pardon, madame, I only meant to speak to the girl."

"How dare you!" Joclyn swung a woven basket at him. "Accost my lady, you cur? You've scared the wits out of her. Get back, ruffian!"

"My apologies." Michael held up palms devoid of weaponry, though he was himself well armed, with his sword at his side. "My lady, forgive me, I did not mean to alarm you. Ask your knight to put down his sword. I would never harm such a beautiful young lady in any way. I only came forward to ask your name."

"What need you to know her name? Get back, knave, or I'll have our defender run you through," Joclyn raged. She looked at Marie, who stood trembling, her face gone deathly pale. "Begone, I said."

Michael could see he would get no further.

"My apologies," he said directly to Marie. She raised her delicate, pointed chin, and her lips pouted as if stung by a honeybee. It struck a blow to his heart to see her so distressed. How he ached to be the one to comfort her.

Not that her chaperone gave him that chance.

Marie's lips parted, her fright giving way to shock. She raised her downcast eyes, looking at the dark knight for the first time. Before her smiled the most handsome man she had ever seen in her life. Beautiful, caring eyes of the deepest blue winked at her. She'd never seen lashes so thick or long, or so very black they looked painted. She felt as if an arrow pierced her heart, it ached so.

She was dumbstruck, not knowing what she should say or do, and she couldn't get a word out anyway, as Joclyn hustled her away. Still Marie stared back at the tall knight. His hair was as black as her brother Royce's. Nay, as black as Thea's. But where they had curls, his fell in soft waves that beckoned this lady's hand to entwine in it.

"I beg pardon, young mistress, forgive me for the alarm I caused you. It was not my intent." He spoke in gentle, deep tones. Marie blushed to the roots of her hair.

"I am all right." Marie put a hand to Sir Louis's arm, and he put down his sword. "You startled me."

"Enough of this foolishness!" Joclyn put herself between Marie and the stranger. "We are going home. Come, Sir Louis."

Marie did not protest her nurse's insistence, but at the market gate, she looked back and saw that the knight still smiled at her. His hungry eyes sent a thrill coursing down her spine. Who was he? She had been hustled away by her guardians before she could find out.

Had she ever met a man like that? Ever? No, she had not, and to be dragged away from him like a child by Joclyn rankled. Was she not old enough to be at court? Was the purpose of her being here to find a husband? Yes!

At the meat market, Marie recovered her wits and halted her procession to send Joclyn to buy three plump chickens and a sausage.

"What need have we to tarry over meat?" Joclyn argued. "Cook sees to that."

"Because I want chickens," Marie said petulantly. "Now, don't be tiresome. Go and get them, Joclyn. Sir Louis and I will wait right here."

"See that you guard my darling well," Joclyn muttered before inspecting the wares of the butchers and fishmongers.

Marie turned to Sir Louis. "Did you recognize that knight that spoke to me?"

"No, my lady. I do not know him."

"Sir Louis, I want to know who he is. He did not frighten me. It was only that he came up from behind me, and you know how skittish I am when someone does that."

"Yes, my lady." Louis knew that to be the truth.

"Find out his name and where he is from. I will wait for Joclyn, and we will go directly home. It is only three blocks. We will be perfectly safe."

"Are you certain, my lady?"

"Yes, Sir Louis. I must know who he is."

All the way home, Joclyn scolded her. The old woman's tirade reached full bloom when they entered the house.

"Nag, nag, nag. Joclyn, when will you stop babying me?" Marie tossed down her basket and put her hands to her ears to block out the nurse's words.

"Well! I never!" Joclyn burst into exasperated tears. "It was you who screamed as if you'd been attacked, then you sent your only protection back to buy a bolt of cloth! I will demand your father send you home. You are not fit for the city or life at court."

"The sooner the better!" Marie declared, and ran outside to the garden to escape Joclyn's scolding and to count the minutes until Sir Louis returned with the information she wanted.

Sir Louis returned at midafternoon. Marie pounced upon him, beside herself with curiosity. "What did you find out, Louis?"

Louis looked about the garden to make certain old Joclyn wasn't nearby eavesdropping. "His name is Sir Michael of Lozere, Lady Marie."

"I don't know that name." Marie frowned, wanting the man to be the most dashing and daring knight of all.

"Yea, mistress. I followed him to the palace, and am quite positive of his identity. Since I saw a gleam in your eye I have not seen before, I tried to find out everything there was to know about him."

"Well, tell me. Don't keep me in such suspense."

"He is vassal to a Saxon duke of much renown. His liege is Roderick of Emory. It was the duke of Emory your Lord Merrault defeated when he became champion."

"Yes, but that was ages ago. What else?"

"They have newly come from Saxony to find wives."

"Really?" Marie's eyes began to sparkle then. Heavens! She had been avoiding court as if it were filled with plague! "Has Michael of Lozere found a wife?"

"Several told me he is more interested in sampling all he sees. The word about is that Sir Michael is a rakish sort. All sweet words and charm, though the Saxon he is bound to is of another sort entirely. There is much gossip about them, m'lady. The duke is viewed as the finest catch to come to court this year. His man, Michael of Lozere, comes a very close second."

"What does the duke look like?"

"As fair as most Saxons are reputed to be, Lady Marie."

"A blond? Then he would not interest me." Marie folded her hands, attempting to appear demure and detached. *How very exciting. I shall go to court this eve and have Papa introduce me properly.*

Marie paced the gallery, anxiously waiting her father's arrival that evening. He sported the deepest deep scowl, and did not look pleased at all.

"Joclyn told me a man accosted you in the markets."

Flustered, Marie didn't know what to say at first. "Well, you know how I have been, Papa, since that day the Vikings made me run in fear of my life. It makes me uneasy when people approach me from behind. I am sure the man meant no harm. He was quite shocked by the assault Joclyn did to him, and Sir Louis put his blade to his heart."

"I heard all of it," Lord Bellamy said tersely, angry for having brought the skittish Marie to court. She jumped at her own shadow. "You are not fit for the duty at court I wished you to do, Marie."

"But, Papa . . ." Marie sputtered.

"No, do not show your courage by attempting to argue with me. You cling to your mother's skirts worse than a babe of five. I am sending you home on the morrow."

"But, Papa!" Marie's face blanched of all color. That was not what she wanted at all.

"I have made up my mind, daughter. Now be silent."

"But, Papa . . . I . . ." Marie wailed as plaintively as Margareth did.

"Silence!" Lord Bellamy roared, cutting her off completely. When he stood to enforce his order, Marie closed her mouth with a snap of her jaw.

Lord Bellamy scowled at her in the most frightening of manners. He was angry and frustrated with her. The incident at the market Joclyn had belabored him with only proved how wrong it had been to bring Marie to Aachen. She was not sturdy enough for the hazards of court life. He had too much on his mind to deal with silly, girlish fears that should have been outgrown by now.

Nor would he spend his evenings cajoling and coaxing a recalcitrant daughter to have a speck of courage. Lord Bellamy had not gotten Marie to court but on three occasions, and each of those times, Roderick of Emory had not been present.

To make matters worse, Lothair had approached the Saxon with an outright order to select his bride from any of the three of Bellamy's remaining unmarried daughters.

The emperor's offer had been bluntly refused. The duke of Emory wanted no alliance that would bind him in any way, shape or form to Lord Bellamy. Privately, Roger of Bellamy harbored no animosity over that. He was as insulted by the emperor's outrageous proposal as the duke of Emory.

An observant man, Roger noted that the duke of Emory took interest only in women who were as fair as he himself was. Considering what black-haired Anne had done to him, the slight could be forgiven.

The more he renewed his acquaintance with the Saxon, the more Lord Bellamy liked him as a man.

Marie tried again to speak to her father. "Papa . . ."

"Marie, you disappoint me. A Bellamy is not a timid soul. Go to your room and pack your belongings. You will go home where you belong, first thing in the morning."

His harsh words sent the girl running from his presence in tears. Roger knew he lacked patience, and wished Lilla had come with him to manage Marie. Joclyn cosseted the girl, while her mother never tolerated feminine sulks and tempers.

Of his four daughters, the only one he'd ever truly understood was Thea. She did not resort to tears at the slightest harsh word. Nor did she sulk for days and pout endlessly. Where Margareth, Andrea and Marie ran to their nurse or their mother, Thea had always stood up to Lord Bellamy, even when it meant she would be turned over his knee. Of his daughters, only Thea did not fear him, and because of that, Roger of Bellamy respected her.

Once he had made the hasty decision to send Marie home, Lord Bellamy would not relent on seeing her sent packing. The next morning, early, all of Marie's trunks were loaded onto a packhorse. She and her maid and her protector knight mounted their horses, and twenty men-at-arms of Bellamy's private regiment set off for Landais to return the girl to her mother. Marie cried and wailed upon her departure. Bellamy exhaled in relief to see her gone.

Chapter Eighteen

At the palace, Bellamy found the emperor in a foul mood, slumped before a model of a fortress on the Lombard border. Lothair invited Hawk to speculate on the prospect of laying siege to such an impregnable fortress, which the emperor had spent a fortune upon constructing.

While breakfast grew cold, the Saxon circled the model, pointing out each and every one of the castle's many and costly flaws. The two-brick, sand-filled curtain wall would be shattered by readily available battering rams, to say nothing of what Roderick's screw-driven trebuchet could do.

The four towers were so high even the strongest archer could not be effective. Because of this, he brought out a weapon neither Lord Bellamy nor the emperor had ever seen before.

"This is a copy I had made from a Swiss design. It's a crossbow that makes our longbows utterly useless."

To prove his point, the Saxon ordered all the doors between the dining hall and the palace wall opened and everyone between to stand aside. Then, he raised the strange wooden contraption to his shoulder, sighted it and released a mechanism that shot an arrow clear across the emperor's dining room and drove the shaft completely through a plastered wall six rooms away.

The sound of the impact cracked like thunder.

The emperor and Bellamy were stunned.

"I acquired a crude version of this arbalest on my way home after Montigney," Emory said, with a quiet menace that made the hackles rise on Bellamy's neck. "Last winter I had time to make modifications to it and had my armorer build them. Every able-bodied man in my fief is adept in its usage. You will notice the time it takes me to reload. As I speak, I am ready to fire again. Not only that, my emperor, this weapon can be braced on a wall and fired indefinitely, and its accuracy is twice that of a longbow.

"The arrows pierce any kind of chain mail used. Which means a hauberk is simply not enough for a man to wear into battle. As a simple hunting weapon alone, it is without question, the most valuable new tool I've ever come across. As a stationary weapon, one man well positioned can pick off hundreds of adversaries."

"Let me see that." Lothair put out his hands to admire the new weapon.

"Mind the trigger, here." Roderick passed it over for the emperor to inspect, then turned back to the scale model and went on at length, finding other faults with the complex.

"What next?" Lothair grumbled. Warfare always seemed to outstretch his imagination. The strength of his army never quite matched that of his brothers'. "Let's talk of other things. Do you find Lady Terese winsome, Roderick?"

"She is fair," he answered bluntly, and sat to eat, not caring that the eggs were cold.

"Well, that's more than you had to say about Diane." The king set aside the crossbow. "I want to see a demonstration of this great arbalest you spoke of. Bellamy, you have excellent hunting near your estates, don't you?"

"The game is plentiful."

"I say we adjourn to the countryside. I want Hawk's opinion of the fortification I commissioned upriver from you."

"I have no interest in seeing Auvergne. I am well aware of the defense works in place at Toulouse, none of which are suited to heavily wooded northern country."

"I rarely go to Auvergne," Lord Bellamy replied. "The king refers to my wife's estate in Picardy. It is there we make our home. The hunting is superb."

"I was not aware you resided that far north," Roderick stated, surprised at that information.

"My wife has always preferred her own estate to the hectic pace of court. I find it advantageous. My children grew up unspoiled and industrious on country life, and to that I credit my wife's common sense."

"Picardy, you say," Roderick said consideringly. "Great hunting there," Lothair insisted. "We will go, Roderick, and while you are there you must take a good look at the three daughters of my chancellor. I wouldn't want to be accused of bias, but should you choose the eldest of the unmarried ones, I will add ten thousand gold crowns and the duchy of Lorraine to her dowry."

"My liege," Bellamy sputtered. "I am not a poor man."

"Only a reluctant one. I know you, Roger. Roderick here shies from taking a bride from a house so closely aligned to mine, and you are the most possessive and selfish of fathers. Your daughters will wither into old maids before you part with them. Your eldest girl was almost twenty before you approved the marriage to Cavell . . . long past the age when good weddings are made."

"There has been no rush to wed any of them, m'lord." Roger replied, a tinge of insult in his tone. "We have had our reasons for keeping our daughters to home."

"I don't question your reasons." Lothair smiled. "I only offer incentive. Give it a thought, Roderick. You could use the gold. I will double it if you make the match within the month."

"Your Majesty," Lord Bellamy said stiffly. "My daughters are not at auction."

"No one said they were." The emperor laughed. "You'd get more than forty thousand if they were. Indeed, they'd bring their weight in diamonds and rare African gold. Do not take insult by my sponsorship. I've known your family all my years. My offer is to Roderick, to sway his mind. Though he's come to find a bride, he's obviously spoiled since last he came to court. Nothing here appeals to him."

"Should I accept the invitation to hunt in Picardy, I will take your offer under consideration, my liege."

"Oh, you will go to Picardy quite soon, I think." Lothair added. "I demand a test of your weapons against my defenses. I am certain Longervais is worthy of challenge. Sir Cavell is my vassal there, a close friend of Lord Bellamy's. Go there, Roderick. Imagine the worst scenario, a siege of the greatest dimension, and project for me what force I need inside to hold the defense."

Roderick was forced to accept. Inspection of the fortress at Longervais, indeed. It was Lord Bellamy's three unmarried daughters the king wanted inspected.

In private, later, as the emperor and Roderick partook of the warm mineral springs of Lothair's bath, the emperor said, "You know, Roderick, I could order you to marry one of Bellamy's daughters."

"And you may order the sun not to rise tomorrow," Roderick responded. "You can order anything, sire. The question is, can you implement it? My life is fraught enough with troubles, without the encumbrance of a woman whose loyalties are questionable, as any daughter's would be who comes from Bellamy's house. He is your man completely, as would be any of the retainers that came with his daughter to my service.

"I also understand your chancellor's daughters are not adventuresome. My fief is far, and we won't attend court frequently. I have little desire to be encumbered by an unhappy girl clinging to her mother's skirts."

"You could well afford to stay a year, or two until your bride adjusts to marriage. Personally, I have great need of you until this treaty at Verdun is finalized."

"My people also need me, sire. I beg to remind you, Your Majesty, that after my defeat at Montigney, you granted me a lifetime dispensation from your service."

The emperor cleared his throat and stirred the mineral water. "Well, that is true enough. I did relinquish all claim upon you. At the time, Roderick, I feared you would not live through the week, much less survive the journey you were bound and determined to make to die at home in Emory."

A wry light gleamed in Roderick's eyes. "Do you regret that I did not die as all planned, my lord?"

Lothair shook his head and smiled. "Nay, Roderick. I have never prayed so earnestly in my own behalf as I did for your soul and continued life after Montigney. It has haunted me long after the deed was done. To my sorrow, Anne was a faithless bitch. God has yet to give the grace to forgive her."

Roderick swung his massive shoulders toward the open arches and stared into the emperor's garden, where a full summer's high wealth of flowers brought peace and beauty to the palace at Aachen, which Charlemagne had built. His hatred for Anne of Aachen no longer ate at his soul. Thea had shown him what love and loyalty truly was.

"Your Majesty, I bear no ill against Anne. The past is dead issue. But I do remind you that I am no longer part of your army, and you are not at war. Charles and Louis are both much weaker than you. If you tend your defenses, you won't have to worry about their encroachment. The best offense..."

"I know, I know." Lothair interrupted him with a dismissive wave of his hand. "You quibble. I invited you to my bath to discuss a bride. One woman is the same as the other."

"If that is the case, why have you put a bounty on Lord Bellamy's eldest unmarried girl?"

The king considered the question at length, studying Roderick patiently. "Suffice it to say, I have my reasons."

"Then why is she not here to court?"

"Althealine of Auvergne has not been to court for several years. Nay, none of Bellamy's daughters have come, except the one he sent back home this morning. Lady Marie's appearances were limited. I suspect the truth is, my chancellor hoards his daughters because he would not have them courtesans. Then, the girls have probably inherited their mother's spirit to some degree. Lady Lilla finds my court exasperating at best. She is a beautiful woman, exceedingly so, who prefers not to compete for the favors of a king or his ministers."

"Lord Bellamy has been blessed, if that is the case."

"Oh, it is a blessing, make no mistake of that, Roderick. Bellamy women don't mix in politics. Which is why I want you married to one of them. I can think of many houses a link to would cause both you and I to lay awake at night, wondering what plot was being hatched against us. A ruler should have someone he can trust completely, should he not?"

"So he should," Roderick agreed, without adding that the mythically beautiful daughters of Lord Bellamy would not receive one whit of his attention. No matter how high the bounty Lothair placed upon their heads.

"Let us leave the bath. Roderick, I have someone I want you to meet." The king reached for a length of Turkish toweling as he climbed out of the bath.

"Not another simpering maid." Roderick clambered out and accepted a towel from the bath attendant.

"No," the king replied conspiratorially. "I think you'll find Eric much more compelling and appealing than a winsome lady's smile."

* * *

The trunk had arrived in the forenoon. Thea did not know of it until she returned from her ride.

"Andrea sent you a gift, dear." Lilla opened the lid, and inside were no fewer than ten dresses of the finest quality.

"How thoughtful of her." Thea knelt and fingered the garments. The exquisite fabrics and designs were without question lovely, but not nearly as nice as those given her by Herewald the Walker. "But she will soon have her baby."

"Yes, but babies change a girl's shape forever, dear. Andrea will not be able to wear a single one of these gowns again."

"You are saying she's gained weight."

Lilla laughed. "Drea has never been keen for fresh air and frequent exercise. I doubt she'll regain the waist needed for any of these dresses."

Thea held a gown to her shoulders and turned to the oval mirror in her mother's room. "These are much too fine for me."

"You will need every one of them."

"These are court dresses. Why should I need them?" Thea stopped herself from saying any more, and turned from Lilla's questioning gaze very quickly. "Has there been word from Papa?"

"There is always word from your father." Lilla tapped her nails against the armrest of her chair, wondering how much she should tell Thea. Roger's letter was on her lap, where Thea could not see it. They were to prepare for company within the week, and a hasty wedding soon after. Lord Bellamy's words were terse and brief. The most compelling statement within the rolled parchment was *By His Majesty's Order.* It was enough to make Lilla's blood run cold.

"He'll be home soon. Judging from Marie's misery and the tone of his letter, you will be forced to attend court whether you want to or not, Thea."

"Ohhhh!" Thea groaned and turned around, looking at her *maman* with baleful eyes. "I would not enjoy it any more than Marie did, *Maman.*"

"It is a duty. Would you defy your father, as well as the emperor?" Lilla noted her daughter's guarded expression.

"No, I will do what I have to do, but I truly have no interest in going. At least with these clothes from Andrea the expense of a wardrobe is unnecessary." Her mother's seamstresses had made certain she lacked nothing. Thea preferred pale colors and shunned having anything made in wool of any sort, fine or not.

"Thea." Lilla smiled at her.

"Yes, *Maman.*"

"Tell me about it."

Thea folded Andrea's gown and returned it to the trunk. "I can't. It is best that I forget."

"I don't think you'll be able to do that until you bring it all out in the open. Did you leave something behind that you cannot bear living without? You are a ghost of yourself."

"I've changed, that is all, *Maman.*"

"We all changed over this. Change is not what I see in your eyes. I see hurt and pain and sorrow. Perhaps forgetting is not the thing you need to do."

"I'll never be able to forget the past, *Maman.*"

"Do you love him?"

"Who?"

"The man whose baby you bear."

"Maman!"

"My darling, you may think I am simpleminded, but there are certain things a woman my age can see. Even as thin as you are, it is obvious."

Lilla had never seen any of her children's eyes look as haunted as Thea's did then. That was confirmation enough, and dreadful for a mother such as Lilla to see.

"I pray you, do not press me. I cannot talk of it."

That was all Thea said. Then, in her inimitable way, she turned and went out doors, where sunshine and flowers could surround her.

Lilla stood. The deepest sigh she'd ever felt rose and came again. She had changed her mind about Thea. When Lord Bellamy returned, she would speak to him regarding their second daughter.

For Thea needed a husband now. She needed to start her life over again. Not that the missing year would ever be erased or forgotten. Lilla wisely knew that would never be the case for Thea. Yet Thea needed to be more than just a loving daughter and a dutiful sister.

What Thea would not say was what Lilla feared the most. Somehow, during her daughter's captivity, she had learned to love the Viking. As farfetched as that might be, Lilla saw too many confirming signs.

What her daughter needed most now was a strong husband who would wipe all traces of the Viking from Thea's mind. Even if she hated the marriage, it would occupy her, fill her days and give her a purpose in life again.

Love might never come to Thea again. Yet Lilla knew the depth of Thea's obedient nature. If her father brought forth a man of his choosing, one who would accept Thea as she was, bearing another man's child, Thea would marry to satisfy her father's wishes.

With that in mind, Lilla opened Roger's letter again.

My dearest Lilla,
Our house is ordered merged with Emory. I have decided Marie would be the suitable match for her compliant nature. The king accompanies me to Landais. We will arrive within a fortnight. See that all preparations are made and Marie advised. Wedding will follow our arrival.

By His Majesty's command, Roger

Lilla formed her own thoughts on the matter. She burned the letter, then rose, gathered a light shawl around her shoulders and went downstairs to assemble her staff and begin the preparations.

One sunny afternoon a week later, Marie saw Thea canter across the drive, and dropped her stitchery to run across the courtyard steps, waving. Immediately Thea drew in the reins on the big dappled roan. "Where are you going, Thea?"

"Up into the forest to pick mushrooms for the gravies. Do you want to come? It is a pleasant day."

Marie touched the ribbons dangling from the gelding's bridle. She looked wistfully toward the gates. "You spend a lot of time riding," she said, with a trace of envy.

"You spend too much time inside. Come, get up behind me, and we'll ride like we used to," Thea offered.

"You would not mind?"

"No, of course not, silly. I would love to have you come along. It would be like before."

Marie hesitated, watching Thea skillfully handle the restive horse. It was not Victory, but then, Victory had been one of a kind. "I had best not."

Thea took her sister's refusal as she always did now. Neither chiding Marie for her lack of courage, nor giving in to the fearful look in her sister's eyes that implored her not to go.

"Well, then, I'll be back soon."

"We could play a game of draughts if you'd stay."

"I'd rather ride."

"Thea—" Marie started to say something, then stopped herself. "Do be careful, will you?"

"Of course, Marie. I'll be back in an hour or so." With those words, Thea galloped off, her skirts flying around her ankles and knees.

"Ach!" Old Joclyn came outdoors to see what was going on between her girls. "There she goes again!" Marie looked to their old nurse and saw the scowl knitting her brow, the twist of her mouth. "At least you have sense to stay to home. Not that one."

Feeling more than just a twinge of envy for Thea's boldness, Marie returned to the hall where her mother was instructing three servants. Marie waited until Lilla had finished giving her directions.

"Where did Thea go, Marie?" Lilla asked.

"Up to the woods to pick mushrooms," Marie said.

"You should have gone. The ride would have put some color in your cheeks."

"Thea prefers to be alone when she rides, *Maman*," Marie answered truthfully. "Why do you let her ride unescorted, when Margareth and I cannot leave the keep without ten men to guard us?"

"Now, Marie, that is not true. Even if it was, Thea deserves her privacy. She is older than you and Margie."

"Is it because she isn't a virgin anymore that she may come and go unprotected?"

"Marie, I'll not have you speak that way. You were right in the first place. Thea prefers to ride alone. I respect her need for solitude. Come, there is work to do."

"Are we expecting company? You have certainly put the servants to great lengths, as if preparing for a siege of guests."

"Does it look that way? Your father returns soon."

"Father is only one person. The cooks are making enough food to feed an army."

"Well, he does come with all his men-at-arms. Who is to say? I like to be prepared."

"I'd like for you to tell me what is really afoot."

Lilla smiled and tapped Marie's nose with a teasing finger. "Remember what is said about curiosity, darling. Now, run out to the garden and bring me in a bushel of flowers to brighten this hall."

Which was all the information Lilla was willing to give Marie or Margareth . . . or Thea, for that matter.

* * *

Garth acquitted himself as almost as fine a mount as Victory. A little older, the gelding liked to run. Thea let him have his head. Joclyn would have been scandalized to see Thea's hems fly around her knees, but that was no different from the way it had always been.

Thea raced past the gristmill and the brook, then turned from the paved road, galloping uphill to the crest that over-looked Longervais Keep.

From the hilltop, the renovations at Longervais were most impressive. Thea rode the ridge, eyeing the once familiar landmark.

The changes in Longervais were most obvious from this southerly approach. Four new towers with conical roofs rose skyward from the massive wall encasing the square keep. A deep earthen embankment had been cut below the founda-tions. A motte fronted that glacis of lowered earth. Thea thought it somewhat reminiscent of Roderick's plan.

A cluster of men and horses gathered at the river. The fa-miliar sight of soldiers didn't alarm Thea. Longervais was the seat of power in the district. The king kept part of his army quartered there.

Thea drew Garth to a halt, raising her hand to shade her eyes, scanning the empty meadow and the collection of men.

"Papa's here!" Thea recognized her father's banners and, squinting hard, she said aloud, "There are Royce and Ja-son!"

Sighting her brothers lifted Thea's spirits. She had not seen either since she returned home. Turning Garth toward the mounted men, Thea galloped across the scarred and pitted field, her scarf and skirts flying.

Lord Bellamy saw her coming and reined in his horse, waving, shouting to her. Thea waved back, digging her heels deeper into Garth's sides.

From his vantage point below the motte bank, Roderick saw the newcomer charge recklessly onto the practice field they had just drained for this test. Alarmed, narrowing his eyes, he saw the rider was a woman.

On the ramparts of Longervais, a clap of thunder sounded in a cloudless sky. Roderick spun his horse around, digging his spurs into the animal's sides, knowing he was the only man close enough to prevent a tragedy. Spurring his horse to a full gallop, Roderick charged the woman on the roan.

He cut across the soggy meadow, intercepting her horse. As he threw himself off his own steed, rolling the woman from her mount to the ground, he recognized her.

He threw his body over hers, covering her completely as the barrage of airborne weapons imploded. Six successive balls of Greek fire erupted over every quadrant of the drenched field.

Thea screamed as she hit the ground. She screamed again, hearing ungodly thunder. Brimstone and fire rained down from the cloudless sky all around her. Her mount screamed in terror and galloped away.

The earth trembled and shook, belching smoke into the air. Dirt, mud and burning grass flew in every direction. A wall of burning water swept up the sodden field. Thea hid her face in the man's chest that covered her.

Clumps of ash and burning sulfur rained heavily on Roderick's back as he smothered Thea beneath his arms and chest. Her screams died of fright.

Neither of them moved until the earth ceased shaking. Little piles of fire sizzled on the water soaked earth.

"Are we dead?" she whispered, clinging to the man, afraid to open her eyes. Her ears rang with thunder echoing in them. She looked up at his blackened, muddy face and gasped, "Roderick!"

"What the hell are you doing here?" Roderick shouted.

"What are you doing here?" Thea yelled right back.

"Thea! My God, Thea!" Lord Bellamy shouted.

The whole meadow surged with men, sloshing through the fiery mud to where Roderick had flattened Thea beneath him. The first to arrive were her father and brothers.

They leaped from their horses as Roderick wiped the mud from his face and eased onto his hip.

"My God, Emory! Thea! Thea, darling, are you well?"

With the thunder still ringing in her ears, Thea couldn't hear the question. But she had sense enough to let go of Roderick of Emory as her father's knee dropped to the earth beside them. He knelt in the mud, afraid to touch the smoldering leather hauberk protecting Roderick's back. A sudden wash of tears streaked from Roger Bellamy's eyes.

"I think I'm only shaken up, Papa." Thea pushed at Roderick's shoulders to dislodge him. Dirt, ash and mud rained off his shoulders and head, pelting Thea where she lay pinned beneath him in the mud.

"Your father?" Roderick whispered in Saxon, his head dropping to Thea's shoulder.

"Yes. Get up, please." Thea was barely whispering. She couldn't move. For that matter, Roderick couldn't either.

There were plenty of men to help her up off the ground. No sooner did Roderick roll off her body than she was swept into Lord Bellamy's arms.

The duke of Auvergne's two sons, Royce and Jason, along with Gregory of Merrault and Hugh of Cavell, stood ready to take the woman into their arms if at any moment her father should weaken.

Her father. Roderick gulped. The ashen-faced Michael of Lozere reached a gloved hand to Roderick, assisting him to his feet. "That was bloody close," Michael said, brushing mud and muck off his liege lord's back.

Recovered somewhat, Bellamy's voice roared a shout. "Thea, for the love of God, what are you doing here?" Now that the fright was over, he gave in to a father's ranting.

During the tense moments that followed, Roderick stood back from the emotional family, brushing dirt away, trying to compose himself. Ironically, only one thought registered: *How many minutes did he have to make his peace with God?*

The maid's two brothers were shaken worse than their father. Minutes passed before anything remotely resembling calm returned to the sodden field. Bellamy composed himself first, rounding on Roderick.

"Sir, I am indebted to you. You risked your life charging into that barrage to save my daughter. Are you all right? I never thought to put a watch to that end of the meadow before we fired the weapons."

"Nor did I," Roderick admitted ruefully. He had taken Thea down hard, and his concern was for her. He drew Thea's hand from Sir Royce's and touched her filthy face, wiping away a smudge of dirt. "Forgive me for my rough unseating of you, m'lady."

"Are you sure you're all right?" her elder brother asked.

"A little shaken is all." Thea thanked God the accident provided reason for the trembling in her limbs. She still could scarcely distinguish a word spoken and, because she did not want to look at Roderick, she wasn't at all certain what his words had been. Mostly, she wanted to stay right where she was, in Royce's protective embrace.

"Oh, sweet Jesu, Thea," Royce murmured, and refused to relinquish her to anyone else. He turned his face down into her dark hair and simply held her crushed against him as tears overfilled his eyes. "Must you always have us in utter fear and desperation for your life?"

Roderick harkened to the brother's anguished croak. He noticed Thea had difficulty following Sir Royce's tender scolding.

"I'm fine," she stubbornly insisted.

"What about me?" the youngest Bellamy demanded in an injured voice. Roderick saw that until the boy moved right in front of her, Thea did not realize he was there. She was not all right.

Once she saw the boy, she smiled bravely.

"Oh, Jason, look at you!" Thea cried. No longer a thin-boned, rangy boy, Jason Bellamy surpassed her height and had sprouted shoulders packed with a man's muscle.

"Jason?" Thea could not believe her eyes. "You look just like Oncle Augustine."

"Ignore the puppy!" Royce growled teasingly.

Forgotten were all the observers as Thea put out her arm and swung it round her little brother's neck. If she hadn't been shaken before, she was now. Crying, she was kissed by both, and returned their greetings fervently.

Roderick stepped farther back from this emotional reunion and found himself face-to-face with Gregory of Merrault. The champion's face contorted thunderously, his black brows beetled with rage. "Did you harm one hair on Thea's head, unseating her, I'll kill you, Emory."

Here was another and much more dangerous enemy, Roderick thought.

"Pardon," Roderick said in a soft, menacing voice that drew no one's attention his way, but held Merrault frozen before him. "I believe I just saved the woman's life, Merrault. Any damage done her in the effort will surely be excused by the fact she still lives and breathes."

"And leave it to you to put her on the ground and yourself between her thighs. Keep away from her, Emory. I intend to make Thea mine."

Their confrontation ended abruptly when Lord Bellamy got hold of his errant daughter and drew her toward the knights. "Your Grace, may I present my daughter Althealine to you. I am indebted to you once again. Thea, this is the duke of Emory, Sir Roderick."

No one thought it strange at all that Thea did not once raise her eyes upward to look Roderick in the face. Her color had risen alarmingly, and the need for introductions and other pleasantries came to an abrupt halt.

"What are you doing riding alone?" her father demanded peevishly. His tone wasn't tempered by relief, but showed a father's deep concern for a daughter's serious lack of sense. Roderick stood idle as Bellamy caught hold of Thea's chin, turned her face toward his and repeated his question, more heatedly.

" 'Twas was a peaceful day till just now. What was that that flew at me? What are you doing here, Papa?"

"Testing the defenses." Lord Bellamy scowled and asked for the third time, "Why are you riding without an escort?"

"Escort, Papa? There's no horse in the stable that can keep up with Garth." Thea answered. "Oh, don't scold me, Papa. Look, here is Royce, as pale as a ghost, and Jason has lost all his courage completely. Did you think I'd be killed by your silly toys of war?"

"You could very well have been maimed. Reckless girl!" Lord Bellamy chided. "Fetch her horse, Matthew. If you weren't as white as a sheet, daughter, I'd take a strap to you for your foolishness. Could you not see that we were about the business of war?"

"What I saw was my brothers, whom I had not seen in a very long time, Papa! Perhaps if you'd stopped by the manor before you came to play your games, I'd have gone the other way when I went to pick mushrooms for supper."

Thea removed herself from Bellamy's strong hold and snatched up her basket. It was a bit the worse for wear. She put two fingers to her mouth and whistled loudly, then cast a sideways glance at Roderick. He stood solemn-faced, thinking her father foolish for allowing her snippy response.

Her horse came snorting and blowing on command, still in a fury. A squire tried to catch his reins, and the horse reared at him threateningly.

"Have a care, Matthew, and let me calm my horse ere he kills you." Thea shooed the squire out of her way. The huge beast calmed for her, though he was skittish and wild-eyed. She had a serious limp in her own gait. She tested his temper greatly, Roderick thought. He waved to Michael to bring his horse and brazenly stepped into the melee, staking his claim.

"You have a reckless daughter, m'lord Bellamy." Without preamble, Roderick swept Thea into his arms and put her on his own mount's back.

"You do not know the half of it," Bellamy complained.

"I should like to hear the other half," Roderick charged as he took the reins from Michael and passed them up to Thea. "Your mount seems upset, m'lady. You will take mine. It is the least we can do."

"Jason, see your sister home, and for the love of God, tell your *maman* to keep Thea out of harm's way," Lord Bellamy commanded in a frustrated voice. She looked back once to take Garth's reins and lead him along. Her brother and another squire took control of her, and they rode off the meadow, much to Lord Bellamy's relief. He turned back to Roderick, needing to thank him for his courageous rescue.

"It was nothing," Roderick said modestly. "I was closest and knew what was coming."

"Aye." Lord Bellamy accepted the knight's modesty. "Still, it could have cost my daughter her life. I am indebted to you."

"Althealine," Roderick murmured. "A most unusual name."

Bellamy fell into step beside the Saxon, who had been joined by his vassal, Michael of Lozere. "Aye, the result of an unsettled argument many years ago. I had wanted the name Caroline. My wife preferred Althea. We compromised. She is the second oldest of the girls. Nineteen this coming Epiphany, I believe."

"She is betrothed?" Roderick had to ask, seeking confirmation of Merrault's claim, though it more than disturbed him to find they were at odds once again over a woman. He knew in his heart that he would kill Merrault before allowing the Frank to marry Thea.

"Nay. Suggestions have been made, and all roundly refused. There is a story to that, but I'd not discuss it here. Suffice it to say you will find Marie as appealing, and infinitely more biddable."

"Marie." Roderick repeated the name he'd heard mentioned so many times to him of late. His eyes sought Michael. His vassal's expression said without words, *We're in deep trouble here.*

"Let us see to the rest of this business, then call it a day," Lord Bellamy said with his usual tireless energy.

Roderick saw no point in arguing. Not now. He had to think on this.

Chapter Nineteen

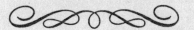

Thea couldn't avoid Joclyn's scolding. The woman took one look at Thea's disheveled appearance and had a fit. Jason placed his sister in the old nurse's care, glad to be done with her. He itched to return to Longervais and the tests of the Hawk's Greek fire. This was the closest Jason had come to a battle.

"What happened to you?" Marie gasped as Thea hurried indoors.

"Papa's come with a regiment of the king's knights. I must warn *Maman.*"

Immediately, Thea gave the news that Lord Bellamy would soon be home. Landais Manor might be spotless, but Thea ordered it cleaned again, quickly. Panic struck her in the kitchens, because Thea saw nowhere near enough meat cooking to feed the men she knew were coming.

They would arrive before sundown. Thea started to join the frenzy of work in the kitchens. Her mother wouldn't hear of that. Lilla ordered Marie and Margareth to see to the spare chambers. Thea was sent to bathe and change.

"Oh dear, suppose it is the emperor!" Thea worried aloud, with Joclyn dogging her heels.

"Mind your tongue. Would they not give us warning if that were so?"

"Who is to say? I did not see him, but it would be just like the man to be there in the thick of it, firing the arbalests himself!'' Thea groaned on the last step up the stairs. Her backside smarted righteously. The unpleasant pain worried her much less than Roderick's presence did. "They were trying out the Greek fire that Saxon has made."

"What was that?" Joclyn demanded.

"Nothing!" Thea slapped her hand over her mouth and told herself to shut up. Lord, what was she going to do?

"Let's get you out of that muddy dress. Just look at you! Thea, I am going to strangle you with my bare hands if you don't use the sense God gave you."

"Joclyn, just see to the water, please. I can undress myself. I am not a child. Go help Mother. She must be beside herself."

"If you think to convince me you are not a child, then put your hair up. 'Tis time you did."

"Go, Joclyn. Let me be. My hair is fine the way it is." Mutinously she thought, *Roderick likes it this way.* The old nurse grunted, but Thea's will was stronger than hers. "If you really want to serve me, go and fetch me a glass of ale. I could use one."

"And where did you pick up the habit of drinking ale? A lady drinks wine, and only in moderation."

"Oh, Joclyn!" Thea scolded right back at her. "Do not tell me what a lady does. *Maman* drinks it, too!"

Joclyn acted scandalized. "Well, I never!"

"'Tis true."

"My ladies do no such a thing!"

"Just send for it." Thea countered. Joclyn was too incensed to bring her the drink, but another servant did. The ale definitely helped calm Thea's nerves. She hurried out of her bath, and was nearly dressed when the sounds of many riders entering the gates announced her father's arrival.

"Are you ready, Thea? Papa's here!" Marie came dressed in a beautiful gown that clung to her curves from shoulder to hips. It was a splendid shade of deepest blue, and over that a mantle of snow-white brocade swept her shoulders

and fell in double streamers down her sides. A brooch of
fiery opals held the mantle pinned in place.

"Almost." Thea struggled with her own mantle, setting
it straight. "I look hideous in this color. God, the emperor!"

"I looked through the gallery and didn't see him. Perhaps he stayed to Sir Hugh's."

"That would be a blessing." Thea hastily crossed herself. She would need all the grace God could give her to get
through this evening.

Marie deliberately didn't tell Thea that the knight Michael of Lozere rode into their courtyard right behind their
father. No, Marie kept every scrap of information about the
man she wanted for herself from her sisters. Marie would
watch her sisters like a hawk tonight. Marie wanted to be
certain it was she who was first introduced to the tall, dark
and handsome Saxon.

If he hadn't come to Landais seeking a wife, he was about
to find out he'd gained one.

"If you don't hurry, Margareth will have all the men
snatched up and wound about her conniving fingers. We
won't even have a partner to the table, Thea."

"I think I'll just stay to my room. The dress—Marie, tell
me, do I look awful?"

"Heavens, no! How could you? You look...oh, drat it,
Thea, you look beautiful as always. I don't stand a chance
with you back home."

"I thought your heart was set on Albert." The resounding affirmation Thea expected did not come from Marie's
lips. "Is there someone else, Marie? You were very quiet
about your affairs at court."

"I had no affairs!" Marie declared, her face coloring pink
instantly. "But I did see someone I liked."

"Better than Albert?"

"Yes. Much better!"

"And this person of interest, is he here?"

"Well . . ." Marie drawled, a secret smile curving her lips into shy beauty. "He is."

"Tell me. What does he look like? His name?" Thea demanded, almost ready to panic if Marie should be infatuated by Roderick of Emory.

"His hair is black and wavy. He's tall, with a face that is a wonder. I know he is a knight who's proven his courage time and time again. Yet what I learned about him was not all good. He has a reputation with the ladies, and I was certain my accidental meeting with him was what caused Papa to send me home so suddenly. We were not introduced, but we will be tonight."

Relief flooded Thea. "Come, we'll go down together. Though it is foolish for either of us to bother, if Margareth beat us to it. What is she wearing?"

"That rose that makes her look nine-and-ten. I could snatch it from her."

"And me in summer yellows. We'll be a bouquet. Let's not get stung!" Thea laughed. "Come, I cannot wait to see Royce any longer, nor Jason, and I would like a hug from Gregory. I was not all that kind to him when he was here last week, nor the time before that, either," Thea admitted ruefully. Lord Merrault had graciously granted her time, two weeks, to think his proposal over. She wouldn't accept it, but she wanted no hard feelings between them, either.

"Were I in your shoes," Marie advised slyly, "I would seek more than a hug, sister."

The day had been a long one. Roderick had resigned himself to the obligation of accompanying the chancellor to Landais. Lothair had commanded Roderick do so, though the emperor declined the additional ride himself.

Roderick had done all he could to avoid it, pleading justifiable soreness and fatigue, but to no avail. There was a saying about being between the devil and the deep blue sea that Roderick had never quite gotten the gist of . . . until that heart-stopping moment when he realized *his Thea* was the duke of Auvergne's treasured Althealine.

In Bellamy's possession as they rode to Landais was the emperor's betrothal contract between Roderick and Bellamy's third daughter, Marie. Lothair had insisted again and again on Althealine, but Bellamy had stood firm against him. It hadn't made any difference to Roderick at the time.

More fool he.

His distrust of the emperor and his chancellor had increased tenfold this afternoon. That damned Merrault made Hawk all the more wary. Today's revelations added more fuel to Roderick's unease. Something more remained afoot, in crafty Lothair's mind.

Lord Bellamy cast many speculative looks toward Roderick this afternoon. Merrault's hostility doubled. Roderick's disquiet mounted. How much did the sly chancellor know? Hawk knew he could trust Bellamy only as far as he could throw him. The feeling was mutual.

Merrault he trusted not at all.

They came at last to Bellamy's manor. Of most curious construction, Landais was a home first, not a defense. It rambled within a short curtain wall, spreading wings in four directions. A turret here, a dormer there, a colonnade between, a hodgepodge of additions that had no cohesive style or form to it.

The chancellor had said it was his wife's childhood home. The original parts of it had been constructed by her ancestor, the Roman emperor Aurelian, when he was proconsul of Gaul. It was a sight for sore eyes, yet boasted a charm to it that few houses could.

As they passed the gates, formal gardens greeted Hawk's eyes. The smell of roses hung in the summery air. Fatigued, Roderick longed for a bath, a meal and a bed. He judged that before this night was over, all hell would break out. His odds of living long enough to enjoy any of his last wishes were between slim and none.

Unsaddling his mount, Roderick looked cautiously to the emperor's guard that always surrounded him. Escaping Lothair's henchmen would not be an easy task. Tonight, it would be impossible.

"We can hope the lord's ale is strong." Michael flashed his smile, speaking in their private Saxon language. "We were advised the hunting was good here, were we not?"

"Aye, so we were." Roderick spoke with a grimness that was contagious. He did not want to walk inside Bellamy's hall. He knew better than to imagine Lady Althealine of Auvergne being pliable.

No, Roderick felt he now knew what John the Baptist must have felt like each time Salome teased him, taking off another veil. His neck felt very vulnerable.

Because they saw to their own horses and the care given was good, Roderick and Michael were of the last to enter the hall. It was larger than Blackstone's.

This portion of the manor had clearly begun as the home of a prominent Roman official. The massive room was surrounded by Corinthian pillars supporting a high vaulted roof.

Directly behind it, an atrium opened onto gardens completely enclosed by additions to the house. Though a huge chandelier was filled with candles, the light was diffused, making the hall itself shadowy.

Three long trestles quartered the hall below the raised dais. A commotion at the base of the stairway to the right of the entrance caught Roderick's eye. He and Michael sidestepped the gathering.

The smell of good food hung in the heavy air. A bevy of servants ran hither and thither, dispensing foaming tankards. A pink-cheeked maid of good proportions handed both Roderick and Michael a mug and went on serving others, looking behind her frequently at the two handsome Saxons.

No one was standing on ceremony in Lord Bellamy's house. Apparently the lord had already invited his men to eat and drink. Most of Roderick's private escort were already doing that. Hawk knew now what a dog felt like on a leash.

The surge of Bellamy's vassals at the stairwell delayed Roderick from getting to a table to be served. He drained his tankard thirstily, viewing the commotion . . . and choked on the last swallow.

Throwing out his free hand to nudge Michael's shoulder, Roderick pointed to the stairs. Royce Bellamy swung a woman in his arms and twirled her around full circle, then lowered her into an embrace and kissed her.

"His wife?" Michael speculated.

Roderick knew better. "Thea," he managed over the ale lodged in his windpipe.

Michael squinted. Smoke from torches and candles made the shadows longer. His dark brows drew together. "We should take our leave, quietly, while we can."

Roderick inclined his head backward to indicate the now familiar guards that shambled after him. Two posted themselves and met his stare without so much as a blinking eye. There would be no leaving. "Did you have any hint of this?"

"Nay." Michael inclined his head toward the clutch of women circling Lord Bellamy. "There is the one I told you of seeing in the market. That is the Marie that escaped us . . . that Lord Bellamy would see you wed on the morrow."

Roderick groaned. "Make your peace with God, Michael. We'll not live to see the morrow."

Bellamy's women were of a similar size. The one with her hand laid on Lord Bellamy's arm was of middle age. A stately woman, beautiful and lovely, whose black hair flowed around her shoulders, unbound and unrestrained. A blaze of white at each temple set her apart from her daughters. The similarity between her beautiful face and Thea's was impossible to miss.

The other two were just as comely. One's heart-shaped face was as innocent and fresh as could be. She wore a rose gown that made the blush on her cheeks seem all the more brighter. A second, dressed in tones of blue, had black braids coiled about her head like a crown. Timid as a fawn, she stayed close to her mother, taking no part in the emotional exhibition involving Thea and the vassals and sons of Lord Bellamy.

"Behold, three unmarried daughters, my liege," Michael said in Saxon.

The apple-cheeked maid came again and swished her skirts before Roderick. Holding out his mug, Roderick said, "We are strangers to this house, wench. What are the names of the daughters of Lord Bellamy?"

"'Tis Thea you see being greeted yonder."

"And the shy one?" Michael asked, intrigued by the girl he'd seen at market in Aachen and scared half to death.

"Lady Marie. They are beauties, are they not?"

"Aye." Michael smiled and held his tankard out to be filled. "We had no idea Lord Bellamy had sired such beautiful daughters."

"Lord is a handsome man," Lolly said brightly. "But the girls favor their mother, Lady Lilla. I'd not be hoping for much if I were you, sir knights. Each of the ladies of this house will marry higher than simple vassal knights. A marriage to a duke is afoot. Margareth is the youngest, wearing rose, and do not be looking to her, for she's too innocent for rogues like you."

"Saucy girl!" Michael laughed at the maid's taunting words. She ambled off, her skirt twitching as she made the rounds, refilling other knights' tankards.

"Most interesting household," Michael observed, not knowing where to let his eyes wander next. The serving girls were nearly as beautiful as the lord's daughters, and doubtless more obtainable. "What do we now, my liege?"

"Have our supper while we can. We should not have long to discover the chancellor's purpose."

Roderick remained on his guard. Michael could not tell what he was thinking. He followed him to a crowded table of lesser vassals, where the shadows of a row of pillars allowed a measure of security.

"We are in grave danger, Hawk," Michael warned.

Roderick thought of that. It was all he had thought of since learning Thea's identity. She had given her word to never cause him harm. Would she hold to her vow when she learned Lothair's plan, that on the morrow Roderick was to wed her sister?

"Aye, we're at great risk," Roderick agreed. One glance around confirmed how sadly he and Michael were outnumbered.

"I'll watch your back," Michael promised.

"Then we will both be run through, as a hot knife passes through butter." As Roderick said as much, the family moved to their seats at the head table, flanking Lord Bellamy. Each of the daughters' admirers hovered about them. Several were close enough to the family to be invited to join them. Merrault was given an honored seat in the midst of the family. Only one of the girls flanked him—Thea.

Roderick accepted the moment of anonymity, knowing eventually Bellamy would remember the true purpose of this excursion to his wife's home.

Roderick burned the whole while he sat watching Thea's dark head bent in earnest conversation with Gregory of Merrault.

The meal progressed. Thea excused herself from the head table and slipped unnoticed outdoors when a troop of acrobats tumbled forward to entertain. Hardly anyone saw Thea leave. Roderick made certain no one but Michael of Lozere saw him follow her.

"Husband, we must speak in private," Lilla said immediately after she had excused Thea from the table.

Lord Bellamy reached for his food. "We have guests."

"Royce is capable of summoning more ale. The house runs itself smoothly, with you in attendance or without. Come to the garden, where I may address my concerns."

Roger waited until they had cleared the hall, having gained the privacy and silence of the courtyard garden. "Speak your mind, Lilla. What is it?"

"While you were absent, Lord Merrault came to visit. He asked Thea to marry him."

"That is great news, wife!"

"No, it isn't. She refused him just moments ago. He has left in a foul temper. Trouble brews there. Thea has become an obsession to him. And another thing, my lord husband—your decision to wed this Saxon lord to Marie troubles me greatly."

"Suffice it to say, it troubles me, as well. That is the way it will be. Margie is too young."

"Thea isn't. To my mind, she is the only choice."

"Thea! Have you lost your mind, woman?" Roger grasped Lilla's arm, drawing her between the pillars at the edge of the balustrade. "How can you suggest such a thing? For God's sake, Lilla, the duke would be within his rights to kill her when there is no blood on the bridal sheet."

"Not if we tell the man the truth. You could even make it worth his while for the loss of a maidenhead."

"Madame, it was you who informed me Thea would refuse all husbands. Did you not just say she's turned down Merrault? Now, you change your mind and argue the opposite. Lilla, desist from this insanity and leave me be. I've had enough of the bartering and begging that goes with arranging one marriage. It is settled and done. The wedding takes place tomorrow at noon at Longervais chapel. You have seen to the arrangements and informed Marie."

"No. I've done nothing of the kind. Nor will I give my consent to this match. Marie will not make that blond giant a good wife, and you well know it, Roger of Auvergne."

"Your consent is not a requirement, woman." Lord Bellamy stiffened, feeling a real battle beginning to surface.

"Did you not make your arrangements regarding Thea and couch them with your parents' agreement?"

"Aye, I did. Yet you have caught me unawares with this Saxon marriage. I cannot abide it, Roger. You know how Marie is. She would live in terror of the duke. I took a good look at him in the hall. Use your head, man."

"I have. He will not accept damaged goods. That, Lilla, is what Thea is."

"Are you implying that your Saxon war god is virgin, and so clean he could cast the first stone?"

Lord Bellamy ground his teeth. Lilla's stubborn expression proved how intractable she was going to be. There was not time to argue this. It was settled, the groom escorted by twenty of Emperor Lothair's most able men. Roger altered his stance and put a gentle hand to Lilla's chin, holding it firmly.

"Lilla, why should we argue? Between you and Thea, I was given no means to see her honor avenged. Now, I ask you, let me be. Do not torment me or make me scold you. I have duties within, the first being introducing the duke to Marie. Come, take my arm and give me your support. In time, we will find Thea a good husband. One who will accept her as she is. Now is Marie's time."

"I cannot stand by you on this. In the first place, the man has reason to show sympathies in Thea's direction. Was not his entire land ravaged by the Vikings? If you would be honest with the Saxon, you might discover there are other possibilities. Secondly, Thea would sympathize with his losses."

"Lilla!" Roger cut her tirade off sharply. "This marriage is a matter of state. Lothair wants the Emory tied permanently to Frankish soil. Which of your daughters will not leave your skirts, woman? Marie! Need I say any more?"

In the shadow of the yews, Roderick held his hand firmly over Thea's mouth, keeping her still and silent while he heard more of the private discussion between Lord and Lady Bellamy. He was doubly glad now he'd followed Thea outdoors and caught her unawares. The kiss of need and desire exchanged between them had stirred his blood. Hers, as well. It was a reckless thing to do. How reckless, he could not have guessed until their privacy was nearly invaded by the lady's parents.

But the parents' exchange gave new meaning to the dangerous position Roderick found himself in. True to her word, Thea had not revealed his identity. The parents blamed Vikings. A measure of relief filled him. It was short-lived, lasting only until the couple went back to the noisy hall.

Thea bit the hell out of his hand. Roderick tossed her across his shoulder and took her deep within the garden, far from overhearing ears and prying eyes. He could tell by the trembling in her struggling body that she was raging, ready to let her temper fly.

Forewarned was forearmed. At least Roderick could say he understood Lothair's plan, now. So the Franks sought to keep him bound by tying him to the apron strings of Lilla of Landais! Thea got a hand loose and pinched his stomach viciously.

"Be still, Thea." Roderick gave her a warning that she'd better heed, and moved farther from the hall. "We will talk, m'lady."

"Damn you, Roderick of Emory," Thea cursed the moment she could, and drove her fist into his middle. "You would marry my sister!"

"I have not married anyone!" Roderick hauled her against his body and kissed her into more compliant behavior. "Nor will I, if this is the plot of the king, to keep me bound to this land when I have my own that needs me far greater than France does. Be still and stop fighting me. What part do you play in this? How much have you told your father?"

"You bastard!" Thea broke loose from him and slapped his face resoundingly. "You deserve that, damn you. You deserve to be run through with a sword. You deserve to be hanged, drawn and quartered. Get away from me, Roderick of Emory. I detest you!''

Thea twisted free. "Thea, if you run from me, I will chase you down."

"*Vous êtes impossible!*" Thea cried. "Leave here at once!"

"I'm not a coward, Thea." His sapphire eyes shone when they met hers.

"Marie could recognize you."

"She hasn't looked at me yet."

"Marry my sister, and it will be your death you invoke." Thea fingered the handle of her Saracen blade.

Roderick glanced at it and smirked. "I see you have armed yourself. Is that the same little toy you used before?"

"You should know from experience how well I keep it honed to cut human flesh." He made her so angry, she could have kicked him. "I will cut your heart out if you dare marry my sister. Go away. Leave us alone."

She turned and fled back to the hall. Roderick's jaw set grimly. He sauntered after her. Their discussion was far from finished.

Chapter Twenty

Lord Bellamy wanted to crack together the heads of every female in his household. First, his wife had accosted and shocked him. Next, Thea had returned to his table in such high dudgeon that she ran Lord Merrault off. Appalled, Bellamy had watched helplessly as Thea's one hope for a respectable future stalked out of the hall.

But that wasn't the half of it.

Marie behaved absolutely deplorably. She witlessly fawned over her husband-to-be's vassal, that hellish rake Michael of Lozere. It took every scrap of Bellamy's control not to grab Marie by her braids and shake better sense into her.

The interminable meal finally ended, and Lilla blithely suggested they all walk in the garden. Roderick came forward to be presented to the ladies and took an immediate shine to Thea, offering her his arm on the stroll through the roses.

Bellamy simmered, incensed by Thea's reaction. A more unmalleable woman than she had yet to be born. She had to be half dragged through the walk, acting as if at any moment she were going unsheathe her Saracen blade and slice the Saxon to ribbons. Roger didn't doubt for a minute that the Saxon duke would enjoy the contest if she did. He never took his eyes off her. What a mess!

They returned to the hall and took seats at the head table. The tense evening continued while minstrels sang. Lilla kept nudging Roger, as if to say, "I told you so." Marie never once looked at Emory. She was all gaga for Lozere. All in all, it was very trying.

Lord Bellamy could not believe the solicitous attention Thea received from the Saxon. At court, women threw themselves before Roderick and never so much as raised the dust at his feet. The more attention the Saxon gave Thea, the blacker Lord Merrault's eyes turned, and the more he drank.

Finally, the ladies withdrew. Roger called for another round of ale at his table. If Roderick truly held an interest in Thea, the time to negotiate was now, before any other woman caught the Saxon's eye.

Knowing exactly what was coming, Roderick held his hand over his tankard, refusing any more of the strong household brew. He sat back, awaiting Bellamy's move.

"You'll not have more?"

"It's a strong brew."

"The way I like it. I use it to judge a man's character."

"Then, by all means, refill my glass, but refill yours, also."

"You're a sly one, Emory."

"I would disavow that." Roderick counted the men at the table, seeing how seriously he was outnumbered. His host raised a quieting hand to the musicians in the gallery, and they put away their instruments. Likewise, his lesser vassals began to withdraw. Soon, the hall emptied while the men at the high board continued to quietly consume their brews. Then, only Lord Bellamy, his sons Royce and Jason, Lord Merrault, Sir Michael and Lord Hawk remained.

"Well, have you nothing to say?" Bellamy inquired.

"It's been a delightful evening." Roderick lifted his tankard, mindful that in any negotiation the first to mention the prize most coveted was the man to lose.

"What think you of the emperor's renovations to Castle Longervais?"

"Is the best-fortified manor I have seen."

"Manor!" Bellamy huffed, clearing his throat.

"Yea," Roderick said in quiet understatement. "That's what it is. Principally built to house a family. Albeit a decidedly strong family, endowed with many men-at-arms. It would take a siege well. Should war ever come to this province, you should move your family there for safety."

"It would be a hard thing to move my Lilla from this old manor. I haven't gotten her to budge much out of it in two score and seven years. She would fight tooth and nail to defend it, and her babies, as well as her ancient and meddlesome mother and father."

"You are rich beyond any measure, to have such a woman."

"It has its benefits. Though I'd be a liar if I said our wills did not clash. She's a strong woman, my lady is."

"An admirable woman. She manages a good house. I was impressed to see a troop of fifty men arrive at suppertime and find food for all with so little warning."

Lord Bellamy chuckled, "She had some warning. I have tried to school my sons in the value of finding a wife with the mettle to accept any challenge. Royce defies me to find such for him. When he's a little older, I'll look about, with my wife's virtues in mind. Between you and I, Hawk, I'd like to know what you will tell the king, now that you've seen the three daughters I have."

"Well, I shall certainly tell him you are a lucky man, for your daughters are very like your wife, indeed."

Bellamy toyed with his tankard, his green eyes hard as iron on Roderick's blue. "I could not but notice that you took a shine to a different daughter than the one on which we had agreed."

"Did I?" Roderick blinked guilelessly.

"Admit it, man, you find Thea charming."

"Was it that evident?"

"Blast it, man! It was Marie I agreed to offer you before we got here. Your man all but snapped her right out from under your nose, and you never batted an eyelash. You never took your eyes from Thea all evening!" Bellamy roared.

The crashing of a tankard and fist on the trestle silenced Lord Bellamy's sons' laughter at his frustration.

"No!" Gregory stood, drawing his sword to expose the dangerous double-edged blade. "You'll not give the finest woman in the land to this cur! I'll not stand for it!"

The silence following Merrault's challenge was dangerously numbing. Roderick lifted his tankard and drained it, having won the first round against the father. He put the cup down empty. Bellamy stood up with the pitcher in hand. His eyes glowed like coals as he stared down the younger man, champion or no. "Thea is my daughter, Lord Merrault."

"You cannot give her to the Saxon. We had an agreement, three years past."

"We had a discussion three years past. No agreement. I told you then, Thea was too young."

"Aye, too young for me, but not too young to be ravished by Vikings! Heathens! Bastards, all! No worse than this Saxon at your table, a wolf invited into the lair."

"Merrault!" As Royce stood, he drew his own sword. "My father might bandy words with you, but I will not. I'll not sit idle while you sully my family's honor."

"I insult no one. I speak the truth. Hard as it may be to your ears, young knight. Tempt me not. It isn't your blood I would taste, but yon Saxon's I am itching to spill."

"You have claimed enough of my blood once." Roderick rose. It seemed inevitable that he must do so. Only so many taunts of Merrault's could be shrugged off.

"Just one minute!" the elder Bellamy roared, seeking order before it could disintegrate. "It has not been agreed, nor even discovered if Hawk even wants Thea. Merrault, do you drink to my daughter's health with us, or do my men evict you from my hall?"

Bitterness filled Gregory's eyes, and his strong mouth worked in anguish, but he would not challenge or fight with the chancellor. He sheathed his sword, turned, and stalked out the door. His retreat came none too soon . . . for Bellamy's household guards returned at the sound of discord and stood ready to heed the chancellor's slightest order. Bellamy waved them out.

"God's teeth, Emory, that man bears you ill."

The understatement made Roderick chuckle. "Aye, and what for, I wonder? He did win the last contest."

"The position, yes, but not the monarch's respect." In the silence after the knight's departure, Bellamy filled his own and Roderick of Emory's cup. "More ale!" He declared a toast, and they stood and drained their tankards. "To Thea!"

A servant ran forward with another filled pitcher and thumped it on the table before his lord. Bellamy filled each tankard. Young Jason toppled over the trestle, head down, black hair spilling onto the wet table.

"Puppy!" His father laughed. "Get him to bed, Royce."

"Oof, he's a heavy lad," Royce complained. "Give me a hand, Lozere."

Michael sought a quiet word with Roderick before helping Royce hoist the youth between them. Once they cleared the hall, Roderick regained his seat opposite Bellamy. They were the last inside the hall.

Bellamy hesitated, clearing his throat before he spoke. "I wanted the boys gone. What I have to say is private, man-to-man between us, Emory. What I tell you, I'll not bear having repeated."

"Speak your mind." Roderick schooled his face, prepared for the worst.

"It grieves me to see you focus on my Thea."

"A father is entitled to his favorite."

"It is not that. Yea, Thea is my favorite. She is her mother's favorite. Her sisters idolize her. Her brothers adore her. This whole damn household has revolved around Thea as if she were the very heart of our family. It has been ever that way since she was born. She was struck by lightning when she was a very small child. It quite scared the life out of all of us. Since then, Thea has always been special to us."

Roderick frowned. "I did not know that."

"Humph. I'm surprised Lothair did not tell you the tale when he waxed so eloquently upon her good traits."

"Nay." Roderick's brow lowered. He was appalled at how little he truly knew about Thea, even after having lived with her intimately for nearly a full year. "Lothair only insists she is a dutiful daughter and will make an excellent wife.

"Oh, aye, she would be that...or she could have been that once." Bellamy starred into his brew, as if the tankard might become a mazer and give him some glimpse of the future or the past. "I could kill Merrault for what he shouted to one and all here this night."

Roderick never took his eyes off the chancellor, but in his heart he felt a knife slice him to ribbons. "I would not hold what the man said against him. Merrault is not in full control of his faculties. Your ale is a potent brew, my lord."

"That is the trouble, sir. Merrault's charge is true. I cannot deny it, though for Thea's honor, I wish that I could. I told you today I had reasons to withhold her. Thea was taken from us. By Vikings who came raiding. She has only just returned."

Bellamy seemed so caught up in his own grief he did not pay strict attention to Roderick's reaction, or lack of one, to those words.

"Sir, I can understand why you said nothing to me of this. I understand your loss. I have met true suffering at the Norsemen's hands. My entire family was slaughtered, except for one male cousin. I still grieve for them."

"Aye, you've been a man beset by tragedy. But then, so has Thea. I deeply regret you did not take a better liking to Marie. She is lovely, truly. Even Margareth would be a good bride, though she is so young I would ply for time for her. But, Thea, well, my lord Hawk, you cannot have her." That

Bellamy's last words were spoken so softly, so regretfully, made them all the more candid.

Round two was Bellamy's.

Roderick raised his mug and put it to his mouth, saluting as the chancellor did the same. He tapped the edge of the tankard on the table for a thoughtful moment.

"Because of prior agreement with Merrault?" he asked.

"Nay, Thea refuses him. I will not press her to a marriage that may not do her good. Merrault may swear he would cherish her, but his bitterness would forever cloud his heart. It's a simple fact of his nature. He was here the night Thea was stolen from my protection, and holds himself at fault that he did not do more to save her."

"Then she is free to accept my *tendre.*"

"Nay, she is not," Bellamy argued contrarily. His eyes sparked with menace. "Hear me, Hawk of Emory. I cannot warrant this daughter's virginity. To be blunt, sir, she has been home so short a while, I have no assurances that she does not carry a bastard in her womb."

Roderick winced, hearing the bitterness in the older man's voice. *Foolish, foolish, foolish, how foolish he had been to make a bargain that led to this.* Raising his head, he set the tankard down and stared hard into a dim corner of the hall.

Lord Bellamy watched the play of emotion across across the musculature of his opponent's face. Anger, hatred, pity, sorrow, all of that he saw flash across Hawk's features before he settled into marblelike acceptance.

"Lord Bellamy, hear me. I have come to France from a homeland that has been devastated, by order of my liege to take a Frankish bride. Nine of every ten in Emory have been slaughtered. We have no children, no laughing little girls, no busy, mischievous little boys. I have been shown a son your king holds hostage against me as assurance for my submission to his will. If your much-loved and cherished daughter Thea is breeding a child this very moment, I will accept that babe as my own. I will give it my name and remove the dishonor of bastardy that would fall on the child. A man such as I needs every son and daughter. Under those terms, would you give me Thea?''

Roger Bellamy's sea green eyes hardened as he stared at Roderick, trying to fathom the depths of the Saxon before him. His words rang true. Bellamy dearly wanted his favorite daughter protected by marriage. His own failure to protect his beloved daughter twisted a raw and painful hurt inside Bellamy's chest. Still, he could not bear having his Thea married so far away as Emory.

"Seek another house. Somehow I will explain to Lothair we cannot come to agreement. You have seen many houses, and if mine falls short, it will make no difference in the long run. Lothair is just getting old and stubborn.''

"Lothair commands I choose from yours. His reasoning is perverse. He seeks kinship to consolidate far-flung lands, all to his purpose of holding his realm together. One of your daughters will be wed to Merrault in time. I have lost Eric. I will not be played for a fool again. And since I must choose from this house, your younger daughters do not suit me. I would not take one who has eyes for another man. The other is too young for the tasks she would face at Blackstone. No. Only Thea suits my needs. Do I tell that to the emperor he will command you to bring Thea to the altar tomorrow.''

"How dare you! You make that threat because Lothair promised you a bounty should you select her.''

"Nay, the gold he's offered does not enter into this. I sense a kinship in Thea that tells me we will deal well with one another. I need a strong woman in my house. Lothair's intrigues sway me not.''

"You know why he does this.''

"As well as you. To keep me here. But I will sail with or without his leave.''

"And take Thea with you. You would force me to give her up, when I have told you all she means to us?'' Bellamy's fist came crashing down on the trestle.

And by showing force, he gave Roderick insight into the father's true objection. Roderick turned his tankard in the slick pool of liquid glazing the trestle.

"Would you object so strongly if I agreed to leave that decision up to Thea?"

Lord Bellamy reacted as if he'd been struck a mighty blow straight in his chest. "You would give your word not to force her to leave this province?"

Roderick thought the question through, carefully considering his answer. "So long as she would remain protected by her family and any infant she bears raised with all the honors of her station and my own, I would not force her to leave this house to come to mine. I give my word to let Thea make the decision to stay or to sail with me."

Lord Bellamy tried to fathom the depth of this offer. "You think to convince her to love you?"

"Who can answer that?" Roderick held open his hands. "It appears that is not a question of love, but a question of trust. If I cannot convince her to trust me, she should stay here in her mother's home. As you have said, she has been taken forcefully from it once."

"Yet you came here to find a wife."

"And I think I have, sir. With your permission."

"Eloquently put. Suppose she refuses? You saw a measure of her strength of will today."

"Aye. As well as a measure of yours as her father. Will she defy you and refuse the match?"

"I will not resort to the means I have used in the past to bring her to heel," Bellamy said thoughtfully. "No, she won't defy me. That would be going too far, even for Thea."

"Perhaps you need only assure her that the marriage would be in her best interest. Hers, as well as my own. I will not hold against her the loss of her maidenhead. In fact, I may cherish her more because of it."

"Then you, Roderick of Emory, may have my daughter Althealine in marriage, with much haste, I pray."

Lord Bellamy stood, raised his tankard and hoisted it, toasting again. "To Thea!"

They both drained their tankards and slammed them on the table, then sat down, facing one another again.

Round three was Emory's.

Roderick toyed with his tankard after it was refilled. "I have been asked by my vassal, Michael of Lozere, to speak for him regarding your other daughter, Marie."

The three girls lay crowded into the same bed, not a one of them asleep.

"*Maman* is going to kill Papa for getting so drunk," Marie hissed, and flipped sideways, taking the blanket off Thea on the other end. Trapped between her elder sisters, Margareth had been weeping half the night.

"I shall never find a husband."

"Oh, be quiet, you ninny!" Marie ordered again.

Thea wished they would both be quiet. She tried to think if she had ever seen Roderick drunk. No, she never had, yet the sounds of shouting and the monstrous din of two lords well into their cups could not be denied. She knew both their voices much too well. Neither one could carry a tune in a bucket.

Lord, from the volume of the shouting, they'd start fighting next. She got up and drew a wrapper about her gown. "Where are you going?" Marie bolted upright.

"To speak with *Maman*."

"I'm going with you!"

"Oh, no, you're not, Marie. You stay here. It's a private talk I intend to have with my mother."

Thea tiptoed through the gallery without looking down at the disgusting performance of two staggering men swinging ale about as if it were soap to lather the floor. At her mother's bedroom, she knocked, then went inside.

"Are you asleep?"

"Who could sleep, with all that racket?" Lilla sat by her fireplace, a stitchery in hand. "Come in, darling, I've been expecting you."

Thea knelt beside her mother's chair. "Can you not go down and put a stop to this abomination?"

"Thea, you know I cannot."

"Then I will."

"Child, your father would take a strap to you for shaming him so."

"What shame does he foist on a guest in his house?"

"Your father will deal honestly with the Saxon, Thea. A few pints of ale will not affect him."

"He will never love me, Mother."

"Why, your father loves you with all his heart."

"Don't be obtuse."

"Thea, you need a husband. You need someone for you to love, who will treat you kindly. What I saw tonight was a rare display indeed. Do not be frightened."

"You think they will agree?"

"I do not have to think. I know they have already agreed. Ach, there go the pitchers against the walls."

"They'll be fighting next."

"Then they will fall down dead drunk right after. Can you not sleep?"

"I don't think anyone in this house is asleep."

"Jason is. Passed out at his father's table."

Thea laid her head on her mother's knee. Lilla stroked her curls soothingly. They waited. Thea was nearly asleep when the door swung open with a mighty crash.

"Where's my wench?" her father shouted.

"Papa!" Thea jumped to her feet, insulted by his words at his entry.

"What are *you* doing here?" Lord Bellamy blinked at his daughter and wife. "Waiting for word, is it? Get you to bed, girl. Your mother and I have to speak among ourselves. Until we do, this is none of your concern."

"I'll stay to hear your discussion," Thea declared.

"Ach!" Her father spun about, divesting himself of his sword with a clatter. "You've raised that one wrong, Lilla, dear. Do ye hear that tongue? Where's my switch!"

"Thea, you are intruding. Go."

"*Maman,* I have to hear for myself."

"You will, all in good time. Now go back to bed."

"Get, get, get." Roger chased her out the door and slammed it at her back.

"Brave knight, terrorizing children," Lilla scolded.

"Oh, be gentle, my love, I feel a monstrous head coming on the morrow. Promise me a house as quiet as church."

"I may hasten your misery by clanging every pan, if you do not tell me what you've done with our daughter."

"Daughters, my love, daughters. Married them, on the morrow. Agreed and pledged and dowered. Damn, that man drives a deadly bargain. To wit, I had to remind the greedy bastard I've one other daughter left to marry."

"Roger of Auvergne!"

"I'm getting to it. Hold your horses, woman. He takes it all. Marie to his vassal Michael of Lozere, Thea to the duke, himself, with no repercussions for the loss of her maidenhead. If there is a babe, it is welcome. The decision to sail with him to Saxony or to stay here at her mother's home is only Thea's to make. What do you think of that?"

"I think you are too addled by ale to tell the truth."

"I am not addled, and every agreement we reached between us is written down."

"By your hand tonight. No one could read it tomorrow."

"Ah, trust me, my dear." Roger wagged a finger. "I have not lost all my wits. My scribe pens a decipherable hand. It was he who took the notes and held the paper when we put our seals upon it. The houses of Emory and Bellamy are merged, twice, my lady. What think you that?"

"I think it time you slept, m'lord." Lilla steered him toward the bed.

"Not without a kiss first." Roger pulled her down on the covers with him. Lilla kissed him with open eyes and saw his, unfocused and close. He was snoring before she raised her head. She turned his legs to the mattress, rolled him over and smiled at his broad back. "And I will take your leave, m'lord, to inform our daughters of the news."

Her news should have been happy news, but within the bedroom the girls were sharing, not a single smile was seen. No, Thea burst into tears, Margareth wailed that she would die an old maid, and Marie ran into the hall, weeping with such joyous emotion, Lilla didn't know which girl to comfort first.

She went to the one who seemed the most distressed, which was Thea, and could make no sense of her hysterical babbling. For all Thea would say was what Marie had said over and over again for the past year. "It is all my fault. I'll never forgive myself."

Chapter Twenty-One

Margareth embraced Thea. "You look so angelic."

"I do not feel it." It was not her gown's fault Thea wasn't feeling angelic. The two layers of cream-colored cloth skimmed her body and floated to her slippered feet like an angel's gossamer robe. Her face lacked all color, and her dark hair, which she never wore bound or covered, was tucked out of sight in a fine net crowned with a circlet of fire opals. "I look ghastly."

"No, you don't." Joclyn swept a mantle of rose silk around Thea's shoulders. It reflected some color onto her pale face.

A belt studded with seed pearls rode Thea's hips, and the last piece of jewelry came from Thea's own casket of jewels, a priceless love-knot brooch of gold and fire opals.

"Words do not describe how beautiful you are." Joclyn dashed away tears that stubbornly kept forming. "Oh, this is not right."

"Hush, Joclyn." Thea patted her old nurse's shoulders, fearing Joclyn would fall apart completely.

"'Tisn't!" Joclyn threw the hem of her apron to her knees and stomped about Thea's room, straightening the clutter. "You just came back. Now you will leave again!"

"We don't have time for this," Thea scolded gently. Her tears had long ago dried.

"You should have someone to love you!" Joclyn wouldn't give it up.

Sighing, Thea looked imploringly at Margareth. She shrugged helplessly, no more capable of managing Joclyn than Thea was. Thea checked Margareth's gown and straightened it. Each of them was aware of time's rapid passage.

"And what is it that has gotten into Marie?" Joclyn went on. "I have never seen her act like this...so forward...so bold."

Thea dared not venture an opinion. She smoothed Margareth's fat braids down her sister's back, satisfied with the ribbons that she had patiently worked into them.

"I will be so lonely without Marie to keep me company."

"It's not easy being the last," Thea told her consolingly.

Lady Lilla swept in regally. She, like Thea, had veiled and encased her flowing hair. Her gown was of a color so rare it made her blue eyes shimmer like sapphires.

"You have outdone yourself, Joclyn!" She drew Margareth forward and looked her over from head to toe. "Charming, sweet and innocent, my darling. Don't look so solemn—your day will come. All things in good time."

Turning to Thea, she fussed with the mantle draped across Thea's shoulders, straightening it. "Are you ready, Thea?"

There was no answer to that question. Thea looked elsewhere, the safe corners of the room, the window, Joclyn's crumpled apron. No, she might not ever be ready. She raised her chin bravely and forced a small smile for Lilla's benefit. "Let's get it done."

"Hardly the words I had hoped to hear." Lilla stroked the smooth cheek of her daughter, cupping it gently in her palm. "It is for the best, darling. Your father's intentions are good. You must not feel we betrayed you."

"Let's go." Thea knew that if she allowed any tenderness now, all her bravado would evaporate. What angered her the most was the vile trick being played upon her unsuspecting family. That Roderick had dragged the innocent Marie into his machinations was more than Thea could bear. Did he think he could silence the truth forever by tying Marie in marriage vows to his vassal? That was wrong. She'd see that the Saxon rued the day.

Joclyn took off her apron and swept her gray head beneath a modest veil, and the women went down to the hall, where the men waited. Only Marie had gone down earlier, too excited to wait patiently upstairs while the rest made ready.

They would go in a formal procession to the chapel at Longervais, where the weddings would take place. Thea looked about, not seeing Roderick or Sir Michael.

In the courtyard, Garth's saddle was laid with a blanket of summer flowers. Hyacinths and fat asters were entwined in Thea's ribboned bridle. Beside him, the gentle mare that Marie always rode was equally ribboned and flowered. Both girls were lifted to their seats by their father, and the decorous ride began, neither fast nor slow, with every mount dancing on frisky feet.

Lord Cavell stood beside Emperor Lothair under the new portcullis, with Cavell's entire household turned out to greet them. Lady Hélène waited upon the steps of the old keep. Her embrace for Thea was loving, for they had not had the chance to renew their friendship.

"I have never forgiven myself for having taken a fever that day," Lady Hélène said as she hugged Thea.

"Do not talk of it, my lady," Thea told her. "It was in no way anyone's fault but my own."

"You haven't changed, except to grow more beautiful than ever, sweet child. Come, enter my house. It is a great honor we are given today."

They went to the chapel, filling it with Bellamys and Cavells and vassals, lords, ladies and servants from both neighboring homes.

Roderick of Emory waited with the priest outside the door of the nave. Beside him stood Michael of Lozere. Thea did not miss the unusual expression in Michael's eyes. She thought she had seen all his moods in the long time she had known him. This was different. He neither smiled nor frowned, only looked to Marie with utter fascination.

Thea didn't dare risk looking at Roderick.

I will kill him, Thea swore to herself. She felt utterly naked without her jeweled dagger on her hip.

Lord Bellamy escorted his daughters to the Saxons and stood between them until that moment when he was asked to relinquish all claims upon them. To Roderick of Emory, Lord Bellamy gave Thea's hand. Marie went eagerly to the man her father had so abruptly agreed to let her marry. Not a whit of which made sense to Thea.

In spite of its being doubled, the wedding seemed the shortest service Thea had ever attended. Once they went inside the chapel to hear the mass, she lost all track of time. The wedding feast followed in Longervais's garden.

Numb, Thea found herself feted and toasted and kissed by every person present at least once, some more often. There were dances and reels and promenades, and a lusty round to flute and drums that made her temples pound. There was drink and food and toasts and boasts and raucous gibes and teases, ribald jokes, and shy, embarrassed blushes from Marie. Thea withdrew mentally from the party, an unwilling participant, more silent than she'd ever been. Not even the emperor could coax a smile from her solemn face when he bestowed upon her the diadem of Lorraine.

Before twilight was upon them, both Garth and the big, bruising charger that Roderick rode were brought forward. A guard of men-at-arms were to escort them up into the mountains, to Thea's father's hunting lodge. Another troop prepared to see Michael and Marie to a cottage loaned to them by Sir Cavell and Lady Hélène.

It came too soon, that moment to ride away from the festivities. From the crowd of well-wishers, Thea broke free and went to Marie, drawing her aside. "Don't be frightened, sister. I will look out for you, always."

"I'm not frightened, Thea." Marie smiled brilliantly. She had never looked happier. "This is exactly what I want."

As she accepted the embrace of her sister, Thea felt Roderick's hand tighten at her elbow...a caution, possibly, a warning...to say nothing, to reveal nothing? She could only guess, for they'd hardly looked at one another at all. As she turned on Michael, Thea's expression must have said plenty, for he stiffened and cocked an eyebrow sanctimoniously. "You'll not be a meddling sister-in-law, will you, Lady Thea?"

"Give me reason to be...once, Sir Michael," Thea warned, with a smile for the benefit of the wedding guests that came nowhere near her eyes.

"Good luck to you, then, Michael." Roderick clapped his vassal on the back, covering the tense moment with Thea. Then, just as smoothly, he turned and swept Thea into his arms. "That's enough of that, I think."

He placed a bold kiss on her mouth, and was roundly cheered for the effort by the celebrators.

"You just wait, Roderick of Emory!" Thea hissed against his teeth.

"But I can't." Roderick sat her on her horse, then quickly mounted his own, while their guard scrambled to gain their seats. Roderick wasn't about to waste another moment. He slapped Garth's flank roundly and set the pace, charging the gates.

Thus hastened away, Thea offered no more than a backward wave to her family. They were soon lost from view by the ten outriders escorting them.

Roderick's expression was as closed to her. Neither had spoken to the other the whole day through, outside of the reciting of their vows. Only Marie had enjoyed the wedding to the hilt.

That morning, in her father's study, Thea had sat before her father's scribe, listening to a reading of the terms of her marriage contract. So many acres of land and a title accompanied each manor and demesne, and a wealth of gold and jewels had been listed first. Then came the unentailed property, ten pledged knights, seventy-five vassals, one hundred serfs, their wives, children, animals and belongings to be transported to Saxony.

Ten Percheron mares and one stallion. Twenty head of brown-coated jersey cows...fine milkers all...one bull, along with hogs and sows and barnyard fowl of every variety, were in the bargain.

The list of household goods would fill every ship Roderick owned twice over. Chests, tables, beds, linens, spices, cottons and wools, Turkish toweling and woven rugs, lamps and beeswax and fine Limousin porcelain, silver services and gold plate, pottery and crockery of every sort imaginable, delivered to Emory.

Not once, but twice!

As the scribe read the list, the packing was being ordered done and transfer made of a goodly portion of Thea's father's wealth. Five of Bellamy's own ships would be dispatched as soon as possible.

It was done.

Roderick of Emory had received the heavy dowry he had came to France to obtain.

The hunting lodge nestled in a glen of tall and stately elms. Its stuccoed and timber-crossed walls and its heavily thatched roof blended into the rustic setting. Ferns filled the forest floor to its walls, their curly heads aflutter in the light summer breeze. Garth trod through it, oblivious of the delicate undergrowth.

Inside the lodge, lamps glowed a welcome. At the clearing, their escort left them to return to Longervais and rejoin the celebration.

Thea and Roderick would be alone at the lodge. Her mother had told her servants had been sent up to prepare it, but would not remain overnight, intruding upon Thea's privacy. The same consideration was being made for Marie and her new husband in a cottage miles across the valley floor. Thinking of her sister being tricked so outrageously made Thea's blood run cold again.

Roderick dismounted and tied his stallion to a post. Before he could turn to offer Thea assistance, she had sprung to her feet. She didn't wait on ceremony, either, leading Garth to the lean-to stalls. She had the saddle uncinched and was reaching for it when Roderick drew her aside.

"I will do that, Thea."

"Oh? Is that the way of it now, m'lord?" Thea yanked on the heavy saddle, determined to do the job herself. A Percheron was not a small mount, nor was the saddle made for it of light weight. Yet Thea yanked it off unaided. It was heavier than she should hoist in her condition, but anger gave her the strength needed to heave it partially over the saddle rack.

Roderick stood aside, seeing she was determined to do things her own way. A murderous look flashed his way, giving eloquent warning of just how serious she was about unsaddling the horse herself.

This was a different Thea from the one he was used to seeing. Or was it?

Head up and an iron rod fitted to her spine, she tramped across the clean straw, heedless of her trailing gown and traveling cloak. From a bin outside the stall she took a bucket of oats and grains and dumped it before her mount. Then she unfastened Garth's bit and bridle and threw it over a peg on the wall.

"See to your own horse, m'lord. My serving days to you are over."

"Thea." Roderick stepped forward to intercept her. They needed to talk, the sooner the better.

"Don't touch me!" Thea recoiled. The viciousness in her tone held Roderick at bay.

"Thea, we..."

"I won't hear it!" She shouted and pressed dusty hands to her ears, shutting him out. "You, sir, have what you came to France to get...a wife with a dowry fit for a king! You will keep your distance from me. Just as you will keep your bargain with my father. I will not be forced to do anything for you again. You went too far this time, Roderick of Emory. I'll never forgive you for this.''

Before he could utter a word, Thea gave him her back and left the stables. She went straight to the lodge and threw open the door, then slammed it at her back.

The resounding bang shattered the peace. Birds and small game protested their alarm. Then a hushed stillness, an unbroken quiet, surrounded the lodge.

Thea was glad Roderick had not pressed for conversation during the day, or further ceremony. It was quite beyond her to be any sort of pleasant. Nor could she have stood another moment of pretending all was right. It wasn't.

She saw the well-laid fire in the hearth, the food and wine awaiting their use on the trestle nearby. Huge bouquets of flowers set about in overlarge clay containers, periwinkle, foxgloves, purplish hydrangeas, asters and colorful eucalyptus lent fragrance to the air.

The lodge had been swept and cleaned and made as luxurious a nest as possible. Every comfort had been seen to before their arrival.

Thea lowered the hood of her cloak, unclasping it and laying it carefully aside, then she sat in the high chair before the fire. Her eyes fixed on the flames. The whole day had rushed by in a blur. Now time came to a standstill. Her words in the stable had been the tip of the iceberg lodged in her chest. Willing herself to remain calm, she clasped the arms of the chair and waited for Roderick to come within.

He took his time about it. No horse had ever been so seriously groomed or bedded down for the night. Thea began to pace, too nervous to eat or be still. The effort to compose her thoughts evaded her.

When the door did open, she was not ready for it. Thea whirled about. Her mantle swept across the hearth as she came face-to-face with her husband. He stood just inside the lodge, the door closed at his back, feet planted firmly apart in an arrogant posture.

Candlelight made his golden skin more striking. His face held that ironlike cold expression she had never been able to fathom. She likened the look to one he must assume before going to war. Well, they were at war. By coming within the lodge, he'd crossed her battle lines.

"Madame, I am at your service." Roderick clicked his heels and bowed to her, sweeping his plumed hat to the floor. He straightened, and his eyes bored into hers.

His hat sailed the length of the room, to land where it might. His magnificent cape went next, and Thea's head swiveled, watching it course like a bird of prey through the smoky air.

Roderick strode with an audible heavy step to the well-laid table, looked it over, then reached for a tankard and filled it to the rim with foaming ale. He put the strong brew to his mouth and drained the glass; then he slammed it down and moved to sit in the same chair where Thea had sat herself, not too long past. He extended his long, powerful legs, crossing them at his ankles.

Looking the very picture of indifference, he laced his fingers and laid them below his ornate buckle on the flatness of his belly.

"Look at me, Thea."

"I am looking at you, damn you. Though we have nothing to say to one another."

"*Au contraire,* wife. First, you will tell me why you did not tell me who you were." He stood at once, towering over her, using his great height as if it were a weapon against her. "Lady Althealine of Limousin, princess of the old kingdom of Landais, marquessa of Guyenne and duchess of Lorraine and the seventeen provinces of the grand duke of Auvergne, daughter of the chancellor to Emperor Lothair, Beloved of Gregory, Lord Merrault, my sworn enemy and most hated foe, craven scion of the emperor's throne, his grand champion and defender. Darling and adored sister to

Sir Royce of Auvergne, Limousin and Guyenne. Mistress of Blackstone Keep, slave to the duke of Emory. Which title would you have me call you?''

Thea winced with each hard-delivered title and scornful appellation. "Will not 'wench' do anymore? I did not wish this to happen. I did not make it so, you did."

"So I did," Roderick replied, in a tone more even than he felt should be possible. "You deny participation in the entrapment your family has implemented against me?"

"It was *not* my doing. The bargain you stuck with my father more than compensates you, while it does nothing to alter the injury done to me."

"Does it, my lady? And suppose I wanted a wife, a true wife, one to live where I live, to go where I go? To shelter and comfort me, as the vows were spoken. *Why didn't you tell me who you were?*"

"It would not have made any difference in how you treated me."

"Is that your reason for enslaving me now in this web of court intrigue?"

"The only intrigue I am aware of is that between you and your vassal, Michael of Lozere. Did you fear Marie would recognize you, Roderick? Is that why you did this?"

"Damn you, Thea." Roderick moved toward her, dangerous and threatening. "Had I known your name, I'd have made certain our paths never crossed again."

Thea flinched. The raw truth hurt so deeply she was surprised she did not bleed. Had she harbored the small hope that this marriage might somehow work? All hope of that died as she read the coldness in his eyes. Unable to maintain eye contact with him, she lowered her eyes as she chose her words with deliberate care.

"We are ill-fated, then, my lord husband." The heaviness in her heart felt too great to hold to herself much longer. "I leave you to your supper and your drink."

She turned from him, withdrawing from the simple hall to the cozy loft above, where a bed had been prepared. A silk gown lay across it for her use. She undressed and washed and put it on with wooden motions, pushing down the hurt that seemed to rage throughout her.

It took deliberate and conscious effort to put herself to bed and to will her mind to turn to sleep. The past year of the harshest self-discipline enabled her to do what she willed. She would not waste tears on today, any more than she'd wasted tears on yesterday.

Chapter Twenty-Two

Roderick had no taste for the food on the table, nor did he have any stomach for the strong ale he'd consumed too much of the night before. He went outside, standing on the forest's edge, able to see through the canopy of trees to the clear, cloudless night sky. A myriad of stars shone down on him, like a blessing. Yet he didn't feel blessed.

Since his return to court, his moments of total privacy had been few and far between. Lothair's ever-present henchmen were away from him now. This night and the two to follow were granted him by the emperor's most devious web spinner—Bellamy.

He saw himself doomed to play the same role over and over again. Now that Lothair had his claws firmly hooked into Roderick's flesh, he'd never let go. The Hawk of Emory was ordained to spend his days riding from keep to keep, fortress to fortress, ever in support of the emperor's defense works, never seeing his homeland again.

Cursing himself for being a thousand times a fool, he could not move forward or go back. How could he ever trust *Lady Althealine?* Empowered though he was by all her titles, he could not go to *his Thea*. Anger simmered and stewed within him—body and soul. What devil's play was this? Where did it end? How entrenched in Lothair's treachery was this woman he had been manipulated into taking for his wife ... this woman who would bear his sons . . . this woman he'd grown to love in ways he'd never loved another.

Why, dear God, couldn't she have just been what she appeared—a sweet and simple maid?

Damn, but she had played him like a harp. With the skill of a master courtesan, she had thrown the lure, and he had swallowed it whole, landing himself vulnerable at her feet.

Groaning, Roderick turned toward the forest, noting how isolated the lodge was. High in the woodlands, they were alone and unguarded, unwatched. He had not felt so free since he'd arrived at Aachen in June.

Today was the third of July. The wind and earth groaned as it did each night. Underbrush rustled as nocturnal hunters stalked their prey. Night birds sang. Owls swooped down upon woodchucks. Not a single man-at-arms stood by, watching him, waiting for Roderick to make the move that would prove him the traitor he was called behind his back at court.

Within his reach were two horses, strong and fleet. Upon them he could make his escape to Saxony. Within the house was a woman he wanted to love and take with him, but could not.

Tonight, spoiling for a fight, he had not given Thea the battle she wanted. The day he set her free, he'd trusted her. He'd feared only the pain she caused his heart. Letting her go had been the hardest thing Roderick had ever done.

He could not forgive her the lie she'd kept between them. And used now as a weapon against him.

He saw the maneuvers of Lothair and Lord Bellamy as suspect. Why did *his Thea* have to be the woman with a bounty of forty thousand ducats on her head? He'd been fooled. He had played right into Lothair's hands.

Roderick would wager his right arm the emperor had known all along who kidnapped his chancellor's daughter.

"Damn and be damned!" Roderick swore out loud. "What a fool I am!"

Roderick turned from the woods and strode inside the lodge. He banked the fire and snuffed the wicks on every candle. The stairs to the loft were narrow, and the ceiling was low. He placed his hand to the edge of it, ducking as he stepped onto the shaved wood planks that formed the sleeping space.

It was a man's retreat, designed and laid out for the comfort of a hunter. The walls were hung with trophies and arms, the low bed under the eaves was wide enough for two. An eiderdown coverlet encased Thea. He heard the familiar sound of her regular breathing that told him she was asleep.

Minding the rafters, Roderick removed his velvet doublet, his hose and trousers, his finest Saxon boots. The water in the basin felt cold, fresh. His palms made rough sounds against his face. He passed a towel over his face and neck, down the expanse of his belly, then cast it aside.

The ropes on the bed groaned and creaked as he moved onto it. The feather mattress swallowed him up, and Thea rolled against him, his weight drawing her to him. Her breathing did not change as he slid one arm beneath her shoulders.

How many times in the past revealing twenty-four hours had he pondered one question: Had this been Thea's plan all along? Had marriage been her ultimate design when she pleaded and bargained with him at Blackstone...imploring him for his word upon hers? And left him heart-broken on the Somme? He feared it was.

She was her father's daughter in all things.

Was not the Frank renowned for his craftiness?

Bellamy also played his hand with expert skill. One daughter the bait, a second a termagant and the third... To what purpose would shy Margareth play? Or was she a pawn held in reserve? In his fear and paranoia, Hawk saw plots everywhere.

Thea stirred against him, turning, pressing her face to Roderick's chest. It had not been a whole month since they

had last made love. In the cabin of his boat, when it had put
to anchor off the coast. One last bittersweet night of lovemaking as a farewell, spent without recriminations, or
words of despair, or sorrow for the parting of the morrow.

Both had given in to the need to see their honor-bound
pledges fulfilled.

One hand of hers lay on his chest, softer now than he'd
ever felt it. A lady's hand, unused to work. She no longer
smelled as earthy and wholesome as the herbs she'd scattered throughout Blackstone. She smelled of attar, sweet and
heady and pampered.

A lady's gown came between them. A lady's honor saw
them wed.

Roderick grasped her jaw and, lifting her face, kissed her
awake. His desire for her had not lessened. If anything, the
heat inside him had been stoked to a consuming, devouring
firebrand.

Impatiently his fingers tore at the satin ties on her gown
and slipped beneath the rare imported silk to find her
breasts. She had never been so barred from him by a gown
or any clothing worn to bed, not even on the coldest winter
night. He lost patience with the garment, tearing it off her
shoulders, hearing her gasp. Then, deliberately, with a viciousness born of frustrated anger, Roderick threw the garment out of their bed.

"You can play the lady where you chose, except my bed."
That was all he said before he pinned her beneath him, covering her body with his, his mouth seeking solace, demanding the one truth that remained between them.

Desire. Torched like a fire struck by violent lightning,
desire encroached on all things combustible within them,
searing its own path. Lust and passion and hard, hard need
drove him to plunge inside her body and slake his desire
until dawn filled the lodge from the open windows below the
loft.

Hazy light filtered upward, and warmth rose like the mist
evaporating from the air. Roderick cupped Thea's face with

the palm of his hand, his eyes searching the green, satisfied waters of her soul for the truth within her.

Distrust lay between them, keeping words at bay.

"Are you hungry?" Thea asked, catching the back of his hand and holding it still against her cheek.

"Starved," Roderick admitted. "Come, we'll break our fast and talk."

Roderick drew her up from the bed, setting her to her feet, and she put on a light cotton shift, nothing more. He donned his breeches and let it go at that. There would be time for dressing later.

She made him a good meal, from the breads and cheeses aplenty on the table and the basket of eggs. Sweet jam flavored of tart summer fruit tempted him, as well as the honey. Thea ate almost nothing of the foods he devoured like a lion. She minded very carefully that her revulsion to breakfast went unnoticed.

"Do you return to court, Roderick?"

"I must," he responded. "The emperor's choice, not mine."

"Have you word from Emory?"

"I've no word to alarm me. Why did you do it, Thea?"

Thea shook her head, unable or unwilling to answer—whichever was her reason, Roderick did not know. He put aside the urge to throttle her. She sighed, and finally those green eyes came up and met his own.

"I understand the rules men make when they war upon each other. I held no claim upon you as your captive."

They were talking of two different things. She, of the acceptance of her ordered role in Saxony. He, of the entrapment her meddling at court and her powerful family ties caused him.

"I cannot forgive you bringing Marie into this."

Roderick stared at her levelly. "What do I say to that? You may blame your father, for all I care. Or, better, look to your own motives, for there lie the serpents."

Roderick's jaw tightened, and he turned his face to the window. The chirping birds filled the morning with song.

"We will clean up here. I will return you to your mother's home this afternoon."

Thea could see it would be useless to argue. As pointless as arguing with her father the morning before. She had mistakenly thought she had a choice in the matter of marrying any man. The last betrayal had been to learn she did not. Her father had pushed the marriage contract to her and commanded her to sign it. Thea had asked only one question. What would he do if she did not? Her father, whom she loved more dearly than any other man on earth, had said not one word as he dropped his hands to his sword belt and began unbuckling the wide leather strap.

As a child, Thea had stood her ground against him and taken the beating he thought her defiance deserved. As a woman bearing a Saxon bastard in her belly, she dared not take the risk. She had signed the contract without another word.

Had she come to this marriage bed bearing the marks of coercion on her body, she feared, her husband would have made the election to kill her father. Did her father know the man he wed her to was the man who abducted her, she feared, he would slay Roderick.

How could she walk this tightrope and survive?

Thea turned a roll into crumbs. "Will I hear from you, Roderick? Will you come see me here in Landais?"

"You would wish to continue a farce? If that be your desire, come to Aachen. I have an apartment within the palace."

Thea's eyes grew wide. She could not admit her pregnancy now—who knew what reaction he would have? "Go to court? And have everyone watching to see my belly distend with child...to hear them whisper behind my back? Speculate? How can you even suggest that? After Anne of Aachen's betrayal to you, how can you even ask that of me?

If you have no pride, then consider mine. No, I will not go to court. I will remain secluded.''

"Meaning you have no wish to pretend there is a marriage between us?''

"You agreed to the terms. My home will be where I want it to be. You may do as you wish at Lothair's court. Secure yourself a mistress. I will see to my own affairs.''

"Affairs!'' Roderick exploded, rising to reach across the table and lift Thea from her seat. "If you would make a cuckold of me, woman, you will find yourself without a choice. The bargain I agreed to was an honorable one. Giving you the choice only as far as a residence. Should you shame me or soil my name, or force me to wear a set of horns, you will forfeit the choice.''

"I was not speaking of taking a lover—'' Thea gripped his wrists as he dragged her harshly forward ''—but alluding to making my own decisions. If you threaten me, Roderick, you'll rue the day. For I can not only make your life miserable and worthless, I can see to it that you are ruined completely. It is within my power.''

"And it is within my power and my right to slap you in the tightest, most secure chastity belt ever devised. Have you thought of that, woman? Play such games with me, and you will rue the day you were ever born. It is my right as your husband. Not your father, your damned emperor, or anyone else could stop me from it. You will come with me to Aachen.''

"I will not. Everyone thinks I was abducted by Vikings. They will be shocked enough that it was I you married, when all know you came for Marie. I will not go to court.''

"Then go home to Blackstone. Inform your family that it is your decision to do so. I have had enough of the damned manipulations of Lothair and your cunning, devious father. If you told them part of the story, you should have told them the whole of it.''

Thea's eyes widened, and her mouth sagged in disbelief. "I have told no one anything.''

"Do not lie to me, Thea. Since I arrived at court, all I have heard pressed to me was a marriage to your house. Though there might have been a dozen more suitable the king raised the stakes on the house of Bellamy a hundred-fold with each passing day."

"It is not my doing." Thea declared. "You would not be alive today if I told the truth to anyone in my family. My father himself would kill you. If you would just think for a moment, you would see that. Papa even went to Louis's court in Saxony on the very chance that he might find some word about me there. Are you so blind you cannot see that?"

"Why the hell didn't you tell me who you were?"

"Who I am, Roderick!" Thea screamed back at him as angry as he. Her teeth rattled from the force of his harsh shake, and then, all at once, Roderick drew her to him, wrapping protective arms around her, holding her close and tight, as if he could never bear to let her go.

"What difference would it have ever made, Thea?" he whispered, his voice a guttural croak against her hair. He thought of that last hint of golden sunlight, and the nymph he'd seen bending over the river. *Even had she shouted her names and titles to the heavens, he would still have stolen her.*

Thea kissed the springy curls on his chest.

"None."

She was willing to admit that truth, and so was he. Remembering how his vassal, Sir Deitert, had believed every word his liege spoke so long ago taught Thea a hard lesson. A man believed what he wanted to believe.

Roderick set her at arm's length and studied her. "So it is. Nothing would have come of it. I do not regret my actions. It has been put to rights now. Any injury done your honor in the past is covered."

"And that makes all well with the world again. The sun still rises in the east and sets in the west. Life goes on."

"Thea, you know what I mean."

"Do I? I tire of guessing your meanings. What is it you really want of me, Roderick?"

"Do I need to say it?"

"Yea, you do, Roderick." Thea held her breath, praying he would say just once that he loved her. Did he do that, all would truly be well again.

"I want you to go home, Thea. I never wanted you to leave, but I gave my word to you. I regret the weakness."

"Because of your word kept, I put my trust in you." Tears glistened in her eyes, but she held them back. Never had she cried before him. She would not do so now.

"Can you not do that again?"

"This time you have entrapped my sister in your plots."

"Thea, it is a love match you witness between Michael and Marie. God help them, but that is what it is."

"I do not believe in such things." Thea revealed all of her disillusionment with those heartbreaking words.

Roderick released her shoulders and stood away to look out an open window at the clearing. "Go and dress, Thea. It is time I took you home, before either of us turns an argument into a blood feud."

"As you wish, m'lord." Thea reverted to a tone that revealed none of her feelings. It was better that way.

The only one not surprised to see the duke and duchess of Emory ride into Landais was Lilla. Among the servants, wagers had been made that not a sound would come from the hunting lodge until the three-day supply of food ran out. Within the family, it was desperately hoped that Thea had found a love match, too.

The look on the faces of the newlyweds put paid to all wagers and dashed all hopes. Thea escaped to her room as soon as she entered the house. Roderick appeared an uneasy guest and made no bones about finding something better to do with his time. He did not stay long, politely answering Lilla's questions about how he had found the accommodations at the lodge.

Within an hour of their arrival, the duke rode to Longervais to continue his examination of it. He spent the evening closeted with Lord Bellamy, discussing and preparing the report on the fortification to suit the king.

Thea came down to supper much quieter and more solemn than before. She retired early, accompanied by her husband. In the morning, Roderick was up early and gone before the women came downstairs.

Over breakfast in the atrium, Lilla gazed at Thea with a mother's growing concern. "Do you wish to talk about it, Thea, or will you continue to hold everything within you?"

"There is nothing to talk about, *Maman*."

"Thea . . ."

It did no good to coax or cajole her daughter. Lilla saw the futility of that. The innate intractability of the child was now fully blossomed into a stubborn woman. The tone of the household changed abruptly when Marie and Sir Michael returned before noon.

There was the honeymoon couple all had wanted to see. The shy looks, the sweetness, the complete intoxication with one another. The joy Lilla so wanted to see was there in Marie's marriage for all to witness and rejoice in. The mother of the two brides consoled herself with the truth that one match had paid off.

There was so much to do immediately after Marie's arrival, for she was going to court, gladly this time. The rush to pack and prepare her things for the next day's departure took much of the notice away from Thea's misery. Only some, for there were servants gathering together the dowries of both girls, and word had come that the first of the ships consigned by Lord Bellamy had arrived at the coast.

Even before the king's guard and the Saxon knights rode off to Aachen, the first of the wagons were taken down to a barge and poled to the mouth of the river at the coast.

Chapter Twenty-Three

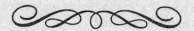

July passed in a warm haze. Thea wandered the gardens morning and evening. To Lilla's experienced eye, her daughter showed all the signs of a woman breeding. Hard as it was to keep quiet a questioning tongue, Lady Lilla managed it. She waited patiently, fearing time would be the judge of whose child Thea bore, her abductor's or her husband's.

Royce returned toward the end of that month. He came to implore Thea to return with him and to join her husband at court. What precisely brother and sister said to one another, Lilla did not know. Royce Bellamy left his mother's house in a fury the likes of which Lilla had never seen.

Lilla confronted Thea, and found her just as visibly upset as her oldest son. "What's wrong? What did you tell Royce that upset him so?"

"Only that I would not go to court and shame my husband by flaunting my belly before God and emperor."

Thea did not realize how bitterly she spoke. She had come home, clinging to a hope that a babe was within her so that she would have something left of Roderick.

How God planned the downfall of woman! Now the babe she had so desperately wanted would be called by all a bastard, even though his rightful father recognized him. Because of her child, she could not go to her husband's side and take her rightful place at court. How could she? The babe had quickened already, yet hardly a month had passed since she and Roderick had spoken their vows. She remembered all too well the shame that the emperor's niece, Anne of Aachen, had put Roderick through. She would not, herself, be the cause of forcing him to battle for her honor. She could spare her husband that.

She did not belong in her own land anymore, but neither could she see herself going to Emory and presenting herself to his people as his lawful wife.

Word came from her father that the inspections of battlements continued. Roderick was supposedly very busy working upon a project of the emperor's. The first two boats had sailed for Saxony. Another was due to leave any day. The fourth ship would carry mostly livestock. The last to sail on the first of September would be Roderick's own ship.

Thea became more withdrawn as the summer waned. Word that the last ship of her father's, bearing her dowry, had left for Saxony came the last day of July. On the first of August, a rider came from Concordia with news that Lilla had long been waiting for—the birth of her first grandchild. Andrea had produced a sturdy boy unexpectedly early.

The joyous news threw Landais into a ruckus. Lilla had planned to be with her eldest daughter when her time had come. Preparations were made to travel to Concordia.

Thea refused to go. Her eldest sister lived much too close to court. She watched her mother, Margareth, Joclyn and half the household leave the next morning. Landais seemed woefully empty after their rushed departure. Sitting to lunch with her elderly grandparents was some consolation and company. Returning to the family's silent wing, Thea felt at such a loss.

She took a basket from the kitchen and made up her mind not to sit and brood over things she could not change. She ordered Garth saddled and brought to her, and left to wander among the summer fields collecting herbs.

When she returned, her basket overflowed with cherry bark and horsetail ferns. Though her mother's loyal vassals greeted her as she rode in, the house seemed so quiet. Thea handed Garth over to a groom and went up the steps into the hall. At the door, Lana greeted her.

"There is a visitor, my lady," the young maid said.

"Oh?" Thea removed her snood and shook loose her hair from its confinement. "Who is it?"

"I do not know his name, my lady. The pilgrim speaks our language very poorly. His name escaped me. I invited him to table, as your mother would have instructed. He awaits within the hall."

"That was good of you." Thea handed Lana the basket of herbs. "Set these in *Maman*'s solar, will you please? I will see to them later."

"Yes, my lady." The girl took the basket and withdrew. Thea entered the great hall and saw the traveling knight seated in the shadows at the end of her father's table. Pilgrims often stopped at her mother's door, and were welcomed and given lodging for the night, if that was their need.

Thea's skirts rustled over the marble floor, announcing her arrival. The knight swung round from the meal placed before him and squinted into the glaring light, spilling into the hall from the sun-filled atrium. He rose to his feet to greet her.

"Welcome to Landais, good knight." Thea smiled politely, speaking slowly for his benefit. "I beg you forgive there being no lady of the manor to greet you when you arrived. My lady mother has gone visiting, and I was out gathering herbs. I am Lady Althealine Emory."

Once she was out of the brilliance of the afternoon's sun, Thea gasped when she recognized the man rising so tall before her. "Sir Deitert?"

"Is this true?" Deitert choked out the words in his poor Frankish. "You are Lady Emory?"

He dropped at once to one knee, his right arm hammering in a salute across his chest. He continued in a hoarse, emotion-choked voice. "My lady, at Aachen I was told that my liege had wed, and was given directions to this house. I am astounded."

"No more than I." Thea responded in the Saxon he had slipped into to make his words clearer. He was overcome for several minutes, his ruddy face gone completely ashen as his mouth worked convulsively to make words of apology that he did not have to speak for Thea's sake.

Gently Thea tugged upon the hands that gripped hers so fiercely. "Sir Deitert, it is all right. I harbor no grudge against you."

"I should have known, little one." Shaken, Deitert rose slowly to his feet. Thea embraced him, assuring him that she bore him no ill will. "You were never what you seemed to be. Is all well with you? What of my liege? Is Lord Roderick here?"

"Nay." Thea shook her head, standing back, her hands upon Deitert's wrists. She smiled, for he looked well, though drawn from his journey, and a little grayer, possibly. "Roderick is not here. He is in Normandy, I believe. What news of home, Sir Deitert?"

"It is good that I have found you. The message I deliver I could only have entrusted to my liege. Word had come back to Emory that he had released the slave he owned. The one we called Thea."

"Aye, that he did," Thea solemnly replied. Sir Deitert's confusion was held in check. He looked about the hall. "You may speak freely here, for only I can divine your Saxon words." Again, Deitert dropped to his knee before her, and gripped her hands tightly between his mammoth paws.

When he spoke again, his words were low and his voice was urgent. "I would have begged my liege on my knees to give me that same woman's whereabouts."

"What is wrong?"

"The children, Emory's babies, are in danger, mistress."

Thea gasped and struck her hand to her breast, her legs buckling beneath her. "What has happened?"

"A fever, my lady, has taken five of our babies, and two of the mothers with them. Yea, I fear it will come within the manor, and my own little Anne and Ellie will not escape the grim reaper's toll of boils and raging fevers."

"Oh, no! What illness is it? A plague?"

"I do not know the illness. I only know my lord's fief is in danger, and this is one our fine defenses cannot stop. All at Emory know 'twas you who save Sir Michael's life when he would have died upon my liege's ship. Will you come? The ship that brought me can see you home in five days' time. We need you, my lady."

"At once, my lord. I will go at once. Tell me, are there many women still with child, this late in summer?"

"Yea, the midwife is busy."

"Have there been ill infants born? Deformed or blind?"

"They did not live," Deitert answered softly.

"I will prepare for the journey, and I must think of some way to get word to my lord husband." Thea's eyes frantically searched Deitert's as she tried to think of all that must be done quickly. "All is not well here for Roderick, Sir Deitert. The emperor keeps Roderick under the watchful eye of a marshal at all times."

She pressed her fingers to her brow, thinking. "Rest, my lord, and make yourself comfortable. I promise not to be too long."

Thea flew to her mother's solar. Inside Lilla's pantry, bottle after bottle had been carefully prepared against all kinds of illness and injury. Roots were dried and herbs hung in great fragrant bunches. Powders were ground and collected in jars. Everything was labeled, and the book of recipes and unguents, powders and poultices rested upon her mother's secretary, as it always did.

Thea packed as much as she could gather, frantic to have a sample of every medicine her mother knew. She took the book, which was more valuable than any tome in her parents' home.

Then she ran to her chamber, gathering up a small packet of clothing for the journey. She turned to the bed where she had slept with Roderick only two nights after their marriage, and stared at it as if somehow she could think of a way to leave him word without giving away to the king or his spies where she had gone.

She knelt by the small trunk that held Roderick's fine clothes from their wedding. He had left it unlocked when he departed, and once his clothes were cleaned and pressed, Thea had returned the fine garments to it. She lifted the lid now, wondering how she could give him a sign that he must find the means to return to Blackstone with all due haste. She stroked her hands across the rich samite of his tunic, fingering the crest embroidered with gold thread.

The proud hawk soared with its wings in full spread, clutching a heart in the grip of its sharp talons.

Quickly she unsheathed her jeweled Saracen dagger from her girdle. More than anything she owned, that knife was a symbol of herself. She pierced the bloodred heart, sliding the blade through the heavy samite so that its point emerged above the hawk's head, pointing due north, toward Saxony.

Then she closed her eyes and whispered a quick prayer that he would see the sign she had left him and understand it. She did not dare leave a written note. Not even to soothe the worry her mother would feel. Then she dropped the lid of the chest and secured the lock, satisfied that only Roderick, who had the key to the lock, would find her sign.

Under the cover of night, Thea's boxes and packets were strapped onto the back of Sir Deitert's horse. Thea had asked for another to carry the excess, and the groom who helped Sir Deitert with the strapping-down saw nothing unusual in this request. Thea dismissed him when the packs were ready.

"I will have to meet you at the gristmill," Thea whispered to Sir Deitert, afraid that her words would be overheard and someone in the house would divine her intent. "There is one exit in the garden that is little guarded. It will take me a half hour, no more, to join you. Go now, sir knight. Godspeed."

Thea saw him off from the steps of Landais as the night shadows lengthened. Sir Deitert rode out through the gates, unmolested by the guards, and then they closed and barred them for the night.

She returned to the hall, pondering what she was doing. For some reason she could not define, she did not want to alert the household to the traveling knight's true purpose. Nor did she wish to tell her grandparents she was leaving or have to explain to them why it was so necessary for her to go. A knot of fear tightened in her stomach at the knowledge that she was endangering the child in her womb to fly to the aid of Roderick's people.

Minutes passed while she wrung her hands in indecision. Death knew no strangers and welcomed all he came upon. What would Roderick do, faced with such a dilemma? She couldn't think. Thea changed into a traveling dress and sturdy boots, then pulled on her cloak.

Quietly Thea ran from the lit hall, disappearing from Landais once again.

Chapter Twenty-Four

The battlement at Le Treport had been selected by the Romans as a suitable place from which to expand their occupation of Gaul across the channel to the Britons.

It did not suit Roderick. He favored the rockier Picard shore, farther northward. If not at the thriving port of Calais, then Lothair should concentrate upon defending against invasion by guarding his waterways. The Somme, for example, Roderick pointed out to Lord Bellamy, was completely unprotected until one came inland to Longervais. Any general with half a mind could circumvent a battle against the fortress.

"What you are saying is that it makes no difference how strong we build our defenses, the enemy will just go around them?" Lord Bellamy snapped.

The hour was late. Their journey was prolonged. He was saddle-weary and hungry. The young Saxon was in little better temper.

"No, I am saying location is everything in every case. Tell your monarch not to throw up walls and castles wherever he has a man of wealth sitting upon some sturdy rock. Longervais is a perfect example of good building, but poor placement.

"It sits in the middle of a narrow valley with hills on either side. Farms and fields surround it. It is inland twenty leagues. A thousand landing places surround it.

"You and I both know walls alone do not make a solid defense. It would have been better if Sir Cavell had been ordered to protect the mouth of the river Somme and build his battleworks there."

"As you have done at Blackstone for Louis?"

"Yea, as I have done *for Emory*." Roderick glumly stared out over the dark forest. He cast a glance over his shoulder to the column of guards that followed Lord Bellamy and him everywhere. Did they but throw chains upon him, he could not be any more imprisoned.

"Enough of this. I'm starving," Bellamy grumbled, and signaled the men to press ahead. "Let us hie to Landais, Roderick. It's a longer ride, but my old bones are in need of wifely comfort and home's fine hearth. Your temper could use the same."

"As you wish, Lord Bellamy." Roderick did not argue. He longed for the ease and comfort only Thea could make him feel. He spurred his horse to match the older man's charge. Behind them, troops thundering to catch up blotted out the sounds of night.

The noise of the horses gave Roderick cover under which he could think his own thoughts. August's heat burned the land from Brittany's shores, Normandy's ragged coast and now Picardy's forests and gently rolling rivers. He was anxious to leave this land.

Michael had remained in Aachen with a fawning bride so enamored of him he could not be trusted to do a single thing save bed the wench.

Roderick had not one man within this complement that he could trust with a message. Lothair, ever inquisitive and manipulative, always wanted more.

It was a fool's journey to press on through the night to Landais. Midnight did not see them out of their saddles.

Lord Bellamy rode as a man possessed. Roderick did not know the countryside well enough to know the chancellor rode to cut hours from their journey. Bellamy traveled as the crow flies, coming over the crest of the western hills, cutting through his hunting grounds.

They came upon the gristmill all at once, and a smooth road, then the white walls of Landais, were right before them. The noisy charge of thirty men on horseback announced their return. Lights flickered inside Landais.

As he dropped from his winded, lathered mount, Roderick let his thoughts dwell upon his woman lodged within the manor. Did Thea rise to greet him? Would she receive him?

He handed his mount's reins to a groom. Bellamy dismounted, kicking his legs, restoring circulation, bellowing like a bull as he approached the open doors of the hall.

His wife stood on the uppermost stair, clutching a thin wrapper round her shoulders. She dropped in deep obeisance to her lord, then rose and threw her arms around Bellamy. Not one of her daughters waited with her.

Deliberately, Roderick turned his back on the embracing couple, not listening to their private words, holding back the hurt because Thea had not bothered to come greet him. He yanked his saddlebag from the back of his mount and slung it over his shoulder, raising the dust from the road out of his clothes.

His legs felt numb. He needed relief, and hunger thrashed his stomach with a vengeance of its own.

The clutch of saddle-weary, dusty men entering the hall gave Roderick anonymity. He found a privy and relieved himself of one burden, took advantage of a bucket of cold water to rinse his face and hands and settled in the hall at a trestle table hastily filled with cold meats, bread, cheese, wine and ale.

His eyes wandered to the servants who rushed platters to and fro. He did not see the face he wanted to see. He was more fortunate than Lord Bellamy. The chancellor's wife had dragged him from the hall before the man had had a chance to wash the dust from his throat.

A serving wench Roderick did not recognize dipped him a curtsy. "My lord Emory," the girl said in deepest tones of respect, offering a pitcher of ale. Roderick held his tankard while she poured. She did not look directly at him. He recognized fear in her manner.

From elsewhere in the quiet house, Lord Bellamy's deepest roar spelled trouble for someone. The men at the table grew quiet, listening, as unable to decipher the meaning of the distant shout as Roderick was. He looked about the tense, very quiet hall. The servants visibly cringed. The scattering of household guards tightened their grips upon their long pikes.

Roderick was the only who moved. He hoisted his tankard to his mouth and drained it, then set it down and pulled a platter of meat to him.

Something was wrong. All summer he'd feared the invisible noose that hung around his throat and threatened his peace of mind. It tightened perceptibly now. The old fox had lost his temper. Roderick could only speculate upon what news a wife might give a man just home from a long, exhausting journey that would bring such a response. Guilt forever pointed its finger at Roderick.

He turned his thoughts to Thea. Where was she? Perhaps she knew what trouble was coming and had been warned off. He could well imagine her and the youngest girl clinging to one another in fear of their father's rage. Roderick could also imagine Thea standing over him, gloating, as he was drawn and quartered.

Roderick had finished the cold meal by the time Bellamy appeared at the atrium doors. He looked haggard, and ten years aged in an hour's time. Before the older man crossed the threshold, his shoulders acquired that proud carriage that gave Bellamy his undeniable nobility.

"My lord Emory." Bellamy approached the foot of the trestle. His voice was forced. "Have you seen to your hunger and thirst?"

"Aye, your table has been well set, my lord," Roderick answered guardedly.

"Then, if I may impose upon Your Grace a little longer this dreadful night, I would have a word with you in my chambers."

Here it comes, Roderick thought, my death knell. As he rose to his feet, he thought again.

It was the emperor's chancellor who was distraught. Bellamy had never looked so shaken. His composure slipped by the second. Hawk had never seen the chancellor in such a state. Wordlessly Roderick followed Bellamy to a private wing within the manse.

His woman, Lady Lilla, stood just within the door of her solar. Her pallor could not be missed. She looked at Roderick with haunted eyes.

"My lady, what has upset you so?"

His question came honestly and unbidden. In her eyes Roderick saw that it was not he who was in danger here. It was someone else very dear to this stalwart lady.

"It is my daughter, Lord Emory." The woman found her voice where her husband could not as he turned to stand beside her and gripped her shoulders. "She has gone."

"Gone?" Roderick asked, blinking uncomprehending eyes. "Your youngest, madame? The little one with apple cheeks?"

"Nay, Thea is gone."

"Gone?" The word echoed in Roderick's throat. The concept escaped him, rattling around in a somehow vacuous cavity where no thought could find purchase. "Gone where? What are you saying? Thea would not go anywhere without having sought my permission."

Lord Bellamy pressed a glass of brandy into Roderick's hand and bade him drink. Roderick thought Lady Lilla more in need of restorative spirits than he. Gently he pressed the glass into her hand, then put his arm around her shoulders.

"Would you tell me of this news, my lady? I fear you are not making any sense to me. May we sit down?"

His body was numb from riding, and his mind was in no better condition. Lady Lilla could not sit, and instead paced the floor of her solar, wringing her hands in a manner familiar to Roderick.

"Andrea, my oldest, gave birth to a son in late July. The babe came early and caught us all unprepared. I took Margareth to Concordia with me. Thea remained at Landais. She would not travel near the court."

Lilla gazed at Roderick with eyes that blazed with a mother's love and fine defense. "I must tell you all, my lord Emory. I must give you the truth as well as I know it. I fear your anger. My husband fears your wrath against us. But, in this, I cannot shirk what I know is my duty."

"Please, tell me what you must, Lady Lilla." Roderick softly encouraged her, for she was not making any sense in what words she did say. Where was Thea? Why didn't she come and greet him?

"It is my fault Thea is the one you took to wife. I thought of all my daughters, she would be the most sympathetic to your cause. You have suffered much in your lifetime. I have grievously misjudged my daughter."

In the silence that followed, Roderick could think of nothing to say. The import of Lilla's words was lost on him in his travel-weary state. "I pray you, go on, madame. What is your point?"

"Thea has gone away with another man, my lord."

Roderick blinked. Utter silence filled the chamber while he attempted to process the mother's words.

"No." He shook his head. "That's impossible."

Lady Bellamy twisted her hands together and flashed an imploring look at her husband. Bellamy rushed to bring another brandy. This time Roderick accepted the glass of potent spirits and bolted it to the back of his throat. Then he gripped the back of a damask-covered chair and stared hard into Lady Bellamy's eyes.

"Madame, I know Thea. She is much too honorable to have gone off with another man. You have your facts wrong. And I take insult at the way you have phrased your words. Thea might be gone, but she would not have gone willingly with another man. The woman loves me."

"My lord..." Lilla sank onto a small, padded stool aghast at his reaction. This was not what she had expected at all.

"Tell me the facts, please. Everything that you know."

Lilla took a calming breath and made the effort to cease her fingers' useless twisting of a bit of linen. "Our first grandchild was born to our daughter Andrea at the end of last month. It had been my intention to be with Andrea, but the babe came early. Hence, when the news came, it caused quite a stir. I took with me nearly all of my most trusted servants. Thea was here alone, with just a handful of remaining staff. The household guards were split, half to accompany me to Concordia.

"After we had gone, a man came to the house. He was not known by any here, and he did not speak to the servants. Thea was out at the time of his arrival.

"When Thea returned to the house, she went to greet the visitor in my stead. Lana said she saw them embrace most tenderly. It appeared they knew each other well. That night, the man went on his way. The next morning, the servants discovered Thea was gone. No one has seen her since.

"We have done as we did before, sent out searchers, knocked upon every door within the land and demanded knowledge of her whereabouts. But she has disappeared, my lord. Gone. My husband and I can only conclude one thing. The man who came to our house was Thea's Viking. She chose to go with him. I am sorry."

Lilla bowed her head as she took a ragged breath, then looked straight at Roderick. "I must tell you something else, my lord. You know of her capture, but I am not certain of what Thea has told you of that time. I know, as a mother knows her children, my daughter Thea fell deeply in love with the man who took her captive. Thea bears the Viking's child."

Roderick kept himself from shouting at the mother, *The man who took Thea was no Viking.* He glared at the mother, totally at a loss for words.

Lady Lilla, hoping to defuse his temper and console him in some gentle way of mothering women, made the mistake of telling him that her daughter was well into her pregnancy and that the baby had quickened in midsummer.

The mother blathered onward, stating how she thought it mostly the baby that had caused Thea's decision to leave without a word of explanation. She had words to the effect that her eldest son had not taken the news of the bastard in Thea's belly very well. Perhaps Thea had feared for her infant's safety.

In the middle of this, Roderick held up his hand, calling for silence. "Madame, please. Spare me. I am saddle-weary and exhausted. Nothing can be gained by continuing to beat a dead horse. In the morning, when I am fresh, I would like to speak with you again."

All of Lilla's intuitive reasoning did nothing for her son-in-law. Lilla retired to her private chamber to handle her own sorrow. Roderick left to sort out his.

Under the circumstances, Roderick could do nothing to solve the mystery of Thea's disappearance that very moment. A servant showed him to his chamber, where a hot bath had been prepared. A full casket of Lord Bellamy's strong spirits was set upon a nearby table to ease Roderick's temper. Every servant in the house crept about on tiptoe, terrified of Lord Bellamy, avoiding Lord Emory.

Landais Manor was like a tomb. Roderick winced with guilt, wondering if this was the way it had been the last time Thea disappeared. For Thea to be gone without a trace or a proper explanation was so uncharacteristic that he simply could not believe it true.

Unable to confide his thoughts to anyone inside the manse, he paced his and Thea's bedchamber after his bath like a man possessed. Of course, her mother had already searched the chamber thoroughly, seeking any clue Thea might have left behind. Roderick did the same, in a useless exercise.

Bellamy's spirits did a fair job of obliterating the ability to think coherently. Roderick eyed the turned-down bed. This was not quite the welcome he'd anticipated. As late as it was, he decided to shelve further thought until the morrow, when his brain was fresh.

But that empty, pristine bed did not appeal to him. He wanted Thea in it. He needed her to be here for him. He kicked the chest at his feet, then howled because he'd injured his bare toes. Hopping on one foot, he swore at the stupidity of a man who would kick a heavy Saxon chest and think to injure it.

That was how he noticed the lock was closed.

He had already searched through Thea's things, looking for a note or some kind of explanation, some sign of struggle or proof of fight from her. She wouldn't have gone willingly with any abductor. God, she had fought him with every ounce of strength she possessed when he took her.

He searched his saddle pack for his keys. Unlocking the trunk, he lifted it. The scent of beeswax and sandalwood filled his nose as he brought a candle's light over the neatly packed contents. Thea's Saracen blade immediately caught his eye. She was never to be seen without it. The knife pierced the heart embroidered on his court tunic. The razor-sharp point of the blade exited from the cloth like a beacon above the hawk's head.

Roderick touched the golden hasp. Thea would not deliberately cut— Roderick abruptly stopped, telling himself what Thea would not do. He traced the sapphires and ruby studded in the ornate handle and ran his finger across the line of the blade. It swept through the heart and rested above the crest of Emory. His heart.

Abruptly he pulled the blade from the fabric and tucked it underneath the folded garments inside the chest. He closed the lid and locked it. Then he blew out the candle and put himself to bed.

He knew where Thea was. She had gone to Blackstone. He closed his eyes and willed himself to sleep. In the morning, he'd begin to deal with the situation as she'd left it to him. There was a mystery to be solved, yes.

The next day, Roderick questioned the young servant who had waited on the pilgrim knight. He questioned the girl at length, probing her mind for forgotten details. What did the man look like? Had Thea called him by any name? The litany went on and on. The men who had guarded the portals, he put through the same paces, as well as the groomsman who had seen to the horses.

He realized in quick order that the stranger who had come to Landais had to have been Deitert. That only compounded the mystery. Why would Deitert have left his post guarding Blackstone? Why had there been no word sent to Roderick the whole summer long? He could not imagine his seneschal being so lax in his duties. What could possibly have compelled Thea to leave in such haste?

Curiously, he came back to Lady Lilla every time, for the mother was the key to the daughter's mind. Lilla was completely baffled. She could not explain her daughter's disappearance except by acknowledging her daughter's love for a Viking. She knew of no one else with whom Thea had formed any alliance. Other than the men who came to Lord Bellamy's house and were known to them, Thea had no special friends, no lovers though she did possess many admirers. So the mother was stumped there, unable to provide more clues to her daughter's disappearance because she had fixated on one fact.

Roderick would have loved to explain to the mother that he was well aware that Thea loved *her Viking*. But he could not reveal he was that Viking without risking his own skin. That, and time itself, left Roderick powerless to reassure Lady Lilla that her daughter had not betrayed the family's trust.

There was nothing left for Roderick to do but to go on. They were at war in every corner of the empire and the emperor expected much from him. Paris had been sacked on Easter Sunday. Bellamy's spies reported that Lothair's treacherous brother, Louis the German, had employed the same Danish Vikings, headed by Ragnar Ladbok, to pillage and harrass all of his brother Charles's lands, as well as Lothair's.

Late summer provided long days and pleasant weather at court. Michael was a changed man, worn to a frazzle by dazzling court life and a tireless, giddy bride.

When he arrived with Lord Bellamy at the Aachen manse, Roderick was highly grateful that the chancellor took one long look at his third daughter's obsessive collection of trinkets, baubles and unrestrained purchases and ordered her to the country. The youngest was gathered from Concordia and sent home, as well. Michael slept for a day and a half out of pure exhaustion.

He woke from his much-needed rest to find only Roderick brooding in silence in Bellamy's hall. "We must talk," Roderick said.

Roderick told Michael of Thea's disappearance from Landais, and his conviction that Dietert had come because things were not as they should be in Emory. And he told of his worries for his small and helpless son, whom Lothair held as a hostage for Roderick's continued cooperation.

"I know that the empire is at war, but this is no longer our fight, Michael. When Lothair released me after Montigney, he quit his claim upon my service forever. You witnessed his oath, and at home I have his seal. That does me no good here and now. So Lothair holds my Eric. Anne is dead. My son should be surrendered to me. We must find a way to take Eric from the emperor," Roderick said plainly. He stared at the cold hearth. "When the time comes to leave, Eric can not be left behind to be used against me."

"You'd be a damned fool if you did. Tell me what you want me to do. You know I am your man," Sir Michael vowed.

"When I make my move, you must go directly to Aachen, secure Eric and bring him home to Blackstone." Roderick couldn't say it any plainer.

"You have only to ask and I will do it," Michael assured him.

Roderick turned his mind to the logistics of leaving France. His boat would moor at the mouth of the Somme on the fifteenth of the month. He intended to be on it, come hell or high water. He didn't care which.

Neither he nor Michael had any word from Emory all summer. Roderick thought it odd that Deitert had not sent a single message to Aachen. Other than a census roll from Friar Laurence, there had been no news. He hadn't liked the count when Lord Bellamy passed the document to him in chambers.

There had been twelve deaths, but no cause was stated. Seven were infants. His thoughts that day had gone to Thea.

He missed her now more than he'd ever thought it possible to miss any woman. Again and again their wedding night at Bellamy's hunting lodge tore through him. How desperate and necessary, how brutal and complete, their joining had been.

Within his arms, Thea, lovely Thea, was the only woman who had ever touched his heart. He longed for her at his side, ached to hold her in his arms, and sorrowed that he could not kiss her. That she was not here with him at court was the most bitter pill he had ever had to swallow.

This vulnerability of love astonished and preoccupied him night and day. He had sworn after Anne of Aachen so thoroughly besmirched his honor never to let any woman within his defenses. But Thea had tunneled her way through to the core of his being. He loved her. He loved her dearly.

He had never known a premonition in his life. But the hair at the back of his neck continued to rise for no good reason whatsoever. Thea needed him. Emory needed him. His wife was in danger. He could feel that in his bones.

He could not rest at night, for every time he closed his eyes he saw her face, worn-out and tired, exhausted by some nameless trouble. He had to get home to Blackstone to protect her, to save her.

As the middle of September approached, Michael feared they would never get to Roderick's ship, much less escape Lothair's henchmen. The emperor managed to put new obstacles in their path daily.

Roderick was so consumed with worry for Thea that he moved like a dead man, blind to all that lay about him.

They accompanied Lothair to Quentowic on the coast, where the emperor was to meet his weakling brother, Charles. Paris had been sacked, Rouen lay in rubble, and the Danes were everywhere, destroying everything. Charles needed a loan from Lothair to buy the voracious Danes off.

Viking longships had sailed up the river Loire on Saint John the Baptist's feast day, the twenty-fourth of June. Sixty-seven longships had landed at Nantes. The Vikings had made easy slaughter of the citizenry, who had flocked into town for the feast day. They had plundered the church, murdered the bishop and his congregation, and gutted the rich salt and wine trading center.

The *Nordmanni* had then rowed downriver with their plunder, booty and slaves, and set up their camp at an abandoned abbey on the Île de Noirmoutier, near the mouth of the Loire.

Charles feared the Norse had every intention of staying forever. They dug into their fortified position, establishing a base from which they continued to raid and harry his kingdom.

In a separate incident, Charles had put together an army to meet Ragnar Lodbok on the shore at Paris, with all due confidence of beating the Norse Vikings who dared to sail so deep inside his country.

But Ragnar had proven to be a terrifying foe. He'd attacked the smaller portion of Charles's army, staged on the west bank of the Seine. Ragnar had defeated the smaller detachment and taken over a hundred prisoners. While Charles and his troops on the east bank watched helplessly, Ragnar had retreated via his ships to the Île-de-France, the island in the middle of the Seine, and hanged every single captive before Charles's horrified eyes.

Paris had been plundered without any army raising a weapon to stop the slaughter or the pillaging. Charles was in dire straits when he sued for peace with his elder brother, Lothair, borrowing five thousand pounds of silver. Ragnar was willing to cease killing and plundering and to act as Charles's protector against *other Viking* attacks, provided Charles met his price.

Lothair, craftier and wiser, agreed to make his younger brother the loan, provided Charles would make the substantial concession of vowing sovereign allegiance to him. Roderick added nothing to the negotiations, not even rising to the bait when a ship of Danish Vikings were sighted off the coast.

"Deuce!" Lothair spurred his mount to the rear of his escort and reined in beside Michael of Lozere. The emperor's face was purple with rage. "What is wrong with your liege lord, Lozere? When did the great Hawk of Emory start thinking with only his balls? What has happened to the man's temper?"

"I believe it is the holding in of his temper that distracts him so, my liege," Michael replied. "You do not know him as well as I."

"Then tell me, what will bring his mind to right? I've gotten Charles to pull in his horns. Now I want to put an end to the antics of that bastard brother of mine in Germany. Louis is the true villain here. He's paying these Vikings to stir up trouble. I'll be damned if I'll cede him one inch of territory now. While I am trying to pull this empire back together, the best seige-maker I know wanders about in a-fit-to-be-tied rage over a skirt."

"Sire, 'twas you who arranged the match," Michael informed him.

Lothair grimaced, kicking his horse into a canter. "I suppose he harbors bitterness, not once betrayed by a slut, but twice."

Michael held his silence, though he cared not at all for the comparison of the king's niece, Lady Anne, to his lord's good lady, Thea.

"Tell Roderick I want him to go to Lorraine at once. I have already sent Merrault and laid siege to Lejeun. I will have it taken by the quickest route, before the first of October. Then, I want all of Lorraine secured. I'll not have Louis breathing down my neck in the spring. By the gods, Louis will come to the table at Verdun and sign, just as Charles will, or I'll have his damned head upon a pole. Tell Roderick those are his orders, by my command."

"Sire, you know we must serve Louis first, since he is king of all the Germans."

"The hell you will, Lozere. You are here, and you will serve the greater power, the empire, first."

"And I beg remind you of the pledge you gave my liege when you thought he lay dying after Montigney. Emory is dispensed from all future service."

"Dammit man, don't quibble with me. I need Hawk to end these plots against me. No better man to bring Louis to heel than the Hawk of Emory. See my orders delivered to your liege."

Lothair spurred his mount and galloped to the head of the column. Michael watched him leave, considering the command he had just been given. Michael finally recognized the emperor's purpose; Lothair wanted his brother's head on a pikestaff, and he expected Hawk to do it.

Michael didn't think a minor bloodletting against a small garrison of stranded Vikings at Lejeun would alter Roderick's frame of mind. The only thing Roderick wanted was his release to return home. All else had ceased to matter.

One good thing came of Lothair's orders. Before hying into battle, both he and Roderick took leave to put their affairs in order. Michael's affairs meant he would go down to Landais and see to Marie. A few sweet kisses never hurt a man going off to war. Surprisingly, Roderick agreed to join him.

Their ever-present vanguard objected to the detour in their destination. Sir Marcus, the king's marshal, vowed the delay would affect the siege at Lejeun greatly.

Roderick said he didn't care—Michael wanted to see his wife. They rode north to Landais, period.

They arrived on the eighteenth of the month, unexpected, and found Landais full to bursting. Lord Bellamy's family had convened in celebration of Lady Lilla's elderly parents' anniversary and Lady Andrea's feast day. The house was so full of guests there was nearly not enough room for Lothair's soldiers.

Sir Marcus had to quarter his men-at-arms at Longervais. Only ten of his knights and squires and he himself were welcomed at Landais. Even so, the troops were banished to an outer barracks, while Roderick and Michael were invited to join the family and sleep within the manse.

Entering the private chambers of the older couple, Roderick got the surprise of his life. Gregory of Merrault sat at the long dining table between the eldest and the youngest daughters. Roderick could not hold back his scorn when he asked outright, "What are you doing here, Merrault? Have you sent another in your place at Lejeun?"

"Lejeun?" Gregory's clear blue eyes widened. "Lejeun? It is nothing but a crumbling turret in the middle of a plain that flooded last spring and has yet to drain."

Sporting a taunting smile, Merrault separated himself from the ladies and strode to Roderick, looking over the two dusty knights in full battle regalia as the taller of the two removed his helm and cradled it in his arm.

"Ah, I see." His sly smile pulled creases in the corners of his dark-lashed eyes. "You have become the emperor's Viking-router now. Lejeun awaits your skill at toppling brick and mortar and beam and spar. Without wife to succor you, work is all you have," he declared with vicious spite. "Is that where you are off to, my friend?"

"Do not call me friend," Roderick warned.

"Enough, my lords." Bellamy put himself between the two men. "This is not the place for old battle scars to split open. It's a joyous time. Welcome, Roderick, Michael, welcome. I am glad you have joined us. Lilla, order more meat and ale for my other sons' enjoyment, as well."

"We have not met, my lord, but I am Andrea." A young woman holding a sleeping infant stepped forward and presented her hand. Andrea was taller than Thea, larger, but just as pretty. The infant in her arms looked hale and hearty, rosy-cheeked and large. "This is my son, Rafael."

Roderick's expression softened somewhat as the baby yawned deeply and nuzzled against his mother's breast. The tiny newborn reminded him of his own son, whom the king held hostage. "He is an angel, Madame Andrea. I congratulate you."

Roderick turned as a small hand touched his arm insistently. He found the youngest Bellamy daughter awaiting his attention. "A word with you, my lord."

Her whisper came at exactly the time Marie found her way into Michael's arms. Amid the squeals of laughter Marie's swamping of Michael caused, Roderick barely heard the youngest sister's soft words.

"I have important news for you." The girl's eyes darted to Merrault's retreating back as he rejoined her parents at the table. She colored to the roots of her hair. "But I cannot speak freely here. There are too many ears that might hear what I say."

Roderick nodded curtly to show that he understood. He reluctantly escorted Margareth back to the table, paid his respects to the elderly couple honored at the head and ate a meal in silence, trying to puzzle this one out. The evening aged. Bellamy grew verbose and talkative.

It was not long before Marie coaxed Michael to retire for the night. Shortly afterward, the elderly couple made their way to their own apartments, and the ladies withdrew with them.

As soon as he was able, Roderick pleaded weariness from the hard ride from Aachen and retired. He was not alone for long. Only a moment or two passed before the softest tap was heard upon the chamber door.

Margareth stepped inside surreptitiously checking at her back to see if she was watched. The maid wore a night rail and a long robe. Her feet made no noise upon the deep carpeting as she came to Roderick.

"What is it you have to tell me?"

Margareth spoke earnestly, but very softly. "I was accosted on my way to the village yesterday. A young man bade me give you a desperate message, and to trust telling it to no one else."

"Who is he?"

"The youth told me his name is Benjamin, and claimed to be your kin. As he was fair and tall like you, thus I believed his claim. He said to tell you, for safety's sake, he has removed your ship to Nez sur Mer. He has twice been attacked. He said you would know of the hidden cove there, and he would wait a week, no more."

Margareth bit hard against her lower lip. Her huge blue eyes looked up to Roderick fearfully. "One other thing, my lord. When news came to me that Lord Merrault was again to the house, I went rushing to my father's chambers to greet him. I overheard Gregory tell my father the emperor has sent him here for the sole purpose of destroying your ship. He told my father you had been sent on a fool's errand elsewhere."

"And so I was," Roderick mused. His brow lowered in a considering frown. "What gain do you seek from telling me this?"

"None, my lord." Margareth's cheeks colored deeply. "I owe you more than I can ever explain. I have always been very jealous of my sister Thea, resenting the affection Lord Merrault bore her. I confess I wanted him for myself. By marrying Thea, you have made it much easier for me to gain the man I wish to have. I do not understand what the emperor asks of Gregory, or why the man I love bears such malice to you. I only know Papa must do as Emperor Lothair commands. So must Gregory, while it is my understanding your debt to Lothair was absolved forever at Montigney. That is how it has been explained to me. You owe His Majesty no more than tithe and men pledged in war. There is something afoot, and I fear you are personally in danger. I must go."

"Wait," Roderick called to her.

"I dare not," Margareth whispered. "Forewarned is forearmed, my lord. I am glad you have come."

The young girl was gone as quietly as she had entered.

Roderick paced across the bedroom floor, his unshed armor creaking, weighting down his steps. Enough of this madness, he told himself. *I am going home.*

Like a man possessed, he whipped off the heavy weight of his armor, dropping the heavy pieces to the floor. He shouted for a servant and ordered a tub filled with hot water to the rim and told the quaking twit before him to hie to Michael's quarters and rout the lout from his bed, no matter what his activity.

Roderick took his bath and sat within the polished tub, thinking. He rose abruptly, dressed in tunic and chausses, donned softer, more pliable boots for riding, not fighting.

A knock upon the door presented him not with Michael, as he'd requested, but with Lady Lilla.

"My servants tell me you are displeased. What service can I provide you, my lord? I would not have it said the hospitality of my house is remiss."

Roderick's eyes locked upon the elegant face of Lady Lilla. Her eyes were clear-sighted, wise, and of a nature he found most unusual.

"There is naught I need, Lady Lilla, save to leave this place and return to my homeland. I am needed there most grievously."

"You are?" Lilla's face bore confusion. "What, pray tell me, stops you from doing what is your duty as you see it? Do not feel yourself obligated to remain here simply because my daughter Marie cannot think farther than her nose. She is a silly, thoughtless girl."

In a flash of intuition, Roderick knew he could trust this motherly woman who held such a good grip upon her life.

"Do not think it as a mere wisp of girl that binds me here, madame. As fond as I am of my sister-in-law, and as valued as Michael's friendship is, it is not their newly wedded bliss that impedes my journey. I am trapped in a ploy of Lothair's making."

"Ah, the fox..." Lady Lilla sighed. She looked out the door she had left open, then turned back to Roderick. "The night is not very cool. Would you mind escorting me through the gardens, my lord?"

"It would be my pleasure." Roderick nodded, liking Lady Lilla anew.

Amid the scent of roses, she smiled at her son-in-law. "For some reason, Duke Emory, you do not seem as troubled as you were when last I saw you."

"No, madame. I am not," Roderick answered.

"Tell me, what business has the emperor with you now? I know he admires your castle-building skills most greatly."

"Madame, I have been sent on a fool's errand. Had I not succumbed to the impulse of allowing my vassal to kiss his bride once more, this night I would be bedding down under the stars, on my way to a site of battle. An impulse alone brought me here, and arriving, I found within your hall the man to whose aid I was going. A most strange coincidence. Lord Merrault is supposed to be neck-deep in a siege."

"Is that what you and he were speaking so abruptly of when first you arrived?"

"Yea."

"And there is no siege?"

"You have the right of it, my lady."

Lilla thought her way around what he had said and what he did not say. "Lejeun is strategically placed, is it not?"

"It would be an excellent position for a battlement of the sort I have raised at Blackstone."

"I see. Is Blackstone bigger than Longervais?"

"Bigger, stronger, better placed."

"Curious." Lady Lilla frowned. She sat down on a bench and smiled at Roderick. "Very curious. May I tell you something?"

"You may say anything to me, madame."

"Lothair has many admirable qualities, but like any ruler, he has devious methods. I have been privy to certain confidences, you understand. While I will not betray my monarch or my country, I look to the intrigues of court with a different eye than most women in my position. The happiness of my husband and my children has always come first. It puzzles me that the emperor sent you to a battle that does not exist.

"It also troubles me that he holds you ignorant of the son Lady Anne bore you. She died, you know, of the pox, at the convent at Solbert. And Lothair keeps the babe, a boy named Eric, to hold you in loyal service to him should Louis move against France. Meanwhile, my husband grows saddle-weary in his own efforts to bring about the peace negotiations begun at Verdun last year. There are no traitors within Landais.

"You, sir, have long ago proven to me your loyalty to our emperor's realm. He asks too much of you. Nor does he deal fairly with you."

"I have no complaints, my lady."

"No. I would like to help you, Roderick. Is your ship not overdue, the one that was to take the livestock set aside for Marie's and Thea's dowry home?"

"It is overdue, but I will not accept further offerings from your coffers to my household. You have given Thea and myself enough, my lady."

Lilla remained quiet, considering him deeply. "I wish I had spent more of my energy delving into my daughter's thoughts. I feel greatly at fault. I so wanted the match between you and Thea to be suitable."

Roderick averted his face to glance down at the flowering rosebushes lining the garden's path. "I believe Thea and I are eminently suitable, lady."

"Do you?" Lilla chose her next words with great care. "Try as I might, I cannot see Thea in a traitor's role. She is always so straightforward, so direct. I try not to deceive myself, as many mothers do. Were she spiteful, she would have shown that nature in little ways. Not once did I ever hear my daughter say one harsh word against you."

Lilla thought deeply. Her brow pleated with concern. Then, revealing how helpless she felt, she looked into Roderick's carefully masked face, seeking any trace of emotion. He would give her not a single clue. She sighed.

"Something has long bothered me. When Thea left, she took one of every medicine I had ever gathered. Now, my lord, you have told me there have been . . . how did you put it?"

"I did not put it, madame. I said I was needed in my land most grievously."

"There have been deaths?"

"Yea. The summer census from my abbey that Lord Bellamy showed me states that twelve of my people have died."

"Is that an unusual number?"

"For a healthy, robust people, yea, it is very unusual."

"I see." Lilla wanted to grind her teeth. The man never let a single scrap of information slip past his lips. She decided to take the bull by the horns and make her own assumptions. What else could she do but throw at him her deepest, darkest suspicions?

"My lord Emory, could it be that my daughter did not betray our trust in her, after all? Do you suspect, as I do, that she went instead to your own land of Emory? If by some chance a messenger bearing bad news came here after seeing the emperor at Aachen, seeking you, and found only Thea and told her the terrible news? Would Thea not believe she was empowered to act in your best interest as Lady Emory and chatelaine of your household? Could she have gone with that messenger? Thea would do something like that without a moment's hesitation if she thought she was needed. Needed specifically because of her skills as a healer."

How neatly the woman's logic and intuition pushed through the maze of puzzling facts and came to a unique conclusion. One that Roderick had hoped she might never consider. His sense of foreboding drummed inside him like a separate heartbeat, calling him home, home, home.

"Most curious." Lilla repeated, deep in thought, her fingertips pressed against each other. Since Roderick did not echo her spoken thoughts, she sighed and looked up at him once again. "You have the most interesting face, Roderick. Do you know you give nothing away? Not a scrap of emotion do you ever betray.

"Another thing, sir, the bad blood between you and Merrault is serious. I know whence it came. A wicked woman at court, who played both of you false. I may sit here in the country, but I do hear of what transpires at Aachen. Lady Anne betrayed you, but somehow, I cannot believe my Thea did. She has never had anything less than a loyal and loving heart."

Both corners of Roderick's mouth moved in a reluctant grimace, neither showing a smile nor actually making a frown. He sat down heavily upon the bench at Lady Lilla's side and gazed into the greenery that was her garden.

"Thea is the bravest woman I know. Did I dare to agree with your insightful assessment of your daughter, madame, I would be forced to make a confession."

"A confession, my lord?"

"Aye." Roderick nodded. "A guilty conscience often troubles even the most hardened soul. I have labored long under certain assumptions, thinking I could easily leave this country of yours and it wouldn't matter about the past."

"I am afraid you leave me mystified. Do you allude to Thea in any way?"

"Are you still convinced your daughter fell in love with her Viking captor?" Roderick laced his fingers together between his knees, his head bent, eyes on the well-turned earth beneath the roses.

"I would not hurt you by uttering those words again."

"You think them true? An honest answer, madame."

"Do not press me, sir."

"I must, for I would have only the truth."

"*Oui*, she did love him, deeply. But, unlike my husband, I do not believe she has cuckolded you."

"I know that she has not, madame. Thea's honor is the most noble thing about her. It protects her, and shines forth for all to see. Even for a fool such as I, who is too blind to see what is placed clearly before his eyes."

That Roderick smiled as he spoke made Lilla regard him with surprise. She rose to her feet, her midnight blue eyes scanning her son-in-law from head to toe.

Almost tonelessly, she whispered, "My Thea loved her Viking with all her heart. Has anyone ever told you, my lord, you could easily pass for kin of Ragnar Lodbok?"

Roderick chuckled. "I should hope my manners are better than his, my lady."

"Oh, they are, indeed. But you do resemble him, with that blond fierceness about you. It is too coincidental, *n'est-ce pas?* A maze to work through. Thea wouldn't tell me anything. Do you know, she used to tell me every thought that came into her head? And you, my lord, met every demand, negotiated long and hard and would not settle for a virgin sister just as well endowed, but had to have the daughter who had been taken from me. Am I near the mark? Will you confirm my thoughts, or only leave me to speculate down the years?''

Lady Lilla was too circumspect to await an answer to her question. She gave the tall Saxon her back and began treading her way down the cobbled path. At a yew tree, she stopped and smiled back at her son-in-law, holding out her hand to him, waiting his escort.

"Come, my lord Emory. We must see you safely gone from Landais. With winter soon to bring its rains and storms, you will not be missed at court. Come."

Closer to the manse, Lilla stopped and again fastened her eyes to those obscure blue beacons that neither confirmed nor denied anything to her.

"I have one question, my lord. Do you love my daughter?"

Roderick studied her at length, then softly answered. "With all my heart. Thea is everything to me."

Lilla's eyes closed, and the most painful sigh entered her chest as her hand pressed against the emotion that rested on her heart. "That has been my prayer, lo these many months. Thank you, Roderick. Godspeed you to her."

Overwhelmed, Lady Lilla drew a linen to her eyes and paused a moment to gather her composure. "Now that the family's feast is over, the hall has been given over to the emperor's man. I will see to their rest, my lord. Leave everything else to me. Trust me."

Chapter Twenty-Five

September 842 A.D.
Blackstone Castle, Emory, Saxony

The nights were the worst. Roderick's hall seemed so oppressive. No matter how many doors were left open, heat remained within the keep, and the fevers raged higher.

It seemed Thea had been nursing sick one after sick one forever. Mothers came with their infants. Fathers trudged up the hill bearing wives fallen to the sickness.

Mostly it was the babies that fell ill with the disease. It had no name Thea could give it. It was an illness of chills and racking fevers, leaving small, helpless bodies wasted by it.

Late summer's heat punished more. Thea prayed for rain to break the harsh drought so determined to ruin them all. Rain did not come.

Those who recovered, Jesse and Elspeth and the friars took care of in the abbey. Thea only saw her two good friends for a short while before her order to isolate the sick from the well was put into effect.

She had everything she thought contaminated burned. The rash on the sick ones' bodies blistered and dried if they were going to live. She had never seen anything like it.

Her mother's book gave her little help. She could treat

symptoms, soothe the rash and the burning skin, but she couldn't cure anyone. Only God could do that.

Sir Deitert stayed to the keep, helping Thea tend the sick and the dying. Sometimes, Thea thought she would go mad, listening to the wailing and crying of sick babies. She could get no rest herself.

The dog days came and dust hung in the air. The humidity doubled.

She renewed her efforts at praying for a storm to break the heat. As September passed, no new patients came up from the village. The sickness was completely contained within the keep. The guards she had ordered Sir Deitert to post at the portcullis gates let no one enter Blackstone.

In the bailey, Henry tended a small graveyard. It had been the masons sent by her father who died first. Thea wondered if they had brought the plague with them, harbored it and spread it to the villagers.

Two of Roderick's pages had died, as well as another mother, a Celt, and her infant, since Thea had come to aid them. In all, twenty-four of Roderick's precious few Saxons were dead.

Those who recovered did so very slowly. Their gaunt frames were sorely weakened. Day by day, some grew better and some began to help with the washing and the sponging of fevered skin.

Thea sat in an alcove, a bowl of broth in her hands, a spoon in her hand, which she was too tired to lift. She gazed out upon the fortress walls. Walls that completely obliterated the little view of the village that once had been available from this lower window.

Roderick's fortress surrounded her. Built to protect those within, it now protected those without. The twenty-foot-high barbican kept the pestilence away from his people.

The breeze that came in the window raised the hackles on Thea's neck. She brushed away a fly, but it came back again and again.

Looking around the hazy hall where all the pallets were spread, she saw what was to her a horrible invasion of the annoying creatures. They could not be driven away. Sometimes they stayed on a sick one so long they left horrible bites.

The one that tormented her own arm came back for a feast. Thea refused to allow the creature to draw her blood. She slapped it down with a wet kerchief, killing it against the stone seat. A dark smear of blood revolted her. As she wiped the seat clean with the wet rag, she looked to the sick hall again.

There were more flies than she could remember there being at Blackstone. Of course, there would be, with so much sickness and heat. Her brow furrowed.

To her mind, flies were a devil's torment, harbingers of sickness and filth. Why hadn't she noticed them before? Where were they coming from? Could she do anything to keep them out? The heat of shutting the keep would kill everyone.

She went upstairs to her room and looked through her mother's book again. Lilla had collected many methods of driving away odious insects. Citronella, from a grass, was useful; juice and the rinds of citrons also.

There was an abundance of citrons in Auvergne, but none in Blackstone. A sickroom should be screened with netting, her mother's book advised. Care should be taken that all refuse was suitably destroyed, buried far away, covered with lime or lye or salts. The sick persons and their quarters should be kept scrupulously clean.

Thea had done all that, she thought. Still, the flies hung thick in the air, a pestilence.

Evening finally came. She and Deitert sat to the trestle pushed to the side of the great hall. Again Thea brushed away a fly that wanted her. Sir Deitert seemed immune to them, or else too tired to care any longer. Thea didn't know how she would have managed, if not for him. He lifted bodies she could not budge, worked unstintingly beside her day and night. He never complained or seemed to mind doing even the meanest of the work.

In the distant north, heat lightning teased the sky.

"How can we get rid of these flies, Sir Deitert?"

"Burn the grounds," he answered. "Release all the animals from the pens and the stables. Flies breed in the manure and the garbage. Have it swept and cleaned."

"Lime the privy." Thea sat up, remembering other ways. "We need only burn the bailey ground."

"Aye, wherever slops have been tossed."

"We must do it, before this plague takes us all. Come, let us go wake Henry."

"No, first, mistress, we must get the sick away from the smoke and the ashes we will cause."

"Where? We cannot take them outside the keep. There have been no more come sick up from the village. It is contained within the keep."

"Aye," Sir Deitert agreed. "They must be taken up to the dormitory. I will raise the battlement doors. It is cooler there than here."

The work of moving the sick ones up two floors was horribly difficult. Some adults could walk, but were so weak they could not stand unsupported. The rest had to be carried.

It was cooler on the uppermost floor. The breeze came strong over the high battlement walls. A draft from the roof swept fresh air down the long room.

Together, Thea and the old knight made every victim as comfortable as possible. To be certain no more flies harassed them, Thea set her mother's precious citronella candles to burning. The scent caused Armina's eyes to flutter. Thea wasn't certain the old woman had the strength to live through the night. She held a cup of potion to her cracked and dried lips.

More than maintenance just didn't seem possible.

Deitert escorted Thea downstairs with a firm hand on her arm. Once the animals were all released out the gates, Thea,

Henry and Deitert worked half the night, sweeping up soiled straw, bringing it out to spread upon the rank-smelling ground.

They spread thick, dry layers of fresh straw upon the refuse until every stored blade inside the castle walls was out in the open upon the grounds.

Guilt assailed Thea as she looked at Deitert and the old groom.

"Is there any other way? If the fire gets out of hand and spreads, Roderick will blame me for destroying all he has worked to achieve."

"If it is the flies that spread the disease, then we have no choice," Deitert said wearily. "We have done it in camps after sieges. Sometimes it is the only way. Go up, mistress. See to the sick ones. Henry and I will do the rest."

Thea couldn't go, knowing that her husband might return to find his home blackened—in ruins again. Roderick would never forgive her for destroying all he had worked so hard to achieve. Then she thought of those who had recovered from the sickness, those Jesse and Elspeth tended as they regained their strength in the abbey. Thea wanted this pestilence gone forever from Emory. If the price of removing it was Roderick's keep, so be it.

Nodding wearily, she acceded to Deitert's order. She went into the hall via the only open door. All the shutters had been closed and secured. In the hall, the pots of sulfur she had set out smoked. The filthy flies sought the high ceiling to escape. Thea went up to the third floor, bringing two more buckets of fresh water with her.

She set the buckets down and closed the door securely behind her, sinking weakly against the cool stone wall.

The smell of burning straw and grass drifted in the arrow slits of the battlement. The scent came, but the smoke did not. Thea could not open any window, lest the smoke billow inside. She found a clean bed and sank down onto it, unable to sleep.

Thunder boomed distantly all through the night. At sunrise, Thea went onto the battery and looked down on the yard. A solid black carpet swept from wall to wall. Smoke stains blackened the barbican.

Until she went downstairs, Thea did not know the enormity of the fire. Not one bucket of water had been thrown to contain or control the fire.

Sir Deitert and old Henry slept, collapsed in utter exhaustion in the great hall, covered with ashes from head to toe.

Roderick's brand-new doors, bearing his emblem of a hawk, had burned through the night. Smoke and red-hot cinders dropped out of the charred and blackened oak onto the threshold. Flames had licked inside the keep, streaking the great hall's newly plastered interior walls, leaving stone marked and all wood consumed. Not a shutter or door or ribbonfold panel remained undamaged on the ground floor.

Blackstone was a worse ruin than it had been the day Thea first came to it.

There weren't any more flies.

With the first floor destroyed, the dreadfully ill people had to be kept upstairs. None died in the days that followed. One gained enough strength to be able to help with nursing the others. Armina recovered enough to complain about the food.

Finally, the rains came. Going to the kitchen to bring up the soup, Thea stopped and listened to the crack of thunder overhead and felt the first drops of cool rain fall upon her skin. Her dress spotted as she watched stone walls, covered with black soot, moisten.

"Let it rain, God," she prayed out loud. "Let it rain for days and days."

She took the pot from the fire and set a lid upon it, then trudged up three flights of stairs. In the dormitory, a dozen people sat upon their cots. Arnulf looked at her and said, "It rains, mistress."

The rain was a godsend. She spooned out stew for those who could handle a more solid meal. Sir Deitert ladled the soups to those who couldn't. The nursing went on.

A small boy sat on his pallet, crying for his mother. His sores had crusted over and, bathing him, Thea applied calamine to his skin. He sucked his thumb and leaned against her and drifted back to sleep. Another child cried long into the night, crying for his mama.

One by one, the fevers broke. One by one, the patients regained their strength. Sir Deitert carried the recovered ones to the sealed gates and unlocked the wicket gate to pass them out.

The men Sir Roderick had charged with the guarding of the keep allowed no distraught mothers or fathers near the gates. Even when the fire had raged all night within the bailey walls, the men had stood at their stations with crossbows in hand. No well person was allowed to enter. To the rear of the keep, twenty-four graves remained unblessed.

When the second toddler was pronounced well enough to leave, Deitert took him in his arms and went down to the gates again. The only key to the portcullis was in his care. As he came to the gate with the recovered child, he saw his liege lord standing at the entrance, his fists locked upon the thick iron grate.

Deitert stopped. "My lord, you have returned."

"Aye," Roderick declared. "Open the gate."

"You cannot come within, my lord," Deitert said.

"You dare to tell me I cannot enter my own home?"

"Nay, my lord. You cannot. Stand aside and let me pass this child out to my guards."

"Look past your nose, man. Your guards are crumpled at my feet, and damned lucky that I haven't bludgeoned them to death. Where is Thea?"

"Within, my lord."

"You crazy old man! Open this gate!"

The child in Deitert's arms began to cry. Deitert consoled him with a pat upon his back and a clucking sound. "There,

there, best get used to hearing that roar, boy. You'll hear it often, the older you get.''

"Deitert!" Roderick screamed in rage, unable to move the gate or even shake it.

One of the clobbered guards shook his head and came round, hoisting himself to his feet. He got water and tossed it on his mate, bringing him conscious.

Both were dazed by the lord's temper and vengeance. Both were more afraid of the disease raging inside the keep than they were of their liege lord's wrath.

"What have you done to my house?" Roderick bellowed. It wasn't the damned house that had him worried so. It was the woman within the keep. Finally, he calmed down, his rage spent in useless temper. When Deitert ordered the two guards to hold him back while he released the boy, all hell broke loose.

Deitert set the wailing child outside the wicket and slammed it shut, locking it before Roderick could break free from the two men holding him. His threats and orders fell on deaf ears. Deitert turned his back upon the locked gate and returned to the keep.

He drank two glasses of dark ale before he went upstairs to help Thea with the seven remaining patients. She lasted one more day, then simply collapsed.

Unable to rouse her, Deitert laid her on a clean cot and waited for the sweats and fever to come. He had been through the sickness himself early, in the plague...a much lighter case than those that came afterward. He feared the intensity of the one Thea might develop.

She slept an entire day, and came around to find only three others within the long dormitory. Armina was back in the kitchen, and the soups coming upstairs were not so good. No boils had appeared on Thea's skin. She sat up, weak from lack of food, bone-weary, and looked to the two children lying upon their beds. The little baby girl who cried so much at night held up her arms, wanting comfort.

Thea gathered the child in her arms and bathed her, fed her, rocked her to sleep. She slept more than the baby did.

She woke up in Roderick's bed. Deitert sat her up against a pile of pillows. He held a silver bowl and spoon in hand, determined she would eat the soup he offered.

"You are the last, my lady. The keep is empty now. Come, eat, you must try to get well."

Thea tried to sort out her head. She touched her skin and found it cool, looked at her forearms and found no spots. "I do not have it, Deitert. I am not sick."

"We cannot be sure of that. Not yet. You are very weak. We must wait and see." He did not tell her that her lord raged in the village. Thea ate the soup and drank the cool water offered her and slept again.

She dreamed of the day Roderick would come home. Dreamed of the way his house would look when all her dowry was settled upon it. Perhaps then he would tell her he loved her. Waking, she remembered the charred walls.

It was better Roderick stayed at Aachen.

Thea cocooned herself in sleep. She felt the baby in her womb move vigorously and awoke to find Armina cackling above her. "This be a fine kettle of fish."

"What fish?" Thea sat up, confused.

"Oh, this room, my lady." Armina set a bowl on a table beside the fine high bed. "Never saw nothing so grand."

Armina's gnarled fingers strayed to the lace-edged linens. "You be a witch, truly. Here's yer soup. Eat it now. Today's the day his lordship's coming in the keep. You should see the machine he's rolled up the hill. Can't say as I blame him wanting in, now that I done seen this. 'Tis a fine bed here to his room. 'Tain't such a fine bed down on his boat."

"Roderick is here?"

"Been here a fortnight. He's scaling the wall. I expect poor old Deitert's going to die."

Chapter Twenty-Six

Armina tried to put the bowl of chowder in Thea's hands. She wouldn't take it. Swinging her feet over the side of the high bed, Thea held on to the carved bedpost for support.

"Why, you're breeding!" Armina cackled. The bowl clattered as she put it down on a polished mahogany night table. "Didn't learn the last time, did you?"

"Oh, you wicked old crone, get out of my way."

Thea struggled to reach the door. Her night rail fluttered around her pale limbs. Armina swept a bony arm around Thea's waist, keeping her from falling to the carpet-strewn floor.

"Wicked? Who be wicked? You witch! I suppose you wants to go downstairs, do you?"

"Don't you dare try to stop me."

"Nay, I wouldn't. This should be some sight to see. The young lord pitted against the old goat that taught him every trick he knowed."

Armina's cackle grated on Thea's nerves, but she needed the old woman's help to manage the stairs. Thea's head wasn't right. It was light and dizzy. The floor swam upward, determined to smack her on the chin.

Holding the wall for support, Armina doing the rest, Thea made it down to the charred great hall, where the stench of blackened wood permeated the air.

Thea gasped when she came out the burned doors and saw the knight standing in full armor with his back to her and his sword drawn. More awful than that was the hideous machine that towered above the closed portcullis.

"Deitert!" Thea called. Her voice simply did not carry anywhere near far enough. Whatever the machine was meant to do, it did. The smashing and ferocious grinding at the iron gates made Thea throw both her hands across her ears and scream.

The old knight heard Thea scream. Deitert swung around. He looked fearsome and noble in his old-fashioned battle regalia, as fierce as any warrior Thea had ever seen. She stumbled toward him, Armina not much help upon the wide stairs. Deitert clanked of metal as he ran to Thea.

He dropped his sword in the ash and caught Thea before she fell to the ground. "My lady, you should not be here."

"Open the gates, Sir Deitert. I order you to open the gates."

Deitert had not lowered his visor, and the tears that glistened on his silvery lashes spoke of a different will from the one Thea had in her mind.

"I cannot, my lady. I am sworn to defend and protect my lord. Do I let him come in Blackstone and touch you, he may die. I cannot let him in to that fate. Hawk is the son I've never had. Better that he and I fight till he drops and is wounded than that he come within the keep and take this disease from you."

"Touch me, Sir Deitert," Thea implored him. "Look at my skin. I am not infected. It is not sickness that affects me, my lord. It is the baby inside me that saps my strength and weakens me to the point where I cannot get up. Sir Deitert, I beg you, open the gates and let my husband in. Touch me, Sir Deitert, see how Lord Roderick's child moves within me. Let my husband come in."

Deitert's gauntlet-covered hand moved to the slight mound where the frail lady's hand lay.

"I am not sick," Thea insisted. "I know I am not sick."

"A few more days and we could be certain."

"We have had enough days. No one has sickened in nearly a month. It is over, Sir Deitert. Go to the gates and raise them."

"Here, here, now." Armina rushed out of the hall with a fur rug to spread upon the steps. She threw it down and took Thea's shoulders from Sir Deitert's, settling her rather roughly upon the covered stone.

"Go on, go on, you old scarecrow. Fight yer liege if you be going to. We ladies will sit here and watch the blood run."

"Armina!" Thea gasped as the old crone squatted beside her.

Deitert stood, hesitating, not knowing whether to follow his heart or his head. He looked at Thea's pale face, then back to the portcullis as it thundered and shook from the impact of the gigantic iron screw crushing it.

"I guess I'd better let him in," he muttered finally, and walked toward the portcullis without his sword or shield.

"Cease yer battering!" Deitert's shout would have woken the dead. The shout that came back from outside the wall was just as ferocious.

"Have you come to your senses, you damned old fool?"

"Nay. 'Tis for good reason you've been kept out, puppy."

Deitert threw off his helm. It clattered on the brick-lined Roman road that went through the portcullis and ended at the keep steps.

"Get your blasted machine out of my face and come fight me like a man. We've a score to settle, whelp!"

Down went a gauntlet with a slap upon the ground. Another followed. Mail crackled as the aventail that protected Deitert's head and shoulders came off. It chinked on the bricks.

Without, the sounds of heavy wheels creaked. Slowly the monstrous machine rolled back from the gate.

From somewhere on his person, Deitert produced the key to the lock that prevented entrance and exit. His sabatons rang upon the bricks as he stomped to the gate and unlocked it. The chains and counterweights rattled in the portcullis, lifting and grinding as Deitert raised the heavy iron gate.

Outside, a crowd watched from a secure distance. Then, right in the middle of the now open gate, stood Roderick of Emory.

"Oh, this is gonna be good!" Armina clapped her hands with glee.

Thea tried to push up onto her feet. The old crone sat her firmly back down. "No, no, you don't, Lady Emory. You sits right here with me."

"Don't you touch me." Thea declared, her anger rising at the old woman's audacity.

"Don't you know nothing? Old Deitert's got a score to settle, and it be you. Now, shut up and leave them be, Yer Ladyship."

Armina's point eluded Thea. Armina calling her *lady* instead of *witch* was shock enough for Thea's brain to process. She touched her brow, feeling how damp it was with perspiration.

Roderick strode inside the bailey with a heavy tread of ringing iron.

Upon his head sat a silvered helm with the hawk of Emory frozen in flight. More metal sheathed his body than Thea had ever seen upon a fighting knight in her entire life. He wore an armored suit that appeared indestructible.

Thea cringed. In his old and rusted chain-mail hauberk, Sir Deitert was doomed. He would never strike a blow to Roderick's well-protected flesh.

It could be no contest at all.

Before her eyes, the old knight drew his last protection over his shoulders, shedding his hauberk.

Lord Roderick loomed before him, threatening and fierce, a burnished shield in one hand, a double-edged sword in the other.

When the worn hauberk clinked on the ash-covered ground, Deitert tore off his stained gambeson. He stood like old, pale marble, fierce and unmoving, naked from the waist up. He was a mountain of flesh, battle-hardened and scarred.

"Well?" Deitert demanded. He put his fists into his meaty sides and glared at his liege.

Thea gasped. Armina laughed with glee, clapping her gnarled hands together. Roderick shouted behind him, and two squires ran through the gate. Ben and Frederick worked like madmen, unfastening plates, unbuckling straps beneath the armor. They took away his helm, the chest piece, the linked armor that protected Roderick's legs, hips and stomach.

His hauberk, beneath the armor, buckled down his back, covering Roderick past his knees. It peeled away like a second skin. His heavy quilted gambeson was the last protection to be removed.

Out of armor, Roderick stood as bare-chested as Deitert. Not an ounce of spare flesh marred his powerful frame. When he moved into a crouch, preparing for hand-to-hand combat, his muscles rippled in the sunlight.

Deitert's awesome physique appeared no less intimidating in size alone, but the hard muscle of his prime was well covered by the solid girth of middle age.

Neither man looked prepared to yield an inch.

"You locked me from my keep," Roderick said accusingly.

"Aye, for good reason." Deitert added an oath that made Thea sit up and take notice. "There was death and sickness inside this keep. 'Twas for your own good I kept you away. So that you would live to receive the beating I intend to deliver to you."

"You have kept me from my woman, my hearth, my home. Did you think to take her for yourself?"

"Aye, the lady is under my protection, and it was damn well time I did that for her. You, you worthless piece of mange, you kidnapped a lady and brought her to Emory. You made her your slave. You abused her fine breeding and delicate nature. You sired your bastard upon her. When you were done with her, you discarded her and went looking for a dowry to suit your greed."

"I married her," Roderick declared.

"Too late, puppy. The day you should have married the maid was the day you brought her ashore. Instead, you shamed us all by declaring a fine lady a whore and your slave before all the people of Emory."

"I did not know she was a lady then."

"Liar!" Deitert shouted. "You knew it in your heart. And I, in my stupidity, by my oath of loyalty to you, turned a blind eye upon her fate. Because of my oath to you, I have compromised my most sacred vows as a true and faithful knight of the holy cause. You and I owe penance to the lady. Prepare to meet justice, Roderick of Emory."

Deitert went forward all at once, charging Roderick, head down, fists flashing. Although braced for the charge, Roderick fell back several paces, taking blows to his midsection.

Thea screamed.

The crowd outside rushed within. Men and women with babies in arms and toddlers clinging to their legs jockeyed with tonsured monks for the best position to see the fight. A cheer rose up from men loyal and sworn to Roderick as the fight in the bailey began in earnest. Their great shout drowned out Thea's useless scream of protest.

"Ah, haha! Give it to 'im, Deitert, that's the way!" Armina croaked.

Thea struggled to her feet. As she wavered unsteadily, her sister Marie threw her arms around her, catching her.

"Marie!" Thea gasped in recognition. "How did you get here?"

"Thea! For the love of God, what are you doing out here in your night rail? You aren't decent. Oh, look! Michael and

I just got here, and he said we were missing the fight. God, Thea, you look horrible. Are you ill?''

"No, only exhausted. Tell them to stop, Marie. Make them stop. Where is Michael?"

"No help there, m'lady. Sir Michael's rolling up his sleeves to take his own vengeance from Hawk." Armina punched at the air, grunting as the blow she mimicked struck solid flesh. The crone paused to look away from the fight and scowled at Marie with deep displeasure.

"Ach! Not another witch! I'm too old to put up with two of ya." She pushed them both toward the gaping hall. "Go on, go on, be timid-like. Don't stay to see His Lordship get his nose wiped good and dirty."

"Help me across the yard," Thea commanded her sister as Armina scuttled back to watch the fight. "I've got to stop this."

"Certainly not." Marie turned Thea the other way and pulled her within the hall. "God, what happened here? This is a disaster!"

"Marie, go stop them!"

"I certainly will not. Roderick of Emory deserves a beating. There's a whole line forming out there to take a piece of him. Now, you sit down right here."

Marie pushed Thea to a bench at the trestle table. She straightened and looked around the hall with a brow raised high. "So this is home sweet home? Really, Thea! You should be ashamed of yourself. Did you have to burn the manse down? I wouldn't like to be in your shoes when Roderick gets himself together after this fight."

"Marie, if it takes the last of my strength, I am going to slap you."

"I don't think you have it in you, kitten. For once, thankfully," Marie quipped. "Is it as bad as this upstairs?"

"I don't know," Thea winced at the thudding and *oof*-ing that continued outdoors. "What is happening? Go look."

Marie did just that, stepping to the blackened portal. "Well, that just goes to prove one should never discount strength just because of gray hair. My, these Saxons are a strong breed. I don't think Papa could put on as good a show."

Thea covered her face with both her hands.

"You're not worried, are you?" Marie asked. "Uh, Hawk's just knocked Michael flat on his back."

"I think it was a mistake for me to come downstairs."

"Possibly. Can you run, Thea? Roderick's coming this way. My, and is he in a temper! Could it be it's time for just deserts? Sister, you have definitely developed a flair for the dramatic."

"Marie, damn you, stop tormenting me!"

Thea gripped the table as she rose unsteadily to her feet. A shadow crossed the portal, and then Roderick stood in the hall. Marie quickly scooted out of his way.

"Thea!" Roderick's shout rocked the rafters.

Thea swallowed, unable to find her voice. Her mouth felt stuffed with cotton lint. He swiveled a half turn and found her with his eyes. A chill swept down Thea's spine. The cold sweat of fear broke out from every pore in her body.

"Answer me, woman! Do you not recognize your husband, your lord and your master?"

"Aye." Thea got that one word out.

Watching, Marie cocked a brow in surprise. *He could give lessons to Papa,* she thought, having to hand that point to Emory. He certainly had mastered the fine art of intimidation with a roar. Marie held her breath, staying still and silent, waiting for Thea's next move.

Thea took her hands away from the trestle, straightened her spine and said without a single waver, "Welcome home, Lord Roderick."

Bravo! Marie silently applauded, then winced as the man started toward Thea.

Thea caught hold of the trestle, backing away from Roderick's advance. He came around the end too fast, and she could not get up any speed at all.

"Is this a sample of how you take care of my property?"

"We did the best we could under the circumstances." Thea came to the end of the trestle. She leaned forward over it, gripping the wood for support. Was it his presence that made her legs tremble so?

She stayed her retreat, caught in a ray of sunlight that spilled down from the arch windows in the gallery.

Her lawn gown, sooty and soiled, was hardly more than gauze. Roderick came out of a strong shadow, advancing with measured step toward her. He halted, caught by the vision presented him. Thea might as well have been wearing nothing at all.

He stiffened, outraged momentarily, recalling that she had been outside on the steps not so very long ago. His eyes moved restlessly across the body so clearly revealed to his eyes by that gauzy nothing of a gown. He shook aside his desire for her.

"Will you continue to run from me, wench?"

"Nay, my lord. I've come to the point where I make my stand. Oh, your eye, Roderick! You're hurt!"

Roderick continued his perusal of her. His battered hands clenched and opened. The urge to take her in his arms overwhelmed him. Only the possibility of her containing the deadly disease held him to his place.

"The old knight packs a solid punch. You can save your tender mercies for his blackened chin."

"You did not kill Sir Deitert?"

"Kill him? I'd as soon sever my own arms. It was a stupid thing to do to lock me out. Were you so afraid of my wrath that you told him to do that?"

"Oh, no, my lord. It was the advice written in my mother's book. To gather all the sick ones within one location and stop the spread of the disease by isolating them. It worked, Roderick. All have recovered now."

"And you, my lady? Deitert swore to me that you were ill."

"Nay, my lord." Thea realized he had stopped advancing toward her. He held his distance. "I am only tired. It has been a hard summer without you."

Thea weakened a little more, swaying against the table. "I must sit down." She reached for the bench, but did not make it. Roderick jumped to catch her.

"God's teeth, woman, don't you ever eat?"

He had her up in his arms in a moment, cradled safely against his chest. Thea managed one arm around his sweaty neck. The second she touched him, she knew it no longer mattered to her if he ever said the words *I love you* to her. His gentle touch said it all for him. He cherished her in more ways than she could ever count. Words were unnecessary after that.

"Oh, Roderick, I thought you would never come. We needed you. I needed you."

Roderick made a displeased noise deep in his chest and strode to the stairs. Thea was hardly more than a feather's weight in his arms. She curled against him, closing her eyes as he mounted the stairs with a purposeful stride.

"Needed me!" he snorted. "It appears to me you have everything well in hand, little Frank."

"Where are you taking me?"

"To my chambers, or do you intend for my entire fief to see you in all your glory? I've trouble enough with my men, without your tempting them as you tempt me."

"I tempt you?" Thea asked. "My lord, you are not angry with me?"

Her head swam dizzily. She closed her eyes, aware of his purposeful movement, unable to protest against it. She was near to fainting when he laid her gently down upon the fine bed that graced their bedchamber.

Roderick tucked her under the coverlet, then pressed a wet linen against her face.

"I don't think you should have got out of bed," he scolded.

"If I hadn't, you'd still be trying to destroy your own gate, my lord."

Thea was patient while he blotted her brow, but then, impatient, she took the cloth from his hand and reached up to take the blood from his face and the dirt from his chin. "I would very much like it if my husband would give me a kiss."

"Your husband has a smashed lip, my lady."

"Oh, Roderick." Thea caught his shoulders and pulled him down to her. "I feared I would never see you again. My love, promise me you will stay home now. I need you here. This fief is impossible without you."

Roderick slipped his arm underneath her. He kissed her forehead, feeling how cool her skin was. Even so, he was fearful of kissing her mouth. Her eyes closed. She truly seemed to have no strength within her.

Unlike Deitert, who had weathered the plague in fair health, Thea seemed consumed by it. He stroked her hair back from her face and realized she was asleep.

That for him seemed to settle it for the time being. He stood up and saw that she was well covered and secure in the center of the bed.

There was an incredible amount of work to get organized. Since she couldn't do it, he would.

In the hall, Armina cackled over the fight, berating Deitert with a blow-by-blow retelling as Elspeth patted wet compresses to his many lumps.

Roderick stopped at the foot of the stairs and squinted with his one good eye at his vassal. Deitert's chin came up, challenging him. Both grunted sourly.

"Well?" Roderick demanded. "Is honor satisfied by the blood you've drawn from me this day?"

"It is possible we may have other occasions to dispute your lack of integrity." Deitert's answer was well-spoken, in spite of the swelling of his lips.

"As I said the day I brought the maid here, she is mine, Deitert."

"Had you called her a maid then, we'd have no quarrel."

"That's telling 'im!" Armina jabbed a fist in the air.

"Armina, shut up," Roderick said levelly.

The old crone snorted and looked at him with grudging respect. She bent her knee, in only the slightest show of obeisance. Deitert chuckled, despite his lumps and bruises. Elspeth hid a smile behind her hand.

The people of Blackstone still milled about the bailey yard. Roderick went out to the steps, and a shout greeted his ears. He smiled and raised his arms for silence.

"I see fewer people here before me than I did when last I stood upon these steps. We have all lost some of our dearest ones again. I need your help, people of Emory. My lady saw to your needs. Now, we must see to hers.

"It will be some days before she recovers enough to come down and greet you herself. I would have her come to a clean hall, to a decent yard and a keep that does not put any of us to shame.

"Will you go and bring your buckets and your brushes, your rags and soaps, and help me put this keep to rights for Lady Emory?"

"Aye, my lord!" The unified shout cheered him.

"Then let us begin."

"Better see to putting meat on your eye first," somebody hollered. Roderick laughed the comment aside.

He turned round to find his sister-in-law studying him rather grimly.

"I suppose that means you expect me to work, too," Marie declared sulkily, then turned back to the hall. With a swish of fine fabric, Marie disappeared up the stairs.

This time the scars of the fire came away much faster. In the days that followed Celts, Franks, Britons and Saxons all worked together. Scaffolding was lashed together and every wall scrubbed until all the soot was removed.

Within the keep, a hive of active women scattered everywhere, washing and cleaning, scrubbing and dusting. As quick as the interior walls dried, men followed, smoothing clean white plaster until all the scars of the last fire were obliterated completely.

Marie found the treasured pieces of Thea's dowry in the vacant chambers on the second floor, still packed and draped in dustcovers. New doors and shutters were carved and hung, and precious sheets of fine glass carefully cut and leaded into frames for the hall's great windows.

Once the keep was clean, Marie brought the treasured furniture out, saw to its dusting and polishing and arrangement. She supervised the hanging of tapestries, the draping of well-made beds and the restoration of good linens.

A fine, polished table was placed on the foot-high dais, and carved chairs for the lord and lady graced it. Lower chairs for their guests were lined up on either side like a regiment.

Thea slept through it all. Through the return of the household from the abbey. Through the arrival of Roderick's son, walking now on chubby legs. Roderick held the boy in his arms, overlooking the sleeping woman on the bed.

"Who is that?" he asked Eric.

The boy was more interested in sucking on a fat thumb, and it wasn't until Roderick had asked the question sternly a third time that Eric deigned to answer. Pointing wet fingers at Thea's sleeping face, he said, *"Maman."*

"Good boy." Roderick turned and handed Jesse the youngster. "Take him to bed, now."

"Yes, my lord." Jesse dipped a curtsy and took the child from the room. Elspeth gathered up a tray of dishes and followed Jesse through the door.

Roderick sat down on the side of the bed. Thea stirred against the pillow at her neck. He drew back the sheeting, raising a brow over the finely made gown she wore. He was home, but slept in a guest room. Everyone in the keep waited with bated breath for spots to rise on Thea's skin. She remained cool, her skin moist and clear. His anxiety over her was too much for Roderick.

His fingers strayed to the laced gown at her throat.

No doubt her sister had put Thea into this latest fashionable contraption. It was beautiful. Of pale cream color, a silky fabric that suited her fine skin so well. Roderick thought it all well and good for Marie to wear her fancy gowns. He had other ideas about what Thea should wear to bed. He opened the gown, parting it as far as it would go.

He saw she was not a whit bigger than she had ever been, still barely a handful of a woman. Her skin was pink and pale; her belly, though, was round and firm. Laying his hand on the bare skin below her navel, he felt the firmness of it. A movement fluttered across his palm.

Roderick pulled his hand back, looking at the swelling, then laid his palm again upon her, his fingers spread completely to span her hipbones. Again, the nudging flutter pushed back, this time the small kick actually moving his thumb.

Roderick's eyes widened, and his brow arched above the smile lingering on his lips. How like Thea to stubbornly hold on to what she viewed as hers. He'd feared she'd lost the baby, that that was the cause of her weakness now.

Thea shifted, curving toward the body heat she felt near her. Her eyes fluttered. Sleep seemed so deep for her, and the struggle to rise from it impossible. A little moan escaped her throat, and her hand came over his. "Roderick?"

"Aye."

"You haven't lit any candles."

"Nay, 'tis cooler without."

"Are you all right?"

"I am fine." Awakening more, Thea snuggled against his warm, furred chest. "Can you feel your son moving?"

"Aye."

"I brought him home with me." Thea's fingers pressed on top of his.

"Thea, I have also brought a son home with me. His name is Eric, and he's not much older than a year. I pray you accept him and learn to love him."

Thea lifted her eyelids and stared into the clear blue of his eyes. "Is Eric Anne's baby?"

"You know of that?"

As always, Thea wondered how much knowledge she could commit to him. "Aye, I knew why Anne was sent to Solbert."

"Then I am glad Eric is home where he belongs. I was frightened for him to remain in the emperor's house. Marie insisted she go with Michael to get Eric when I left France. She talked the emperor into releasing Eric to us."

"Ah..." Thea smiled. "There is some of Papa in Marie too, then. Roderick..." Thea paused. "My lord...I have always known why the emperor gave us Lorraine. It will be Eric's birthright. Tomorrow, I'll get up and put your house to rights. I am sorry about the fire."

"Deitert explained it all."

"Roderick?"

"Thea."

"How did you get home?"

Roderick chuckled. He undressed and lay down beside her, gathering her closely in his arms. "You remember the night of the wind and the thunder when you ran away?"

"Vaguely I remember being so foolish, once, my love."

"Ah, what sweet words you say, little Frank. Well, I often puzzled over how you came by your skills and witches' brew. I no longer question the obvious. 'Twas your lady mother who saw to it that our feisty emperor's guards and servants and loyal vassals all took a long-needed night's sleep. I know whence you gained your skills."

"*Maman?*"

"Aye, a brave lady, that one, as brave as her lovely daughter Thea. I love you, sweetling. I don't think you realize how much I do love you, Thea. I never thought a woman would become so important to me. Aye, I am bewitched, just as that old hag says I am."

Thea leaned back in his arms, studying his so-serious face, and wondered for just a moment if he realized what he had said. But then, she knew her husband well enough to know he measured his every word. A smile tilted the corners of her mouth. She decided it was more prudent for her not to remark upon his testimony of love. She no longer needed to hear the words spoken to her. His actions spoke as loudly.

"I thought the emperor would keep you for years," she finally said.

"He would have, but he didn't account for Lady Lilla."

"Oh, *Maman*. She must be so worried about me."

"Nay, Thea, she knows exactly where you are. Do not be surprised if she comes to visit in the spring. After all, now she has two daughters living in Blackstone."

"You told them? Papa, too?"

"Nay. Your *maman* is wiser than I regarding your papa. She will tell him the truth sometime during the winter. Preferably when a long cold spell will keep him to home and out of harm's way."

"Oh, dear." Thea used his neck to lift herself up against his chest. She sought his mouth, kissing his lips.

"Don't start another fire, Thea."

"No, my lord. I only want to stay here in your arms, where I am safe and warm. Will you help me out of this gown? Marie insists I dress as she does."

"I shall ban her from my chamber."

"Ban Armina, too."

Roderick chuckled deeply. "The old hag tells everyone about your fine bed. She still claims you are a witch, and we shall not discuss what your sister thinks of her."

Thea stretched, feeling toes that tingled at the end of her legs, fingers that were slowly stirring to life again. She drew in a great gush of air, her stomach and chest pressing against

Roderick as she did so. The opened gown fell from her shoulders.

"My lord!" She stretched against him. "Is that what I think it is?"

"Hush, Thea, be still, and do not remind me." Roderick pulled her gown back over her shoulders. It did shield her from him.

"It has been a long time since our wedding, my lord."

"Don't remind me."

"I think I should. That is, unless you have replaced me in some way. I have a duty to you, do I not?"

"Thea."

"Yes, my lord?"

Roderick lay frozen still, unable to move as her lips pressed against his scarred chest. "Nay, Thea, you must rest."

"My lord Emory. I have slept a mighty long time. Do not deny me. I would have the same pledge given between us now as I once gave you and have never forgotten. Here in your chamber, in your hall, your kitchen, anywhere in your land, I will never deny you. I would have the same from you, my lord. Do not deny me."

"Ah, Thea. I will never deny my love for you again." Roderick sighed deeply and, lifting her from his chest, he turned her into the soft, down-filled mattress and took her mouth completely with his own. "Be it ever so between us, now and forever more."

* * * * *

Author Note

The year 841 A.D. was a tumultuous year for the three grandsons of Charlemagne, who became kings. Their sire's empire had been divided into three kingdoms. The ruling brothers squabbled for power and fought repeatedly until peace was finally reached between them by the Treaty of Verdun.

Lothair forced his younger brothers to accept his dominion as Holy Roman emperor. Throughout their sibling struggles, Vikings assaulted the whole European theater, seeking wealth, trade, land and kingdoms of their own. It was a very adventuresome time when terrible Viking longships sailed up the river Seine.

Charles the Bald set a precedent that was to follow for hundreds of years of paying the first Danegeld, seven thousand pounds of silver to Ragnar Lodbok.

Curiously, once he reunited the old kingdom by treaty in 843, Lothair lost interest in ruling and stepped down so that his son, Louis, could assume the emperor's crown. Lothair retired to a monastery, where he lived the rest of his days in peace.

The old kingdom of Saxony still exists today as a state of Germany.

HARLEQUIN SUPERROMANCE®

a heartwarming trilogy by *Peg Sutherland*

*Meet old friends and new ones on a trip to
Sweetbranch, Alabama—where the most unexpected
things can happen...*

Harlequin Superromance #673 *Double Wedding Ring* (Book 1)

Susan Hovis is suffering from amnesia.

She's also got an overprotective mother and a demanding
physiotherapist. Then there's her college-age daughter—and
Susan also seems to have a young son she can't really
remember. Enter Tag, a man who claims to have been her
teenage lover, and the confusion intensifies.

Soon, everything's in place for a Christmas wedding.
But whose?

**Don't miss *Double Wedding Ring* in December,
wherever Harlequin books are sold. And watch for
Addy's Angels and *Queen of the Dixie Drive-In*
(Books 2 and 3 of Peg Sutherland's trilogy)
this coming January and February!**

Harlequin® Historical

WOMEN OF THE WEST

Don't miss these adventurous stories by
some of your favorite Western romance authors.

Coming from Harlequin Historical every month.

Don't miss any of our Women of the West! WWEST-1

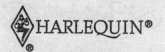

HARLEQUIN®

CHRISTMAS ROGUES

**is giving you everything you want on
your Christmas list this year:**

- ☑ -great romance stories
- ☑ -award-winning authors
- ☑ -a FREE gift promotion
- ☑ -an abundance of Christmas cheer

This November, not only can you join ANITA MILLS,
PATRICIA POTTER and MIRANDA JARRETT
for exciting, heartwarming Christmas stories
about roguish men and the women who tame
them—but you can also receive a FREE gold-tone
necklace. (Details inside all copies of
Christmas Rogues.)

CHRISTMAS ROGUES—romance reading at its
best—only from HARLEQUIN BOOKS!

**Available in November wherever
Harlequin books are sold.**

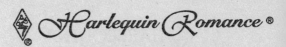

Harlequin Romance ®

New from Harlequin Romance
a very special six-book series by

MIDNIGHT SONS

DEBBIE MACOMBER

The town of Hard Luck, Alaska, needs women!

The O'Halloran brothers, who run a bush-plane service called **Midnight Sons**, are heading a campaign to attract women to Hard Luck. (*Location: north of the Arctic Circle. Population: 150—mostly men!*)

"Debbie Macomber's *Midnight Sons* series is a delightful romantic saga. And each book is a powerful, engaging story in its own right. Unforgettable!"

—Linda Lael Miller

TITLE IN THE MIDNIGHT SONS SERIES:

HARLEQUIN  PRESENTS®

Dark secrets...

forbidden desires...

scandalous discoveries...

an enthralling six-part saga from a bright new talent!

HEARTS OF FIRE
by Miranda Lee

This exciting family saga is set in the glamorous world of opal dealing in Australia. *HEARTS OF FIRE* unfolds over six books, revealing the passion, scandal, sin and hope that exist between two fabulously rich families. Each novel features its own gripping romance—and you'll also be hooked by the continuing story of Gemma Smith's search for the truth about her real mother, and the priceless Black Opal....

Coming next month:

The story concludes with

BOOK 6: *Marriage & Miracles*

Gemma's marriage to Nathan couldn't be over! There was so much that was unresolved between them.... And, most importantly, Gemma was still in love with Nathan. She also had an extraspecial secret to share with her husband—she was expecting his baby.

Harlequin Presents: you'll want to know what happens next!

Available in December, wherever Harlequin books are sold.

Harlequin® Historical

Claire Delacroix's UNICORN TRILOGY

The series that began with

UNICORN BRIDE

"…a fascinating blend of fantasy and romance."
—*Romantic Times*

and

PEARL BEYOND PRICE

"…another dazzling Delacroix delicacy." —*Affaire de Coeur*

now continues with the November 1995 release of

UNICORN VENGEANCE

"An irresistible romance…" —*The Medieval Chronicle*

If you would like to order your copy of *Unicorn Bride* (HS #223) or *Pearl Beyond Price* (HS #264), please send your name, address, zip or postal code along with a check or money order (please do not send cash) for $4.50 for each book ordered ($4.99 in Canada), plus 75¢ postage and handling ($1.00 in Canada) payable to Harlequin Books, to:

In the U.S.	In Canada
3010 Walden Avenue	P.O. Box 609
P. O. Box 1369	Fort Erie, Ontario
Buffalo, NY 14269-1369	L2A 5X3

Please specify book title(s) with your order.
Canadian residents add applicable federal and provincial taxes.

HUT-3

New York Times Bestselling Author

PENNY JORDAN

Explore the lives of four women as they overcome a

CRUEL LEGACY

For Philippa, Sally, Elizabeth and Deborah life will never be the same after the final act of one man. Now they must stand on their own and reclaim their lives.

As Philippa learns to live without wealth and social standing, Sally finds herself tempted by a man who is not her husband. And Elizabeth struggles between supporting her husband and proclaiming her independence, while Deborah must choose between a jealous lover and a ruthless boss.

Don't miss CRUEL LEGACY, available this December at your favorite retail outlet.

 MIRA The brightest star in women's fiction

MPJCL

HARLEQUIN SUPERROMANCE®

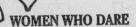

WOMEN WHO DARE
They take chances, make changes
and follow their hearts!

Christmas Star
by Roz Denny Fox
Harlequin Superromance #672

Since her childhood, Starr Lederman has always wished on
what her mother called the Christmas star—the first star out
on those December nights just before Christmas. Now her
adopted daughter, SeLi, does the same thing.

But SeLi isn't wishing for toys or video games. She's
out for the serious stuff—a dad for herself. Which
means a husband for Starr. And SeLi's got a man all
picked out. Clay McLeod, rancher.

Clay's not looking for a wife, though. Especially not a woman
as independent and daring as Starr. A woman *he* believes is
having an affair with his brother. His married brother.

But at Christmastime, things have a way of sorting
themselves out....

Available in December, wherever
Harlequin books are sold.